SHADOWS IN THE

There was a long leather thong knotted around the intruder's waist. Now, untied, it could be seen to be a sling, with a soft leather pouch at its center. A smooth, heavy stone went into the pouch and the figure rose a little, beginning to swing the simple weapon in a wide slow circle, using a minimal wrist movement and gradually building up speed.

The sentry became aware of a foreign sound in the night. It began as a deep-throated, almost inaudible hum, and slowly grew higher in pitch. The change was so gradual that he wasn't sure at what point he became aware of it. It sounded like an insect of some sort . . . a giant bee, perhaps. It was difficult to detect the direction the sound was coming from. Then a memory stirred. One of the other sentries had mentioned a similar sound some days previously.

Clang!

An unseen missile smashed into the head of his spear. The force of the impact snatched the weapon from his loose grasp, sending it cartwheeling away from him. His hand dropped instinctively to the hilt of his sword and he had it half drawn when a slim figure rose from behind the table to his left.

Read all of the adventures of

RANGER'S APPRENTICE

THE RUINS OF GORLAN

THE BURNING BRIDGE

THE ICEBOUND LAND

THE BATTLE FOR SKANDIA

THE SORCERER OF THE NORTH

THE SIEGE OF MACINDAW

ERAK'S RANSOM

THE KINGS OF CLONMEL

HALT'S PERIL

THE EMPEROR OF NIHON-JA

THE LOST STORIES

And the companion series

THE OUTCASTS

THE INVADERS

THE HUNTERS

RANGER'S APPRENTICE

BOOK SEVEN: ERAK'S RANSOM

JOHN FLANAGAN

PUFFIN BOOKS
An Imprint of Penguin Group (USA) Inc.

PUFFIN BOOKS

Published by the Penguin Group

Penguin Young Readers Group, 345 Hudson Street, New York, New York 10014, U.S.A.

Penguin Group (Canada), 90 Eglinton Avenue East, Suite 700, Toronto, Ontario M4P 2Y3, Canada
(a division of Pearson Penguin Canada Inc.)

Penguin Books Ltd, 80 Strand, London WC2R 0RL, England

Penguin Ireland, 25 St Stephen's Green, Dublin 2, Ireland (a division of Penguin Books Ltd)

Penguin Group (Australia), 707 Collins Street, Melbourne, Victoria 3008, Australia
(a division of Pearson Australia Group Pty Ltd)

Penguin Books India Pvt Ltd, 11 Community Centre, Panchsheel Park, New Delhi–110 017, India

Penguin Group (NZ), 67 Apollo Drive, Rosedale, Auckland 0632, New Zealand
(a division of Pearson New Zealand Ltd)

Penguin Books (South Africa), Rosebank Office Park, 181 Jan Smuts Avenue,
Parktown North 2193, South Africa

Penguin China, B7 Jiaming Center, 27 East Third Ring Road North,
Chaoyang District, Beijing 100020, China

Penguin Books Ltd, Registered Offices: 80 Strand, London WC2R 0RL, England

Published in Australia by Random House Australia Children's Books in 2007
First published in the United States of America by Philomel Books,
a division of Penguin Young Readers Group, 2010
Published by Puffin Books, a division of Penguin Young Readers Group, 2011

7 9 10 8 6

THE LIBRARY OF CONGRESS HAS CATALOGED THE PHILOMEL EDITION AS FOLLOWS:
Flanagan, John (John Anthony).
Erak's ransom / John Flanagan.—1st American ed.
p.   cm. — (Ranger's apprentice ; bk. 7)
Summary: On a mission to pay the ransom of a new ally, apprentice Will and his friends find themselves
in a desert wasteland awash with enemies.
ISBN: 978-0-399-25205-1 (hc)
[1. Apprentices—Fiction. 2. War—Fiction. 3. Deserts—Fiction. 4. Fantasy.] I. Title.
PZ7.F598284Er 2010
[Fic]—dc22   2009011665

Puffin Books ISBN 978-0-14-241525-2

Text set in Adobe Jenson

Printed in the United States of America

ALWAYS LEARNING   PEARSON

For Rachel Skinner.
(I hope you're sitting down when you read this.)

BOOK SEVEN: ERAK'S RANSOM

Author's Note

I had almost completed writing *Ranger's Apprentice Book 6: The Siege of Macindaw* when I realized I had neglected an important period in Will's and Halt's lives.

Books 1–4 deal with Will's early years as an apprentice. Books 5 and 6 describe his first mission as a graduate Ranger. But there was a gap between them. I realized that as Will approached the moment when he would become a Ranger in his own right, he would be troubled by the worry that he wasn't ready for the responsibility that this would entail.

In addition, I wondered about Halt. As a graduate Ranger, Will would move on to his own fief. How would Halt deal with the loss of his cheerful, lively influence—one that had become so much a part of his day-to-day existence?

These questions were too important for me to ignore. So this book goes back a little in time, to the period before Books 5 and 6. It's set a few months prior to the moment when Will is due to graduate. Halt is making his own plans to fill the empty space that Will's imminent reassignment will leave in his life. Will is beginning to worry that he's not ready to move away from the comforting shelter of Halt's presence.

Other characters, too, are chafing at the changes that have taken place in their lives. Principal among these is Erak, Oberjarl of the Skandians. And it's Erak's restlessness and dissatisfaction that precipitate the chain of events described in this book.

John Flanagan

1

THE SENTRY NEVER SAW THE DARK-CLAD FIGURE GHOSTING through the night toward Castle Araluen.

Merging with the prevailing patterns of light and shade thrown by the half-moon, the interloper seemed to blend into the fabric of the night, matching the rhythm of the trees and cloud shadows as they moved with the moderate wind.

The sentry's post was in the outer cordon, outside the walls of the massive castle, by the southeastern tower. The moat rippled gently behind him, its surface stirred by the wind so that the reflections of the stars in the dark water were set shimmering in a thousand tiny points of light. Before him stretched the massive parkland that surrounded the castle, carefully tended, immaculately mown and dotted with fruit and shade trees.

The ground sloped gently away from the castle. There were trees and small shady dells where couples or individuals could sit and relax and picnic in relative privacy, sheltered from the sun. But the trees were small and they were well spaced out, with plenty of open ground between them so that concealment would be denied to any large attacking force. It was a well-ordered compromise between the provision of privacy and relaxation and the need for security in an age when an attack could conceivably happen at any time.

Thirty meters to the left of where the sentry stood, a picnic table had been fashioned by attaching an old cart wheel to the sawn-off stump of what had been a larger tree. Several rustic benches were placed around the table and a smaller tree had been planted to one side to shade it at noon. It was a favorite spot for the knights and their ladies, affording a good overview of the green, pleasant parklands that sloped away to the distant dark line of a forest.

The intruder was heading toward this table.

He slipped into the shadows of a small grove forty meters from the bench, then dropped belly-down to the ground. Taking one last look to get a bearing, the dark figure snaked out of the shadows, facedown, heading for the shelter of the table.

Progress was painstakingly slow. This was a trained stalker who knew that any rapid movement would register with the sentry's peripheral vision. As shadows of clouds passed over the park, the crawling figure would move with them, rippling unobtrusively across the short grass, seeming to be just one more moving shadow. The dark green clothing aided concealment. Black would have been too dark and would have created too deep a shadow.

It took ten minutes to cover the distance to the table. A few meters short of the objective, the figure froze as the guard suddenly stiffened, as if alerted by some sound or slight movement—or perhaps just an intuitive sense that all was not quite right. He turned and peered in the general direction of the table, not even registering the dark, unmoving shape a few meters from it.

Eventually satisfied that there was no danger, the sentry shook his head, stamped his feet, marched a few paces to the right then back to the left, then shifted his spear to his left hand and rubbed his eyes with his right.

He yawned, then settled into a slump, his weight resting more on one foot than the other. He sniffed wryly. He'd never get away with that relaxed posture on daylight sentry duty. But it was after midnight now and the sergeant of the guard was unlikely to come and check on him in the next hour.

As the sentry relaxed again, the dark figure slid the last few meters to the shelter of the table. Rising slowly to a crouching position, he studied the situation. The sentry, after his shuffling and stamping, had moved a few meters farther away from the table, but not enough to cause a problem.

There was a long leather thong knotted around the intruder's waist. Now, untied, it could be seen to be a sling, with a soft leather pouch at its center. A smooth, heavy stone went into the pouch and the figure rose a little, beginning to swing the simple weapon in a wide slow circle, using a minimal wrist movement and gradually building up speed.

The sentry became aware of a foreign sound in the night. It began as a deep-throated, almost inaudible hum, and slowly grew higher in pitch. The change was so gradual that he wasn't sure at what point he became aware of it. It sounded like an insect of some sort . . . a giant bee, perhaps. It was difficult to detect the direction the sound was coming from. Then a memory stirred. One of the other sentries had mentioned a similar sound some days previously. He'd said it was . . .

Clang!

An unseen missile smashed into the head of his spear. The force of the impact snatched the weapon from his loose grasp, sending it cartwheeling away from him. His hand dropped instinctively to the hilt of his sword and he had it half drawn when a slim figure rose from behind the table to his left.

The cry of alarm froze in his throat as the intruder pushed back the dark cowl that had concealed a mass of blond hair.

"Relax! It's only me," she said, the amusement obvious in her voice. Even in the dark, even at thirty meters' distance, the laughing voice and the distinctive blond hair marked her as Cassandra, Crown Princess of Araluen.

2

"IT MUST STOP, CASSANDRA," DUNCAN SAID. HE WAS ANGRY. SHE could see that. If it hadn't been obvious from the way he paced behind the table in his office, she would have known it from the fact that he called her Cassandra. His usual name for her was Cass or Cassie.

And today, he was thoroughly annoyed with her. He had a full morning's work ahead of him. His desk was littered with petitions and judgments, there was a trade delegation from Teutlandt clamoring for his attention and now he had to take time out to deal with a complaint about his daughter's behavior.

She spread her hands palm-out before her—a gesture that mixed frustration and explanation in equal parts.

"Dad, I was just—"

"You were just skulking around the countryside after midnight, stalking an innocent sentry and then frightening the devil out of him with that damn sling of yours! What if you'd hit him, instead of the spear?"

"I didn't," she said simply. "I hit what I aim at. I aimed at the spearhead."

He glared at her and held out his hand.

"Let me have it," he said, and when she cocked her head, not understanding, he added, "The sling. Let me have it."

He saw the determined set to her jaw before she spoke.

"No," she said.

His eyebrows shot up. "Are you defying me? I am the King, after all."

"I'm not defying you. I'm just not giving you that sling. I made it. It took me a week to get it just right. I've practiced with it for months so that I don't miss what I aim at. I'm not handing it over so you can destroy it. Sorry." She added the last word after a pause.

"I'm also your father," he pointed out.

She nodded acceptance of the fact. "I respect that. But you're angry. And if I hand over my sling to you now, you'll cut it up without thinking, won't you?"

He shook his head in frustration and turned away to the window. They were in his study, a large, airy and well-lit room that overlooked the park.

"I cannot have you stalking around in the dark surprising the sentries," he said. He could see they had reached an impasse over the matter of the sling and he thought it best to change his point of attack. He knew how stubborn his daughter could be.

"It's not fair to the men," he continued. "This is the third time it's happened and they're getting tired of your silly games. The sergeant of the guard has asked to see me later today and I know what that's going to be about." He turned back to face her. "You've put me in a very difficult situation. I'm going to have to apologize to a sergeant. Do you understand how embarrassing that will be?"

He saw the anger in her face fade a little. "I'm sorry, Father," she said. She was matching his formality. Normally, she called him Dad. Today it was Cassandra and Father. "But it's not a silly game, believe me. It's something I need to do."

"Why?" he demanded, with some heat. "You're the Crown Princess, not some silly peasant girl, for pity's sake! You live in a castle with hundreds of troops to protect you! Why do you need to learn how to sneak around in the dark and use a poacher's weapon?"

"Dad," she said, forgetting the formality, "think about my life so far. I've been pursued by Wargals in Celtica. My escorts were killed and I barely escaped with my life. Then I was captured by Morgarath's army. I was dragged off to Skandia, where I had to survive in the mountains. I could have starved there. After that, I was involved in a full-scale battle. Those hundreds of guards didn't exactly keep me safe then, did they?"

Duncan made an irritated gesture. "Well, perhaps not. But—"

"Let's face it," Cassandra went on, "it's a dangerous world and, as Crown Princess, I'm a target for our enemies. I want to be able to defend myself. I don't want to have to rely on other people. Besides..." She hesitated and he studied her more closely.

"Besides?" he queried.

Cassandra seemed to consider whether she should say more. Then she took a deep breath, and plunged in.

"As your daughter, there's going to come a time when I should be able to help you—to share some of your load."

"But you do that! The banquet last week was a triumph..."

She made a dismissive gesture with her hands. "I don't mean banquets and state occasions and picnics in the park. I mean the important things—going on diplomatic missions in your name, acting as your representative when there are disputes to be settled. The sort of things you'd expect a son to do for you."

"But you're not my son," Duncan said, a little too softly.

Cassandra smiled sadly. She knew her father loved her. But she also knew that a king, any king, hoped for a son to carry on his work.

"Dad, one day I'll be Queen. Not too soon, I hope," she added hastily and Duncan smiled his agreement with the sentiment. "But when I am, I'll have to do these things and it'll be a little late to start learning at that point."

Duncan studied her for a long moment. Cassandra was strong willed, he knew. She was brave and capable and intelligent. There was no way she would be content to be a figurehead ruler, letting others make the decisions and do the hard work. He sighed.

"You're right, I suppose," he said. "You should learn to look after yourself. But Sir Richard has been teaching you the saber. Why bother with the sling—and why learn to sneak around unseen?"

It wasn't uncommon for highborn young ladies to study swordsmanship. Cassandra had been taking lessons from the Assistant Battlemaster for some months, using a lightweight saber specially made for her. She turned a pained expression on her father.

"I'm all right with the saber," she admitted. "But I'll never really be an expert and that's what I'd need to be to hold my own against a man with a heavy weapon. It's the same with a bow. It takes years of practice to learn to use one properly and I just don't have the time.

"The sling is a weapon I already know. I learned to use it as a child. It kept me alive in Skandia. I decided it would be my weapon of choice and I'd develop my basic skills until I was really expert."

"You could do that on a target range. You don't need to terrorize my sentries," Duncan said.

She smiled apologetically. "I admit I haven't been fair to them. But Geldon said the best way to practice was to make the situation as real as possible."

"Geldon?" Duncan's eyebrows slid together in a frown. Geldon was a retired Ranger who had an apartment of rooms in Castle Araluen. Occasionally, he acted as an adviser to Crowley, the Ranger Corps Commandant. Cassandra flushed as she realized she'd given away more than she intended.

"I asked him for a few pointers on unseen movement," she confessed, then added hurriedly, "but he didn't know about the sling, I promise."

"I'll speak to him later," Duncan said, although he had no doubt she was telling the truth. Geldon wouldn't be fool enough to encourage her in the irresponsible practice sessions she'd devised.

He sat down, breathing deeply for a few seconds to let his anger subside. Then he said in a more reasonable tone, "Cass, think about it. Your practice sessions could conceivably put you, or the castle itself, in danger."

She cocked her head to one side, not understanding.

"Now that the sentries know what you're up to, they might just ignore the occasional noise or sign of movement outside the walls. If they were to see some dark figure creeping through the night, they'd assume it's you. And they might be wrong. What if an enemy agent was trying to infiltrate the castle? That could result in a dead sentry. Would you want that on your conscience?"

Cassandra hung her head as she considered what he had said. She realized he was right.

"No," she said, in a small voice.

"Or the opposite might happen. One of these nights, a sentry might see someone stalking him and not realize it's only the Crown Princess. You could get killed yourself."

She opened her mouth to protest but he stopped her with a raised hand.

"I know you think you're too skilled for that. But think about it. What would happen to the man who killed you? Would you want him to live with that on his conscience?"

"I suppose not," she said glumly, and he nodded, seeing that the lesson had been learned.

"Then I want you to stop these dangerous games of yours. If you must practice, let Geldon work out a proper plan for you. I'm sure he'd be willing to help, and it might be harder to slip by him than a few sleepy sentries."

Cassandra's face widened in a smile as she realized that, far from confiscating her sling, her father had just given his permission for her to continue her weapons practice.

"Thanks, Dad," she said, the eagerness obvious in her voice. "I'll get started with him later today."

But Duncan was already shaking his head.

"There's time for that later. Today I need your help planning a trip—an official trip. I want you to decide who should accompany us. And you'll probably need to have new clothes made as well—proper traveling outfits and formal gowns, not that tunic and tights you're wearing. You say you want to help, so here's your chance. You organize everything."

She nodded, frowning slightly as she thought over the preparations she'd have to make, the details she'd have to arrange. An official royal trip took a lot of planning and involved a lot of people. She was in for a busy couple of weeks, she realized. But she was glad that his attention had been diverted from his earlier annoyance.

"When are we going?" she asked. "And where to?" She'd need to know how far they were traveling so she could organize their overnight stops along the way.

"In three weeks' time," the King told her. "We've been invited to a wedding at Castle Redmont on the fourteenth of next month."

"Redmont?" she repeated, her interest obviously piqued by the name. "Who's getting married at Redmont?"

3

HALT RAN HIS FINGERS THROUGH HIS SHAGGY HAIR AS HE studied the list of names. "Gorlog's beard!" he said, using a Skandian oath he had become quite fond of. "How many people are here?"

Lady Pauline watched him serenely. "Two hundred and three," she said calmly.

He looked up from the list, appalled. "Two hundred and three?" he repeated and she nodded. He shook his head and dropped the sheet of parchment on her desk.

"Well, we're going to have to pare it down," he said.

Pauline frowned slightly in concentration as she considered his statement. "We could possibly get rid of the three," she said. "I'm not sure that I really need the Iberian ambassador and his two idiot daughters at my wedding."

She took a quill and scored out the last three names on the list, then looked up at him and smiled brightly.

"There. All done. Wasn't that easy?"

Halt shook his head distractedly, taking the list again and scanning through it. "But . . . two hundred people? Do we really need two hundred people to get married?"

"They're not getting married, dear. We are," she said, deliberately misunderstanding him. He scowled at her. Normally, Halt's scowl was a fearsome thing. But it held no terrors for Lady Pauline. She raised one eyebrow at him and he realized he might as well drop the scowl. He went back to the list, jabbing his forefinger at one section.

"I mean . . . I suppose the King has to come," he began.

"Of course he does. You are one of his oldest advisers," she pointed out.

"And Evanlyn—well, Cassandra. She's a friend. But who are all these others? There must be fifteen in the royal party!"

"Seventeen," Lady Pauline said. "After all, the King can't travel without his retinue. He and Cassandra can't just hop on their horses and turn up one day, saying, 'We're here for the wedding. Where do we sit?' There's a certain amount of protocol involved."

"Protocol!" Halt snorted derisively. "What a load of rubbish!"

"Halt," said the elegant diplomat, "when you asked me to marry you, did you think we could just sneak off to a glade in the woods with a few close friends and get it done?"

Halt hesitated. "Well, no . . . of course not."

As a matter of fact, that was exactly what he had thought. A simple ceremony, a few friends, some good food and drink and then he and Pauline would be a couple. But he felt that it might not be wise to admit that right now.

The engagement of the grizzled Ranger and the beautiful Lady Pauline had been the talk of Redmont Fief for some weeks now.

People were amazed and delighted that this seemingly ill-matched yet well-respected pair were to become man and wife. It was something to wonder about, to gossip about. Little else had been discussed in the Redmont dining hall for weeks.

There were those who pretended not to be surprised. Baron Arald of Redmont was one of them.

"Always knew it!" he told anyone who would listen. "Always knew there was something going on with those two! Saw it coming years ago. Knew it before they did, probably."

And indeed, there had been occasional vague rumors over the years that Halt and Pauline had been something more than friends in the past. But the majority of people had dismissed such talk. And neither Halt nor Pauline ever said anything about the matter. When it came to keeping secrets, few people could be more tight-lipped than Rangers and members of the Diplomatic Service.

But there came a day when Halt realized that time was slipping past with increasing speed. Will, his apprentice, was in his final year of training. In a few months he would be due for graduation and promotion to the Silver Oakleaf—the insignia of a full-fledged Ranger. And that meant Will would be moving away from Redmont. He would be assigned a fief of his own and Halt sensed that his day-to-day life, so full of energy and diversion with Will around, would become alarmingly empty. As the realization had grown, he had unconsciously sought the company of Lady Pauline with increasing frequency.

She, in her turn, had seen his growing need for company and affection. A Ranger's life tended to be a lonely one—and one that he could discuss with few people. As a Courier, privy to many of the secrets of the fief and the Kingdom they both served, Pauline was one of those few. Halt could relax in her company. They could discuss each other's work and give counsel to each other. And there was, in fact, a certain history between them—an understanding, some might call it—which went back to a time when they were both younger.

To put it plainly, Lady Pauline had loved Halt for many years. Quietly and patiently, she had waited, knowing that one day he would propose.

Knowing also that, when he did, this incredibly shy and retiring man would view the prospect of a very public wedding with absolute horror.

"Who's this?" he said, coming across a name he didn't recognize. "Lady Georgina of Sandalhurst? Why are we inviting her? I don't know her. Why are we asking people we don't know?"

"I know her," Pauline replied. There was a certain steeliness in her voice that Halt would have done well to recognize. "She's my aunt. Bit of an old stick, really, but I have to invite her."

"You've never mentioned her before," Halt challenged.

"True. I don't like her very much. As I said, she's a bit of an old stick."

"Then why are we inviting her?"

"We're inviting her," Lady Pauline explained, "because Aunt Georgina has spent the last twenty years bemoaning the fact that I was unmarried. 'Poor Pauline!' she'd cry to anyone who'd listen. 'She'll be a lonely old maid! Married to her job! She'll never find a husband to look after her!' It's just too good an opportunity to miss."

Halt's eyebrows came together in a frown. There might be a few things that would annoy him more than someone criticizing the woman he loved, but for the moment, he couldn't think of one.

"Agreed," he said. "And let's sit her with the most boring people possible at the wedding feast."

"Good thinking," Lady Pauline said. She made a note on another sheet of paper. "I'll make her the first person on the Bores' Table."

"The Bores' Table?" Halt said. "I'm not sure I've heard the term."

"Every wedding has to have a Bores' Table," his fiancée explained patiently. "We take all the boring, annoying, bombastic people and sit them together. That way, they all bore each other and they don't bother the normal people we've asked."

"Wouldn't it be simpler to just ask people you like?" Halt asked.

"Except Aunt Georgina, of course—there's a good reason to ask her. But why ask other bores?"

"It's a family thing," Lady Pauline said, adding a second and third name to the Bores' Table as she thought of them. "You have to ask family and every family has its share of annoying bores. It's just part of organizing a wedding."

Halt dropped into a carved armchair, sitting slightly sideways with one leg hooked up over the arm. "I thought weddings were supposed to be joyous occasions," he muttered.

"They are, so long as you have a Bores' Table," she replied. She chewed on the end of her pen, considering yet another list. "Now, let's see that everyone has a role to play. Best man: Will, of course. And Gilan is your second groomsman. Alyss and Jenny, bridesmaids. Horace can be the usher."

"What does an usher do?" Halt asked. She smiled at him.

"He ushes. You know, *Friend of the bride? Friend of the groom?* He'll be good at that. Crowley has offered to give me away, which is sweet of him. And Baron Arald will perform the ceremony." She laid down the pen and sat back with a satisfied sigh.

"And that's everyone."

"Wouldn't *protocol*," Halt laid special stress on the word, "suggest that the King might have some official role?"

Pauline rolled her eyes in frustration. Halt was right, of course. And she sensed that he was enjoying her mistake a little too much— the innocent look in his eyes confirmed it. She took up the pen again, frowned for a moment, then said triumphantly, "Patron-Sponsor! We'll make him Patron-Sponsor!"

"And what does a Patron-Sponsor do?" Halt asked. She shrugged.

"No idea. I just made it up. But I'll think of something." She added the King's name to the list in her neat script, making a note to inform the King's Chamberlain about the concept of a Patron-Sponsor. No problem there, she thought. Lord Anthony was an old friend. Without looking up from her work, she said casually, "You will be getting a haircut, won't you?"

Halt ran his hand through his hair. It was getting a little long, he thought.

"I'll give it a trim," he said, his hand dropping unconsciously to the hilt of his saxe knife. This time, Pauline did look up.

"You'll get a haircut," she said. Her gaze was steady and unwavering.

"I'll get a haircut," he agreed meekly.

4

IT WAS GOOD TO BE BACK RAIDING AGAIN, ERAK THOUGHT
contentedly.

Life as Oberjarl had its attractions, he had to admit. And it was
pleasant to receive a twenty percent share of all booty that the raiding fleet brought in to Hallasholm. But Erak had been born to be a
sea raider, not a tax collector and administrator. Several years of sitting around the Great Hall at Hallasholm, going over receipts and
estimates with Borsa, his hilfmann, had left him bored and feeling
the need for distraction. Whereas his predecessor, Ragnak, could
look at taxes levied on ships' captains and inland farmers with an
undisguised acquisitive glee, Erak felt vaguely uncomfortable with
the amounts that were piling up in his coffers. As a wolfship captain,
his sympathies had always lain more with those who might seek to
evade paying their full tax rather than the Oberjarl and the eagle-
eyed hilfmann who levied it.

Eventually, he had dropped a massive pile of scrolls—estimates,
returns, harvest figures and detailed inventories of goods and booty
captured by his jarls—into Borsa's lap and announced that he was
going raiding again.

"Just one last raid," he said to the indignant hilfmann. "I'll go mad if I sit here behind this desk any longer. I need to be back at sea."

Reluctantly, Borsa conceded the point. He had never been the warrior type himself. He never understood why the big, ruffian-like sea captains who were invariably elected Oberjarl didn't share his passion for studying figures and detecting undeclared income. But he knew they didn't. Even Ragnak, in the early days of his rule, had continued to go on occasional raids. It was only later, when he became lazy and a little avaricious, that he found enjoyment in remaining at Hallasholm and counting his riches, over and over again.

Erak then sent for Svengal, his former second in command who had taken over the helm of *Wolfwind*, and informed him that he was assuming command again, for one more raid.

Some men might have been displeased by the prospect of being demoted to first mate. But Svengal was delighted to see Erak back in control. The two men were good friends and Svengal knew that Erak was by far the better navigator.

So here they were, off the Arridi coast, approaching the small trading town of Al Shabah, doing their best to approach quietly.

Al Shabah was one of the towns that provided supplies, equipment, timber, cordage and canvas to ships entering the Constant Sea. It was an unremarkable place, built on a promontory above a small beach, with a man-made harbor on the northern side, accessed by stairs. At this time of year, ships of the trading fleets had begun to make their way into the Constant Sea in increasing numbers, bringing trade goods from the islands to the southwest in the Endless Ocean. As they came, they stopped at Al Shabah, or one of its sister townships, to replenish water, food and firewood and to repair any damage caused by storms.

When they sailed out of the harbor, they left behind a bewildering variety of gold coin and bullion used to pay their bills. Every so often, in response to a secret message from the town, an armed caravan from the inland capital of Mararoc would arrive and collect the treasure from the towns, taking it back to the Emrikir's vaults.

The first caravan of the year was due in another two weeks, Erak knew. The schedule was a closely guarded secret, for obvious reasons. If potential attackers had no idea whether the treasure had been removed or not, it reduced the risk of attack. No right-minded pirate would risk his life in the hope that there *might* be treasure in the town's strong room. Secrecy and uncertainty were Al Shabah's best defense—particularly when the alternative would mean maintaining a large and expensive garrison for the entire year.

But secrets can be uncovered, and a week earlier, eighty kilometers down the coast, Erak had paid an informant forty reels of silver to gain a copy of the schedule. It told him that while other towns had already been emptied of their riches, Al Shabah's coffers were still temptingly full—and would remain so for some days to come.

There was a small standing garrison in the town—no more than forty men. Forty sleepy, overweight, comfortable Arridi townsmen, who hadn't fought a real engagement in twenty years or more, wouldn't provide much resistance to thirty yelling, fiendish, bloodthirsty, gold-crazed Skandians who would come screaming up from the beach like the hounds of hell.

Peering though the darkness ahead, Erak could see the lighter patch of land that marked a small sand beach at the foot of the promontory. Instead of approaching from the seaward side, he had taken *Wolfwind* deep into the bay that ran beside the promontory. Approaching along the shoreline, the ship was hidden against the dark background of the land and they were actually approaching from the landward side of the town. When they went ashore, at the beach, they would be at the foot of a hill leading to the rear wall.

Most lookouts, he reasoned, would be concentrated on the walls looking out to sea.

High above, the white buildings of the town itself were also becoming distinguishable in the rising sun. There were no lights, he noticed. No beacons or even torches to illuminate the path of the sentries who must be patrolling. He shrugged. Not a bad idea, he thought. A burning torch might make a sentry feel safe and secure, but it ruined his night vision and made it almost impossible to see anything beyond the few meters illuminated by the torch.

Erak heard the gentle breaking of waves on the beach. There was no surf to speak of, just small wavelets tumbling over themselves. Swinging the tiller smoothly, he set the ship on a forty-five degree approach to the sand. He raised his free hand, palm up, in a pre-arranged signal and sixteen oars rose dripping out of the water. There was an occasional grunt of exertion as the rowers lifted their oars to the vertical and then carefully lowered them to stow them alongside the rowing benches. Two clattered noisily, the sound seeming to be magnified by the silence around them. Erak glared at the offending oarsmen. He'd speak to them later—when he could speak more forcefully than the present situation allowed.

There was a grating sound from for'ard and he felt a dragging vibration through the soles of his feet as the keel ran onto the sand. Four men were poised on the bow gunwales, about to leap into the shallow water and make the ship secure.

"Go easy, line handlers!" Svengal whispered hoarsely.

The men, who would normally have dropped noisily into the knee-deep water, remembered at the last moment and lowered themselves carefully. Taking two bow ropes with them, they ran up the beach, feet squeaking on the sand, and hauled the ship a little farther up onto dry land.

They secured the bow ropes into the sand with hinge-bladed

sand grapnels, then faced inland, hands on their battleaxes, alert for any sign of attack.

Erak peered up at the town above them. Still there was no sound of any alarm, no sign of guards or patrols. The whitewashed buildings, looking almost ghostly in the predawn light, loomed silently above the wolfship.

More men were lowering themselves over the bow now, and others were carefully retrieving shields and battleaxes from beside the rowing benches and passing them down to others, who took them with exaggerated care and piled them on the beach above the high waterline. The shields, which were kept stowed on the outer gunwales along the length of the ship, had been covered with dark cloth to make them less conspicuous. The men stripped this off, found their respective weapons and stood ready for their captain.

Erak passed his shield and ax down to one of the men standing in the shallow water, then lowered himself over the gunwale as well. He stretched down to arm's length and released his grip, falling only a few centimeters before his feet hit the wet sand. He took his shield and ax back from his crewman and moved to where the thirty men stood lined up. The four line handlers who had been first to land would remain with the ship.

Erak couldn't help smiling as he felt a small thrill of adrenaline course through him. It was good to be back, he thought.

"Remember," he told the raiding party, "keep the noise to an absolute minimum. Watch where you're putting your feet. I don't want you missing your step and sliding down the hill in your own personal avalanche. We want to get as close as we can before they spot us. With any luck, and from the look of things, we'll be inside the town before anyone raises the alarm."

He paused, looking around the tough bearded faces before him. There were a few answering nods. Then he continued.

"On the other hand, if we are spotted, all bets are off. Start yelling to raise the dead and go at 'em. Make 'em think there's an army out here come to see them off."

Often, he knew, a sleeping garrison could be paralyzed by fear at the sound of a yelling, screaming body of attackers.

He looked around. There was a rough path at the foot of the hill, winding up toward the silent, sleeping town above them. He gestured toward it with the head of his ax.

"There's our way to the top," he said. Then, hitching his shield up on his left shoulder, he uttered the time-honored Skandian leader's call to action.

"Follow me, boys."

5

THE PATH WAS NARROW AND UNEVEN, AND THE CLIMB WAS STEEP.
But the Skandians, in spite of their bulk, were in excellent physical
condition and they maintained a brisk pace behind their leader.
There were a few grunts of exertion from time to time and
occasionally a stone would be dislodged from underfoot to go rattling
down the hillside.

But on the whole, the thirty raiders made little noise as they
jogged up the path toward Al Shabah.

Everything was a compromise, Erak thought. Just as he'd taken
the lesser of two risks by approaching along the bay's coastline, rather
than from farther out to sea, where the ship stood a better chance of
being spotted, now he had to balance speed against stealth. The longer they took to reach their objective, the greater the chance became
that their presence would be discovered. That would make the fight
a lot harder. By the same token, if they rushed up the path full speed,
they'd also increase the chance of being heard.

So the best way was to steer a middle course, maintaining a
steady jog.

Their sealskin boots thudded softly on the sand and stone underfoot. It was more noise than he would have liked, but he estimated

that it would remain unheard even if there were listeners at the top of the cliff.

There was a bad moment when one of the men immediately behind Erak lost his footing and tottered, arms waving desperately, at the edge of the steep slope leading down to the sea. Fortunately, his ax was in the carry loop on his belt, otherwise his arm-waving might have separated some of his friends from their heads.

He let out an involuntary cry and his shuffling feet released a volley of stones and rocks that clattered down the hillside. In the instant that he was about to follow them, an iron grip caught hold of the collar of his sheepskin vest and he felt himself heaved back onto firm ground by the Oberjarl.

"Gods above! Thanks, chief . . ." he began. But a huge hand clamped over his mouth, cutting off further words. Erak thrust his face close to the other man and shook him, none too gently.

"Shut up, Axl!" he whispered fiercely. "If you want to break your neck, do it quietly or I'll break it for you."

"Sorry, chief. I just . . ." he muttered, and Erak shook him again.

"Shut up!" he hissed. Then, releasing his grip on the other man's collar, he glanced anxiously toward the cliff-top, waiting to see if there was any sign that the rower's clattering and yelling had been heard.

The entire raiding party waited in silence for several minutes. Then, as there was no sound of the alarm being raised above them, there was a general release of tension.

Erak pointed upward and led the way again, jogging steadily up the steep slope. A few meters from the crest, he signaled for the men to halt. Then, gesturing to Svengal to accompany him, he covered the remaining distance to the top in a crouch, cautiously peering over the crest as he reached it. Svengal, a meter or so behind him, mirrored his actions and the two big Skandians knelt side by side, taking stock of the situation.

Al Shabah stood some forty meters away, across a bare patch of ground. The town was surrounded by a low stucco wall, a little over two meters high. Even if there were sentries patrolling, it would present no real obstacle to the Skandians. They were skilled at scaling walls like these. Two men would stand at the base of the wall, holding a length of an old oar handle between them, at waist height. The rest of the group would take a running start, one at a time. As each man stepped up onto the oar handle, the two men holding it would heave upward, sending their shipmate soaring up the wall. It took practice to get the timing right but it was one of the skills all Skandians practiced from boyhood.

Today, there would be no need for it.

An arched gateway stood four meters to their right. The gate was open and the entrance was unguarded.

"Too easy," grinned Svengal.

His captain frowned. "That's what I was thinking," he said. "Where are the guards? Where are the lookouts?"

Svengal shrugged. In spite of the absence of any guards, both men were still keeping their voices low, speaking barely above a whisper.

"We've caught 'em with the back door open, chief," he said. "The guards, if there are any, are probably around at the front of the town, facing the ocean. That's where they'd expect an attack to come from."

Erak rubbed his chin suspiciously. "Maybe," he said. "Wait here while I take a closer look."

Rising into a half crouch, he moved across the open space toward the wall. At every second, he expected to hear a challenge. A shout. Or an alarm bell ringing. But Al Shabah was silent. Reaching the

wall, he edged his way along it to the open gate. With one fluid movement, he flicked his massive battleax clear of its belt loop and hefted
it in his right hand, then, moving with deceptive speed for someone
so bulky, he sprang through the open gateway, quickly facing right
then left, ax ready, shield up to protect his left side.

Nothing.

The flat-roofed white houses stretched away from him down a
narrow street. The few windows were black squares in the whitewashed stucco. The doors were firmly closed. Nothing moved.
Nobody stirred. Al Shabah seemed deserted.

Erak hesitated a few seconds. It seemed wrong. There should be
a guard. Even one man patrolling the wall. Then he shrugged.
Maybe Svengal was right and the Arridi guards were concentrated
at the seaward side of the town. Perhaps all the lookouts were straining their eyes for the first sight of an approaching ship. Or maybe
they'd just grown complacent. It had been over twenty years since a
Skandian ship had raided here. The secrecy surrounding the timing
of the treasure caravans had kept the coastal towns safe. It was only
the fortuitous acquisition of the timetable that had led Erak to plan
this raid.

He shook his head. Maybe he was getting too skittish. Maybe
the time he'd spent lolling around Hallasholm was making him behave like a nervous maiden aunt. Abruptly, he made up his mind,
moved back to the gateway and signaled Svengal and the others to
join him.

The soft thud of sealskin boots across the sandy ground awoke
no response from the town. Svengal glanced inquiringly at his leader.

"Where to now, chief?"

Erak gestured with his ax. "Town center. We'll follow this street.
It seems to be heading in the right direction. Keep your axes ready
and your eyes peeled."

He led the way again and the raiding party followed in two files, peering around them at the silent houses. From time to time, the last two men in the line would do a sweep, turning through a full circle to make sure enemy troops weren't coming up behind them, and studying the flat roofs of the houses that stood to either side of their path for a sign of enemies. But there was nothing to be seen.

The street wound its way toward the center of the town, eventually opening up into a small square, where a large building faced them, taking up one entire side of the square. This would be the town headman's official quarters, Erak guessed. He searched his memory for the name of the building—the khadif, he remembered. The equivalent of a town hall or a tax house in other towns.

Half a dozen narrow streets opened onto the small square. The buildings that formed the other three sides—probably shops, eating houses and inns—were colonnaded with deep verandahs that would give welcome shade from the heat of the sun during the middle of the day. As he had the thought, Erak glanced to the east, where the sky was already lightening with streaks of pink. The front of the khadif facing the square was also colonnaded. The building itself was the only two-story structure in sight. Like the others, however, it had a flat roof, hidden by a decorative façade designed to give an added feeling of dominance to the building behind it.

In the center of the square stood a small fountain. Its reservoir was currently full of water, but the mechanism that allowed the water to flow from its central spout appeared to be turned off.

Erak stepped out into the square, his men following. As they exited from the narrow street, they formed into a more compact diamond formation, with the Oberjarl, Svengal and Axl at the lead point of the diamond. A few of them swung their axes experimentally as they crossed the square toward the two-story building. Still there was no sound from the town. The growing light cast their shadows in elongated, fantastic forms behind them. Erak stepped up onto the marble porchway before the khadif's big double doors. He studied them briefly. Solid, he thought. Hardwood with brass binding and a good strong lock. Still, Skandians carried their own keys for doors like this and he motioned to two of his brawnier rowers to step forward.

"Axes," he said, gesturing to the door.

The men grinned at him. One of them set his ax down for a moment, spat on his hands, then seized the ax in a two-handed grip. Erak stepped away to give the man room for a good roundhouse swing at the lock.

"Stop right there!"

The command rang out across the square and the Skandians turned in surprise. A figure had appeared from one of the side streets leading into the open space. A few of the raiders cursed in alarm. Erak's eyes narrowed and he felt a sinking sensation in the pit of his stomach. It had all been too easy, he thought.

The newcomer was tall and slim, dressed in the ornate fashion of an Arridi warrior. Flowing white shirt and trousers, doubtless of fine linen, were covered by metal-studded leather body armor. A long curved sword hung at his side and a circular shield made of metal—probably brass—was on his arm. The shield, Erak noted, was equipped with a sharp central spike. It was a weapon of attack as well as defense. A simple acorn-style helmet, also spiked, surmounted a small roll of fine cloth that wrapped the man's head. Probably, Erak thought, it was designed to avoid the contact of sun-heated metal on skin during the middle of the day.

The helmet was highly burnished, and a shining silver curtain of chain mail hung from it, protecting the wearer's neck at the sides and back. That and the highly polished metal on the armor were enough to show that this was a senior officer.

As they watched, a double file of warriors equipped in similar, if not as expensive, fashion quickly jogged out of the side street, fanning out to either side of their leader. Erak estimated that there were at least forty of them. There was a surge of movement from his own men as the Arridi warriors appeared.

"Keep it steady," he growled at them. Out of the corner of his mouth, he said to Svengal, "We're outnumbered."

"Not by too many," Svengal replied. He too had been counting the opposition. "I think our boys can take these fancy nancies without too much trouble."

Unlike Erak, he hadn't bothered to keep his voice low and it carried across the square to the Arridi officer. They saw his narrow, bearded features split by a smile as he heard Svengal's comment. He raised a silver whistle to his lips and blew once.

There was a grinding sound of heavy timbers dragging on stone and the Skandians saw each of the half dozen streets that led into the square suddenly blocked by heavy timber barriers pushed out from the walls.

"Didn't notice them," Erak said quietly to Svengal. They must have passed by one of the barriers as they entered the square but he'd been too busy to realize its significance.

"You appear to be trapped," the Arridi said.

Erak set himself a little more firmly and brought his shield up to the defense position. His men mirrored the action. "So do you," he replied.

Again the other man smiled. The white teeth were very obvious in his dark, bearded face.

"Ah," he said. "But how many archers do you have with you?"

He raised the small silver whistle to his lips and blew one long shrill blast. There was a shuffle of movement overhead and as Erak watched, the rooftops of the three sides of the square facing them were suddenly alive with archers. He had no doubt there were more on top of the khadif's flat roof as well. Even without counting he could see there were close to one hundred men, all armed with short recurve bows, each of them with an arrow nocked and drawn, aimed at the defiant group of Skandians.

Erak glanced grimly along the line of bowmen. The bows were short-range weapons. On a battlefield, he might have ignored them. But here, in the confined space of the town square, they would be deadly.

"Don't anybody move," he said quietly. One false move now could mean a volley of arrows sent in their direction.

Axl, beside him still, growled in frustration. His fighting blood was up and he didn't like the threat of a hundred arrows aimed at him. His instinct was to strike out and damage somebody.

"They can't get us all, chief," he said. "At least we can do for pretty boy here."

The tall Arridi smiled at the words, his hand dropping casually to the hilt of the curved saber he wore. Erak knew a fighting man when he saw one and in spite of the highly polished accoutrements, he had the feeling that this one was a dangerous warrior.

"Shut up, Axl," he said, not for the first time that morning. The Arridi took a pace forward. He raised his eyes to the men on the rooftops and made a hand signal. The archers released the tension on their bows, although Erak noticed they kept the arrows nocked and ready.

"There's no need for us to fight," he said. His voice was deep and pleasant. His tone was reasonable and unthreatening. "There's only one of you we're interested in. Hand him over and the rest of you can go free."

"And who might that one man be?" Erak asked, although he felt he already knew the answer to the question.

"Erak. The one they call the Oberjarl," the Arridi answered him.

Impulsively, Axl took a pace forward, raising his ax threateningly.

"You'll have to go through the rest of us to take him!" he shouted defiantly. Erak heaved a deep sigh and shook his head in irritation.

"Well done, Axl," he said. "You've just told them I'm here."

6

Undoubtedly, Baron Arald thought with a deep sense of pride and satisfaction, this would go down as the wedding of the year. Perhaps of the decade.

Already, it had all the hallmarks of a roaring success. The Bores' Table was well attended with a group of eight people, currently vying to see who could be the most uninteresting, overbearing and repetitive. Other guests glanced in their direction, giving silent thanks to the organizers who had separated them from such dreadful people.

There had been the inevitable tearful flouncing and shrill recriminations when the girlfriend of one of the younger warriors from Sir Rodney's Battleschool had caught her boyfriend kissing another girl in a darkened corridor. It wouldn't be a wedding reception without that, Arald thought. He sighed with contentment as he surveyed the colorful scene in Redmont's dining hall, where brightly dressed couples sat at tables, while Master Chubb's minions hurried through the room, delivering a bewildering variety of delicious foods: roasted meats and fowls, platters of steaming vegetables, spiced specialities of the kitchen, amazing and fantastic creations in pastry so light that it seemed to explode into featherlight fragments at the first taste. And, he thought with immense satisfaction, there were puddings and fruit yet to come!

The ceremonial side of the day had gone off perfectly, he thought, thanks in no small measure to his own performance as celebrant. He felt that his rich and carrying tones as he recited the marriage formula to the happy couple had added just the right touch of gravitas to the proceedings.

As one would expect of a seasoned orator like himself, he had lightened the mood with a particularly witty sally about the secret passion that had burned between Halt and Lady Pauline for these past twenty years—a passion apparently unremarked by anyone save himself. The joke was based around a rather clever play on words in which he referred to Pauline's unceasing affection for the often absent Ranger as her "love without halt."

He had paused after the joke to allow the audience a few moments to laugh. The fact that nobody did was a mild disappointment. Perhaps, he thought, his humor was too subtle for the masses.

Pauline, of course, had been a stunningly beautiful bride.

The woman's poise and taste were unsurpassed in the Kingdom. When she appeared at the bottom of the aisle in Redmont's audience hall, attended by young Alyss and Jenny, there had been a mass intake of breath from those assembled—a muted "aaaah" that ran around the room.

Her gown was white, of course, a clever formal variation on the elegant Courier's uniform that she normally wore. Simplicity, he thought. That was the key to good fashion. He glanced down at his own purple velvet doublet, decorated in bright blue and gold diamond-shaped lozenges, highlighted by silver embroidery, and had a moment of doubt that perhaps it was just a shade too busy. Then he dismissed the thought. The bulkier male figure could stand a little extra embellishment, he decided.

But Pauline had really been stunning. With her gray-blond hair swept up on her head and a simple gold necklace at her throat, she had glided down the central aisle like a veritable goddess. Her attendants were suitably alluring as well. Alyss, equally tall and elegant, wore a variation on her mentor's gown, but in pale blue. Her blond hair was down, falling naturally to her shoulders. Young Jenny, the second bridesmaid, couldn't compete with the other two for height and elegance. But she had her own charm. Small, with a rounded figure and a wide friendly grin, she seemed to bounce down the aisle where the others glided. Jenny brought a natural sense of exuberance and fun to any proceedings, Arald thought. Her yellow gown reflected her sunny disposition and approach to life.

As for the groom's party, Crowley had really come up trumps. Naturally, everyone had been wondering what Halt would wear. After all, nobody could remember seeing him in anything other than the muted greens, browns and grays of a Ranger's cloak. Discussion reached fever pitch when it was heard that, a few days before the wedding, he had actually visited Redmont's barber for a haircut and beard trim.

Then Crowley had revealed his surprise—an official formal uniform for the Ranger Corps that would be worn for the first time at the wedding by Halt, Will, Gilan and himself.

In keeping with Ranger tradition, the basic color was green—a dark leaf green. In place of their dull brown jerkins and breeches and cowled camouflage cloaks, each Ranger wore a belted sleeveless tunic over a white silken shirt. The tunics were made from the finest leather and all of them were the same rich leaf green. High on the left breast, woven in metallic thread, was a miniature oakleaf insignia—silver for Halt, Gilan and Crowley, bronze for Will.

Dark green breeches and brown, knee-high boots in soft leather added to the effect, while the broad belt that gathered the tunic at the waist supported an ornate version of the Rangers' standard-issue double scabbard. The formal model was black and shining and chased with silver trim. Halt's contained two specially made knives, a saxe and a throwing knife. They were both perfectly balanced and the hilts were chased in silver as well. They were Crowley's wedding gift to his old friend.

"I know you won't wear them in the field," he'd said. "But keep them for formal occasions." He, Gilan and Will wore their day-to-day, utilitarian weapons.

The final touch, everyone agreed, was a small piece of genius. If Rangers were known for anything it was their long mottled cloaks— a garment into which they could virtually disappear when the need arose. Such a cloak would be out of place at a formal occasion, so Crowley had replaced it with an item that reflected the sense of the original. Each Ranger wore a short cape. Made in dull satin, it bore the mottled green-brown-gray pattern of the cloak, with an arrangement of four stylized arrows, picked out in silver thread, running diagonally down it. The cape was offset to hang from the right shoulder, reaching only to the waist. In one stroke, it represented the cloak and the quiver of arrows that all Rangers wore at their right shoulder. Everyone agreed that the four Rangers looked impressive and handsome in these new uniforms. Simple and stylish once again, thought Arald, before suffering another momentary qualm about his own outfit.

He turned to his wife, the very beautiful, redheaded Lady Sandra, and gestured at the brightly colored doublet.

"My dear," he said, "you don't think I'm a bit ... too much in this, do you?"

"Too much, darling?" she repeated, trying to hide a smile. He made a doubtful little gesture.

"You know . . . too colorful . . . overstated. Coming the peacock, as it were?"

"Do you feel overstated, my lord?" she asked.

"Well, no. But perhaps . . ."

"You are Baron of Redmont, after all," she said, now managing a completely straight face. He looked down at himself, considered carefully, then, reassured, nodded his thanks to her.

"No. Of course not. You're right, my dear. As ever. My position deserves a little bit of pomp and show, I suppose. No . . . you're right. I'm perfectly fine. Just the right tone, in fact."

This time, Lady Sandra had to turn away, finding something urgent to say to the person sitting on her opposite side. Arald, reassured now that he hadn't committed a fashion gaffe, went back to his musing over events so far.

After the official ceremony, the guests had proceeded from the audience hall to the dining hall and taken their seats. Tables had been carefully placed with regard to rank.

The wedding party was seated centrally on the dais, of course. Arald, Lady Sandra, Sir Rodney and the rest of the Redmont officials were to their left at another table. The King, as Patron-Sponsor of the event, occupied a third table, along with Princess Cassandra and his entourage.

When people had taken their places behind their chairs, those at the three tables on the dais entered and stood ready—wedding party first, then the royal party, then Arald's group. King Duncan motioned for all to sit and there was a scraping of chairs throughout the huge room. Duncan remained standing. When the commotion of shifting chairs and shuffling feet finally died down, he spoke, his deep voice carrying easily to all corners.

"My lords, ladies, gentlemen . . ." he began, then, seeing every doorway into the room crowded with faces belonging to castle staff and servants, he added with a grin, "and people of Redmont Castle." There was a ripple of amusement through the room. "Today I have the honor of being Patron-Sponsor of this very happy event."

Arald had leaned forward attentively and craned around to see the King at the other side of the dais. This position of Patron-Sponsor was new to him. He had been wondering for some weeks what it entailed. Perhaps now he would find out.

"I must admit," Duncan continued, "I was a little curious to know what the duties of a Patron-Sponsor might be. So I consulted with my Chamberlain, Lord Anthony—a man for whom the mysteries of protocol are an open book."

He indicated his Chamberlain, who inclined his head gravely in response.

"Apparently, a Patron-Sponsor's duties are relatively clear-cut." He reached into the cuff of his sleeve and produced a small sheet of parchment on which he had written notes. "As Patron-Sponsor, I am charged with . . ."—he paused and consulted the notes—"adding a sense of royal cachet to proceedings today."

He waited while a ripple of conversation ran around the room. Nobody was quite sure what adding a sense of royal cachet really meant. But everyone agreed that it sounded impressive indeed. Lady Pauline's mouth twitched in a smile and she looked down at the table. Halt found something of vast interest in the ceiling beams high above. Duncan continued.

"My second duty is . . ."—again he consulted his notes to make sure he had the wording correct—"to provide an extremely expensive present to the bride and groom . . ."

Lady Pauline's head jerked up at that. She leaned forward and turned to make eye contact with Lord Anthony. The Chamberlain met her gaze, his face completely devoid of expression. Then, very slowly, one eyelid slid down in a wink. He liked Pauline and Halt a great deal and he'd added that duty without consulting them. After certain events in the past, he thought he owed at least that much to Halt.

"And finally," Duncan was saying, "it is my duty to declare this celebration officially open. Which I now do, with great delight. Chubb! Bring on the feast!"

And, as the assembled throng cheered, he sat down and the feasting began.

"I liked your speech," Alyss said to Will as the puddings were cleared away. He shrugged.

"I hope it was all right," he said. As best man, he had proposed the toast to Halt and Lady Pauline. It was a mark of his growing maturity, thought Alyss, that he had the confidence to speak from the heart of his deep affection for his teacher and friend. As a member of the Diplomatic Service, she was a trained speaker herself and she had admired the way he hadn't shied away from voicing his true feelings, yet avoided cheap sentimentality. She'd glanced once at Halt during the speech and saw the grim-faced Ranger furtively wiping his eye with a napkin.

"It was a lot better than all right," she assured him. Then, as she saw him starting to grin, she jogged him with her elbow. "What?"

"I was just thinking, I can't wait to see Halt in the bridal dance with Pauline. He's not known for his fancy stepping. He should be quite a sight to behold. A total fumble foot!"

"Is that right?" she said dryly. "And how do you think you'll manage it?"

"Me?" he said in some surprise. "I won't be dancing! It's the bridal dance. The bride and groom dance alone!"

"For one circuit of the room," she told him. "After which they are joined by the best man and first bridesmaid, then by the groomsman and second bridesmaid."

Will reacted as if he had been stung. He leaned forward to speak across Jenny, on his left, to Gilan.

"Gil! Did you know we have to dance?" he asked. Gilan nodded enthusiastically.

"Oh yes indeed. Jenny and I have been practicing for the past three days, haven't we, Jen?"

Jenny looked up at him adoringly and nodded. Jenny was in love. Gilan was tall, dashing, good-looking, charming and very amusing. Plus he was cloaked in the mystery and romance that came with being a Ranger. Jenny had only ever known one Ranger and that had been grim-faced, gray-bearded Halt.

Well, there was Will, of course. But he was an old friend and held no sense of mystery for her. But Gilan! He was beautiful, she thought.

And he was hers for the rest of the reception, she promised herself.

Will felt a sense of panic as he heard the orchestra playing the opening bars of "Together Forever," the traditional bridal dance. Halt and Pauline rose from their seats and people stood and applauded, craning to watch as he led her down the stairs from the dais to the main floor, where a space had been cleared for dancing.

"Well, I'm not dancing," Will said through gritted teeth. "I don't know how."

"Oh yes you are," Alyss told him. "Let's hope you're a fast learner."

He glanced at her and saw no prospect of escape. "Well, at least I won't be the only one," he said. "Halt will be terrible too."

But what nobody in the assembly knew was that for the past ten days, Halt had been taking dance lessons from Lady Sandra. He had always been well-balanced, coordinated and light on his feet, and it had taken just a few hours for the Baron's wife, an expert herself, to turn him into a consummate dancer. Now he and Pauline glided around the room as if they were born to dance together. There was a gasp of surprise from the crowd, then an enthusiastic roar of applause.

Will felt Alyss's surprisingly firm grip on his forearm as she stood and brought him to his feet beside her.

"Let's go, Fumblefoot," she said.

There was no escape, Will knew. He preceded her down the stairs, giving her his arm as she descended. Then he faced her uncertainly.

"Arm there," she said. "Other arm, idiot. Now hand there ... okay, ready? We're going to start with your left foot. On three. One. Two ... What the devil is he doing here?"

She was looking over his shoulder toward the main entrance to the hall, where a commotion had broken out. There was a huge, unkempt figure standing just inside the door, arguing with the servants posted there, who were trying to restrain him. His fleece jacket and horned helmet marked him as a Skandian. Heads had turned toward the noise and, already, Horace was heading down the aisle to take charge. But after a few paces, he stopped in surprise, recognizing the man at the same time Will did.

"It's Svengal," Will said.

7

HORACE REACHED THE ARGUING GROUP JUST INSIDE THE MAIN door and quickly quieted things down, reassuring the servants and guards that the Skandian was a friend, and not about to make a one-man attack on Castle Redmont. Will watched as the tall warrior spoke quickly to Svengal, then led him away to a side room. As they went, Horace turned, caught Will's eye and made an unmistakable gesture for him to join them.

Gradually, the people in the hall relaxed as it became apparent that the incident had been resolved and there was no immediate danger. The orchestra, which had tailed off at Svengal's appearance, picked up the melody once more and eyes returned to the bridal couple. Will saw that Halt and Lady Pauline had paused and were standing motionless in the middle of the dance floor. He crossed quickly to them.

"Finish the dance," he said quietly. "I'll take care of it."

Halt nodded his gratitude. The last thing he wanted was any kind of disruption to Lady Pauline's special day.

"Find out what he wants," he said.

Will grinned. "Maybe he's brought you a wedding present."

Halt jerked his head toward the back of the room.

"Get going," he said. Will grinned again and turned away, taking Alyss's hand as he passed.

"Come on," he said, leading her off the dance floor with him. He glanced up to catch Gilan's inquiring look as the tall Ranger led Jenny down from the dais. Will jerked his head toward Halt and Pauline and mouthed the words, "Keep dancing."

Gilan nodded. The less disruption to the normal run of events, the better, he realized.

Pauline saw the quick exchange between the two young Rangers, then watched as Will picked his way through the tables, Alyss accompanying him. She admired the speed with which he had reacted, the way he was taking over the situation.

"He's growing up," she said to Halt as they began to dance again. Gilan and Jenny now circled the floor with them as well. Then Duncan and Cassandra joined them, followed by the Baron and Lady Sandra. That was the signal for other dancers to crowd onto the floor. Within a few minutes, most people had forgotten that a travel-stained, weary Skandian had just crashed the wedding party.

King Duncan steered his way toward Halt and Pauline, Cassandra moving lightly in time with him.

"Halt? Any idea what's going on?" he said out of the corner of his mouth.

"Will's finding out now, your majesty," Halt replied and the King nodded, satisfied.

"Keep me informed," he said, and he and Cassandra circled away. They were replaced by Arald and Sandra, as the Baron plowed through the crowded dancers. Whereas Duncan and Cassandra had circled gracefully, Baron Arald took a direct route, rather like a purple, blue and gold battlehorse. Regrettably Lady Sandra had never been able to pass the finer points of the dancer's art on to her husband.

"Halt?" he said as they approached.

"Will's checking, sir," Halt told him, and the Baron nodded.

"Good. Keep me informed."

He and his wife moved off. Halt glanced quizzically at his partner, having to look up slightly to do so. Pauline was tall for a woman.

"As soon as I know anything myself," he said.

As they reached the entrance to the hall, Alyss stopped and turned Will toward her.

"Perhaps I should go back to the table," she said. "This Svengal doesn't know me and he might feel more comfortable talking if there are no strangers present."

As a Courier, her instincts for intrigue were finely honed and Will sensed she was right. There was obviously something out of the ordinary going on. Svengal's abrupt appearance proved that. He nodded and briefly took her hand in both of his.

"You could be right," he said. "Besides, it will look better if one of us is back at the party."

He squeezed her hand then released it. She smiled at him, turned, and slipped back through the crowded room. Will watched her go, then moved away toward the small anteroom where Horace had taken their unexpected visitor.

Svengal was slumped wearily on a bench as Will entered.

"Will," said the Skandian with a tired smile, rising stiffly to shake hands. "Sorry to barge in at a time like this."

Will glanced up at Horace.

"What's going on?" he asked. From Svengal's downcast, weary manner, he gathered it was not good news.

Horace shrugged. "I thought we'd wait for you. Save him saying everything twice. What's going on out there?" He indicated the hall with a quick head gesture.

"It's all back to normal. You got things settled before too many people had a chance to notice. Good work."

Horace made a small self-deprecating gesture and Will took another look at the Skandian.

"You look just about done in, Svengal. Are you all right?"

Svengal had slumped back onto the bench. He grinned ruefully, easing his aching back.

"I've felt better," he said. "I've spent two days and most of last night on one of your blasted horses—all the way from Castle Araluen to here. I can hardly move my legs or back."

"Araluen?" Horace interrupted. "What were you doing there?"

"We sailed *Wolfwind* up that same river we took last time. I thought it was the best place to look for you all."

Will and Horace exchanged glances. "I imagine that set the cat among the pigeons," Will said. There was a treaty in place between Araluen and Skandia, but even so, the unexpected sight of a wolfship so far inland could only have caused alarm.

"We flew Evanlyn's pennant," Svengal told him. "We still had it in our flag locker. Is there anything to drink around here?"

Will held up his hands in apology. "Sorry. You could probably use something to eat as well," he said.

Svengal nodded several times. "Yes. That would be good too. Haven't eaten in a while."

Will called to a page who had been stationed outside the door. The young boy put his head around the door frame, staring curiously at the massive Skandian, who grinned at him.

"Bring us some wine . . . no, wait!" Will said as the boy began to dart away. The page returned. "Get us a plate of food as well. A big plate. A platter, in fact. Lots of meat and bread. Don't worry about vegetables or greenery." He knew that Skandians had a deep-seated contempt for salads as a food source.

"Bring the wine in a flagon," Horace added. "Not one of those dainty glasses they're using outside. And hurry!"

"Yes, sirs," the page said. He raced away.

"So tell us," Will said, "what brings you here in the middle of Halt's wedding?"

Svengal shook his head in apology. "Didn't know about that," he told them. "We've been at sea for months now. We need help and you were the only people we thought could give it."

"We?" Horace asked.

"Erak and me. Well, Erak really. He told me to come here and find you—and Halt."

"So he's still in Hallasholm, I take it?" Will said. He was aware that Erak had turned his ship over to Svengal when he had assumed the office of Oberjarl. But Svengal shook his head.

"He's in Arrida," he told them. "He's been captured by the Arridi and they're holding him ransom."

"What?" Will's voice rose to a higher pitch than he'd intended. He paused and composed himself. "What the devil is he doing in Arrida?"

"We were raiding," Svengal explained. "He was bored with sitting around talking to Borsa all day."

"I can imagine," Will put in. He still harbored resentment for the Skandian hilfmann, who had assigned him to life as a yard slave—an almost certain death sentence in the bitter Skandian winter.

"Get over it," Horace told him and jerked a thumb at Svengal. "Let's hear the story."

But the page chose that moment to return with a platter loaded with chicken legs, pork chops and a small mutton leg. There was also a tankard of wine on the tray that he set down. Svengal looked greedily at the food and drink.

"Oh, go ahead," Horace told him.

Svengal drank a third of the wine in one draft, then grabbed the mutton and tore off enough with his teeth to feed a small family. He chewed and swallowed for a few moments, his eyes closed blissfully as the food and drink sent energy coursing through him.

"He was hungry," Will muttered. Svengal said he'd been riding for two days—not a popular way of traveling for Skandians. It was becoming obvious that he hadn't stopped to eat. The sea wolf swallowed a last piece of mutton and took another gigantic gulp of wine. He wiped grease and wine from his whiskers with the back of one massive hand, then let go a belch loud enough to wake the dead.

"I take it he likes our food," Horace said. Will rolled his eyes impatiently.

"Svengal," he said, "get on with it. How did Erak get himself captured? And how did you get away? What in God's name were you doing in Arrida? And—"

Svengal held up a grease-smeared hand. "Hey, two or three questions at a time, all right? As I said, Erak was bored. He wanted to go to sea again. So he decided to go on one last raid." He paused, considering. "Well, he said it would be his last but I doubt it. I reckon he—"

"Get on with it!" Will and Horace chorused together.

"Oh . . . yeah, sorry. Well, we planned a raid."

"In Arrida?" Horace said incredulously, and Svengal regarded him, an injured look on his face.

"Yes. In Arrida. After all, we're not allowed to raid here these days, are we? We have to go farther afield."

Will and Horace exchanged glances. "I suppose that's our fault," Will said. "Go on, Svengal."

"Anyway, we planned to hit a town called Al Shabah. It's a trading town where they provision ships and we figured—well, Erak figured—there'd be a lot of money there. You see—"

"Svengal," Will said, "I'm sure there were excellent reasons for raiding this El Shibah . . ."

"Al Shabah," Svengal corrected him, eyeing a chicken leg then reaching for it.

"But just get on with what happened, all right?"

"Well, we landed before dawn and everything seemed deserted. No guards. No lookouts. We made our way into the town and then we realized they'd been waiting for us. There were over a hundred troops in there—frontline troops too. Not the usual amateurs you find in those little towns. They were expecting us. They even knew that Erak was coming. They called him by name, knew he was Oberjarl. Said he was the only one they were interested in."

"Let me get this straight. They ambushed all of you? The entire ship's crew?" Horace frowned at the thought.

Svengal nodded. "They let the rest of us go because they needed us to collect the ransom. They even returned our weapons once we were back on board. Said they didn't want us captured by pirates while we were fetching the money." He snorted in bitter amusement. "Ironic, isn't it?"

"How much is this ransom?" Will asked.

"Eighty thousand reels," Svengal said. The two young men whistled.

"That's a lot of silver," Horace said.

Svengal shrugged. "Erak is Oberjarl, after all."

Will was frowning as he thought over what Svengal had said. There was something he didn't understand.

"Svengal, eighty thousand is a lot of money. But surely Erak could put his hands on that amount. As you say, he is the Oberjarl. Why did you come here for it?"

"Erak told me to come here. It could take the best part of a year for us to get to Skandia and then back to Arrida with the money . . ." He trailed off, the thought not quite completed.

Will nodded. "That makes sense," he said. "And I'm sure King Duncan will lend the money. After all, Erak saved his daughter's life." He sensed that Svengal had something else on his mind, something he was reluctant to say.

"But?" he prompted, and the sea wolf sighed heavily.

"Erak didn't want me to go back to Skandia with the news that he was a captive," he said. "He's pretty sure that he was betrayed by one of our own people."

8

∞∞∞∞∞∞∞∞∞∞∞∞∞∞∞∞∞∞

"Betrayed?" King Duncan said. "Why would his own people betray him? Last I heard, Erak was a popular choice as Oberjarl."

It was the following morning and even Baron Arald's spacious office in Castle Redmont was looking slightly crowded with the numbers present. In addition to the King and his daughter, Lord Anthony, Crowley, Halt, Pauline, Baron Arald, Sir Rodney, Horace, Gilan, Will and Alyss were all seated around the central desk, where Arald had given precedence to the King. Svengal, exhausted by his ride from Araluen, was still sleeping off the effects of the journey. Although, Will thought with grim humor, the effects might be longer lasting than he expected. A novice rider, Svengal would be stiff and sore in every muscle and joint when he awoke.

The previous evening, after Will had reported the basic facts of Svengal's arrival, it had been decided to leave detailed discussion till the morning. The wedding celebration had continued as if there had been no interruption. That had been Lady Pauline's decision. As she had said to Halt some weeks earlier, this was a big occasion for many of the guests—perhaps a once-in-a-lifetime opportunity to brush shoulders with royalty.

"Let them enjoy themselves," she had said. "We can deal with this in the morning."

Halt smiled at her as she said it. It was confirmation of the Baron's good judgment in appointing her to a high diplomatic position.

Pauline also had an ulterior motive. She knew full well that this would be one of the few occasions in her life when she could persuade Halt to dance with her and she had no intention of letting it pass merely because Oberjarl Erak had carelessly got himself captured by the Arridi. It was, she thought, a matter of retaining a sense of perspective.

So the dancing and feasting had continued. Then, just before midnight, an open carriage pulled by two white mares had arrived at the entrance to the dining hall. The newlyweds led a procession down the central aisle and were cheered aboard by a horde of well-wishers. In addition, hundreds of others had arrived from the village itself, where the Baron had contributed two steers to be roasted and several kegs of ale for a giant outdoor feast.

These newcomers lined the path to the gatehouse, where the massive drawbridge and portcullis were open. Others waited outside, on either side of the road winding down the hill toward the forest. As the carriage passed by, they pelted it with flowers and cheers in equal amounts. Halt, who had spent his life in covert activities, moving unseen and unnoticed through the country, found it a novel and uncomfortable experience to be the center of attention. He felt strangely exposed without the comforting concealment of his camouflage cloak and slumped low in his seat, trying to disappear into the plush cushions. Lady Pauline, on the other hand, sat upright and waved regally to the cheering people. And since the vast majority of those who arrive to gawk at any wedding go to see the bride in any case, his reticence went largely unnoticed.

"Where will they be going?" a blacksmith's wife asked of nobody in particular as the carriage clattered down the hill.

A housewife next to her—one of those people who always know the answer to every such question—replied with smug certainty.

"I've heard that, deep in the woods, there's a special love nest been built for them. A bower of flowers and precious materials where they'll spend the night." Her imagination fired by her own statement, she then added authoritatively, "What's more, there are specially trained songbirds in the trees and pure white deer will be grazing in the clearing for my lady's enjoyment."

The actual facts were more mundane. The carriage would stop at the little cabin just at the fringe of the forest, where Halt and Pauline would wait until the crowd had dispersed. Then they would board another, less ornate, carriage drawn by two nondescript bays and return to the castle, where Arald had set aside a suite of rooms as their permanent residence.

So here they all were, discussing the remarkable turn of events that Svengal had brought to their door.

"Erak's popular with the majority," Will told the King, in answer to his question. "But there's a small faction in Hallasholm who would like to see him lose his position. Small, but vocal and persistent."

"I assume our treaty has something to do with this?" Crowley asked. When Halt had led the Skandians to victory over an invading Temujai force, he had capitalized on the situation by creating a treaty where large-scale raids on Araluen were discouraged by the Oberjarl. In Erak's case, "discouraged" translated pretty much as "forbidden."

"It doesn't help, that's for sure," Will said. "And the anti-Erak faction are using it as a lever to create dissension among the others. But it goes deeper than that."

"If there's an anti-Erak faction," Lady Pauline said, "one assumes that they must also have their own leader in mind. Who might that be? Do we know?"

"We do," Will told the room. Although he and Horace had both been privy to Svengal's news, they had decided that Will would conduct the briefing for the others. It was part of a Ranger's training to know how to assemble and report facts as cohesively as possible. "It's a man called Toshak, a crony of Slagor's."

His eyes met Cassandra's as he said the name and he saw understanding dawning there. Slagor had tried to have Cassandra executed when she and Will had been among the Skandians. Later, she had discovered his part in a plot to betray the Skandian forces to the Temujai.

Alyss saw the byplay between Will and the blond princess. Her lips tightened slightly but, trained diplomat that she was, she swiftly composed her features before anyone noticed.

"Slagor?" the King said. "But surely he's dead. Erak had him executed for treason at the end of the war, didn't he?"

"I tried to convince him not to," Cassandra put in. "I thought it was a bad idea and I felt . . . responsible, I suppose."

The King shook his head. "No. It's unpleasant, my dear, but it had to be done. Slagor betrayed his country in time of war. You can't leave people like that unpunished. He deserved what he got and you have nothing to blame yourself for."

"The princess has a point, however," Halt said. And as the others looked at him, he went on to explain, "Executing a criminal often makes a martyr of him. Once he's dead and gone, people all too often forget the crimes he's committed and start to see a more sanitized version. A person like that starts to be seen as a victim, then as a figurehead for anyone who has an ax to grind. No pun intended," he added, remembering that Slagor had been beheaded.

Will nodded in agreement. "That's pretty much the way Erak sees it, according to Svengal. Toshak, the leader of a rebel clique, doesn't give a fig about Slagor's fate. He's using him as a symbol to further his own purpose. Which is to take over as Oberjarl."

The King nodded slowly. It made sense. "Which is why Erak doesn't want Svengal going back to Skandia with the news that he's been captured—and that it'll cost the Skandians eighty thousand reels to get him back. It might be quicker and cheaper just to elect a new Oberjarl."

Sir Rodney had listened to the conversation so far without speaking. Now he frowned thoughtfully and posed a question.

"Given that there may be people who want Erak out of the way, that's still no proof that they were involved in his capture, is it?" he asked. "After all, that might just have been good luck on the part of the Arridi."

Will nodded. "That could be right, Sir Rodney. But there's more to it. The Skandian raiding fleet meets before any raiding season and assigns territories by lot. So the other captains—and Toshak was one of them—knew Erak's ship would be raiding that part of the coast."

"Still," Crowley said, "Rodney has a good point. It could have been simple luck on the Arridi's part that allowed them to ambush Erak. They could have heard a wolfship was in the area and set up the trap—arranging to sell him the false timetable. There's no hard evidence that Toshak was involved."

"Except for one thing," Horace put in. He felt Will was being besieged on all sides and might need a little help. "They weren't just waiting for any wolfship. They knew it was Erak who was coming and they knew he was the Oberjarl. Only a Skandian could have told them that."

Rodney and Crowley both nodded thoughtfully, seeing the logic in the argument. Cassandra was watching her father anxiously. She felt they were getting off the real point.

"We'll lend Erak the money, won't we, Dad?" she said. Her father looked up at her. He was inclined to do so, but he hadn't totally made up his mind. Eighty thousand was a lot of money. Not a crippling amount, admittedly. But it wasn't a sum you would just throw away.

"I'm sure Erak is good for the money, your majesty," Halt said. He had already decided that, in the unlikely event that Duncan wouldn't agree to the loan, he would go and shake Erak free of the clutches of the Arridi tribesmen.

"Yes, yes," Duncan said, still considering. "And the actual amount is sure to be less. The Arridi would be insulted if we didn't haggle a little."

"I owe Erak my life, Father," Cassandra said quietly, but firmly. The use of the word "father" alerted Duncan to the fact that she was beginning to think he might be reluctant to help Erak. Before he could say anything, she continued. "Not just when he helped Will and me to escape. But later, when Slagor exposed my true identity and tried to have me killed, Erak was ready to get me away then."

Duncan raised a hand to calm her down. He could hear her voice rising in pitch and he didn't want a confrontation with so many people present.

"Cassie, I fully intend to pay the ransom. It's the mechanics of the whole thing that are a little difficult." He could see that this statement satisfied his daughter, but she looked puzzled, so he went on. "For a start, I'm not putting eighty thousand reels—or whatever the final amount might be—on a wolfship and waving good-bye as it sails off for Arrida. There's too great a chance that it could be lost . . . storms, shipwrecks, pirates. It's too risky."

Lord Anthony coughed apologetically. "There's always the Silasian Council, your majesty," he said, and Duncan nodded in his direction.

"That's what I was thinking, Anthony."

The Silasian Council was a cartel that traded in currencies, rather than in goods. They provided a means by which countries could exchange funds without the risk of dispatching actual cash or bullion on long perilous journeys. Countries deposited money with the Silasians, who paid interest to the depositor. They also undertook to deliver any amounts that might require transfer—either in fact or as deposits from one country's account to another. The council took a percentage of each transaction as its fee and guaranteed safe passage of funds as part of its service. The risk of loss during transfers was more than covered by their fee.

"Are the Arridi signatories to the Silasian agreements, Anthony?" Duncan asked his Chamberlain now. Lord Anthony's face twisted in thought.

"I doubt it, your majesty. At the last listing, they weren't there."

"In which case, we'll have to arrange for the Council to do an actual cash delivery. That means someone will have to negotiate the terms and the final amount with the Arridi and get them to agree to the arrangement, and the fee to be paid to the Silasians."

Fees were usually paid by both sender and receiver.

"I can do that, your majesty," said Halt quickly. But the King shook his head.

"No. I'm afraid you can't, Halt. There's a protocol involved. We're dealing with the ransom of the ruler of a country. And on the practical side, there are negotiations to be carried out. That needs someone of high rank—a national seal-bearer. It is a matter of national funds, so it needs someone of royal rank. Ideally, I should go myself."

Halt shrugged. That would be fine with him.

Then Duncan added, in a frustrated tone, "But I can't at the moment. I'm supposed to be organizing the peace talks between four of the six Hibernian kings. They'll fall apart if I don't arbitrate among them."

"Then give me your seal and I'll go in your place. We'll say I'm your long-lost cousin," Halt said. He had very little patience for the proper way of doing things. Duncan sighed and looked at Crowley.

"Have you never explained to your wild man how the system of royal seals and signets works in the civilized world, Crowley?"

Crowley raised his eyebrows. He suspected that Halt had engaged in numerous fraudulent activities to do with royal seals over the past twenty years. But this time, they couldn't take the risk.

"The royal seal can only be used by a member of the royal family, as you know, Halt," said Lord Anthony. "If you were to use it, any negotiations you carried out, and any agreements you reached, would be fraudulent and therefore void. If that were exposed, it would take years for Araluen to regain the trust of other countries. We can't risk that."

Halt snorted, his usual reaction to formalities and protocols. Lady Pauline placed a calming hand over his own and he looked at her and shrugged apologetically. Then, trying to keep his voice reasonable, he asked, "Couldn't you give me a warrant to act on your behalf, signed over your seal?"

"If it were another country—Teutlandt or Gallica, for example—that's exactly what I'd do," Duncan replied. "But unfortunately, even though the Arridi speak the common tongue, they have their own alphabet and written language, which bears no resemblance to ours. We have nobody who can write or read it and presumably they have nobody who can read ours. So a warrant authorizing you to act on my behalf might just as well be a shopping list with my seal at the bottom." Duncan paused, chewing his bottom lip in frustration. "No. I'll have to go myself," he said. "But it'll have to wait till I've dealt with the Hibernians."

"There must be some other way," Halt insisted.

"The answer is staring us all in the face," Cassandra said. "I'll go."

9

"YOU WILL NOT. IT'S OUT OF THE QUESTION," THE KING ANSWERED brusquely.

Color rose in Cassandra's cheeks as he spoke. Controlling her anger with a great effort, she spoke very calmly.

"Why? Why should it be out of the question? Our family, our country, owes a debt of honor to Erak. The Skandians are our allies because of him. So why shouldn't I be the one to negotiate his release?"

"Because—"

"You've said that the task requires a seal-bearer. A member of the royal family. Well, I don't see any others around here. Why shouldn't I go in your place?" She paused, then added with greater intensity, "Dad, this is exactly what we were discussing a few weeks ago. One day I'll be Queen. If I don't start taking on some of these duties now, I'll never be ready to be a real queen—someone you'd be proud of."

"Cassandra, you will not go and that's an end of it. Now let's stop this discussion. It's embarrassing."

She sensed the weakness in his argument and knew what was behind it.

"It's only embarrassing because you know you're wrong about this. I owe Erak my life. I have a right to help rescue him."

There was a matching flare of anger in the King's face now and she sensed that she had scored a point. There was no rational reason why she shouldn't undertake the mission. His objection to it was purely personal. It was understandable, she realized. But it was wrong.

"The problem is, Cassandra," he said, also working to keep his voice calm, "you're . . ."

"A girl," she interrupted.

He shook his head doggedly. "That wasn't what I was going to say. I was going to say you're inexperienced and young. You've never carried out negotiations like this."

"I negotiated the Skandian treaty," she shot back, and he shook his head like a clumsy bear frustrated by a small dog nipping at its heels.

"You had Halt to advise you then," he said, and she answered immediately, giving him no respite.

"And he can advise me on this," she said. She looked at the Ranger. "Halt, you'd come with me, wouldn't you?"

"Of course I would, your highness," he said. Unlike the King, he saw no good reason why Cassandra should not go on the mission. In Skandia, she had proved to be brave and resourceful. And she was no shrinking violet. She'd shown that in the battle line against the Temujai, when she had continued calmly directing her group of archers while the fierce horse soldiers overran her position. He had no doubt that she could look after herself.

"Halt . . ." the King began, looking angrily at his old friend. But Lord Anthony now interjected as well.

"Actually, your majesty, there is a certain merit in the idea. The Arridi are a matriarchal society. Succession is through the mother's line. So they have no objection to dealing with women—

unlike some countries. That makes the princess an excellent choice as your representative."

The King came to his feet abruptly. The heavy high-backed chair he had been sitting in teetered for a moment on its back legs with the force of his movement. Then it crashed back onto a level footing again.

"I will thank you all to stay out of this!" he said, in an overloud voice. "This is a family matter. It is between my daughter and myself and it is of no concern to any of you! Is that absolutely clear?"

The last four words were delivered in a shout and there was an awkward silence in the room for several seconds. Then Baron Arald spoke.

"No, your majesty. I think you're wrong," he said firmly. The King's furious gaze swung to him. Arald met it unflinchingly.

"Baron Arald, this does not concern you. Do you understand?"

Arald shook his head. "No, sir. I don't. On the contrary, it does concern me. It concerns all of us."

"I am the King, Baron Arald, and I say this matter is private."

Will watched Baron Arald with some awe. He had seen the burly knight's courage in battle several times but this was something different. This was a far greater form of courage—the moral courage to speak out when your conscience told you to do so.

"And those two statements contradict each other, your majesty. Because you are King, this matter cannot be private. Because what concerns you and your family concerns the country. In the past, you've said you valued my advice—"

"Well, I don't value it now!" the King snapped.

Arald shrugged. "If you only value my advice when I agree with you, you don't value it at all," he said bluntly. The King flinched as if Arald had struck him. He realized that the other man was right. But still . . .

"Arald, you don't understand. You don't have children. She's my daughter and this will be a dangerous journey . . ."

Cassandra snorted derisively but Arald glanced quickly at her to silence her, then spread his hands in understanding. "Granted, your majesty. Just as it was dangerous when you led the army against Morgarath. Just as it was dangerous when Rodney and I fought the Kalkara. This is the price we pay for our privileged rank. We enjoy the privileges because, when the time comes, we have to face the danger. And your daughter is no exception. She knew that when she and Will destroyed Morgarath's bridge and allowed themselves to be captured."

The King was a relatively young man but at the mention of that terrible time, his face seemed to grow haggard and old. That had been the worst time of his life, he thought. He sat down slowly. Arald softened his tone a little.

"Your majesty, you're right, I have no children, so I can't fully understand how you feel. But your daughter is also right. She will be Queen one day and she wants to rule in the fashion you've set. There is a risk in all of this. But Cassandra is willing to take it and so must you be."

King Duncan looked up and swept his gaze slowly around the room. Cassandra, he saw, was defiant as ever. Arald's face was set and determined. Halt and Crowley's faces were inscrutable in the shadows of their cowls. The two younger men were both a little wide-eyed—obviously uncomfortable at the emotions that had been bared in the room. There was still a hint of admiration in Will's eyes, however, as he continued to stare at the Baron. Rodney was nodding in agreement with Arald's statements, while Gilan made a show of studying his nails. Anthony's face was apologetic but determined. Alyss was obviously trying to mask her feelings, but it was clear that she shared the boys' discomfort.

Pauline alone was composed and calm. There was no sign of agreement in her expression. Duncan sensed a possible ally.

"Gentlemen, Cassandra, Alyss, I wonder would you mind giving me a few moments alone with Lady Pauline," he said.

There was muttered acknowledgment of his request and the ten other people filed out of the room, leaving the King and the Courier alone. As the door closed behind Will, the last to leave, Duncan turned to the tall woman sitting opposite.

"What am I to do, Pauline? How can I talk sense into them? You have to help me with this." He did his best to maintain a reasonable, nonargumentative tone.

"Your majesty," Pauline replied evenly, "if this is why you asked me to remain, you might as well send me away with the others. I agree with Arald. You are wrong on this."

"But she's just a girl . . ." he began.

"So is Alyss. Yet I've already sent her on several quite dangerous missions. Is your daughter any more valuable than my assistant?"

"She's the Crown Princess!" he said angrily, and Pauline raised an eyebrow.

"And as such, she has a greater duty to the country than a mere orphan like Alyss. The Baron is right. Those of us who enjoy great privilege have the greater duty. And Cassandra's privilege is second only to yours."

Duncan stood and began to pace around the room. Pauline remained sitting, but she followed him with her eyes.

"When you appointed me to a high position in the Diplomatic Service, did you hesitate because of my gender?"

"Of course not," he replied. "You were the best person for the job."

She nodded acknowledgment of the compliment. "You are the first ruler to accept women in positions of responsibility, without regard to the fact that they are women. And without worrying that your decisions might place them in danger from time to time."

"I value ability above all else," he said. "Man or woman."

She spread her hands in a small "there you have it" gesture.

"Then value it in your daughter. She is an exceptional young woman. And she's not one to sit simpering by the fire while the menfolk do all the dangerous work. She's proved that already. She's already done more, seen more than most men will manage in their entire lives. The girl has a taste for adventure and you won't break her of it.

"Personally, when I see the character and courage of the person who will succeed you, I thank the good lord for it. You're a good king, your majesty. And she'll be a good queen. But you have to give her the chance."

King Duncan's shoulders slumped as he realized she was right. He allowed himself a tired grin in her direction. He spread his hands in a gesture of surrender and returned to the high-backed chair.

"What ever made me think you'd be on my side?" he asked her. Lady Pauline allowed herself a smile in return.

"We're all on your side," she replied. "You were the only one out of step." She paused, then urged him gently, "Shall I call the others back in?"

He nodded. "Why ask me? It's all of you who are making the decisions."

The group filed back into the room, taking their former positions around the desk.

They cast curious glances at Lady Pauline, trying to gauge what had passed while they'd been waiting in the anteroom outside. But the diplomat was skilled in hiding her feelings and gave them no hint as to what had been decided.

Duncan sat, his elbows on the table, his head in his hands, while he marshaled his thoughts. When the usual shuffling and moving and settling into seats was done, he looked up at the group surrounding him.

"Very well," he said at length. "I've decided. Cassandra will carry out the negotiations with the Arridi . . ."

There was a quick intake of breath from his daughter, then she hurriedly rearranged her features, on the chance that he might change his mind. He glanced at her and nodded. Then he fixed his gaze straight in front of him again.

"Halt, you'll go with her as her chief adviser. Help her in the negotiations and protect her."

"Yes, sir," Halt said impassively.

"Will, you'll go too, of course," the King said. "You've kept her safe before. Do it again."

"Yes, sir," Will said, grinning broadly. He had assumed that he would accompany his mentor but one never knew. Then it got even better.

"Horace, just in case they can't manage it between them, you're going as Cassandra's personal bodyguard. Understand?"

"Yes, your majesty," Horace said, and he and Will exchanged grins. Will mouthed the words "like old times" and Horace nodded. Cassandra beamed at the two of them and moved a little closer. Off to one side, a frown touched Alyss's face.

"Right. Now, in addition to the three of you, I'll want to send a reasonable force as well. Say, twenty armed men from the Royal Guard." The King paused as Halt raised a hand to interject. "Yes?"

"Sir, we won't need them—" he began, but the King interrupted him.

"This is not a matter of your ego, Halt. I'm not happy about sending my daughter on this mission in the first place and I do insist you need an adequate force to protect her. You three aren't enough in my estimation."

"I agree, your majesty. But you're forgetting we'll have thirty fully armed Skandians with us as well. They're the best fighting men in the world."

Horace couldn't help himself. He grunted in agreement, then hastily made a gesture of apology for interrupting. The King looked from Halt to Horace, then back to Halt again.

"You trust them?" he asked bluntly, and Halt nodded.

"With my life, your majesty."

Duncan fingered his chin thoughtfully. "It's not your life I'm worried about."

"I'd trust them with my life too, Dad," Cassandra said calmly.

Halt added further reassurance. "I'll have Svengal swear a helmsman's oath that he and his men will protect her. Once they've done that, you'd have to kill all thirty of them before you even got near Cassandra."

Duncan drummed his fingers, considering. Eventually, he gave in. "All right then. But I want to make sure." He looked keenly around the room. "Gilan, you'll go too."

"Yes, sir!" Gilan said eagerly. The prospect of a mission with Halt and Will was very appealing to him. But Crowley was frowning.

"That's highly unusual, your majesty," he objected. "You know the old saying: 'one riot, one Ranger.'"

The saying stemmed from a legendary event in the past. A minor fief had risen up against their cruel and avaricious lord, with hundreds of people surrounding his manor house, threatening to burn it to the ground. The panicked nobleman's message for help was answered by the arrival of a single Ranger. Aghast, the nobleman confronted the solitary cowled figure.

"They sent one Ranger?" he said incredulously. "One man?"

"How many riots do you have?" the Ranger replied.

On this occasion, however, Duncan was not inclined to be swayed by legend. "I have a new saying," he replied. "One daughter, two Rangers."

"Two and a half," Will corrected him. The King couldn't help smiling at the eager young face before him.

"Don't sell yourself short," he said. "Two and three-quarters."

10

THE FOLLOWING DAY, THE THREE RANGERS, ACCOMPANIED BY
Horace and Svengal, were on the road, headed for Castle Araluen.

The others had watched with broad grins as Halt self-consciously
kissed his new wife good-bye. Lady Pauline took their separation
philosophically. When she had accepted Halt's proposal, she had
known that their life together would be interrupted by urgent missions and sudden departures. Still, she thought wryly, it might have
been nice if this particular departure had been a little less sudden, a
little less urgent.

Alyss had stood beside her, waving with her as the five mounted
figures cantered down the winding road that led away from Castle
Redmont. Pauline glanced sidelong at her protégée and couldn't resist the tiniest vestige of a smile at Alyss's set face.

"Why so glum?" she asked innocently. Alyss looked up at her,
grimacing.

"He's going off with her again," the young girl said. No need for
Pauline to ask who she might mean. Alyss and Will had been seeing
a lot of each other in the past year, she knew. They had become very
close. Now it obviously bothered Alyss that Will was setting out on
a mission with Cassandra once more. Alyss knew that the Ranger's

apprentice and the princess shared a special relationship. She just wasn't sure how special it might be.

"I've been trying to work out a reason for me to go along with them," she added, a little disconsolately.

"To keep an eye on your investment?"

Alyss nodded. "Exactly. I thought I could volunteer to go as a companion to her—and as a diplomatic adviser. I'm good at negotiations, you know."

"That's true." Pauline considered the idea. "In fact, it might have been worth suggesting. I would have supported the idea. Why didn't you?"

Alyss looked away from her now, watching the small group gradually dwindling from sight. Or rather, Pauline surmised, she was watching one member of the small group.

"Two reasons. I decided Will and Halt and the others didn't need the responsibility of another female to look after. If I were there, it would mean that much less protection for Cassandra. And she is the Crown Princess, after all."

"And the other reason?" Pauline prompted her. Alyss grinned a little ruefully.

"I thought I might succumb to the temptation of hitting her over the head with an oar," she said. "Which would not have been a good career move."

Pauline grinned in her turn. "And she is the Crown Princess, after all," she parroted.

The riders had disappeared into the fringes of the forest. Pauline slipped her arm inside Alyss's and led her away from the battlements where they had been standing.

"Don't worry too much about it," she said. "Admittedly, there is a strong bond between Will and the princess. That's inevitable, after all they've been through . . ." Her tone of voice indicated that there was more to be said. It was Alyss's turn to prompt.

"But?" she said.

"But Will made a choice several years ago when he opted to remain a Ranger. He knows that a Ranger's life won't mix with life at court. A princess and a Ranger just aren't a good match. And it would be twice as difficult when Cassandra eventually becomes Queen."

"Whereas," said Alyss, "there's a lot to be said for Rangers and Couriers marrying?"

Lady Pauline allowed herself a slow smile. "Oh, indeed. Of course, the Courier has to accept that the Ranger will often be called away on urgent missions."

"And he'd better accept that I'll have missions of my own," said Alyss, abandoning the pretense of talking in the third person.

Pauline patted her arm gently. "That's my girl," she said.

"Why couldn't I go with the others?" Cassandra asked, for perhaps the twentieth time.

She was in the rooms that had been set aside for her use at Redmont, hastily cramming clothes into her leather traveling valises. Duncan raised an eyebrow at her cavalier treatment of the fine silks and satins she was handling.

"Perhaps you should let your staff attend to that," he suggested, seeing that she would never get the lids closed on the jumble of gowns, cloaks, overdresses, petticoats and scarves that reared up out of the cases. Cassandra made an impatient gesture.

"That's my point. They could have packed all this up. I could have ridden ahead with Will and Horace."

"And deprived me of a few last days in your company," Duncan said gently. She instantly regretted her impatience. He was worried about sending her to Arrida, she knew. He had made no pretense that he wasn't. And she knew he would worry from the moment she left until the moment she returned, safe and sound.

As she had the thought, she realized that she would miss his calm and confident presence while she was away. And his warmth. They might squabble from time to time but it didn't change the fact that they loved each other deeply.

She stepped toward her father and put her arms gently around his neck, drawing him to her. "Sorry, Dad," she said softly. "I'd like a few days with you too."

"The others have to get the ship ready," he reminded her. "Riding back with me won't hold you up in the long run."

He patted her shoulder. He could feel a pressure building in his eyes as tears started to form. He would miss her. He would worry about her. But above all, he knew, he would be proud of her. Proud of her courage, her sense of duty, her spirit.

"You'll make a great Queen," he said.

Svengal lay groaning on the turf. His thighs were sheer agony. His buttocks ached. His calf muscles were on fire. Now, after he had tumbled off the small pony he was riding and thudded heavily to the turf on the point of his shoulder, the shoulder would hurt too. He concentrated on trying to find one part of his body that wasn't a giant source of pain and failed miserably. He opened his eyes. The first thing he saw was the face of the elderly pony that he had been riding as it peered down at him.

Now what made you do a strange thing like that? the creature seemed to be asking.

Gradually, as Svengal's focus widened, he became aware that other eyes were staring at him. Three Ranger horses, for a start, and above them, three Rangers, all with the same puzzled expression. Only Horace and his larger horse looked vaguely sympathetic.

"You know, it beats me," Halt said, "how these people can balance on the deck of a ship that's going up and down and side to side three or four meters at a time, yet put them on a placid old pony that's as gentle as a rocking horse and they're instantly trying to get off again."

"I wasn't trying to get off," Svengal told him. He slowly rolled over and rose to his knees. His muscles shrieked in protest. "Oh, by the Great Wallowing Blue Whale, why does everything hurt!" he said. Then he continued his original thought. "That brute of a horse bucked me off."

"Bucked you off?" said Gilan, hiding a grin. "Did anyone see Plod here do any bucking?"

Will and Halt shook their heads. To his discredit, Halt was enjoying this just a little too much. During the Temujai invasion, he had been on board a wolfship sent to verify Slagor's treachery. Svengal had been one of the crew members most amused by the reaction of Halt's stomach to the motions of the sea. Halt had a long memory, Will had learned.

"He bucked, I tell you," Svengal insisted, standing more or less upright and groaning again. He couldn't quite straighten at the waist. "I felt a distinct movement."

"He turned to the left," Gilan told him.

"Suddenly," Svengal insisted.

"Plod never did anything suddenly in his life," Halt said. "At least, not in the past fifteen years of it."

"That's why we call him Plod," Will put in helpfully. Svengal glared at him.

"That's not what I call him," he said venomously. The three Rangers exchanged amused looks.

"Well, yes, I'll admit we have heard some colorful language this morning," Gilan said. He turned to Halt. "Who is this Gorlog character, by the way? And does he really have horns and teeth and long shaggy hair?"

"He's a very useful person," Halt told him. "You can invoke him by all of those different features. He's the very soul of variety. One never gets bored with Gorlog around."

Svengal during this breezy interchange was eyeing the battleax hanging from Plod's saddlebow. He wasn't sure if he'd rather use it on the pony, or on the three Rangers who were enjoying his predicament so thoroughly.

Horace decided it had all gone far enough. He slipped down from Kicker's saddle and caught Plod's trailing bridle, leading him toward the aching Skandian.

"You three don't have a lot of sympathy, do you?" he asked. The three Rangers exchanged glances again, smiling at each other.

"Not really," Gilan agreed cheerfully. Horace dismissed them with a wave of his hand and turned to Svengal.

"Come on. I'll give you a boost." He held out his hands, forming a stirrup to help Svengal into the saddle. The Skandian backed away, holding his aching back with one hand.

"I'll walk," he said.

"You can't walk all the way to Araluen," Horace said reasonably. "Now come on. The best thing you can do when you've had a fall is get back in the saddle again." He looked at the three Rangers. "Am I right?"

Three cowled heads nodded. They looked like green and gray vultures, Horace thought.

"Get on again?" Svengal asked. "On that?"

Horace nodded encouragingly.

"You're telling me that the best thing I can do, after this fiend

from hell has lurched and spun and jumped and broken every second bone in my body, is to get back on and give him another chance
at me?"

"That's right. Come on. I'll boost you up."

Painfully, Svengal limped forward, raising his right foot and placing it in Horace's cupped hands. The next part, the sudden convul-
sive leap upward, involving all his thoroughly abused major muscle
groups, was going to hurt like the very devil, he knew. He looked into
Horace's eyes. Honest. Encouraging. Free of guile.

"And I thought you were my friend," he said bitterly.

11

"LOWER AWAY!" CALLED SVENGAL. "SLOWLY NOW! EASY DOES IT! A little more . . . Olaf, take up the slack there! Bring him left! Hold it! A little more . . . that's it!"

Tug, suspended by a large canvas sling that passed under his belly, showed the whites of his eyes as he soared high into the air, then swung out over empty space to be lowered gently into the last of the horse-holding pens that had been constructed in *Wolfwind's* midships.

The wolfship appeared at first glance to be nothing more than a large open boat. But Will knew this was a false impression. The central decked section that ran between the rowing benches was actually comprised of three separate watertight compartments, which gave the ship buoyancy in the event that a wave swamped it. The large sealed compartments also served as storage space for the booty that the crew "liberated" on their raids. Now one of these compartments was being used to accommodate the three Ranger horses and Horace's battlehorse, Kicker. The decking had been removed and four small pens had been constructed for the horses. The job had been carried out so quickly and efficiently that it was obvious the Skandians had done it all before.

The pens were a tight fit but that would be all to the good if the ship struck bad weather. The horses would be less likely to slip and fall. In case of extreme conditions, Svengal and his men had prepared more canvas slings that would support the horses and prevent them from falling.

Will slipped into the pen now with Tug and released the lifting sling that had been attached under his belly. He tied the little horse's halter to a ring in the front of the pen. Abelard, in the next pen, nickered a greeting. Tug looked nervously at his master.

Horses aren't supposed to fly, he seemed to be saying. Will grinned, patted his nose and gave him half an apple.

"Good boy," he said. "You won't be in here for long."

The crew were dismantling the shear legs they had assembled to lift the horses on board. The whole operation had gone smoothly. Kicker was the most highly strung of the horses, so he had gone aboard first. It was felt that he might panic at the sight of his brothers sailing in the air, legs dangling. If he didn't know what was coming, Halt said, he was more likely to behave. As each horse was lowered into the shallow well in the deck, his rider was waiting with soothing words and reassurance. Will scratched Tug's ear once more and climbed out of the pen.

"You've done this before," he said to Svengal. Since Skandians didn't ride horses as a rule, there was only one explanation for it.

Svengal grinned. "Sometimes we come upon abandoned horses on the shore. It'd be cruel to leave them, so we take them on board until we can find them a good home."

"Abandoned?" Will said. Svengal was all wide-eyed innocence.

"Well, nobody has ever asked for them back," he said. Then he added, "Besides, after what I've heard about Halt and the Temujai horses, I wouldn't make too big a fuss about it if I were you."

Many years ago, Halt had "borrowed" some breeding stock from the Temujai herds. The present-day Ranger horses bore an unmistakable resemblance to those borrowed animals. Sad to say, Halt had yet to return them.

"Fair point," said Will. Then, glancing up at the dock, he said, "Looks like we're almost ready to go."

Cassandra and her father were approaching down the dock, followed by a small retinue of friends and officials. Duncan had his arm around his daughter's shoulders. His face showed his lingering concern over the wisdom of this trip. Cassandra, on the other hand, looked eager and alert. She was already feeling the many constraints of life in the castle slipping away. In place of the stylish gowns she was normally required to wear, she wore tights, knee-high boots, a woolen shirt and a thigh-length belted leather jerkin. She wore a dagger in her belt and carried a lightweight saber in a scabbard. Her other baggage followed behind, carried by two servants. The time she had spent in Skandia had taught Cassandra the value of traveling light. She beamed a greeting as she caught sight of Will and Horace leaning on the rail of the ship. The two boys grinned back at her.

Svengal, with surprising agility for a man of his bulk, stepped lightly onto the rail of the ship, jumped ashore and approached the royal pair. Out of deference to the King, he raised his knuckled hand to his brow in salute. Duncan acknowledged the gesture with a quick nod of the head.

It has to be said that Skandians weren't big on protocol and the niceties of court speech. Svengal was a little at a loss as to how he should address the King. Skandians never called anyone "sir," as that implied that the speaker was somehow inferior to the person he was addressing. Likewise, formal titles such as "your majesty" or "my lord" didn't sit comfortably with the egalitarian northerners. In their own society, they solved the problem by using the other person's title or position: skirl, jarl or Oberjarl. No Skandian ever called Erak "sir" or "my lord." If they wanted to show respect, they addressed him by the word that described what he was—Oberjarl. If that was good enough for his own ruler, Svengal thought, it should be good enough for the Araluen King.

"King," he said, "you have Skandia's gratitude for the help you're giving us."

Duncan nodded again. It didn't seem necessary to say anything in reply. Svengal looked now at the slim blond girl at the King's side.

"And I know how difficult it must be for you to send your daughter on a mission like this."

"I won't deny that I have misgivings, Captain," Duncan replied this time. Svengal nodded rapidly.

"Then I give you this oath. My helmsman's oath—you're familiar with the helmsman's oath, King?"

"I know no Skandian would ever break it," Duncan said.

"That's true. Well, here's the oath, and it binds me and all my men. We will protect your daughter as if she were one of our own. So long as one of us is alive, no harm will be allowed to come to her."

There was a low growl of assent from the members of the crew, who had gathered at the ship's shoreward rail to watch the proceedings. Duncan looked around at their faces now. Scarred and weather-beaten, framed by hair wrapped in untidy pigtails and surmounted by horned helmets. Duncan was a big man, but the Skandians were built on a massive scale. They were bulky, hard muscled and well armed. And the faces showed one more thing—determination to uphold their leader's oath. For the first time in the past three days, he felt a little better about the whole situation. These men would never desert his daughter. They would fight tooth and nail to defend and protect her.

He raised his voice a little, so that his answer was aimed not just at Svengal, but at the entire crew.

"Thank you, men of *Wolfwind*. I don't believe my daughter could be in better hands."

The sincerity in his voice was obvious, and again there was a fierce growl of assent from the Skandians.

"One thing, however. I think from this point, until you reach Al Shabah, it might be safer if Cassandra were to travel incognito. She has decided to resume the name most of you know her by— Evanlyn."

Will nudged Horace in the ribs. "Thank goodness for that. I could never get used to calling her Cassandra. I get tongue-tied around her when I'm reminded she's a princess."

Horace grinned. It didn't bother him either way. But then, stationed at Araluen as he was, he was more used to seeing Cassandra on a day-to-day basis.

Evanlyn, as she would now be known, hugged her father one more time. They had already gone through prolonged good-byes in private. Then she glanced up at the pennant streaming from the masthead—her personal pennant depicting a stooping red hawk.

"In which case, we'd better have that down for the time being," she said.

As one of the crew moved to the halyards to lower the flag, her father muttered to her, "Make sure you get it back this time. I'm not sure I like the idea of a gang of freebooters sailing under your pennant."

She grinned and touched his cheek with her hand. "You're right. It could be embarrassing at a later date."

She moved away from him and stepped lightly aboard the ship, taking Axl's hand to steady herself as she did so.

"Thank you," she said. He flushed and nodded, mumbling something indiscernible as she moved to the stern, where her companions were waiting.

"Anything else?" Svengal asked, and Halt pointed to the east.

"Let's get going," he said.

"Right! Up oars!" Svengal's voice rose into the familiar ear-shattering bellow that Skandian skirls used when giving orders. The rowing crew clattered onto their benches, retrieving their oars and raising the three-meter-long oak poles vertically into the air.

"Cast off and fend!"

The line handlers cast off the bow and stern lines that had held *Wolfwind* fast to the jetty. At the same time, three other crewmen placed long poles against the timbers of the jetty and pushed the ship clear, setting it drifting out into the current. As the space between ship and shore widened, Svengal called his next order.

"Down oars!" There was a prolonged clatter of wood on wood as the sixteen oars were slotted into their rowlocks down the sides of the ship. The blades were cocked forward toward the bow, poised just above the water, ready for the first stroke.

"Give way all!" Svengal ordered, seizing the tiller. The oars' blades dipped and the rowers heaved themselves backward against the oar handles. *Wolfwind* surged forward through the water and the tiller came alive in his hand. The bow oarsman on the port side called for another stroke and the speed increased as a small bow wave began to chuckle at the wolfship's prow. They were under way at last.

12

⟨⟨⟨⟨⟨⟨⟨⟨⟨⟨⟨⟨⟨⟨⟨⟨⟨⟨⟨⟨⟨⟨⟨⟨⟨⟩⟩⟩⟩⟩

THE TRIP DOWNRIVER WAS UNEVENTFUL. SEVERAL TIMES, THEY saw farmworkers and travelers stopping on the banks of the river to gape at the sight of a fully manned wolfship slipping quietly by. Once or twice, horsemen had set spurs to their horses after the first sighting and gone galloping away, presumably to sound the alarm.

Will smiled at the thought of villagers huddled behind a stockade or in one of the defensive towers that had been built at strategic sites, waiting for an attack that would never come.

Even though there had been no Skandian raids for the past three years, the memories of those who lived near the coast were long, and centuries of raids were not forgotten quickly. There might be a treaty in place but treaties were abstract concepts written on paper. A wolfship in the vicinity was a hard reality, and one likely to create suspicion.

Finally, *Wolfwind* slipped out of the sheltered waters of the estuary and turned south into the Narrow Sea. The Gallican coast was a thin dark line on the horizon, more sensed than seen. It could well have been a cloud bank. The wolfship rose and fell with the gentle slow rollers that passed under her keel. Evanlyn, Will and Horace stood in the ship's bow, feeling the regular rising and falling movement beneath their feet.

"This is quite pleasant really," Will said.

Evanlyn smiled at him. "As I recall, you said much the same thing last time—just before that storm hit us."

Will grinned ruefully in reply. "How was I to know?"

Horace looked a little anxious. "A storm?" he said. "Was it bad?"

"The waves were huge," Will said. "They came through two or three times the height of the mast there."

Horace looked at his old friend, polite disbelief in his eyes. But Evanlyn hurried to support Will.

"No, really, Horace. They were huge. I thought we were going to die."

"I was *sure* we were going to die," Will added.

Horace gazed anxiously around him. Up until now, he'd been enjoying the light, easy movement of the ship.

"Well, I hope we don't hit anything like that today," he said.

Will shrugged casually. "Oh, don't worry. *Wolfwind* can handle anything the sea can throw at her."

He leaned back, breathing in the salt air. He was enjoying himself, and it was good to be spending time with Evanlyn once more.

Their paths had diverged after their return from Skandia and he knew that she had been disappointed, even hurt, by his decision to remain a Ranger, turning down a commission in the Royal Scouts. He had been offered the commission only after Evanlyn had pleaded with her father to find a way of keeping Will at Castle Araluen. She had seen his refusal as a rejection of her and, the few times they had met socially since, she had made a point of assuming royal airs and maintaining a frosty distance from him. Now, in the rough-and-ready atmosphere of a wolfship, with so many reminders of their past adventures around them, those barriers seemed to be melting away.

"Are you all right?" Gilan asked Halt. It was the third time he had asked the question. And as he had on the previous two occasions, Halt replied in a tight voice.

"I'm fine."

But something was wrong, Gilan sensed. His former mentor seemed unusually distracted. There was a small frown knotting his forehead and his hands gripped the ship's rail so hard that his knuckles showed white.

"Are you sure? You don't seem all right." In fact, Halt was looking rather pale, behind the beard and below the shadow of his cowl. "Is something bothering you?"

Halt's pale angry face turned to him. "Yes," he said. "Something is bothering me. I am being constantly asked 'Are you all right?' by an idiot. I really wish—"

Whatever it was that he wished was cut short abruptly and Gilan saw his face set in determined lines as he clenched his teeth tightly. The fact that the interruption coincided with a larger than usual lurch from *Wolfwind* was lost on the younger Ranger. He cast a worried look at his old teacher. Halt had loomed large in his life for years. He was indefatigable. He was all-knowing. He was the most capable man Gilan had ever known.

He was also seasick.

It was something that always afflicted him for the first few hours of a sea journey. It was the uncertainty, Halt knew. It was all mental. When the ship lurched or heaved or rolled, he was caught unprepared—unable to believe that something so large and substantial could be tossed around so much.

Deep down, he knew that the current conditions weren't too

bad. But in the first few hours of a sea journey, Halt's mind queried the fact that any moment might see a bigger wave, a more sudden lurch, a fatal roll that would go too far. He knew that once he became accustomed to the idea of the ship moving and recovering, moving and recovering, he would come to terms with his stomach and his nerves. But that would take several hours. In the meantime, he thought grimly, whatever his reason might tell him, he'd be well served if he stayed close by the railing. He wished that Gilan would leave him alone. But he couldn't find a way to suggest such a thing without hurting the younger man's feelings. And that was something that Halt, gruff and bad-tempered and unsmiling as he might appear to be, would never countenance doing.

Svengal, large, noisy and hearty, appeared at the railing beside him, breathing the salt air deeply and exhaling with great sighs of satisfaction. Svengal was always glad to be back at sea—an attitude that Halt thought bordered on lunacy.

"Mmmmm! Smell that! There's nothing like the sea air to brace you up, is there?" he boomed. Halt glanced suspiciously at him. Svengal didn't meet his gaze. Instead, he peered out at the sparkling water. "Nothing like it!" he told them. He took a few more deep breaths, studiously ignoring Halt's condition, then finally said to Gilan, "You know what I don't understand?"

Confident that Svengal was about to answer his own question, Gilan saw no need to reply beyond raising his eyebrows.

"I don't understand how people can ride all day on one of those jerking, lurching, jumping, bucking fiends from hell without the slightest problem . . ." He jerked a thumb at the four horses in their midships stalls. "But put them on a smooth, solid, barely moving ship's deck and suddenly their stomachs want to turn themselves inside out at the slightest little roll."

He grinned at Halt, remembering the Ranger's lack of sympathy when the pony had thrown Svengal during the ride back to Araluen.

"Halt?" said Gilan, realization dawning. "You're not seasick, are you?"

"No," Halt said shortly, not trusting himself beyond one syllable.

"Probably need a bite of breakfast to settle your stomach," Svengal said helpfully. "Get something solid inside you."

"Had . . . breakfast." This time, Halt managed three syllables—but with some difficulty. Svengal affected not to notice.

"Cabbage is good. Especially pickled cabbage. Sits on the gut nicely," he said. "Goes well with a nice piece of greasy bacon. You should try that if you . . ."

But before he could finish, Halt lurched toward the ship's rail and hung over it. Dreadful noises were torn from him. Svengal, still affecting a look of innocence, turned to Gilan, hands spread and eyes wide.

"What in the world is he looking for? Has he lost something, do you think?"

13

After two days at sea, Halt was mercifully in control of his stomach once more. That didn't stop an evilly grinning Svengal from asking after his health at every possible opportunity, or offering him choice tidbits from the wolfship's limited larder.

"Chicken leg?" he said, an innocent grin splitting his face. "Bit greasy but good nevertheless. Just the thing to stick to a man's ribs."

"Svengal," Halt said for the tenth time, "I am over it. Are we clear on that? I am over being seasick. And I am definitely over your attempts to make me heave my insides over the railing."

Svengal looked unconvinced. He knew Halt's strength of mind and he was sure that he was bluffing—that, deep down, the Ranger's stomach was still in turmoil. All it needed was a little suggestive prodding.

"If it's not to your taste, I've some lovely puréed chestnut sauce you could smother it in," he suggested hopefully.

"Very well," Halt agreed, "give me the chicken leg. And fetch me the chestnut sauce—and some pickled cucumbers while you're about it. Oh, and you'd better bring me a large tankard of dark ale if you have any."

Svengal grinned, convinced that Halt was bluffing. Within a few minutes he had the requested food laid out on a small folding table by the steering position. He watched expectantly as Halt bit into the chicken, chewed slowly and swallowed. Jurgen, one of the crew, filled a mug with dark ale and set it down as well, then stood by with the small cask, ready for further instructions.

"All well then?" Svengal asked hopefully. Halt nodded.

"Fine. Bit overdone and stringy but otherwise all right." He took a deep draft of the dark ale, which he knew was Svengal's favorite and which he knew was in limited supply. He thrust the tankard out to Jurgen.

"More," he said briefly. The Skandian uncorked the cask and let a stream of the dark foaming ale run into the tankard. Halt drank again, draining most of the beer. He wiped the back of his hand across his lips.

"Not bad. Not bad at all," he said, and held the tankard out again. The smile on Svengal's face started to fade as he saw more of his favorite tipple gushing into Halt's tankard. A joke was a joke, he thought, but this was starting to get expensive.

"How many casks of that do we have left?" he asked the crewman.

"This is the last, skirl," came the reply. He shook the cask experimentally to check how much was remaining and Svengal's practiced ear could tell from the hollow splashing sound that it was less than half full. Or, as he thought in his suddenly anxious state of mind, more than half empty. Halt took another long pull and held the nearly empty tankard out.

"Better top me up," he said.

"No!" Svengal's anxious cry stopped the crewman as he began to raise the cask once more. "Leave it, Jurgen."

Jurgen nodded, hiding a grin himself. He liked Svengal. But like all Skandians, he also appreciated a good practical joke. He admired the way the short-shanked Araluen had turned the tables on his captain.

"You're sure?" he asked. "He seems to be enjoying it."

Halt belched lightly in confirmation and took another bite of the sauce-smeared chicken leg.

"He's enjoying it too much," Svengal replied shortly. He cast an aggrieved look at Halt. "Some people don't know when a joke has gone too far."

Halt smiled malevolently at him. "So I've noticed," he replied. "So tell me. Are we done with the questions about my health and the state of my stomach?"

"Yes," Svengal muttered darkly. "I was only worried about you, that's all."

Injured dignity was not a look normally associated with Skandians, but as Svengal stalked away, nose in the air, he almost managed to pull it off.

14

THE ARRIDI COAST WAS A THIN BROWN LINE OFF THE STARBOARD
side as *Wolfwind* slipped smoothly through the water. It was strangely
quiet now that the crew had been able to ship their oars and set the
big square sail. For the past four days, the wind had blown steadily
from the east, directly opposite to their direction of travel. But as the
sun had risen on this, the fifteenth day of their journey, the wind had
shifted to the south. Svengal had the yardarm raised and braced
round to an angle of forty-five degrees to catch the wind. The
wolfship tried to turn downwind immediately. But Svengal's firm
control of sheets and tiller kept the bow pointed east. *Wolfwind* still
crabbed to the north, inevitably, but the conflicting forces created by
the wind in the sail, the resistance of the keel in the water and the
turning force of the rudder resolved themselves into an east-northeast
course for the ship.

And even if she was losing some ground to the north, she was
making better progress to the east than she would have under oars.
Svengal knew that a wise captain conserved the strength of his oarsmen as far as possible.

Halt, Evanlyn and Svengal were deep in conversation now in the
stern part of the ship, discussing plans for the coming negotiations.

Horace was crouched beside Kicker in his pen, working to remove a stone that had become wedged under the battlehorse's shoe. They had taken the horses ashore several times, on deserted stretches of beach, to exercise them and stop their muscles from softening. Will stood alone in the very bow of the ship, chin resting on his forearm as he leaned on the bulwark. For perhaps the tenth time in as many days, he was feeling uneasy about what the future might hold.

But not about the negotiations for Erak's release. He was certain that they would proceed smoothly and successfully. After all, Halt would be beside Evanlyn to guide her and advise her of any possible pitfalls.

And that was the crux of it, he realized. He had spent the better part of the last five years relying on Halt, trusting his judgment, following his lead. Just as they would all be doing when the ship finally reached Al Shabah and they went ashore to rescue Erak. Halt's presence, his foresight, his skill, his innate ability to solve any problem that raised itself, was an enormous source of security for Will. He was firmly convinced that there was nothing Halt couldn't do, no problem that he couldn't solve.

And soon, Will knew, he would be leaving that protective umbrella and striking out on his own. In three months' time he would face his final assessment tests—designed to ascertain whether or not he had what it took to be a successful Ranger.

For the past year, this final assessment had loomed large in his mind. He had seen it as the culmination of his training, the final hurdle that he must leap before he received the Silver Oakleaf— symbol of a graduate Ranger. And he'd looked forward to it with some impatience.

But now, he realized, the assessment would not be the end. It would merely be the beginning of a new and even larger phase of his life. The real assessment would follow. And it would never cease, for as long as he remained a Ranger. Every day he would be tested. He would be called on to make life-or-death decisions—sometimes without enough time to consider them properly. People would look to him for advice and leadership and, suddenly, he doubted that he could provide it. He realized now that he wasn't ready for the role. He could never be like Halt—so calm, self-assured, experienced.

So incontrovertibly right about everything.

He wasn't Halt. He was Will. Young, impulsive, green as grass. Without really thinking about it, he had somehow assumed that once he had graduated, he and Halt would continue to live in the comfortable little cabin just inside the edge of the forest. But Halt's marriage meant that those days were nearly over and Halt had realized it, even if Will hadn't. Halt had already moved into the apartment that he and Lady Pauline shared at the castle, although he would continue to use the cabin in the forest as a base for his observation of the goings-on in the fief.

At first Will had viewed the change in circumstances with equanimity. The idea of having the cabin mostly to himself had a certain appeal. He could invite friends over for meals. Horace, if he happened to be visiting Redmont, as he did from time to time. And Alyss.

Alyss, he thought. Yes. It would be pleasant to sit by the fire in the cozy little cabin with the beautiful, tall blond girl, talking over old times and new developments in their jobs. She was already a graduate Courier and being sent on missions by her mentor, Lady Pauline. Alyss enjoyed sitting with him, listening to him play the mandola, nodding her head in time to the beat.

Unlike Halt, he thought with a wry smile, who groaned and fidgeted whenever Will produced the little instrument from its hard leather case.

But then, he realized, that would not be the way his life went.

He wouldn't be in the cabin, with or without Halt. He wouldn't be anywhere near Castle Redmont. Once he graduated, he would be assigned to another fief, one of fifty throughout the Kingdom. He could be sent hundreds of kilometers away from everyone and everything he knew. And when he got there, people would expect him to know what he was doing. They would look to him for guidance and advice and protection.

In short, they would think he was like Halt.

And he knew all too well that he wasn't. He sighed deeply at the thought.

"There's a happy sound," said a cheerful voice at his elbow. He started with surprise. Even engrossed in his thoughts as he had been, he would have expected to be aware of anyone approaching him so closely.

Anyone but Gilan, he corrected himself. Possibly Halt, but definitely Gilan. The young Ranger seemed to be able to move in total silence when he chose to. He was the Ranger Corps' recognized master of unseen movement.

Gilan leaned now on the rail beside Will, looking at him curiously.

"Something on your mind?" he asked quietly. Gilan knew from his own experience that there were some problems that an apprentice didn't want to ask his mentor about. He knew, too, that he was in a unique position. As a former apprentice to Halt himself, he could understand most of the doubts that might be going through Will's mind. In fact, Gilan had a pretty shrewd idea as to why Will was sighing.

"No . . . well, I suppose, sort of . . . well, yes," Will said.

Gilan's smile widened. "And there's a choice of three answers for me. Never let it be said that you don't answer a question thoroughly."

Will essayed a smile in return, but it was a wan little effort.

"Gil," he said finally, "when you were about to take the silver, did you think you were . . ." He hesitated, not sure how to put it, then tried another tack. "I mean, did you feel sort of . . ."

He was about to say "inadequate" but he couldn't imagine the word applying to Gilan. Gilan had a claim on Will's respect that was second only to Halt's. He was an expert archer, like all Rangers. But unlike any of the others, he was also a master swordsman. He alone of the fifty serving Rangers carried a sword in addition to the regular Ranger weapons. He was also, as Will had just been reminded, an expert in the art of silent movement. And he was respected among the Corps by other Rangers, far senior to him in years. On several occasions, Will had heard Crowley and Halt discussing Gilan's future in the Corps and he knew that Gilan was marked for high office.

The fact that this might have something to do with Gilan's being Halt's former apprentice didn't occur to Will. But certainly the word "inadequate" would be an insult to someone so capable and skilled.

Gilan studied the troubled young man beside him and felt a surge of affection for him.

"Were you going to say 'unready'?" he asked, and Will seized on the word gratefully. It was less insulting than the one he had nearly used.

"Yes! Exactly! Did you feel unready for it all?"

Gilan nodded several times before answering. His smile became a little wistful as he thought back to those days years ago when he felt exactly the same doubts he was sure Will was feeling now.

"You know, a year before my finals, I was quite sure I knew it all."

"Well, yes. Of course," Will said. Gilan would have been more than ready a year before most apprentices. Then he realized that a year ago, he had felt exactly the same way. He turned to look at the tall Ranger.

"Then," Gilan continued, "in my last few weeks, I realized how much I didn't know."

"You?" Will said incredulously. "But you're—"

Gilan held up a hand to silence him. "I started thinking, 'What am I going to do without Halt to advise me? What will I do when he's not around to clear up the mistakes I make?' And the whole thing had me shaking in my boots.

"I thought, 'I can't possibly do this job. I can't be Halt! How can I ever be as wise and clever and, let's face it, as downright sneaky as he is?' Is that pretty much the way you're feeling now?" he concluded.

Will was shaking his head in amazement. "That's it in a nutshell! How can I be like Halt? How can anyone?" Again, the enormity of it all weighed down on him and his shoulders slumped. Gilan put a comforting arm around them.

"Will, the very fact that you're worrying about it says you'll be up to the job. Remember, nobody expects you to be Halt. He's a legend, after all. Haven't you heard? He's eight feet tall and kills bears with his bare hands . . ."

Will had to smile at that. Halt's reputation throughout the Kingdom was pretty much the way Gilan had stated it. People meeting him for the first time were surprised to find he was actually a little smaller than average.

"So you can't possibly live up to that. But remember this, you have been trained by the very best in the business. And you've been privileged to stand beside him for the past five years and see how he approaches a problem. Believe me, a lot of that rubs off. Once you have your own fief, you'll soon realize how much you do know."

"But what if I make a mistake?" Will asked.

Gilan threw back his head and laughed. "A mistake? One mistake? You should be so lucky. You'll make dozens! I made four or five on my first day alone! Of course you'll make mistakes. Just don't make any of them twice. If you do mess things up, don't try to hide it. Don't try to rationalize it. Recognize it and admit it and learn from it. We never stop learning, none of us. Not even Halt," he added, seriously.

Will nodded his gratitude. He felt a little better. He cocked his head suspiciously.

"You're not just saying this to make me feel better, are you?" he asked.

Gilan shook his head. "Oh no. If you don't believe me, ask Halt to tell you about some of my whoppers. He loves reminding me of them. Now let's go see what they've been talking about so seriously."

And with his arm around the younger man's shoulders still, he led him away from the bow and back to the small group by the tiller. Halt glanced up as they approached, caught a look from Gilan and had a pretty good idea what they had been talking about.

"Where have you two been?" he asked, his tone light.

"Admiring the view," Gilan told him. "Thought you might need some advice from the two wisest heads on board."

15

WOLFWIND SLIPPED THROUGH THE NARROW OPENING IN THE breakwater that protected Al Shabah Harbor. She was under oars, and the sail had been gathered and furled to the yardarm. At the peak of the mast flew Evanlyn's pennant—four meters long, undulating slowly in the offshore breeze to display a red hawk on a white field.

Even if the red hawk device itself were not recognized, the extreme length of the pennant and its shape—broad where the hawk device was shown, then narrowing rapidly until it split into two swallow tails a meter from its end—were enough to indicate that the ship was carrying a royal delegation—an ambassador at least, or perhaps even a member of a royal family. Svengal had ordered the pennant unfurled when they were still a kilometer offshore, making it clear that his ship had no warlike intent.

In spite of that fact, the crews of the dozen or so merchant ships that were anchored in the harbor or tied up to docks had armed themselves and stood ready along their bulwarks to repel any attempted attack by the Skandians. Sailors in this part of the world, and most others, for that matter, knew the Skandian reputation all too well. The presence of a royal standard did little to allay their suspicions.

Wolfwind, lean, narrow and deadly looking, slipped past the first of the anchored ships, for all the world like a wolf slinking among a flock of fat, nervous sheep.

"Looks like we have a reception committee," Halt said, indicating the main wharf that ran along the inland side of the harbor. There, they could see a body of men drawn up—perhaps fifty in all—and from time to time, the sun glinted off burnished armor or weapons. A green banner was waving from the pier—the international signal that they were cleared to come alongside.

Svengal leaned on the tiller and the bow swung toward the inner harbor. The bow oarsman called the stroke and the wolfship moved smoothly up the harbor.

"I'd better get my reception clothes on," Evanlyn said. She slipped below, into the small triangular cabin at the stern of the ship. There was barely head room for her to stand erect there, but at least she had a little privacy. A few minutes later, she reemerged. She had replaced her usual leather tunic with a longer one of dull red satin, which came almost to her knees. It was beautifully embroidered and carried a small red hawk device on the left breast. A broad leather belt gathered the red tunic at the waist. Will noticed idly that the belt was decorated with what seemed to be interwoven leather thongs, threaded in and out through slits in the belt itself, and crisscrossing for its entire length.

The long boots and hose remained, as did the white silk shirt she wore under the tunic. On her blond hair, hastily brushed and gathered, she wore a red, narrow-brimmed hat with a long bill. A single hawk's feather was set in the hatband.

She wore a necklace Will had never seen before. It was made of dull gray stones, all the same size. They didn't look to be expensive or even semiprecious. More like smooth marble, in fact. Maybe she wore it for luck.

Evanlyn tugged the tunic straight, removing a few last wrinkles where the belt had cinched it too tightly. She cleared her throat nervously.

"How do I look?" she asked Halt.

He nodded approval. "Just the right blend of practicality and formality," he replied.

She flashed a quick grin at him. She was nervous, Halt saw.

"Svengal and I will do the talking for the time being. These will just be minor officials—the harbormaster and so forth," he said. "Your turn will come when we meet with the Wakir. For the time being, look arrogant and condescending."

She started to smile, realized that such an expression didn't fit his instructions and instead arched her eyebrows and raised her chin, tilting her head back imperiously so she could stare down her nose at him.

"How's that?" she asked. She thought she saw the faintest trace of a grin in the shadows under his cowl.

"That's perfect. You could have been born to it."

"Don't make me smile or I'll have you flogged," she said quietly.

Halt nodded. "You could be catching on too fast," he said. Then his attention was drawn to the business of docking the ship.

Svengal was a flamboyant ship handler and he brought her in fast. At the last moment, he growled an order and the oarsmen backed water fiercely, taking most of the way off her.

"Oars!" he called, and the dripping blades rose out of the water, coming vertical before the oarsmen laid them down in their brackets. There was the usual clatter of oak on oak.

The ship ghosted in for a few more meters. They were at an angle of about thirty degrees to the dock and one of the crew threw a line from the bow. An Arridi dockworker quickly grabbed it, wound it once around a bollard and began to haul in.

A few seconds later, another rope soared over the water from the stern. This too was seized and the men on shore began to haul the wolf-ship alongside. The crew threw felt and wicker fenders over the side to protect the ship's scantlings from the hard stone of the wharf. As the ropes were made tight fore and aft, *Wolfwind* rocked gently alongside the jetty, the fenders groaning and creaking slightly as she did so.

The railing of the ship was a meter or so below the level of the wharf. Evanlyn started toward it but Halt's low voice stopped her.

"Stay where you are. Look imperious. We have to be invited ashore first."

The armed men they had seen from farther out were ranged along the wharf now, in two ranks, facing the wolfship. They all had their shields slung ready for action and their hands hovered close by the hilts of their swords. An officer detached himself from the line and strode toward the wharf's edge. Svengal recognized him.

"This is the bantam rooster who ambushed us in the town square," he said, in what he thought was a whisper. Halt glanced at Svengal sardonically.

"I'm sure he's thrilled to hear you say so," he replied.

The tall Arridi warrior stopped now, a few paces back from the edge of the wharf. Halt studied him keenly and came to the rapid conclusion that this was a man to be reckoned with. There was an air of assurance about him. Halt sensed that he was not a man to bluster or bluff. He knew what he was doing and he would bear watching, the Ranger thought.

The Arridi gave them the traditional desert greeting, touching his right hand to his lips, then his forehead, then his lips again. The gesture was born from the old tribal saying for first meetings, Halt knew: "We will eat. We will consider. We will talk."

The correct protocol was to return the gesture but Svengal didn't know that. He waved his hand vaguely in the air in a clumsy parody of the man's graceful movement.

"You're back, northman." The tones were deep and cultured. The voice was calm and unruffled. Its owner had learned the skill of projecting his words without seeming to shout them.

"I've come for the Oberjarl," Svengal said. He wasn't one for the niceties of protocol or beating round the bush.

The Arridi smiled. "Svengal, isn't it?"

Svengal nodded pugnaciously. "Aye. It is. But you've got the advantage of me." He felt uncomfortable, standing below the other man, forced to look up to him. He wondered where the Arridi had learned his name and decided that Erak must have mentioned it to him. In their previous encounter, there had been no introductions. Svengal and the crew had been held prisoner separate from Erak, until the day of their release, when the Oberjarl gave Svengal his instructions about the ransom.

"I am called Seley el'then by my people," the Arridi told him. "Foreigners usually find it more convenient to shorten the name to Selethen. I am a captain in the Arridi Guard."

"Well . . . enchanted," Svengal replied brusquely. He recalled the word from some dim memory of lessons in politeness that he'd been given when he was younger. He assumed it was appropriate. Selethen's face remained expressionless but Will was sure he could see a trace of a smile in the dark eyes.

"We didn't expect you back so soon," Selethen said. Then he gestured to the long pennant that still floated lazily in the slight breeze. "Nor did we expect you in such company. Surely you haven't had time to return to your home country? Whose flag is that flying at your masthead?"

Halt thought it was time somebody gave Svengal some help. The

Skandian was a master at navigation and seamanship, but his nego-tiating skills were limited to brandishing an ax and bellowing, "Hand over everything you've got." A smoother approach was called for here.

"Captain Svengal is a friend of the royal family of Araluen," he said, stepping forward. As he spoke, he slipped his cowl back so that his face and features were no longer in shadow. "That pennant is an Araluen Royal Standard, belonging to my lady here."

He indicated Evanlyn, who was doing her best to look disinter-ested and condescending at the same time. The Arridi glanced at her and she felt his keen eyes on her. She thought a contemptuous toss of the head might be in keeping. She tossed it contemptuously.

Selethen switched his gaze back to Halt.

"And your lady is?" he queried.

"My lady is prepared to negotiate the terms of the Oberjarl's release with your leader," Halt told him smoothly. "Erak, too, is a close friend of the royal family of Araluen."

He felt it was best to keep the captain guessing as to Evanlyn's real identity and position. Uncertainty such as that could work for them. And there was no real need to reveal her title to an underling.

Selethen considered this fact for a few seconds. Obviously, it was an unexpected turn in the proceedings. His face, however, showed no sign of the rapid thinking and evaluation that was going on behind his calm, unflustered look. Eventually, he spoke again.

"Unfortunately, the Wakir is not available today," he said. He faced Svengal again. "As I said, we did not expect you to return so soon. Unless . . ." He let the thought tail off.

"Unless what?" Svengal wanted to know. The Arridi inclined his head apologetically.

"Unless you had gathered some of your countrymen and came back here to release him by force," he said.

Svengal grunted. "The thought did occur to me."

This time, they all saw the smile on Selethen's dark face.

"I'm sure it did. However, the fact remains that it is impossible to arrange a meeting with the Wakir at such short notice. We could not contemplate such a thing before tomorrow."

Halt nodded agreement. "Tomorrow will be fine." He hesitated. "Could we perhaps see Oberjarl Erak in the meantime?"

Selethen was already shaking his head before he finished the request. "Unfortunately this is not possible either. But I can offer her ladyship comfortable quarters until tomorrow. We have a guesthouse that will certainly be more comfortable than a Skandian raiding ship."

He indicated a substantial two-story building set back a little from the waterfront. Unlike the solid, featureless warehouses along the quay, it had shaded balconies and wide doorways and windows on the upper floor.

"There is room there for your ladyship and her immediate party," he said. "The ship's crew will have to remain on board, I regret to say."

His even tone told them that he didn't regret it too deeply. Halt shrugged. No town would want thirty fully armed Skandians coming ashore. He was certain that the bulk of the Arridi soldiers currently on the wharf would remain there to keep an eye on things.

"Fine by me," Svengal said gruffly. There was no way he would be willing to leave his ship empty and undefended while he was in a potentially hostile port. He'd rather they kept an eye on *Wolfwind*. Any Skandian ashore was always mindful that his ship was his only line of retreat.

"Then if you would follow me?" The Arridi captain gestured in the direction of the guesthouse and began to turn away. Evanlyn's crisp voice stopped him.

"Captain Seley el'then! Aren't you forgetting something?"

He turned back, impressed by her tone of command and by the fact that she had mastered the full form of his name perfectly, after having heard it only once. He bowed deeply.

"My lady?" he asked, and she strode forward to the rail of the ship, holding out her right fist to display a large signet ring on the second finger.

"Surely you'll need to convey my seal to your Wakir before he can consent to our meeting?"

Again, her pronunciation was perfect as she managed to add the slight guttural sound to the initial letter of Wakir. Selethen nodded apologetically and produced a small wax impression box. It was about the size of a box that would contain a ring. It was made from gleaming ebony and had a snap-hinged lid.

"But of course, my lady," he said. He passed the little box to Halt, who hinged back the lid and handed it to Evanlyn. Inside was a layer of firm wax. She pressed her ring into it now, leaving the clear impression of her hawk device. Then she snapped the lid shut to protect it from damage and handed it back to Halt. The Ranger passed it back to Selethen, who tucked it away into a pouch on his belt.

"Now perhaps I could show you to your accommodation?" he said.

Halt and Gilan stepped up onto the wharf as Selethen drew back to allow them access. They turned and held their hands down to Evanlyn and she stepped up lightly after them. Will and Horace followed. Svengal, after a few brief words of instruction to Axl, mainly along the lines of, "Nobody is to come aboard," brought up the rear.

Selethen eyed the three figures in the gray and green cowled cloaks, taking in the massive longbows that each of them wore slung over their shoulders.

Strange, he thought. I must find out more about these.

He gave a quiet order and a file of ten soldiers detached themselves from the wharf contingent and led the way toward the guesthouse. As Horace passed Selethen, the two warriors eyed each other and like recognized like. Selethen saw the broad shoulders, the tapered hips and the easy balanced stride. A long straight sword hung at the Araluen's belt.

This one I understand, thought Selethen. He would make a dangerous enemy.

At the same time, Horace was taking in the slim build, the athletic movement and the long curved sword that hung at Selethen's side.

This one would be a bit of a handful, he thought.

They were both right.

16

THEY SPENT A COMFORTABLE NIGHT IN THE GUESTHOUSE. A dozen of Selethen's men remained on guard outside, but the visitors were allowed to leave the house and walk around the immediate vicinity if they chose to.

They were served food and drink—fruit juices and water in the latter case. The food was delicious—cold fowl of some kind, served with salad greens with a distinctive sharp lemon dressing and fresh flat bread. Horace tore at a leg of the fowl and crammed vast amounts of the bread into his mouth.

"This is all right," he said enthusiastically. "We're doing well for prisoners."

"We're not prisoners," Halt reminded him. "We're a diplomatic delegation."

Horace nodded. "I keep forgetting," he said, spraying bread crumbs in all directions. Halt quickly backed away. Then the warrior's attention was distracted by the half-dismembered bird on the platter before him and he rummaged through the pieces.

"Any more legs?" he asked of no one in particular.

"If they invent a four-legged chicken," Will said, "Horace will think he's gone to heaven."

Horace nodded in agreement.

"Four-legged chicken," he said. "Great idea. We should get Master Chubb onto that."

He found another leg and wasted no time ripping large shreds from it with his teeth. Gilan watched him with some curiosity.

"I don't recall him eating this much when we were in Celtica," he said.

Horace grinned. "We didn't have this much to eat in Celtica," he said. "Besides, I felt a little overawed and nervous in the company of you mysterious Rangers."

"They don't make you nervous anymore?" Evanlyn asked, her eyes smiling as she sliced a peach in half. The fruit really was delicious, she thought. Perhaps it had something to do with the hot climate.

"Not in the slightest," Horace said. He was grinning now but he did remember that there was a time when he had been distinctly unsure of himself in the presence of Rangers—first with Gilan and Will in Celtica, then later in company with Halt as they crossed Gallica. Odd to think that now they were his closest friends. "I've learned since then. Halt's really a pussycat," he added.

Will and Gilan both snorted in an unsuccessful attempt to conceal their laughter. Halt's eyebrow rose fractionally as he regarded the grinning young man.

"A pussycat," he repeated.

Svengal had been watching this exchange with interest. Now he joined in with a loud guffaw.

"More like a battered old tomcat, I'd have thought," he said. Halt's withering gaze swung to the big Skandian, who remained resolutely unwithered.

"Everyone's a comedian all of a sudden," Halt said. "I think I'll go to bed."

He exited the room with what little dignity remained to him.

◆   ◆   ◆

Breakfast was served in the internal courtyard the following morning an hour after sunup. The air was fresh with the morning sea breeze, but already they could feel the coming heat of the day.

The three Rangers were delighted to find, among the platters of flat bread, sliced fruit, preserves and jars of juice, a pot of hot, rich black liquid.

"Coffee!" Gilan said reverently, pouring himself a cup. There was brown sugar to sweeten it and he spooned it in, while Halt and Will also helped themselves. Evanlyn shook her head at the sight of them.

"If a person ever wanted to capture you three," she said, "he'd just have to bait the trap with a pot of coffee."

Will nodded. "And we'd go gladly," he agreed. Then he said to the others, "This is really good coffee."

"Should be," Halt said, leaning back with his cup and putting his booted feet on the low table in front of him. "The Arridi invented it. Everyone sleep well?"

In fact, most of them had slept patchily, unused to the sensation of a bed that didn't roll and pitch rhythmically beneath them. But the mattresses had been soft and the bedrooms were cool and well ventilated. They were discussing the phenomenon that Svengal described as "land wobbles," which most seafarers feel when they first go ashore after a long voyage, when one of the servants entered and bowed to Halt.

"Captain Selethen is here, sir."

"Ask him to come in," Halt said, removing his feet from the table and rising to greet the Arridi officer as he entered the courtyard. As before, Selethen made the hand gesture to lips, brow and lips in greeting.

"Good morning, my lady, and gentlemen. Is everything satisfactory?"

Halt returned the hand greeting and motioned the captain to a seat.

"Everything is excellent. Will you join us for coffee?" he offered, but Selethen shook his head regretfully.

"Sadly, I have duties to attend to." He glanced at Svengal. "Your men have been given breakfast, Captain," he said. "There is no need to check."

Svengal nodded. The previous evening, he had made a point of visiting the ship to make sure his men were being looked after. They had their own supplies on board, of course, but he felt they should be fed by the Arridi, as they were part of an official delegation.

"Thank you," he said gruffly. Selethen turned back to Halt and Evanlyn now.

"His Excellence the Wakir will be delighted to receive you at the tenth hour," he said.

Evanlyn glanced uncertainly at Halt and he made a discreet hand gesture, signaling her to answer.

"That is suitable to us," she said.

Selethen smiled and drew himself to attention.

"I will escort you," he said. "I will be back fifteen minutes before the tenth hour. Please be ready to leave at that time."

Evanlyn said nothing, looking away with a disinterested expression. Princesses didn't respond to orders, Will realized.

"We will be ready," Halt said. He and Selethen exchanged the graceful hand gesture of greeting and farewell once more and the Arridi backed away a few paces before turning to leave. Horace, watching, marveled at the ease with which Halt fitted in to situations like this. He said as much to Will when the two of them returned to the room they were sharing, and he was a little surprised at his friend's gloomy response.

"I know. He's amazing, isn't he?" Will said. "He always knows exactly what to do and say."

Horace looked at him curiously, wondering at his less than enthusiastic manner. He had no idea that Will had been thinking exactly the same thing, and comparing himself to his master—a comparison that he found less than favorable. Once again Will was wondering how he would ever cope as a Ranger in his own right.

Fifteen minutes before Selethen was due to return, Halt summoned Will and Gilan to his room.

The two younger men entered curiously, wondering what their leader had in store for them. As it turned out, it was a pleasant and very welcome change to their equipment.

"Leave your cloaks here," Halt told them. They noticed he was not wearing his. "They're designed for the Araluen climate, not Arrida. And there's not a lot of forest and greenery around these parts."

He was right, Will thought. The green and gray mottled cloaks were designed to blend into the background colors of their fertile homeland, not the dry, sunbaked vistas they found themselves in now. The heavy wool was decidedly uncomfortable in the Arridi heat. Yet they were part of a Ranger's uniform and Will was reluctant to discard his.

Halt was opening a pack he had brought from the ship. He withdrew a folded garment from it now, shook it out and passed it to Gilan.

It was a cloak, a cowled Ranger's cloak, Will saw. But instead of the random green and gray colors they were used to, this one was unevenly mottled in varying shades of light brown. Furthermore, he realized as Halt produced a second cloak and handed it to him, it was made of heavy-duty linen, not wool.

"Summer issue," Halt said. "Cooler in the heat and a lot better if we have to blend into the background here."

Gilan had already swung his cloak around his shoulders. He looked at it, impressed. It was definitely more comfortable than the winter-weight cloak he had laid across the back of a chair. Will donned his, examining the coloring at closer quarters. He liked the familiar feel of the garment, the confidence that came with the ability to blend into the countryside and seem to disappear. That ability had become very much part of his life in recent years.

"Where did you get these from?" he asked. Halt regarded him quizzically.

"We have visited these parts before, you know," he said. "Crowley had the Castle Araluen quartermasters make some up the moment he heard we were coming here."

He waited while Gilan and Will moved the cloaks experimentally, eyeing each other and studying the unusual colors, seeing how they would blend into the landscape of rock and desert that surrounded Al Shabah.

"All right, ladies," he said, "if you're finished with the fashion show, let's go meet the Wakir."

17

Flanked by an escort of a dozen Arridi warriors, the small party followed Selethen as he led the way toward the center of the town, where the khadif, official residence of the Wakir, was located.

As they moved away from the harbor, and the cooling influence of the sea breeze, the temperature began to rise. It was a heavy, dry heat and the three Rangers were grateful that they had switched to their new cloaks.

The Rangers, Horace and Evanlyn kept their eyes straight ahead, as befitted the dignity of a diplomatic mission. Svengal felt no such inhibitions. He looked around curiously, getting a feeling for the town. The approach to the town square was similar to the one he had taken some weeks earlier in Erak's company, even though they had been approaching from the opposite side of the town. The narrow street wound through the same featureless whitewashed buildings. The roofs were flat and from time to time he saw curious brown faces peering over the balustrades at the small party, no doubt attracted by the solid tramp of their escort's feet on the street.

He studied the houses they passed. There were few windows, balconies or other openings looking onto the street. But now that he had seen the inside of the guesthouse, he realized that Arridi houses tended to look inward, onto shaded central courtyards, where the inhabitants relaxed.

They arrived at the open space of the town square. As they passed out of the narrow street into the wide paved area, Svengal noted the wooden barricades hinged back against the walls on either side. Obviously they were a permanent installation. Pity he hadn't noticed them last time, he reflected, or realized their significance.

Selethen led them across the square. The fountain that Svengal had noticed on his previous visit was now running and he could hear the musical splash of falling water.

Funny how just the sound of running water made a man feel a little cooler somehow, he thought. He was about to share this insight with the others but, for the first time, he noticed their fixed, unwavering expressions and realized that it might not be the time for idle chitchat.

They stepped up into the cool shade of the colonnaded terrace. The massive brassbound doors were open this time and Selethen stood to one side, gesturing for them to precede him. His troops fanned out to either side of the door.

Evanlyn led the way in, with Halt a pace behind her. Gilan, Will and Horace walked three abreast and Svengal hurried to catch up with them, falling in step with Horace.

"Quite a place they've got."

The young warrior grinned at him.

After the hard morning light outside, reflected from the multitude of white buildings, it was dim inside, and it took a few seconds for their eyes to adjust. But it was pleasantly cool as well, Svengal noted gratefully.

They were alone in a vast room, obviously the Wakir's audience hall. Around three sides were other rooms and second-floor galleries, where the doors to yet more rooms were visible. But the central hall itself took up the entire two-story height of the building. It extended upward to a vaulted roof, where cleverly designed glazed openings and baffles allowed indirect light to enter the room without incurring the penalty of the heat that would come with direct sunlight.

The walls were painted in the ubiquitous white, while the floor was tiled in elaborate mosaics, with an overall light blue pattern. The coolness of the tiles underfoot seemed to radiate upward, contributing to the comfortable temperature in the large room.

The fourth side of the room, the one they were facing, was the site where the Wakir received delegations. There was a tall wooden chair, carved in intricate patterns and much decorated with gilt and red paint, standing in a central position, on a slightly raised dais. Several low benches, presumably for those seeking audience, were arranged to either side.

Evanlyn stopped a few paces into the room, waiting for further developments. She looked straight ahead, knowing that it would be a mistake to turn to Halt for advice. That would show any unseen observer that she was unsure of herself, and not in command of this expedition. She knew that if Halt wanted to give her advice, he would do so in an unobtrusive way. For the moment, he was content to follow her lead. He stopped half a pace behind her and to her right. The others halted as well.

Selethen stepped to her side and said quietly, "The Wakir will be arriving in a few moments."

He gestured toward the raised dais. His intent was obvious. They were to move forward and await the Wakir's arrival.

"When he does," Evanlyn said in a clear, carrying voice, "we shall join him."

Will saw the slight movement of Halt's head as the Ranger nodded approvingly. There was a matter of protocol, and even more important, dignity, here. They had discussed the local system of rank and nobility on the ship. The Wakir was the local ruler, with authority over the province of Al Shabah, and answerable to the Emrikir, the national ruler. That made him the equivalent of a baron in Araluen. And since the Al Shabah province was an important one, this Wakir would be a senior baron, equivalent to someone like Arald.

But Cassandra was a Crown Princess and far superior in rank to any local ruler. It would not be seemly for her to stand waiting while the Wakir took his time arriving. Of course, as the head of a delegation, she had to show some deference to his position. She could not, for example, insist that he come to her at the guesthouse.

Stopping here, just inside the entrance to the audience hall, was a compromise that served both her dignity and that of the Wakir. Halt glanced at the Arridi captain as he registered her statement. He thought he saw a small light of approval there as well. It occurred to him that perhaps Evanlyn's sense of self-worth and confidence was being tested—and this would probably not be the last time it happened.

"I shall inform His Excellency," said Selethen. This time, Halt was sure he saw the slightest trace of a smile on the dark face before the tall warrior moved away.

He disappeared into one of the many side doors. There would likely be galleries and hallways running the length of the building, Halt thought, as well as offices and rooms for the Wakir's staff.

"Well done," Halt said to Evanlyn in a low voice. She didn't turn to look at him but from the three-quarter viewpoint he had, he saw her cheekbones move and knew that she had allowed a faint smile to touch her face.

"Wasn't sure what to do," she murmured back to him.

"Trust your instincts," he told her. She knew more about these situations than she realized, he thought. She'd spent years at Duncan's side. "When in doubt," he added, "be pompous."

"Don't make me laugh, Halt," she said out of the corner of her mouth. "I'm as nervous as a cat here."

"You're doing fine," he said. As he said it, a door opened at the far end of the room, on the left-hand side, and half a dozen men emerged, led by a man who could only be the Wakir.

He was a disappointing figure, Will thought. So far, he only had experience of Selethen and his soldiers. They were tall and lean and had the look of trained fighting men about them. The Wakir looked like a clerk—a hilfmann, he thought, remembering his despised antagonist at the Skandian court.

The Wakir was a good head shorter than any of the others in his entourage. A head-and-a-half if compared to Selethen, who, as a mere captain of the guard, had brought up the rear. The Wakir was also a little overweight—no, Will corrected, he was fat—a fact that could not be concealed by the flowing robes he wore. And the face beneath the oversized turban seemed to have been formed from soft clay, molded hastily to form features, with a squashed lump of a nose set in the middle. He looked around uncertainly, saw the Araluen delegation, and took his seat on the carved, decorated chair. He had to sit well forward to make sure that his short legs actually touched the ground. Had he sat back, they would have swung, childlike, some five centimeters from the polished wood floorboards of the platform.

"Regular giant, isn't he?" Horace muttered out of the side of his mouth.

"Shut up," Halt replied, in the same fashion.

"Children, children," Evanlyn said quietly in mock admonishment. Will regarded her with admiration. She stood straight-backed and confident. She was handling all this with great skill and aplomb,

he thought, as if she were born to it. Then he shrugged mentally. She
had been born to it. For a moment, he had another flash of his own
inadequacy. Then, as Evanlyn stepped out toward the dais, he hurried to fall in step with the others.

Their boots rang on the tiled floor, echoing off the bare walls as
they proceeded down the large room. Evanlyn stopped just short of
the dais, waiting to be announced.

Selethen stepped forward, between her and the Wakir.

"Your Excellence, may I present the delegation of Princess
Cassandra of the Kingdom of Araluen. Princess, may I present His
Excellence Aman Sh'ubdel, Wakir and overlord of the province of Al
Shabah."

Evanlyn inclined her head deeply. She'd been told by Lord
Anthony that strict protocol required a woman to curtsey in this sort
of situation. But she'd told him that she'd be damned if she would.

"Excellence," she said, holding the bow for several seconds, then
looking up.

The Wakir gestured for her to approach and as she stepped toward the low dais he said, "Please be seated, my lady."

Evanlyn froze in midstep. A small frown crossed her face.

"I am Crown Princess of Araluen, Excellence. As such, I am addressed as 'your highness.' Or, if that isn't acceptable to your own
dignity, 'Princess Cassandra' would be suitable."

Good girl, thought Halt, although his face remained inscrutable
as ever.

The Wakir seemed a little flustered by her reaction. He glanced
to one side and for a moment, Evanlyn had the distinct impression
that he was looking to Selethen for guidance. She had an urge to
look at the captain as well, but she knew she must keep her gaze
fixed on the Wakir.

"Of course, of course! A slip of the tongue. Apologies, Princess . . .

your highness," he said, waving a hand to dismiss his unintentional gaffe. "Please, please, sit with me."

For a moment, Evanlyn fought an overwhelming urge to giggle as she wondered what he'd do if she took him literally and hopped up to sit on his knee on the massive carved chair. She struggled to keep a straight face, forcing herself to regain complete composure. Her hesitation served her well, however, as the Wakir took it as a further sign of her displeasure. He rose from his chair. Will had to hide a smile as he saw how awkward this movement was. The short-legged Arridi ruler had to skid his behind forward to the edge of the seat, then virtually drop to the floor. Having been shorter than most of those around him all his life, Will enjoyed seeing someone else struggling with the problem.

"Sit, your highness, please!" he repeated, and Evanlyn nodded her consent, moved to a richly upholstered bench that Selethen placed before her and sat gracefully. The Wakir nodded. He climbed back aboard his seat, wriggling his backside again to get into position, cast another sideways glance, then licked his lips nervously. Evanlyn thought she might as well take charge of matters.

"We've come to discuss the ransom of our friend Erak, Oberjarl of Skandia," she said. Her voice was high and clear. "We understand you have set a sum for this?"

"We have," the Wakir replied. "The sum required is . . ." Again he hesitated and again there was that sideways shift of the eyes. Evanlyn frowned. The man seemed very unsure of himself, she thought. Then he continued. "Eighty thousand reels of silver." There was a renewed tone of confidence in his voice now that he spoke the figure, as if it had just been confirmed for him.

Evanlyn shook her head. "Too high," she said firmly. The Wakir jerked back in his seat in surprise.

"Too high?" he repeated, and Evanlyn nodded. She was conscious of Anthony's briefing on this matter. They'll expect you to bargain, he had said. It's a virtual insult if you don't.

"We're offering fifty thousand," Evanlyn told him calmly. The Wakir's hands flew about his head in an agitated fashion.

"Fifty thousand? But that's . . ." He hesitated and Evanlyn finished for him.

"Our offer."

The Wakir's hand played with his chin, tugging at the loose flesh below it. His eyes took on a crafty look.

"All very well to offer such a low price, your highness. But how do I know you are capable of paying even that much? How do I know you are authorized?"

"You have my seal," Evanlyn said simply. She had seen the seal box that she had returned to Selethen the previous day. It was sitting on a side table beside the Wakir's chair. He looked at it now, picked it up and opened the hinged top.

"Aaah, yes. Your seal," he said, studying it.

"It identifies me as Princess Cassandra of Araluen," Evanlyn replied, and Halt, listening intently, detected the slightest note of suspicion in her voice.

Again the Wakir fingered his chin.

"So you say. But this seal, of course, could belong to . . ." He looked around the room, waved his hand indefinitely and finished, ". . . anybody."

Evanlyn sat back on her bench for a few seconds, her mind racing. She knew that countries kept a register of official seals and she knew that Arrida was on the list of countries with which Araluen had exchanged such information. Before she had left Araluen, Duncan and Anthony had assured her that in the last exchange, some six months prior, her seal had been included with Duncan's as a matter of course. The Wakir should know that. If he didn't, it could mean only one thing . . .

Abruptly, she rose from her chair and turned to her five waiting companions.

"Let's go," she said crisply.

She didn't hesitate, but strode decisively through them. They hurried to follow in her wake, her boot heels loud on the tiled floor. Behind them, there was a buzz of activity on the dais. Will glanced back and saw the Wakir had come to his feet again, and was gesturing uncertainly toward Selethen. The captain stepped forward now and called after her.

"Princess Cassandra! Please wait!"

Evanlyn stopped and turned deliberately.

"Wait?" she asked, and he moved toward her, hands stretched out in an imploring gesture. "Why should I wait to be insulted any further? You've had me dealing with an impostor. I'll wait in the guesthouse, but only as long as the next tide. If the real Wakir doesn't make himself known by then, we're leaving."

Selethen hesitated, then his shoulders relaxed and he smiled ruefully.

"My apologies, your highness." He turned to the tubby little figure on the dais. "Thank you, Aman. You did your best."

The fake Wakir shrugged disconsolately. "I'm sorry, Excellence. She caught me by surprise."

The suspicion that had been growing in Evanlyn's mind was confirmed. She raised an eyebrow at the captain.

"Excellence?" she repeated, and he shrugged.

"Aman is my accountant," he said. "As I think you just guessed, I am Wakir of Al Shabah. Now perhaps you could come back and we'll begin to negotiate in earnest."

Evanlyn hesitated. She was tempted to stand on her dignity. Then she thought about Erak and realized that every second of delay would cause him discomfort and uncertainty.

"Very well," she said and walked back to the dais. The four Araluens and Svengal followed her. As they marched back up the audience hall, Horace leaned down to Will and whispered in his ear.

"Is she good at this, or what?"

18

SELETHEN LED THEM OUT OF THE LARGE AUDIENCE HALL TO a smaller chamber set to one side. There was a low central table surrounded by thick, comfortable cushions. Arched, unglazed windows looked out onto a shaded verandah while a slow-moving fan, obviously kept in motion by an unseen servant, swung back and forth overhead, keeping a cool breeze circulating through the room.

Selethen gestured for them to sit. This time, Will realized, there was no position of power for the Wakir. He sat on the same level as his guests. Two of his soldiers remained in the room, standing impassively to either side of the door. At a signal from one, servants emerged through a far archway and placed bowls of fruit on the table, along with a coffeepot and small cups. Evanlyn hid a smile as she saw the three Rangers' eyes light up at the sight of the last items.

"My apologies for the playacting outside," Selethen said smoothly. He looked slightly amused by the whole proceeding, Will thought. Evanlyn showed no sign of any reciprocal amusement.

"Was it really necessary?" she asked coldly, and Selethen inclined his head.

"I'm afraid I felt it was, your highness," he said. Evanlyn went to speak but he continued, "You must appreciate that I needed to be sure I was dealing with someone who has full power to negotiate. After all, I expected Svengal here"—he nodded toward the Skandian, who was trying to make himself comfortable sitting cross-legged on a cushion—"to return some months hence with the ransom money. A delegation from Araluen, arriving so soon and apparently acting on his behalf, was definitely a surprise. I suspected a trick."

His gaze flicked to Svengal again. "No offense," he added, and the Skandian shrugged. If he had been able to think of a worthwhile trick to release Erak, then he would have tried it.

"You had my seal," Evanlyn told him. "Surely that was proof enough." It wasn't a question. It was a statement. Selethen inclined his head thoughtfully.

"I recognized the seal, of course. But I knew nothing of the person who carried it. After all, a seal can be stolen or even copied. I was faced with the prospect of negotiating with a young woman. I needed to be sure that you were the real princess. That's why I had Aman impersonate me. I knew you'd probably see through the deception. But if you were planning trickery of your own, you'd pretend to go along with it. Only a real princess would have the courage and dignity to call my bluff and walk out as you did."

He smiled at Halt. "Your princess has a strong nerve. She'd make a great Arridi."

"She makes a great Araluen," Halt replied, and the Wakir acknowledged the statement.

Then he rubbed both his hands together and smiled eagerly.

"So now, perhaps we can negotiate!" he said.

The haggling took most of the rest of the morning. Selethen returned to his base figure of eighty thousand reels. Evanlyn countered with an offer of forty-five thousand. When he gave her a hurt look, and pointed out that earlier she had begun at fifty thousand, Evanlyn told him that he had tried to trick her and her dignity now demanded a lower figure as a starting point.

The bargaining continued. Selethen raised the fact that keeping Erak guarded and cared for had already cost his province a considerable amount of money.

"Those soldiers could have been gainfully employed elsewhere," he told her. "The Tualaghi bandits raid our villages constantly."

Halt looked up at the name. Crowley's briefing to him had relied on intelligence that was over a year old. He had been under the impression that the Tualaghi, a wild desert tribe of bandits and robbers, had been successfully suppressed. Apparently, if the Wakir was to be believed, they had regained some of their traditional strength. It was a fact worth knowing, he thought—unless it was just a bargaining ploy on Selethen's part.

Evanlyn expressed her sympathy for the expenses incurred. But her tone left no doubt that she was less than concerned about it. In reply, she countered with the expense of her trip to Arrida—and the cost of maintaining her own retinue.

"Very few expeditions enjoy the presence of three Rangers," she said. "Their skills are very much in demand in my homeland."

It was Selethen's turn to react to a word. His eyes narrowed thoughtfully as she said "Rangers." He knew there had been something about those three cloaked men. They had the appearance of simple woodsmen, archers or hunters. Yet there was an air of self-assurance about them all, and the older one, the princess's principal adviser, spoke with a depth of authority that one would never expect from a simple archer. Rangers. Yes, he had heard the term. There were rumors about the Araluen Rangers—stories told by seafarers who had visited their country. They were vague and unsubstantiated, and doubtless exaggerated, to be sure. But enough to make him look at them with renewed interest.

"Let it be remembered that your friend and ally came here as a raider," he said. "He planned to rob Al Shabah's treasury." His subtle use of the words "friend and ally" conveyed the vague implication that the Kingdom of Araluen had given some kind of tacit approval to Erak's raiding. It gave him a step up onto the moral high ground. "There must be some penalty exacted for that intention."

Evanlyn conceded the point—she could hardly do otherwise. She countered with the fact that nothing had actually been stolen, but Selethen had won that round and she was forced to raise her bid to fifty-five thousand. He said he would consider—consider, mind you—a sum of seventy-eight thousand.

And so it went on. Selethen was clearly enjoying the process. Bargaining was a matter dear to any Arridi's heart. And, after a while, to her own surprise, Evanlyn found she was enjoying herself as well. The man was charming and good-humored. It was impossible to take offense. And she had to admit that he was very handsome, in an exotic, swashbuckling fashion.

Eventually, they reached a tentative agreement. The figure was sixty-six thousand, four hundred and eight reels of silver, to be paid in the form of a warrant on the Silasian Council. The odd figure of four hundred and eight reels was reached when Selethen complained that the Silasians would take their commission from the end figure. The fact that delivery of the silver was absolutely guaranteed allowed him to give a little on the figure. But he still resented the commission.

He wrote the final amount on a parchment and nodded several times.

"I will consider this for the next hour," he said.

He rose, offering his hand to Evanlyn to assist her. Even though she was as lithe and athletic as a cat, she took it, enjoying the contact. She saw Horace's slight frown as she did so and smiled to herself.

A girl can never have too many admirers, she thought. Will, she noted, seemed unperturbed by the fact that she retained hold of Selethen's hand a little longer than politeness dictated. But then, Rangers were trained to look imperturbable. He was probably seething with jealousy, she thought.

The others rose to their feet as well, Svengal grunting as he heaved his bulk upright.

"I will have you escorted back to the guesthouse," Selethen told her. "I will bring you my answer in an hour's time."

In spite of the delay, she knew that the figure would be accepted. Halt had told her before they left the guesthouse that the façade of considering it for an hour was simply part and parcel of Arridi bargaining.

She smiled and bowed her head. "Thank you, Excellence. I look forward to your decision."

Back at the guesthouse, as they sat around the table in the courtyard, Svengal shook his head impatiently.

"Why do they have to go through all this rigmarole?" he asked. "We know they're going to accept the figure. They know they're going to accept it. Why not just say so and be done with it?"

"It's a kind of compliment," Halt told him. "It makes it seem that you've driven such a hard bargain that they can't accept immediately. They have to appear reluctant. They enjoy subtleties like that."

Svengal snorted. Like most Skandians, he preferred the direct approach. The tortuous intricacies of diplomacy left him cold.

Gilan grinned. "I liked his subtle implication that we were somehow involved in the raid."

Halt nodded. "You mean his reference to our being 'a friend and ally'? It was a nice touch."

Svengal was still annoyed over what he saw as an unnecessary waste of time. In addition, he was bored, tired of behaving diplomatically and looking for an argument to pass the time.

"Well, in a way, he's right. All this is partly your fault, you know," he said.

Halt leaned forward in his chair, eyebrow raised. "Our fault?"

Svengal made a vague gesture. "Yes. After all, if you hadn't insisted that we stop raiding your country, we never would have been here in the first place."

"Pardon me if I disagree," Evanlyn said. "You surely can't be trying to blame us for Erak's habit of charging ashore waving an ax and grabbing everything that isn't nailed down." She realized as she said it that it might sound a little harsh, so she added with a note of apology, "No offense, Svengal."

Svengal shrugged. "None taken. It's a pretty accurate description of Erak on a raid, as a matter of fact. But the point remains . . ."

Whatever that point might have been was never made clear, as a servant appeared at that moment, informing them of Selethen's arrival. The Wakir followed a few meters behind, smiling as they rose from their chairs around the table.

"Agreed," he said, and there were smiles all around the table.

"That's wonderful, Excellence," Evanlyn told him. "I have a warrant against the Silasian Council in my baggage. All it needs is for the amount to be filled in and for me to add my seal. We can do that straightaway."

Selethen nodded contentedly. "Whenever it's convenient, your highness," he said. "There's no hurry."

Fortunately, there would be no problem with both sides understanding the warrant. The Silasian Council's warrants were well-known throughout the area and although Araluens and Arridi used a different written language, both nations used the same numbering system. The figure agreed and signed to by Evanlyn would be unmistakable.

"I'm sure Erak wouldn't agree," Halt said. "When will we be able to see him and give him the news?"

Selethen hesitated.

"Ah . . . yes. We will bring him to you," he said.

"Today?" Halt asked, noting the tone of hesitation in the other man's voice.

"Perhaps it might take a little longer than that," Selethen said. Halt looked at him suspiciously.

"How long?" he asked very deliberately. Selethen gave him his most disarming smile. Halt remained resolutely un-disarmed.

"Four days? Perhaps five?" Selethen said.

Evanlyn and Halt exchanged exasperated glances.

"Where exactly is he?" the princess asked Selethen. There was a definite cutting edge to her voice, Will thought. Selethen seemed to agree. His disarming smile became a little less confident.

"On his way to the fortress at Mararoc," he said. "It's four days, on a good horse."

19

"When were you planning on sharing this information with us?" Halt's voice was deceptively calm.

Selethen shrugged. "Once the bargaining was complete. I had him removed from Al Shabah when your ship was first sighted. There was always the chance that we might not reach an agreement, and in that case, I wanted the prisoner where his crew couldn't attempt a sneak attack to rescue him." He glanced at Svengal. "No offense."

The Skandian drew a deep breath and let it out very slowly. He was obviously making a huge effort to control himself.

"You know, one of these days, I'm actually going to take offense if people keep throwing out these slurs. And then things are going to get rather ugly. When we Skandians do take offense, we do it with a battleax."

Selethen inclined his head. "In that case, accept my deepest apologies. In any event, now that the bargaining is successful, I'll send word to Mararoc and have the Oberjarl brought back here. As soon as the warrant is sealed and delivered to me."

"Oh no. I don't think so," Evanlyn said immediately. "I'm not handing over the best part of seventy thousand reels until I've seen the goods are undamaged." For a moment, she was about to say "no offense" to Svengal for referring to his Oberjarl as "goods." In light of his previous statement, she thought it wiser not to.

They had reached an impasse. The two negotiators stared at each other stubbornly. Will finally broke the silence.

"Why don't we all go to Mararoc to fetch him?" he asked Selethen. "The princess can reassure herself that Erak is all right and hand over the warrant there."

It was significant, he thought, that both Evanlyn and Selethen looked immediately to Halt for a response. The older Ranger was nodding.

"I think it's a good idea," he said. It was a fair compromise. And in addition, he could see there were advantages to traveling inland in Arrida. Very few Araluens had ever ventured more than a kilometer from the coast and a Ranger's thirst for strategic knowledge was insatiable. He looked at Selethen. "I assume you'll ensure the princess's safety?"

"We'll take an escort of fifty of my men," he agreed.

"And my crew," Svengal put in. "After all, we've sworn to protect the princess."

This time, however, Selethen didn't agree.

"No," he said flatly. "I'm not allowing an armed force of Skandians to go marching across Arrida."

"There's only thirty of them," Svengal said ingenuously. Selethen smiled grimly.

"Thirty Skandians," he said, "are the equivalent of a small army."

Svengal had to grin modestly at that assessment. Selethen switched his gaze to Halt.

"I can't allow it," he said simply.

Halt nodded. "He's right, Svengal. You wouldn't allow a hundred Arridi warriors to go wandering around Skandia, would you?"

Svengal chewed his mustache thoughtfully and eventually he had to agree that Halt was right.

The Ranger saw him wavering and added, "And I think the five of us, along with Selethen and fifty warriors, should be enough to keep the princess safe."

Evanlyn coughed lightly and they all looked at her.

"I think the princess," she said archly, "would prefer it if you didn't discuss her as if she weren't in the room." She smiled at Svengal then and added, "I'm happy to release your men from their oath for the short time it will take us to get to Mararoc."

Then she turned to Selethen.

"So when do we get started?"

They left in the predawn grayness the following morning. Selethen pointed out that the Arridi preferred to travel in the hours before noon, by which time the sun has reached its full strength. None of the Araluens saw any reason to disagree with him.

The sea breeze followed them for the first kilometer or two. The early morning was fresh and cool and they covered ground quickly. Selethen had supplied Evanlyn with a horse—one of the local breed favored by Arridi warriors. It was taller than the horses the three Rangers rode—finer boned and more delicate looking. Its coat was smooth, in contrast to the shaggy little horses. It had a short muzzle and a handsome, intelligent face. Obviously bred for flashing speed in short bursts, thought Halt as he admired the beast. And undoubtedly able to cope with the heat and dryness of the desert.

The Arridi leader had offered Horace a similar mount but Horace had chosen to stay with Kicker.

"He knows my ways," he said, smiling.

There was a long, thin band of orange creeping above the low hills in the east as they rode inland. The sea breeze faded away as they got farther from the coast but the air was still chilled. The clear nights in the desert allowed heat to escape into the atmosphere. Nights were surprisingly cold while the days became hot and searing.

"I thought deserts were supposed to be all sand," Horace said to Will, surveying the hard, rocky surface they were crossing.

Selethen heard the comment and turned to him.

"You'll see plenty of that when we reach the Sand Depression," he said. "The ground we're crossing now is the coastal plain. Farther inland there's a belt of sand dunes that stretches for thirty-odd kilometers before we reach the escarpment. Then we'll climb several hundred meters to the site of Mararoc."

"So we'll see plenty of the country," Horace said cheerfully.

The three Rangers exchanged quick glances. Selethen was no fool. He saw the quick look that passed between the three Rangers and resolved to keep a close eye on them. There was no current animosity between their countries. But who knew when that might change?

The previous night, Halt had called Will and Gilan to his room. "This is a great opportunity to learn something about the inland areas of Arridi," he said. "After the first few kilometers, whatever maps we have in Araluen are sheer guesswork."

Will and Gilan had listened eagerly. Rangers were obsessed with information gathering, and knowledge of the topography of the country could be vital if there were ever any future confrontations with the Arridi.

"Take notice of any major land features—cliffs, hills, tors, wells. Particularly wells. When we rest, note them down. We'll compare notes each evening, to make sure we keep it as accurate as possible. Then we'll draw a chart of the day's progress. Do you both have your northseekers?" he asked.

The two younger men nodded. The northseekers were magnetized slivers of steel set in a protective container and free to swivel as the magnetic field of the earth dictated. Their use and value had originally been discovered by the Skandians. All Rangers carried them.

"Then use them," Halt went on. "But try to make sure Selethen doesn't notice too much of what we're doing."

The glaring eye of the sun had slid up over the rim of the earth now—a vast red ball rising into the sky. It interested Will that at this time of day it was possible to discern the sun's movement. One moment it was just broaching the horizon, the next it was soaring freely. And already its heat was starting to bite, dispelling the remaining chill of the dark hours.

"Don't like the look of that," Svengal muttered. He was riding a heavyset workhorse. The slender Arridi breed would have been too light to carry his bulky frame over a long journey. Selethen looked at him curiously and the Skandian pointed toward the sun.

"When you see a red sunrise like that at sea, you start looking for a harbor," he said.

The Wakir nodded. "Same in the desert. It often means a storm. But not always," he added, smiling reassuringly at Evanlyn.

During the hours before dawn, they had ridden as a group, with Selethen's men riding in a ring around them. Now that visibility had improved, he blew on a small silver whistle and the troop took up its daylight positions. A squad of five riders cantered forward until they were a kilometer in advance—still in sight but able to give ample warning of any impending attack. They spread out into line abreast, each man several hundred meters from his neighbor.

Another five dropped back and formed a similar screen to the rear. The remaining forty men split into two files riding on either side of the command group, a hundred meters out and on parallel paths. It was one advantage of traveling in such bare, featureless country, Halt thought. Selethen could deploy his men across a wide space without having to keep them bunched up on a track.

The other notable feature of the formation was that it precluded the men talking among themselves and missing any possible threat. The horsemen in the two parallel files were all facing outward, he noticed, their eyes scanning the horizon.

He nudged Abelard up level with Selethen's pure white stallion.

"Expecting trouble?" he asked, nodding at the wide-flung screen of men protecting them. Selethen shrugged.

"Always expect trouble in the desert. Then you usually won't meet it."

Halt nodded appreciatively. "Very wise," he remarked. "Who said that first?"

Selethen allowed himself a thin smile. "A very wise man," he said. "Me."

He glanced around. He could see the younger of the three Rangers making a note on a small sheet of parchment, staring intently at a hill in the distance with a distinctive hooked shape to its peak. He decided there was little he could do to stop this activity.

"You mentioned the Tualaghi," Halt said. He nodded meaningfully at the protective screen around them. "I'd heard you had them pretty well under control."

Selethen shook his head in exasperation. "Nobody can keep those devils under control for too long. What do you know of them?"

Halt shrugged. "They're raiders. Bandits. Assassins," he said.

Selethen nodded grimly. "All of that and worse. We call them the Forgotten of God, the Blue-Veiled Riders. They despise the true religion. They worship devils and demons and they're committed to murder and robbery and pillaging. The trouble is, they know the desert like the backs of their hands and they can strike and fade away before we have a chance to retaliate. They have no honor and no sense of pity. If you are not one of them, you are not human. Your life is worthless."

"But you did manage to defeat them at one stage?" Halt prompted.

"Yes. We formed an alliance with the Bedullin." Selethen saw the question forming on the other man's lips and went on to explain. "They're a desert nomad tribe. Warriors. Independent and very proud. But they're honorable people. They know the desert nearly as well as the Tualaghi and they joined with us in a temporary alliance to bring them to heel."

"Pity you couldn't make it permanent," Halt said.

Selethen looked at him. "Indeed. But as I say, the Bedullin are proud and independent. They're like hawks. You can use them to hunt for you for a while. But they're always really hunting for themselves. Perhaps it's time I approached them again to put the Tualaghi back in their place."

Halt noticed that the Wakir was looking more and more often to the southern horizon. He followed the man's gaze and could see a thin dark line there.

"Trouble?" he said. Selethen flashed him a reassuring grin.

"Maybe. But at least the Tualaghi won't worry us. They rarely move in groups of more than ten. Fifty warriors would be too big a force for them to attack."

"Quite so," Halt murmured. "Yet a wise man should always expect trouble, didn't you say?" Unconsciously, his hand touched the string of the massive longbow slung across his shoulders. Selethen noticed the action. He glanced at the southern horizon again. The dark line had thickened noticeably. And it seemed closer. His hand went to the silver whistle inside his shirt.

"I think I'll call the outriders in a little closer," he said. "Visibility could become a problem before too long."

Svengal had urged his sturdy horse up alongside them. He gestured to the approaching storm.

"Seen that?" he asked, and Selethen nodded. "When we get hit by one of them at sea, it's full of wind and water and rain so thick you can't breathe. What's in that one?"

"Sand," Selethen told them. "Lots and lots of sand."

20

There was a new urgency in Selethen's manner as the outriders closed in, in response to his signal. He looked around the foreigners, ensuring they were all wearing the keffiyehs he had given them when they set out from Al Shabah. These were desert headdresses—essentially simple squares of cotton, folded into a triangle, then draped over the head so that elongated tails hung down either side and at the back, providing protection from the sun. They were held in place by a twisted coil of camel hair rope.

Now he quickly showed them how the elongated tails could be pulled across the face then quickly twisted over each other to cover the nose and mouth. It was a simple but effective form of head protection in the desert.

"You'll need them," he said. "Once the sand wall hits us, you'll be unable to breathe without them." Will glanced to the south. The thin dark line he had noticed a few minutes ago was now a thick band that spread from one side of the horizon to the other. In fact, he realized, the southern horizon seemed to have moved closer. He glanced north to confirm the fact, then back again. The sandstorm was blotting out the horizon to the south. It was a dirty brown color at the base, almost black. And now he could see that it towered thousands of meters into the air, blocking out the sky. The storm itself was rapidly becoming the boundary of their world.

Selethen stood in his stirrups, looking for any available shelter.

"There!" he called. "There's a shallow wadi. The bank will give us a little protection."

He urged his horse toward the wadi, a dry gully that cut through the hard rocky ground. The walls were barely three meters in height but they would offer some protection, at least. They hurried to follow him. He halted a few meters short of the edge to allow them to pass by.

"My God," said Horace, "look at how fast it's moving!"

They looked up. The dirty brown wall of swirling sand now completely blocked their sight to the south. There was nothing but the storm and it was quickly advancing on them. It was moving like the wind, Will thought. Then he realized, it was the wind.

He glanced up and caught Evanlyn's eyes on him. They exchanged a worried look and he knew they were both thinking of the same thing—the massive storm that had swept down on them when they were prisoners on *Wolfwind* years before. He tried to grin reassuringly at her but at that moment the first breath of the storm struck them—unbelievably hot and fetid and laden with flying, invisible grains of sand.

Tug plunged nervously as the sand whipped his face and flanks. Will kept a firm hand on the reins. Usually, Tug only needed him to hold them lightly but in these conditions, he knew, his horse would respond better to the sense of control that a firm pressure on the bit would impart to him.

"Take it easy, boy," he said. "It's just sand."

The wind was now a living presence around them, keening horribly. And the light was dying. Will was startled to find that Evanlyn, less than five meters away, was now a shadowy, indistinct form in the dimness. The others were no clearer.

Selethen rode in among them and they pressed closer to him to hear him, horses tossing and whinnying nervously. He unwound the protective keffiyeh from his mouth and shouted his instructions.

"Ride down into the wadi. Dismount and turn your horses' tails to the wind. Try to cover their heads with your cloaks if you can. Then we'll..."

Whatever he was going to add was lost in a giant fit of coughing as he drew in a mouthful of fine flying sand. He doubled over, pulling his headdress across his face again and waving them toward the wadi.

Halt led the way. Will's sense of panic rose as he realized that his mentor would be out of sight in a few meters if he didn't hurry to follow him. He was conscious of other blurred figures close to him as Gilan, Horace, Evanlyn and Svengal all followed suit. Farther away there were vague forms moving in the storm and he realized these were the Arridi troops moving to the shelter.

The dim shadow that was Halt and Abelard seemed to sink into the ground and he realized that they must have reached the rim of the wadi. Tug, seeing them disappear, became nervous, sensing that the ground before him was unsafe. He whinnied shrilly and balked, resisting Will's efforts to urge him forward. The wind was screaming around them, terrifying in its intensity and power, disorienting the little horse. Never before had Tug refused Will's command, but now he stood his ground. The wind prevented his hearing the reassuring tones of his trusted master's voice and he sensed danger somewhere ahead. He had seen Halt and Abelard disappear and he was trained to protect his master in situations like this. He braced his forelegs and stood fast, head down into the screaming, flaying wind.

Will saw the shadowy figure of Horace move past him, recognizable only because of the fact that Kicker stood hands taller than Tug. Someone else moved past him too. He had no idea who it was. Conditions were getting worse, as unbelievable as that might seem. The wind was like the blast from an oven, the air superheated, and the millions of flying, stinging sand particles tore at any piece of exposed skin. The grains forced their way into clothing, under the face masks of the keffiyehs, into boots, inside collars and into any crevice in the skin—eyelids, ears, nostrils were full of it and Will coughed rackingly.

He found the action of coughing caused him to inhale more sand than he expelled but it was unavoidable.

He couldn't stay here like this, he realized. And he couldn't leave Tug. He would have to dismount and lead him, hoping that the sight of his master would calm his fears enough for him to move. He took a firm grip on the reins and swung down to the ground. Ordinarily, he would have trusted Tug to stand still when he dismounted. But he knew the horse was close to panic in this screaming, hellish, sand-laden wind.

He slipped his right arm up under Tug's neck, caressing him and speaking to him, all the time keeping a firm hold on the reins with the other hand. It seemed to be working. Tug's braced forefeet relaxed and he allowed himself to take a faltering few steps in response to Will's urging.

"Come on, boy. It's all right. It's only sand." He tried to croon the words reassuringly but he was startled by the sound of his own voice, which came out as a dry, faltering croak. He doubted that the horse could hear him, but he felt that the contact of his right arm and the proximity of his body was keeping the little horse under control.

He stooped as he led Tug forward, trying to see the point where the ground dropped away into the wadi. It was all he could do to make out the ground itself amid the flying debris of the storm.

He glanced up at Tug's face. The little horse's eyes were shut tight against the wind. Fine sand and dust had crusted over the moisture around the eye sockets and lids.

Where in blazes was that bank? He stumbled forward, awkward with the resistant weight of Tug's body. He pulled the reins firmly and the horse yielded a little, taking three more hesitant steps forward. He realized that Tug's instinct was to turn tail toward the wind, protecting his eyes and nostrils from the whipping sand. But he had to keep forcing the little horse forward to the meager shelter offered by the wadi's banks. He had a sense that the storm had not yet reached its peak.

Sand whipped across his eyes, blinding him, and he released his hold around Tug's neck for a moment to try to wipe them clear. It was a futile effort. He gasped and spluttered, suffocated by the storm. He pulled on the reins once more and stepped forward, head bowed against the screaming darkness around him.

And felt his foot fall into empty space.

Off balance, he teetered on the brink of the wadi bank, flailing his free arm in the air to try to regain his stance. His whirling arm struck Tug across the nose and the little horse reared back in surprise and alarm.

The reins came loose from Will's grip as Tug jerked away. He wheeled instinctively away from the wind. His senses, normally so keen and finely honed, were deadened by the all-pervading scream of the storm. Seeking for some sense of Will, he took a pace, then another, whinnying shrilly in alarm. But he was heading in the wrong direction.

Will floundered to his feet. He tried to call to his horse but his voice was barely a croak now. He thought—thought—he could sense a presence in the storm a few meters away. He stumbled toward it, knowing it was Tug.

But the vague shape, nothing more than a half-perceived denser mass in the darkness surrounding him, moved away and he lost sight of it. He stumbled forward, the wind behind him now.

"Tug!" he tried to shout. But the sound was inaudible even to his own ears, drowned by the triumphant shriek of the massive wind. He stretched out a hand and touched nothing but flying sand.

Then, miraculously, he saw a shadow looming out of the dark mass of wind and sand and debris.

"Tug!" he gasped. But a hand grabbed the collar of his cloak and pulled him forward.

Dimly, he realized that he was face-to-face with Selethen.

"Get . . . down!" the Wakir shouted at him, dragging him toward the rough ground. Will fought against the iron grip.

"Horse . . ." He managed to force the word out. "My horse . . ."

"Leave . . . him!" Selethen spoke slowly and deliberately so that he could be heard above the storm. Now he was urging his own horse, trained for and accustomed to these conditions, to its knees, all the time holding Will's collar with his free hand. The Arridi horse lay on its side, head curled around into the shelter of its own body. Will felt a foot slip between his feet to trip him and he and Selethen crashed to the ground together, the Arridi dragging him into the scant shelter provided by the horse's body.

"Tug!" Will screamed, the effort searing his parched throat with agony. Selethen was fumbling with his cloak, trying to drag it over both their heads to protect them from the sand. He leaned over to speak directly into Will's ear.

"You'll die out there!" he shouted. "He's gone! Understand?"

Dully, Will realized that he was right. He would have no chance of finding his horse in the whirling brown mass that surrounded them. He felt a great stab of pain in his heart at the thought of his horse—alone and terrified in all that horror—and he sobbed uncontrollably, great racking sobs that heaved and shuddered through his entire body.

But there were no tears. The heat and the choking sand and dust denied him even that small comfort.

21

THE STORM FINALLY PASSED. WILL HAD NO IDEA HOW LONG IT had battered them, screamed at them, tortured them. It felt like hours.

While it had raged, it was as if his senses shut down so that he was conscious only of the screaming, tormenting voice of the wind. In the sudden silence that greeted its passing, he became aware of other sensations. There was something heavy across his legs and body, and on top of the cloak that Selethen had pulled over their heads. He felt Selethen moving and he wriggled, fighting against the constricting weight as well, realizing it was sand piled up on them, thrown there by the rampaging wind.

Selethen coughed beside him and managed to throw a corner of the cloak clear. Dirty yellow-brown sand cascaded in on them both. Will rolled to his back and shoved the cloak away from his face, managing to look down at himself.

There was no sign of his body or legs. There was nothing but a sand-covered hump. He struggled to sit up, shoveling the weight from his lower body with his hands. Beside him, Selethen was doing the same thing.

The earth seemed to move behind him and he twisted around,

startled, in time to see Selethen's horse rolling and heaving to get its
feet under it. The stallion forced its way upright, sending a huge pile
of sand crashing onto the two men who had sheltered behind him.
Then, upright, the horse shook itself mightily.

Will heaved himself backward into the clear space left by the
horse's body and felt his legs coming free. With a final effort, he
broke clear of the sand's grip and staggered to his feet.

Below them, in the wadi bed, others were doing the same. The sand
surface heaved in a score of places, as if in response to some minor
earthquake, and bodies began to break clear. Sheltered by the bank, the
others had fared better than he and Selethen. The covering of sand that
lay across them was not so deep or heavy. The horses, able to stand tail
on to the wind and sheltered by the wadi bank, were in better condition. At least they hadn't been half buried.

He looked around into Selethen's face. It was coated and crusted
with the fine clinging yellow sand. The eyes, red-rimmed and sore,
stared out of it like holes in a grotesque mask. Will realized that
he probably looked no better. The Wakir shook his head wearily. He
took a water skin from his horse's saddlebow, wet the end of his
keffiyeh, and began to clean the clogged sand away from the animal's
eyes, crooning softly to him. The sight of the horse responding trust-
ingly to his rider's ministrations brought a horrible realization back
to Will and he looked around frantically, hoping against hope that
he would see another hump in the sand—a hump that would resolve
itself into the shaggy-haired form of Tug as he struggled to his feet.
But there was nothing.

Tug was gone.

Gone somewhere out in the wasteland of the desert. Will blundered a few paces away from the wadi's edge, tried to call his name.
But the dryness and the sand in his throat defeated the effort and no
sound came. A hand touched his shoulder and he turned as Selethen

thrust the water skin at him. He took a mouthful, rinsed it and spat. Then another, feeling the warm moisture soak into the soft tissue of his throat.

He realized that Selethen himself hadn't drunk yet and he handed the water skin back to him, watched as he rinsed, spat, then swallowed a mouthful or two himself. Finally, he lowered the skin.

"You . . . all . . . right?" he asked haltingly. Will shook his head, pointing vaguely to the desert behind them.

"Tug," he said miserably. Then he could say no more. He heard boots slipping and sliding in the sand and turned to see Halt climbing wearily up the wadi bank. His face was covered and yellow-crusted as well. His eyes were red-rimmed and sore.

"Are you all right?" he repeated Selethen's question. Then, his eyes darted from side to side and a horrified look came over his face. "Where's Tug?" he asked fearfully. Will bowed his head, feeling tears trying to form. But, as before, his body lacked the moisture to allow them.

"Gone," he said bitterly. He could only manage the one syllable. He waved his hand to the desert.

"Gone?" Halt echoed him. "Gone where? How?"

"The horse panicked and broke free in the wind," Selethen told him. Will looked up at Halt, his eyes haunted, shaking his head.

"I lost him!" he blurted out. "I let go of the reins! It's my fault . . . my fault!"

He felt Halt's arms go around him, felt himself drawn into the older man's embrace. But there was no sense of comfort for Will. There was no way anyone could lessen the pain he felt. His horse, his beloved Tug, was gone. And he had been the one who let go of the little horse's reins. He had failed Tug when his friend was panicked and frightened and most in need of his master's help and support.

And finally, the tears did come, streaking runnels through the yellow dust that caked his face as he put his head on Halt's shoulder and sobbed uncontrollably. Dimly, he heard the voices of his friends as they gathered wearily around, the questions they were asking and the dreadful, final, awful answer that Halt gave them.

"Tug's gone."

Two words. Two words that silenced them instantly. Gilan, Horace and Evanlyn knew how much Tug meant to Will. They knew the special relationship that formed between a Ranger and his horse. And while Svengal couldn't really appreciate it, he equated it to the sense of grief a Skandian would feel at the loss of his ship and he too felt for his friend.

Selethen watched, uncomprehending. Like all Arridi, he loved horses. But he knew that in a harsh land like this, losses were inevitable. Broken limbs, thirst, the sun, marauding desert lions and the sand cobras that lurked in any damp or shaded corner could all kill a horse in an instant. Such losses were regrettable. But they had to be borne. He glanced at the sun, now past noon.

"We'll rest here for a few hours," he said. "We'll continue on later this afternoon when it cools down."

He ordered his men to light a fire and make coffee. He doubted that anyone would have the appetite for a meal after the ordeal they had gone through. But coffee would restore them, he knew. He watched as the older Ranger led his apprentice away, finding a scant piece of shade under the wadi bank and lowering him to sit.

The princess and the young warrior went to approach them, offering comfort, but the older man waved them away. Now was not the time.

The boy would be exhausted, Selethen knew. They all were. A storm like the one they had been through allowed no rest for anyone caught in it. The muscles, the nerves, the mind were tensed to breaking point. The fear was overwhelming, particularly for someone who had never been through a sandstorm before. The physical and emotional exhaustion were devastating.

The other Ranger, the one they called Gilan, had moved to where the troops were lighting a fire. He waited until the coffee was ready and then took a cup back to the huddled form under the wadi bank. He squatted beside the youth and held the cup out to him.

"Here, Will," he said softly. "Drink this."

Will waved the cup away feebly. He was sunk deep in misery. Gilan pushed it forward again, more forcefully, nudging him with it.

"You'll need it," he said. "You'll need your strength if we're going to find Tug."

Halt looked up at him, startled by the words.

"What did you say?" he demanded, but Gilan was unfazed by the question.

"I'll go with him," he replied. "We'll find Tug."

For the first time, Will raised his head, taking the cup and looking at Gilan over the rim. There was a very faint spark of hope in his eyes. Very faint, Gilan saw, but present.

Halt stood abruptly, taking Gilan's arm and drawing him to his feet. He led the young Ranger a few meters away.

"What are you talking about?" he said in a low tone. "Tug is gone. He's dead."

Gilan shook his head. "We don't know that. He might be lost, but how can you say he's dead?"

Halt raised his hands in a perplexed gesture, pointing to the piles of windblown sand around them. "Did you just go through that storm with us?" he asked.

Gilan nodded calmly. "Yes. And I survived. So did Blaze. Seems to me you're being a little hasty in assuming Tug is dead. Ranger horses are a tough breed."

Halt conceded the point. "All right. Let's assume you're correct. He's alive. But still, he's lost somewhere out there. God alone knows where."

"Lost," Gilan repeated. "And lost can be found. We have to take the chance. You'd do it if Abelard was lost," he added and Halt, about to reply that the task was hopeless, stopped himself. "I'll go with him. Give us two days. We either find Tug in that time or we catch up with you at Mararoc."

"No, Gil. You're not coming. I'll go alone."

Both men turned, startled at the sound of Will's voice. It was as much the conviction in his words as the words themselves that surprised them. Will, devastated with grief a few minutes ago, now had a ray of hope handed to him. And he had seized it eagerly.

"We can't weaken Evanlyn's escort any further. We all took an oath to the King to protect her," he said. "Of all of us, I'm the one we could spare most, so I'll go alone. Besides," he added, "I lost him and it's up to me to find him."

"Don't be ridiculous!" Halt snapped. "You're a boy!"

Will's face, dust- and tearstained, set in stubborn lines as he faced his teacher, the man he respected and revered above all others. He drew breath to speak but Gilan put up a hand to stop him.

"Will, before you say anything, give us a moment here, please," he asked. Will hesitated, seeing the stubbornness in Halt's face that matched his own. But Gilan nodded once and he agreed, withdrawing back to his position by the wadi bank.

"Halt," said Gilan in a reasonable tone, "let me put a hypothetical case to you. If Blaze were lost and I decided to go and find him, would you try to stop me?"

"Of cour . . ." Halt began automatically. Then his sense of reason asserted itself. "Of course not," he amended. "But you're a fully trained Ranger. Will is just a boy."

Gilan smiled at him. "Haven't you noticed, Halt? He's been growing up. He's not the skinny fifteen-year-old you took under your wing anymore. He's already a Ranger in all but name."

"He's an apprentice," Halt insisted. Gilan shook his head again, smiling at Halt.

"Do you seriously think he's not going to pass his final assessment?" he asked. "It's a formality, and you know it. He's already more capable and skilled—and smarter—than half a dozen Rangers I could name."

"But he's too young to . . ." Halt couldn't finish the sentence. He knew that what Gilan was saying was the truth. The logical part of his brain knew that. But the emotional part wanted to protect his young apprentice and keep him safe. If Will went off alone into the desert, who knew what perils he'd be facing? Gilan put a hand on Halt's shoulder. It was a strange sensation, he thought, advising the man he respected more than any other.

"You knew the time would come when you'd have to let him go, Halt. You can't be around to protect him for the rest of his life. That's not why you've trained him to be a Ranger. You tried to do that with me, remember?"

Halt looked up sharply at that. Gilan was still smiling as he answered Halt's unasked question.

"In the last few months of my apprenticeship, you started mother-henning me something terrible," he said. "Remember that man-killer bear we had to track down? You tried to leave me back at Redmont under some pretext or other."

Halt frowned, thinking hard. Had he really done that? He had to admit that he might have. He thought now about Will and he agreed with Gilan. The boy—the youth, he corrected himself—would certainly be accepted as a graduate Ranger within a few months. There was nothing left for him to learn. The assessment was a formality.

"Would you trust him with your life, Halt?" Gilan interrupted, and Halt looked up at him.

"Yes," he said quietly. Gilan patted his shoulder once more.

"Then trust him with his own," he said simply.

22

WILL SELECTED A HORSE FROM THE TEN REMOUNTS TRAVELING with their escort. He was a roan and the smallest of the Arridi horses. It was an unconscious choice and he realized afterward that he had probably picked a smaller horse to make himself feel more at home.

"His name is Arrow," the Arridi horsemaster told him. He smiled at the massive longbow slung over Will's shoulder. "An appropriate choice. And a good one. You have an eye for horses."

"Thank you," Will said, taking the horse's bridle and giving the girth straps an experimental tug. He'd been taught never to rely on other people's judgment when it came to a horse's tack. The Arridi watched approvingly.

There were two full water skins slung over the saddlebow and a small tent and blanket rolled up and fastened behind the saddle. Will's own camping gear had disappeared into the storm with Tug. He led Arrow back to the small group of his friends. The horse resisted at first, turning back to his own familiar comrades and whinnying. Then as Will pulled firmly on the bridle and spoke encouragingly to him, he went along obediently.

Horace shook Will's hand wordlessly, then took the horse's bridle while Will went around the group, making his farewells. Evanlyn hugged him, tears in her eyes.

"Good luck, Will," she whispered into his ear. "Stay safe. I know you'll find him."

Gilan shook hands firmly, looking into his friend's eyes with a worried expression on his face.

"Find him, Will. I wish I was coming with you."

Will shook his head. "We've been through this already, Gilan." He didn't elaborate on the point because he knew if Evanlyn realized he was going alone so that she would be safer, she would object fiercely.

Svengal was next. He grabbed the slightly built Ranger in a typical Skandian bear hug. "Travel safely, boy," he said. "Find that horse and come back to us."

"Thanks, Svengal. Just make sure you don't waste any time setting Erak free. I'm sure he's an impatient prisoner."

A smile touched the huge Skandian's battered face. "We might be doing his jailers a favor when all is said and done," he replied. Will grinned and turned, finally, to Halt.

When the moment came, there was nothing either of them could say and he embraced the gray-bearded Ranger fiercely. Finally he found his voice.

"I'll be back, Halt. With Tug."

"Make sure you are."

He and his mentor slapped each other's backs several times— the way men do when they can't find words to express their emotions. Then he stepped back as Selethen approached. The Wakir inspected the horse and the equipment slung on it and nodded approvingly. Then he held out a rolled parchment.

"This is a map of the area, marking the wells, landmarks and the route to Mararoc." He hesitated. He'd spent the last fifteen minutes copying his own chart and he knew what a valuable strategic document it could be in the hands of a foreigner. "I have your word that you'll never try to reproduce this or copy it in any way?"

Will nodded. "My solemn word," he said. That had been the condition under which Selethen had agreed to provide him with a chart.

"You're sure you'll be able to find your direction?" Selethen asked. Will touched his jerkin to make sure his northseeker was secured in its inner pocket. The magnetic needle was something the Arridi knew nothing about. They navigated by the stars during the night and during daylight hours by a complicated set of tables that related to the sun's movement, altitude and position at different times of the year.

"I'll be fine. Thanks, Selethen."

The Arridi nodded. He still felt that this was an unnecessary fuss to go to over a horse. But he realized that these Araluens felt very differently about their mounts.

"Chances are your horse would have run with the wind behind him. That means he was headed a little north of northeast." He unrolled the map and indicated the direction. "That should take you past the Red Hills here." He pointed to a section of hilly terrain on the chart. "There are two wells on the other side of the hills. Horses can smell water from a great distance. If your horse caught the scent, he could be at one of these. You should reach this one by tomorrow afternoon."

Due to the difference in written language, landmarks such as the wells were drawn as icons on the chart. Will nodded his understanding.

"My guess is, if he found water, he'd stay close by it. If he's not there, I can't advise you what to do next," Selethen said. Will said nothing, studying the map, then looking up from it into the empty space to the north.

"Light a fire at night. There are lions in the desert and a fire will keep them at bay. You'll know if there's one around." He glanced at the roan horse. "Arrow will tell you quickly enough. He's what the lion will be hunting."

"Anything else to look out for?" Will asked.

"Sand cobras. They're deadly. They look for shade and moisture—as most living things do in the desert. They blend in with the sand and you don't know there's one around until it rears up. When that happens, you have less than two seconds before it strikes."

"And what do I do if I'm bitten?" Will asked. Selethen shook his head slowly.

"You die," he said.

Will raised an eyebrow. That wasn't exactly the answer he'd been looking for. He shook hands with Selethen, rolled the map up and tucked it inside his jerkin.

"Thanks, Selethen. I'll see you in a few days."

Selethen touched his hand to mouth, brow and mouth.

"I hope the god of journeys wills it so," he said.

Will turned to the others, forced a grin and took Arrow's rein from Horace.

"Better be off," he said with mock cheerfulness. "Can't keep the sand cobras waiting."

He swung easily into the saddle and turned Arrow's head to the north, trotting away from the little camp by the wadi. When he had gone a hundred meters, he looked back—and immediately wished he hadn't. He felt a huge lump of sadness in his throat and breast at the sight of his friends. Evalyn, Horace, Gilan and Svengal were all waving sadly. Halt didn't wave. He stood a little apart from the others, watching his apprentice ride away.

He continued to watch until well after the horse and rider had faded into the shimmering desert haze.

"Come on, Halt. Selethen says it's time we were moving." Gilan placed a gentle hand on the older man's shoulder. Halt had remained where he stood when Will left, staring across the heat-shimmering ground, willing his apprentice to travel safely.

Halt started at Gilan's words and finally turned away from his vigil. He had continued watching to the northeast, long after Will was out of sight. He was a little surprised, and quite touched, to see that Gilan had saddled Abelard for him. But he was still heavy-hearted as he walked to where his horse waited.

Abelard and Blaze seemed to sense Tug's absence as well, he thought. In other horses, that might have been a fanciful notion. But Ranger horses, like their riders, were a close-knit breed. And, of course, Abelard and Tug had been in each other's close company for nigh on five years. Halt sensed the restlessness in his own horse, the urge to turn toward the north where he sensed his young friend had gone. He patted the soft nose and spoke gently.

"He'll find him, boy. Never fret."

But as he said the words, Halt wished he could believe them himself. He was worried and apprehensive for Will—in no small part because his apprentice had gone into a countryside about which he, Halt, knew little himself. Normally he would have been able to advise and counsel him of the dangers he might face. This time, he was allowing him to venture into a great unknown.

He swung into the saddle and glanced around the faces of his companions. He saw his own doubt and worry reflected there and he realized that for their sake, if nothing else, he must adopt a more positive stance.

"I don't like it any more than you do," he told them. "But let's look at the positive side of things. He's well armed. He's well trained. He's got a good horse. He's an excellent navigator and he has his north-seeker and Selethen's map. He'll be fine."

23

IN DAYS TO COME, HALT WOULD BERATE HIMSELF SAVAGELY FOR the problem that Will was about to face, and for the danger it placed his young friend in. He should have known, he told himself. He should have realized.

When Halt thought about it, with the crystal clarity that comes with hindsight, he realized that he had spent years living in a castle named Redmont—or Red Mountain. It was so called because the rock that comprised its massive walls lent the castle a reddish tinge in the afternoon light. The rock was ironstone, and it contained a high percentage of iron ore.

Halt knew that Will would be traveling through an area named the Red Hills. In his own mind, he told himself he should have made the connection: ironstone, Redmont, iron ore and Red Hills.

The hills were, in fact, the site of massive deposits of iron—so rich that at times the ore itself was visible in large veins on the surface. The red coloration was the result of rust formation. The problem for Will was that as he rode by these huge iron deposits—and some of the hills were almost completely composed of iron ore—his magnetic northseeker needle would deviate from the earth's magnetic field as it was attracted to the metal around him.

Selethen knew of the iron, of course. Most of the iron the Arridi used was quarried from this area—principally because it was so easy to access, requiring no deep shafts or complicated equipment. But the Arridi knew nothing of the secret of the northseekers, and the three Rangers had been careful to keep them hidden. So Selethen had no way of knowing that Will's navigation would be severely affected by the iron as his needle deviated first one way, then the other.

Between them, the two men had the knowledge that might have kept Will safe. But neither of them realized, so neither of them said anything.

It might have become apparent to Will if he simply rode with his eyes glued to the northseeker. If that had been the case, he might well have noticed that from time to time the needle swung and deviated wildly. But that wasn't how he was trained to navigate cross-country. After all, one can't ride through potentially dangerous territory staring down at a magnetic needle.

Instead, Will would rein in and hold the northseeker at eye level until the needle settled in its final position. Then he would turn the graduated ring round the rim of the northseeker until the needle coincided with the N mark. Then, peering through the aperture sight on the side, he would line his eye up with the NE marking, all the while keeping the northseeker facing the N marking. Looking through the aperture sight, he would search for a prominent landmark maybe five or ten kilometers away, in the northeast, then ride toward it. As he reached that landmark, he would repeat the process, finding another landmark that lay to the northeast of his position and riding toward that.

The fact that each time he went through this process, he was deviating farther and farther to the east of his desired course was never apparent to him.

Had he been in Araluen, he might have sensed the sun's position wasn't quite right and become aware that there was a problem. But he was lulled by the knowledge that, this far south, the sun would appear to be in a different position. He trusted the northseeker, as he had been taught to do.

And the farther he rode, the more off course he became.

Once he had passed by the Red Hills, the problem was solved and the needle returned to a true north position. But by then the damage had been done and he was miles from where he thought he was.

Will rested during the middle hours of the day, as Selethen had taught him. There was no shade to be found, with the sun almost directly overhead and very few trees larger than a shrub anywhere in sight. He pitched his small one-man tent to create a haven of shade and crawled into it, leaving the ends open to allow air to pass through. Not that there was much movement in the desert air at midday.

Arrow, unfortunately, had to put up with the direct heat of the sun. But the horse was bred to it.

Sitting cross-legged under the cramped shelter, Will spread out Selethen's chart and studied it for perhaps the tenth time that day.

He marked his starting position then, with his forefinger, traced a line to the northeast, through the Red Hills and onto the barren, sunbaked plain where he now found himself. Estimating the distance he had covered, he selected a point on the map.

"I should be . . . here," he said. He frowned, looking back along the northeast track. If that were the case, he should have seen a prominent landmark late in the morning—a large flat-topped hill close by to the east of his track.

But there was no sign of it. He thought that he had sighted such a hill an hour previously, but it had been a dim, shimmering sight in the overheated distance. And it had lain well to the west of his track.

Could he have gone so far off course? He shook his head. He had been meticulous in taking his bearings and selecting the landmarks that he rode toward. He could accept that he might be several hundred meters off course. Even half a kilometer. But in all his navigation training exercises he had never made such a large error.

The flat-topped hill that he thought he'd seen must have been five or six kilometers to the west of where he was now. He tapped the map thoughtfully. Of course, he told himself, there might well be more than one flat-topped hill in the desert. In fact, there certainly would be. Perhaps the one Selethen had marked had been worn down by wind and weather until its shape wasn't quite so well-defined. He folded the map and put it away. That must be it, he told himself. He must have simply missed it. There were other landmarks he'd see the following day—a balancing rock and a line of steep cliffs, pockmarked with caves. He'd just have to keep a keener eye out for them.

He sat through the next few hours of stultifying heat. How the horse stood it, out in the open, he had no idea. In fact, Arrow, trained for the conditions, had found a scrap of shade beside a low-lying bush. He lay down on his side with a complaining, grunting sound. He placed his head, with its sensitive skin around the eyes, muzzle and mouth, in the deepest part of the meager screen offered by the branches.

The sun passed its zenith and began to descend toward the western rim of the desert. Will crawled wearily out of the tent. He couldn't be said to have rested and he felt completely wrung out by the heat. He'd taken his two water skins into the tent with him. Had he left them out in the direct sun, the water would have heated until it was too hot to touch. Worse, some of it would have evaporated away through the skins, which could never be made completely watertight.

There was a folding leather bucket tied to his saddle pack and he untied it now, snapping it open. Arrow heard the noise and struggled to roll to his feet, shaking himself to clear the sand from his coat. He walked patiently to where Will was carefully pouring water from one of the skins into the bucket. Will was impressed to see that the horse made no attempt to drink before he raised the water to its mouth.

As Arrow began slurping noisily at the water, Will found himself licking his own lips in anticipation. His mouth and tongue were thick and gummy and he himself was longing to drink. But he'd been trained to look after his horse first and he waited till Arrow finished drinking before raising the water skin to his own lips. He took a long draft, held it in his mouth, swirled it around, then let it trickle slowly down his throat. The water was hot and had a bitter, leathery taste from its container. But it was like nectar, he thought. He finished the last of the mouthful, thought about taking another drink, resisted the thought and forced the stopper home.

As Will took a sack of grain from his saddlebags and poured some into the bucket, he wondered what Tug was doing, where he was and if he was safe. He set the receptacle down for Arrow and listened to the grinding of the horse's jaws as he ate.

Will had a few dates and a piece of flat bread. It was stale now and quite hard but he ate it anyway. He wasn't in the slightest bit hungry, a fact he put down to the ovenlike heat of the day. But he knew he had to eat something to keep up his strength.

He took another quick sip of the water. Arrow's head came up at the sound of the stopper being removed from the neck. Will thought he sensed a feeling of reproach in those big, liquid eyes.

"You're used to this. I'm not," he told the horse. Arrow seemed unimpressed by his excuse. He put his nose back down into the bucket, his big tongue searching for any leftover grains in the bottom.

Will looked at the sun and estimated that he'd have another hour or so before he'd have to start making camp. Already, his shadow was a ridiculous, elongated shape that stretched out behind him, undulating over the broken ground. He knew that Selethen would start and finish his day's march in darkness. The Arridi wasn't reliant upon seeing landmarks in the distance through the aperture sight of a northseeker.

Will, however, needed to be able to see—both the landmarks that he steered by and the features marked on the map. He thought again about that flat-topped hill and felt a worm of doubt worrying away inside him. He couldn't have missed it, could he?

He saddled Arrow, packed up his tent, blanket and the rest of his gear and tied it on behind the saddle.

"We'll ride for another hour," he told Arrow. The horse was neither pleased nor displeased by the news and stood patiently while Will swung up into the saddle. Once there, he took out the northseeker, aligned it and peered through the sight. A sand and salt pillar, some three meters high with crystals glistening in the low angle sun, gave him a convenient reference point. He clicked his tongue and urged Arrow into a walk.

As the sun sank lower, the land features to his west became more backlit and indistinct. He thought he saw the line of cliffs—although they seemed a little low to be described as such. They were more of a raised bank, he thought. And it was impossible to see if they were pockmarked with caves, as the chart indicated. The facing bank was deep in shadow by now and he couldn't make out detail like that. Still, he thought, they could be the cliffs marked on the chart. And they could be pockmarked with caves. He told himself they were. They had to be.

But again he felt that worm of doubt.

The giant red ball of the sun was close to the horizon when he decided it was time to stop. He had to gather firewood and he needed light for that. He hobbled Arrow and walked to an outcrop of low, dry bushes, drawing his saxe knife with his right hand. His bow was in his left and he used it to reach out and shake the bush violently, as he had seen Selethen's men doing. Sand cobras lurked in the shade under such bushes, and he intended to scare any out before putting his hand into a potential death trap.

But there were none and he gathered a sufficient supply of firewood. The bush's branches were full of oil and they would burn with a bright, dry heat for a considerable time before being consumed.

He built the fire but didn't light it. Then, with that immediate task taken care of, he unsaddled Arrow and piled his gear to one side. He glanced at the sky and looked at the tent beside his saddle and bedroll.

"No need for it," he said finally.

He spread out his bedroll and blanket and sat on them, wincing as one of the desert's multitude of stones dug into his rump. His taste buds ached for a cup of coffee but he didn't have the water to spare. He contented himself with another swig from the water skin and a handful of dates. Seeing Arrow's watchful eyes, he rose, groaning as his knees took the strain, and moved to feed and water the horse.

The sun finally disappeared and the day's heat began to leach out of the desert. By midnight, it would be close to freezing, Will knew. He checked Arrow's hobbles, then returned to his bedroll. He was exhausted. The heat of the day had been a palpable force and it seemed to have beaten against his body, leaving him feeling battered and worn out. The darkness grew and the stars began to blaze above him.

As more and more of them blinked on, he lay back, an arm behind his head, to study them. Normally he found the stars a welcoming, friendly sight. But not tonight. Tonight his thoughts were with Tug, lost somewhere in this pitiless desert, without water or food, and with Halt and the others, far away to the southwest. He thought sadly about the cheerful conversation by the campfire, and cups of thick, sweet coffee. He licked his lips.

Arrow stirred and, in the distance, Will heard a low, grunting cough. He knew that was the sound that a lion made. He would have expected a majestic, earth-shattering roar. But this asthmatic coughing grunt was the reality. He looked at the horse. Arrow stood straight, ears pricked, eyes showing a lot of white.

"Better light the fire," Will said reluctantly. He stood painfully, moved to the stacked wood and kindling he had prepared earlier and went to work with flint and steel. Within a few minutes he had a small, bright fire burning. He led Arrow a little closer to it. The horse moved awkwardly in its hobbles but Will couldn't risk removing them and losing him.

"Settle down," he told him. Within a few minutes, Arrow had. His head drooped again, his ears relaxed.

Will stretched out and pulled the blanket up around his chin. Accustomed to sleeping when the opportunity arose, he dropped off almost at once.

The moon had risen when Arrow's startled whinny jerked him awake. For a second or two there was an awful sense of disorientation while he wondered where he was. Then he remembered and came to his feet, his bow in one hand and an arrow in the other, eyes searching the thick darkness around them.

He heard the coughing grunt again and it seemed that it could be a little closer. He stirred the fire, added a few more branches and sat down, his back against his saddle, the bow across his knees.

He hitched the blanket up around his shoulders and settled

himself, resigned to the fact that he would have to keep guard sitting up and dozing fitfully, while every muscle and bone in his body ached for him to stretch out and relax.

"No rest for the wicked," he said. It was going to be a long, cold, uncomfortable night.

24

As Will had guessed, Selethen had kept his party moving in the predawn hours each day.

They would wake hours before dawn when the Arridi escort would prepare cooking fires, making coffee and toasting the flat bread over the coals. Selethen noticed that a change had come over the party of Araluens since the young Ranger had left them two days previously. No longer did they joke and laugh around the campfire while they drank their morning coffee. They were subdued, concerned for their missing companion.

It was easiest to notice with the three younger members: Horace, the princess and the young Ranger, Gilan. Halt, meanwhile, had grown even more grim-faced and taciturn than normal.

Not that the two remaining Rangers were any less diligent in observing their surroundings and taking covert notes as they passed landmarks. He was sure they were memorizing and noting prominent features so they could reproduce a map of the route from Al Shabah to Mararoc. Will might have given his oath never to reproduce the chart Selethen had given him, but the others were bound by no such promise. He was concerned about that, but decided there was little he could do to stop them.

For the first few hours, in the predawn dimness, they rode in their usual close-knit formation. Then, as the sun performed its spectacular arrival, the screen of cavalry around the central party moved out to take up their daylight traveling positions.

On the second day, a few hours after sunup, they came upon the tracks of the party preceding them—the party who were taking Erak as a hostage to Mararoc. Prior to that point, of course, any sign left by the riders ahead of them had been obliterated by the massive storm that had swept over the desert. Now, they realized, they were within two days of them.

"They'll be moving more slowly than we are," Halt said. He knew that Selethen had sent Erak with one of the regular caravans that traveled between Al Shabah and Mararoc, carrying trade goods from the coast to the inland city. Such caravans already had an armed escort and it made sense to kill two birds with one stone. But of course, the heavily laden pack mules and freight camels would slow the party down.

Gilan swung down from his saddle and knelt beside the marks in the hard ground. He made out faint impressions of hooves here and there—all but invisible to an untrained eye. From time to time there were more obvious clues of the party's passage, in the form of piles of dung. Gilan poked at one with a stick, breaking it up to study the moisture content inside. Rangers used such clues to determine how fresh the tracks might be—moisture in horse dung or sap in the broken stem of a twig snapped by a passing animal. But they were unused to the blinding heat and dryness of the Arridi desert and the effect it had on moisture content.

"Hard to say how old it is," he said finally. Halt shrugged.

"It'd dry out a lot faster here than farther north. We know it can't be more than two days old. It's been left there since the storm passed through."

Gilan nodded. "You're right. But if I were to see that back home, I'd say it was three to four days old. It's worth knowing for future reference, I suppose."

He straightened, brushing dust off his knees, and swung up into Blaze's saddle once more. He glanced toward Selethen and saw that the Wakir had stopped his horse as well and was fiddling with the ties that held his bedroll in place behind the saddle. The Arridi horse was turned at forty-five degrees to the direction of travel and Gilan had no doubt that the Arridi leader's eyes beneath the shadow of his keffiyeh were trained unwaveringly on himself and Halt.

"He's watching us," he said quietly, and Halt nodded, without looking in Selethen's direction.

"He always does. I think we make him nervous."

"Do you think he knows we're keeping a chart of the route?"

"I'd bet my life on it," Halt said. "Not much gets past him. And I'll bet he's racking his brains to find a way to stop us."

As they moved off, Selethen seemed to finish retying the thongs. He touched his stallion with his knee, turned back to the course his outriders had set and trotted forward.

"What do you make of him?" Gilan asked. This time Halt did look at the tall Arridi warrior before he answered. He was considering his opinion, Gilan knew, weighing up what he knew about the Wakir with what he sensed about him. Finally, Halt replied.

"I like the look of him," he said. "A lot of these local officials are always on the lookout for bribes. Corruption is almost a way of life in this country. But he's not like that."

"He's a soldier, not a politician," Gilan said. He had a fighting man's usual distrust of politicians and officials, preferring to deal with men who knew what it meant to fight for their lives. Such men often had an inherent honesty to them, he thought.

Halt nodded. "And a good one. Look at this formation he's got us in. At first glance, it looks like we're straggling across the desert like Brown's cows. But we can't be approached from any direction without those outriders spotting something."

"His men seem to respect him," Gilan said. "He doesn't have to shout and bluster to get things done."

"Yes. I've hardly heard him raise his voice since we've been on the march. That's usually a sign that the men believe he knows what he's about."

They fell silent for a few minutes, both studying the white-cloaked, straight-backed figure riding on his own, twenty meters ahead of them.

"Not too friendly, though," Gilan said, grinning. He was trying to keep Halt talking, in an attempt to keep his old teacher from worrying too much about Will, gone somewhere into the unknown wastes of this desert. Halt sensed his intention and appreciated it. Talking with Gilan gave him some moments of respite from the constant nagging worry he felt about the boy who had come to mean so much to him. Without intending to, he let out a deep sigh. Gilan looked quickly at him.

"He's all right, Halt," he said.

"I hope so. I just think . . ."

Whatever it was that Halt thought was lost as something drew his attention. There was a cloud of dust moving toward them from the front—one of the outriders, he realized, as he managed to see more clearly through the heat shimmer and made out the dark figure at the head of the dust cloud, and could see the individual puffs kicked up with each stride of his horse's legs.

"What do we have here?" he said quietly. He touched Abelard with his knee and moved up to ride beside Selethen, Gilan following a meter or so behind him.

"Messenger?" he asked.

Selethen shook his head. "It's one of the screen. They must have seen something up ahead," he told them. The rider was closer now and they could make out detail. He swerved his horse slightly as he made out the tall figure of the Wakir and rode directly toward him.

"Vultures," said Gilan suddenly. While the others had been intent on the rider approaching, his keen eyes had sought ahead of them. Halt looked up now, but Gilan's eyes were younger than his. He thought that perhaps he could see black specks circling high in the sky ahead of them. Or it could just be his mind telling him he could see them now that Gilan had said they were there.

Any doubt was removed when the rider came closer, reining in his horse in a sliding cloud of dust.

"Excellence, we've seen vultures ahead," he reported. Selethen waited. His men were well trained and he knew there would be more to the report.

"I've sent Corporal Iqbal and two men ahead to reconnoiter," the man continued. "In the meantime, I've halted the forward screen."

Selethen nodded acknowledgment. "Good. We'll continue until we come up with the screen. By then Iqbal might have something to report. Return to your post," he added. The messenger wheeled his horse, touching mouth, brow and mouth in a hasty salute, then clattered away back the way he had come, raising more of the fine dust. Selethen glanced at the two Rangers.

"Better safe than sorry. Those vultures mean there's something dead up ahead. There's no knowing if whatever it was that killed them is still around."

Halt nodded agreement. It made sense. The desert was a dangerous place to travel, and Selethen was too good a soldier to go blundering in unprepared just to see what had attracted the vultures.

"There's a lot of them," Gilan pointed out. "That could mean there's been a lot of killing."

"That's what I'm afraid of," Selethen replied.

Selethen's fears were well founded. They came up to the scene of the battle an hour later. Not that it had been much of a battle—it was more of a massacre. Horses, mules, camels and men were scattered about the desert, lifeless shapes surrounded by darkening patches of dried blood that had soaked into the sand.

It was the trading party from Al Shabah, and they had been wiped out to a man.

As the new arrivals cantered in among them, the heavy black vultures left their feasting and flapped lazily into the air. Halt motioned for Evanlyn and Horace to wait behind. He and Gilan dismounted and walked among the bodies with Selethen.

The men and animals had been killed, and then hacked in a senseless frenzy. There was barely a body with just a single killing wound. The freight packs had been ripped open and their contents scattered on the ground. Anything of value had been taken. Then the predators had done their awful work.

"When, do you think?" Halt asked. Selethen looked around, his normally impassive face dark with rage and frustration.

"Earlier this morning, I'd say," he replied, and Gilan, kneeling beside one of the bodies, nodded confirmation to Halt.

"The big predators, the cats and jackals, haven't got to them yet," Selethen explained. "They tend to prowl at night, so it must have been after dawn today. And the vultures are still gathering."

Halt had walked away as Selethen was talking, studying the scene more closely. Selethen glanced up at the slowly wheeling black birds above them, riding effortlessly on the currents of heated air that rose from the desert floor.

"Any idea who might have done it?" Gilan asked, and Selethen studied him for a moment, regaining control of his emotions.

"The Tualaghi," he said briefly, almost spitting the word out. "All this"—he indicated the hacked bodies—"is typical of their handiwork." He shook his head, puzzled. "But why? Why would they attack a well-armed party? There were over twenty soldiers in the escort. Usually the Tualaghi prey on small parties. Why this?"

"Maybe someone paid them," said Halt as he returned from his survey of the desolate scene. The Wakir looked at him now, frowning.

"Who? Who'd pay them?" he challenged.

"Whoever betrayed Erak in the first place," Halt told him. "Take a look around. There's no sign of him. Whoever killed your men took him away with them."

25

Will's mistakes were beginning to compound. As they did, the danger grew progressively greater.

The first mistake, and the one that led to all the others, he was still unaware of. That was the fact that for the greater part of the first day, misled by his inaccurate northseeker, he had been traveling far to the east of his intended course. When the influence of the iron deposits in the Red Hills was finally behind him, and his northseeker returned to a true heading, the damage was already done. With every kilometer, he had diverged farther from the course that he thought he was taking. Now he was traveling parallel to it, but kilometers from where he thought he was.

His second mistake was to convince himself that he had seen the landmarks he was seeking. Admittedly, he had seen no flat-topped hill. But he told himself that he must have passed it without recognizing it, rationalizing to himself the fact that its shape had undoubtedly changed over the years from the distinctive profile that Selethen's chart indicated.

The low bank that he had seen late the previous afternoon bore no real resemblance to a line of cliffs. But, needing to believe that he had seen the cliffs, he convinced himself that he really had. He had seen no caves, and the chart showed that the cliffs had been honey-combed with them. Instead, he reassured himself that the caves were invisible because they had been shrouded in late afternoon shadow.

Now, to settle the question once and for all, he should see a bal-ancing rock formation some time in the next few hours—a formation where a large rock stood precariously on top of a smaller. At least, he told himself with a growing sense of foreboding, a feature like that would be unmistakable.

Unless the big rock had fallen off the smaller one overnight, he added grimly.

He needed to see that formation because his water supply was becoming alarmingly depleted. The first water skin was empty. The second was less than half full. He had tried to ration himself severely but the heat simply drained energy from him so that he had to drink or fall senseless to the ground.

He consoled himself with the thought that, once he saw the bal-ancing rocks and fixed his position, the water problem would be solved. A few kilometers from those rocks, a soak was marked on the chart—a small depression in a dried-up riverbed where water seeped slowly to the surface. Once there, all he would have to do was dig down a meter or so and wait while water filled the hole. It might be muddy and unpleasant, but it would be drinkable. And with his water skins refilled and his location established once and for all, he would be able to strike out for one of the wells.

Sometime in the next few hours, he simply *had* to see the balancing rock formation or he was lost—figuratively as well as literally. He had to trust his map and his northseeker and continue to believe that sooner or later, he would see those rocks. He simply had no alterna-tive course of action.

It was this growing fatalism that led to his final, and most serious, mistake. Obsessed with the need to find the balancing rocks and validate his course of action so far, he continued to ride through the hottest hours of the day.

Experienced desert travelers like Selethen didn't do this, he knew. But Selethen could navigate by the stars and didn't need daylight to sight landmarks and reference points. That meant he could afford the time spent resting in the middle of the day. But Will had an urgent need to find that water soak.

So he rode on, the heat battering down on him like a physical force as the sun rose higher in the sky. The air itself was superheated and almost scorched his throat and lungs when he breathed it in, sucking the very oxygen out of the air so that he gasped and panted for breath.

The glare was another constant torture, forcing him to look into the shimmering distance with his eyes screwed almost shut.

Beneath him, Arrow plodded on, head down, feet dragging. Will was alarmed by the horse's rapid deterioration, having no idea that his own condition was even worse.

"Time for some water, boy," he said. His voice was little more than a croak, forcing itself out through his dry throat and mouth.

He swung down from the saddle, his body stiff and awkward. He staggered a few paces as he touched the ground, having to steady himself against the horse's flank. Arrow stood unmoving, head drooped almost to the ground. Then he shifted his weight to his left side, seeming to favor his right front hoof. Already, after only a few seconds standing, Will could feel the blazing heat of the ground burning up through the soles of his boots. For Arrow's unprotected hooves, it must be torture, he thought.

"I'll take care of that in a minute," he told the horse. "First we'll drink."

He fumbled with the ties attaching the folding leather bucket behind the saddle and dropped the bucket onto the ground. He laughed briefly.

"Just as well it wasn't full," he told Arrow. The horse didn't respond. Setting the bucket down carefully, making sure he had placed it on a flat surface, Will took the remaining water skin and unstoppered it carefully. He was painfully aware of how light it was now. As he poured carefully, Arrow's head turned toward the sound. The horse made a low grumbling noise in his throat.

"Hold your horses," he said. Then he laughed. It seemed absurd to say that to a horse.

He had the strange sensation that he was standing to one side, watching himself and Arrow. He shook the ridiculous notion away and held the bucket for Arrow to drink.

As ever, he felt his own mouth and throat working as he watched the horse drink. But, whereas the previous day his mouth had been thick and gummy-feeling, today it was dry and swollen, all excess moisture gone from it.

Arrow finished, his big tongue futilely searching the seams of the bucket where a few last drops might be hidden. Will had become accustomed to the horse's almost philosophical acceptance of the amount of water he was given. This time, however, Arrow raised his head and nosed insistently around the water skin slung over Will's shoulders. It was another indication of how their condition was worsening. The horse's training was being overcome by its need for water.

Will pushed the questing muzzle away. "Sorry, boy," he said, almost incoherently. "Later."

He took two small sips himself, holding each one in his mouth, making it last, before letting it trickle down his throat. Then, reluctantly, he re-stoppered the water skin and laid it in the scant shade of a thornbush.

He raised Arrow's left front hoof to examine it. The horse grumbled and shifted awkwardly. There was no visible injury, but when he laid his palm on the soft center of the hoof, he could feel the heat there. The desert ground was burning Arrow's unprotected feet. Will understood this even more now that he was standing on the sand himself. The heat was all around them. It beat down from the sun, hit the desert floor and struck upward again.

He untied his blanket from behind the saddle and cut it into squares and strips. Then he wrapped the little horse's hooves with pieces of the blanket, padding the underside with several folded layers, and tying the whole thing in place with thin strips. He'd be cold without a blanket when night fell, he knew. But he'd be in a worse spot if his horse became lame.

Arrow seemed to be standing more comfortably, no longer leaning to his right side. Will took his bridle and led him a few paces, walking backward to watch his gait. The horse didn't seem to be favoring either side now, he saw with some relief.

Retrieving the water skin, Will slung it over his shoulder and prepared to mount.

Then he stopped and patted Arrow gently on the neck.

"I'll walk for a while," he said. "You've been doing all the work."

He took out his northseeker and checked his course, seeking a bearing point. There was a cone-shaped hill in the middle distance and he set off for it.

Arrow trudged after him, head down, his hooves now making a strangely muffled sound on the desert sand.

Burdened by the inescapable heat, Will took off his cloak and draped it over Arrow's saddle. He rolled up his shirt sleeves and, for a few moments, he felt a little cooler. But it was an illusion. The cloak, like the flowing garments of the Arridi, helped the body retain moisture. Without it, and exposed to the sun, he began to dehydrate even more rapidly than before.

In addition, his bare arms began to redden, then to burn, then to blister. But by the time he might have realized his mistake, Will was no longer capable of intelligent thought. His system was shutting down. And still he hadn't seen that elusive formation of balancing rocks. They were an obsession with him now. They had to be here somewhere and he had to see them. Soon, he told himself. Soon. He had now been riding and walking for over four hours with no sign of them.

He turned to face Arrow.

"Have you seen them?" he asked. Arrow looked at him disinterestedly. Will frowned.

"Not talking, eh?" he said. "Maybe you're a little hoarse."

He cackled briefly at his own wit and, for a moment, he had that uncomfortable sensation again—that he was standing to one side watching himself and the horse stumble across the desert. He became aware of the water skin slung across his shoulders.

"Need a drink," he said to Arrow. The thought struck him that the water skin was weighing him down. If he drank some more, it would be lighter. And he would be able to move more easily.

He drank deeply, then became aware of Arrow's accusing eyes on him. Guiltily, he re-stoppered the skin and set off again.

It was then that the realization hit him. Selethen had given him a false map. There were no cliffs pockmarked with caves. There was no flat-topped hill. Of course, the Wakir wouldn't hand him such a valuable strategic document! Why hadn't he seen it before? The swine had given him a false chart and sent him out into the desert to die.

"He tricked us," he told the horse. "But I'll show him. We must be close to that soak by now. We'll find it and I'll go back and ram his map down his lying throat."

He frowned. If the map were false, there would be no water

soak just a few kilometers away. He hesitated. Yet there must be a soak. There had to be! Then his thoughts cleared.

"Of course!" he told Arrow. "He couldn't falsify the whole thing! Some of it must be true! Otherwise we'd have seen right through it straightaway! That's real cunning for you."

That problem solved, he decided that he could afford to give Arrow some more of the precious water. But the effort of untying and assembling the folding bucket seemed too much. Instead, he let the water trickle into his cupped hand, laughing softly as Arrow's big tongue licked at it. Some of it spilled, of course, soaking instantly into the baking sand. But it didn't matter. There would be plenty more at the soak.

"Plenty more at the soak," he told the horse.

He replaced the stopper and stood swaying beside Arrow. The problem was, he thought, without another drink, he might not have the strength to reach the soak. Then he would die, all because he refused to drink the water he already had. That would be foolish. Halt wouldn't approve of that, he thought. Coming to a decision, he removed the stopper and drained the last of the water. Then he set off, staggering, beckoning Arrow to follow.

"Come on, boy," he said, the words sounding like the harsh croaking of a crow.

He fell. The ground burned his hands as he tried to break the fall and he didn't have the strength to rise.

He lifted his head and there . . . He saw it!

The balancing rock, just as Selethen had drawn it! It was only a few hundred meters away and he wondered how he could have missed seeing it before this. And just beyond that would be the soak, and all the water he could drink.

He couldn't stand. But he could crawl that far. He began to crawl toward those beautiful balancing rocks.

"How do they do it? Why don't they fall over?" he marveled. Then he added, with a chuckle, "Good old Selethen! What a map!" He looked behind him. Arrow stood, feet wide apart, head hanging, not following.

"Come on, Arrow!" he called. "Plenty of water this way! Come on! Just to the rocks! The wonderful, wonderful balancing rocks! How dooo they do it? Step right up and see!"

He didn't realize that his words were an indecipherable croak. The water he'd just drunk hadn't been enough to compensate for the amount he had lost in the past five hours.

He continued to crawl, dragging himself over the rough, stony ground—the stones cutting his hands and the heat burning them. He left bloody handprints behind him—handprints that quickly dried to a dull brown in the insufferable heat. Arrow watched him going with dispirited eyes. But the horse made no move to follow him. There was no reason to.

There were no balancing rocks and Will was crawling in a giant circle.

26

SELETHEN LOOKED UP QUICKLY AT HALT'S WORDS, A FROWN creasing his forehead. "Who would pay them to do such a thing?" he asked. "And why would they do it?"

Halt met his gaze evenly. He knew the Arridi was angry and emotional over the death of so many of his men—and he sensed that his feelings were fueled by a long-standing hatred of the Tualaghi tribesmen. The situation was a dangerous one and he would have to choose his words carefully. The more he knew about what had gone on here, he reasoned, the better he could convince Selethen of what he was about to say. He turned and spoke quietly to Gilan.

"Take a look around. See if you can figure out what happened."

The younger Ranger nodded and moved off. Only then did Halt address Selethen's question.

"I'd say that whoever betrayed Erak to you in the first place is behind this," he replied.

"That'd be Toshak." Svengal had approached unnoticed. He had been searching the scene for his Oberjarl's body and had come to the same conclusion as Halt.

Selethen looked from Halt to Svengal, then back again. Now there was another emotion showing on his face—suspicion.

"Who is this Toshak?" he challenged. "I've never heard the name. And why would he pay to have your Oberjarl abducted?"

"For the same reason he betrayed Erak to you in the first place. He wants him out of the way," Halt said. He saw Selethen was about to ask another question but he continued, talking over the other man. "It's politics," he said. "Skandian politics. There's a small group of Skandians who resent Erak and would like to see him deposed."

He saw a first glimpse of understanding in the Arridi's face. Arrida was rife with political intrigue and Selethen accepted this as a plausible explanation. But he wasn't fully convinced.

"I repeat. I've never heard of this Toshak person. I take it he's a Skandian, like you?" He addressed the last question to Svengal, whose face darkened into a scowl.

"He's a Skandian. But he's nothing like me."

Selethen nodded, accepting the distinction. Svengal's anger, matching his own, was possibly the most convincing aspect of Halt's argument. But Selethen had seen a flaw.

"If this Toshak wants your leader out of the way, why bother to have him captured and abducted? Why not simply kill him with the rest of these people?"

But Halt was already shaking his head before Selethen finished voicing the question.

"He needs time," he replied. "I said his group is a small one. Most Skandians are content with Erak as their Oberjarl. So Toshak and his friends need time to build resentment and uncertainty. A dead Oberjarl wouldn't serve their purposes. The other Skandians would simply elect a new one straightaway—probably one of Erak's friends. Maybe even Svengal here."

"Gods forbid that," Svengal said earnestly. Halt allowed himself a grim smile at the big Skandian.

"But if Erak is missing, held prisoner somewhere—and it can be

claimed to be the result of his own incompetence—then Toshak
and his group can start a whispering campaign to get people doubt-
ing his ability, and his suitability to be their leader. Particularly if, at
the same time, his captors are demanding a large ransom from the
Skandians. Skandians don't like that sort of thing."

"Indeed we don't," Svengal agreed. "That's why the chief told me
to go to Araluen for help in the first place."

Selethen looked around the group and nodded. He had wondered why Svengal had returned with a group of foreigners to pay
the ransom. So far, the only reason he had been given was that Erak
was a friend of the Araluens. Now he could see a more plausible
explanation for their involvement. A quick resolution to the problem
would act in Erak's favor. The more the situation was dragged out,
the more opportunity there would be for his enemies to sow dissent
among his countrymen.

"Given enough time, the dissenters could create the right conditions to put forward their own candidate as Oberjarl—probably
Toshak himself," Halt said.

Selethen paced back and forth, stroking his beard with one hand
as he considered Halt's arguments. Abruptly, he stopped and turned
to Halt again.

"It's possible, I suppose . . ." he said. The word "but" was left hanging, unsaid, in the air by the tone of his voice. Halt waited, determined
that he wouldn't be the one to voice the obvious doubt. Like Selethen,
he could see another possible explanation for the carnage around
them. But before he raised that, Selethen had another question.

"You say your countryman Toshak is behind this. That he betrayed your leader in the first place?" he questioned Svengal. The sea
wolf nodded and Selethen continued. "Yet I have never heard of him.
Our informant was a fisherman from a small village down the coast.

More of a smuggler than a fisherman, as a matter of fact," he added. "He's accustomed to moving unseen through the waters around our coast. He saw your ship and brought word to us."

Svengal said nothing. But once again Halt had a ready answer.

"You'd hardly negotiate with a Skandian. If Toshak had tried to approach you, he wouldn't have got a word in before the first volley of arrows was on its way. Of course he needed a go-between. And it would have been relatively easy for him to make contact with a smuggler. Chances are, your informant was also the one who sold Erak the false timetable for the money transfers."

"Yes, that's reasonable, I suppose." In spite of his words, they could all hear the tone of doubt in Selethen's voice.

"But I keep coming back to another possible explanation for all this."

He waved his arm distastefully around the scene of death and destruction. Halt waited impassively. Make him say it, he thought. Don't say it for him or you'll give it credibility.

"I agree with you, this could be the work of Skandians—or of Tualaghi in the pay of Skandians. But there's another possible reason why Erak's body isn't here. This was a rescue party. The people who killed my men did it to set Erak free. Even now, he could be heading for the coast and another ship."

"Do you think we'd willingly put ourselves in your hands if we'd planned that?" Halt asked.

"I think it's exactly the sort of double bluff that you might consider," Selethen told him. "You negotiate with me while you organize for another party of Skandians to rescue your friend. If they're successful, you save sixty-six thousand reels. If they're not, you can continue as before, and deny all knowledge of the rescue attempt."

Halt said nothing for a few seconds. As he had realized before, politics and plotting were very much a part of life in Arrida. And this was exactly the sort of convoluted reasoning that would seem logical to Selethen. He knew that his next words were going to be vital to the success of their mission. While he gathered his thoughts, trying to muster the best possible argument to restore Selethen's trust, Horace stepped forward. As Halt and Selethen and Svengal had been talking, Horace and Evanlyn had edged closer, listening. Now the young warrior thought it was time he spoke up.

"One question . . ." he said. All eyes swung to him. Halt held up a hand to stop him from going any further. The subtleties of negotiation, the fine cut and thrust of complex argument, were not the young man's strongest suit.

"Horace," Halt said, a warning tone in his voice, "this might not be the best . . ."

But Horace was holding up his own hand to silence Halt. His face was determined and set in a tight frown.

Halt knew he was angered by the suggestion that they had engaged in the sort of underhanded scheme Selethen had described. He didn't need Horace's injured sense of dignity muddying the waters here. But the young man was plowing ahead, regardless.

"A question for the Wakir," he said. Evanlyn, beside him, mirrored Halt's worried expression. Horace might be about to put his foot in it, she thought. But Selethen made a gesture for Horace to continue and it was too late.

"Your question is?" he said smoothly.

"How could we have known?" Horace asked. His tone was blunt and challenging. Selethen frowned, not understanding immediately.

"How could you have known . . . what?" he asked.

Horace's face was flushed now, partly with indignation but also because he realized that he was the center of attention. He never enjoyed that. But he felt his point was a valid one and deserved to be made.

"How could we have known that Erak was with this party?"

For a moment, nobody understood. Selethen made a confused little gesture with both hands.

"I told you," he said. Standing back and watching, Halt felt an immense surge of warmth for the warrior. Sometimes, he thought, Horace's direct approach could be far more effective than a long, involved dissertation.

Horace nodded. "You told us the night before we left Al Shabah. You told us when the negotiations were complete. Not before then. Up until then, you know we believed Erak was being held in Al Shabah. So, in the eight hours we had, how did we organize for this other group of Skandians to dash out into the desert, find the Tualaghi and bribe them to intercept a caravan we had only just heard of?"

"Well . . . you could have . . ." Selethen hesitated and Horace pressed his advantage.

"And you know that none of us left the guesthouse on that final night. So how did we do it? I mean, Halt's good at these things, but that's beyond even his abilities."

Halt thought it was time he stepped back in. Horace had made his point and it was a telling one. Now was the time to drive it home, before he blundered.

"He's right, Selethen, and deep down, you know it," Halt said. The Wakir's attention was back on him now and Halt knew it was time to force Selethen to either commit to them or to take a position against them. Very deliberately, he said, "Tell me, Selethen, leaving aside the fact that we couldn't have organized this in the time we had, do you honestly believe that we are capable of that sort of duplicity?"

Selethen went to speak, then hesitated. He looked at the small group of foreigners. The warrior Horace and the raider Svengal were fighting men. There was no guile or deceit in either of them. They would be dangerous enemies to face on a battlefield, he knew. But they would fight honestly and bravely.

Then there was the princess. During the negotiations, she had shown her courage and forthrightness as well. In fact, he thought ruefully, if there had been any false dealing at all, it had come from him. First in having his servant impersonate him and secondly in the fact that Horace had just pointed out—in his not telling them that Erak had already left Al Shabah.

That left Halt and Gilan. Unmistakably, Halt was the leader of the group, in spite of the girl's rank. Undoubtedly, he was a thinker and a planner. Yet Selethen sensed a core of decency and honesty in the man. Instinctively, he found himself drawn to the short, gray-haired Ranger.

It was obvious that the others respected him and trusted him. And, perhaps most important, liked him. Horace and Svengal might be straightforward and uncomplicated, but they were not fools. Horace had just proved that.

Selethen bit his lip thoughtfully, considering Halt's question. Then he replied.

"No. I don't think that."

Halt was tempted to let go a huge sigh of relief. But he knew that would be a mistake. Instead, he simply nodded once, as if he had held no doubt as to what Selethen's answer would be.

"Then let's get on with it," he said briskly. "What do we plan to do about all this?"

"I'll send a party out after them once we reach Mararoc," Selethen asked. "For all the good it will do."

Bitter experience had taught him how the Tualaghi operated. They would attack a caravan, then simply melt away into the desert. The Arridi were essentially town dwellers, without the skills in tracking and desert craft to follow the raiders. The Tualaghi knew these wastelands like the backs of their hands and they knew how to disappear into them. Oh, Selethen would send a party in pursuit. But it would be a gesture only. After two or three days they would lose track of the Tualaghi war party and return, exhausted, dusty and frustrated. It had always been this way, he thought. If he had some of the Bedullin with him, they would have a chance. The Bedullin were hunters and trackers and they knew the desert every bit as well as the Tualaghi, their sworn enemies. That was how he had defeated the Tualaghi some years previously—by forming a temporary alliance with the Bedullin. But they were a proud, independent people and they wouldn't stay tied to the Arridi apron strings once the Tualaghi had been brought to battle and defeated.

"Why not go after them now?" Halt said.

Selethen smiled at the man's naiveté. "Because they will fade away into the desert. That's what they do."

"Then we'll track them down. That's what we do," said another voice.

It was Gilan. He had returned from surveying the scene of the one-sided battle in time to hear Selethen's last words.

Halt turned to him. "Find anything?"

Gilan pursed his lips, then pointed to each location as he mentioned it.

"They were hidden behind those rocks to the east," he said. "Maybe eighty or ninety of them. Most of them on horses but some on camels. They had a diversion party to the north—perhaps ten riders. They swooped in, feinted an attack, then turned and ran.

When the escort broke ranks and went after them, the main party hit them from behind."

Selethen looked at the young Ranger with new respect. "You can tell all that just by looking at the ground?"

Gilan grinned at him. "As I said, it's what we do," he replied. "So what do you say? Do we go after them or slink back to Al Shabah?"

His tone was intentionally provocative. He sensed that the Wakir was looking for a reason to go in pursuit of the Tualaghi—to teach them once and for all who ruled this country. And he was right. Selethen's mind was racing. This could be just the chance he had been looking for.

"We'll be outnumbered," he said thoughtfully.

"But we'll have the element of surprise on our side," Halt countered. "You normally wouldn't go after them, would you?"

Selethen considered. Eighty Tualaghi, the young Ranger had said. And he had fifty well-trained, well-armed veterans at his command, as well as the Araluens. Horace and Svengal would give a good account of themselves, he knew. In fact, the more he thought about it, the more he thought that he'd enjoy seeing Svengal carve his way through a Tualaghi war party with that battleax he carried. And the two Rangers both carried massive longbows slung over their shoulders. He was willing to bet they were not just there for decoration. He had the distinct feeling that those two cloaked men could do a lot of damage. There was one problem. He couldn't afford to weaken his forces any more. He'd need every man he could find.

"What about the girl?" he said. If she were to go back to Al Shabah, he'd have to spare men to escort her. That would weaken his force even further.

"She'll come with you," Evanlyn said in a determined voice.

Selethen looked at Halt, his eyebrows raised in a question. Halt smiled grimly. He'd seen Evanlyn's courage in battle before. And he knew she was able to take care of herself with the saber she wore at her belt. On the voyage from Araluen, she'd practiced with Horace and Gilan, both masters of the sword. She'd held her own. She wasn't in their league, of course, but she was capable. Evanlyn wouldn't be a burden, he knew. She might well prove to be an advantage.

"She'll come with us," he said.

27

THE BITTER COLD OF THE DESERT NIGHT WOKE HIM. HE WAS FACE-down, shivering violently as the heat leached from his body. It wasn't fair, he thought. The blinding heat of the day and the near freezing temperatures of the night were combining to rob the last vestiges of strength from him. Shivering took energy and he had none to spare.

Will tried to raise his head, and failed. Then, with a massive effort, he rolled over onto his back, to find himself staring up at the brilliant stars blazing down from the clear night sky. Beautiful, he thought. But strangers to him. He wanted to crane around and look to the north, where he would see the familiar constellations of his homeland, lying low on the northern horizon. But he didn't have the strength. He'd just have to lie here and die, watched over by strange stars who didn't know him, didn't care for him.

It was very sad, really.

There was a strange clarity to his thinking now, as if all the effort of the day, all the self-delusion, was gone and he could view his situation dispassionately. He knew he was going to die. If not tonight, then certainly tomorrow. He would never stand another day of that furnacelike heat. He would just dry up and blow away, carried on the desert wind.

It was very sad. He'd like to have cried about it but there was no moisture for tears. With his newfound clarity of thought, he felt a nagging sense of annoyance. He wanted to know what he had done wrong. He didn't want to die wondering. He'd done everything correctly—or so he thought. Yet somewhere he had made a mistake—a fatal mistake. It was a pity that he had to die. It was annoying that he didn't know how it had come to this.

He wondered briefly if the map Selethen had given him had been false and remembered that thought occurring to him during the preceding day. But he dismissed it almost immediately. Selethen was an honorable man, he thought. No, the map was accurate. The mistake had been his and now he would never know what it had been. Halt would be disappointed, he thought—and perhaps that was the worst aspect of this situation. For five years, he had tried his best for the grizzled, unsmiling Ranger who had become like a father to him. All he ever sought was Halt's approval, no matter what anyone else in the world might think. A nod of appreciation or one of Halt's rare smiles was the greatest accolade he could imagine. Now, at this final hurdle, he felt he had let his mentor down and he didn't know how or why it had happened. He didn't want to die knowing that Halt would be disappointed in him. He could bear the dying, he thought, but not the disappointment.

A large shape moved near him, blotting out a section of the sky. For a moment, his heart raced in fear, then he realized it was Arrow. He hadn't hobbled the horse for the night. He'd wander off and get lost or be taken by predators. He tried to rise once more but the effort defeated him. It was all he could do to raise his head a centimeter or two from the hard, stony ground underneath it. Then he dropped back, defeated.

He wondered what had happened to Tug. He hoped that somewhere, his horse was all right. Maybe someone had found him and was caring for him now. Not that they'll ever manage to ride him, he thought, and chuckled soundlessly at the mental picture of Tug bucking off every rider who tried to mount him.

Arrow began to move away from him, the soft shuffling sound of his padded hooves puzzling Will for a moment, before he remembered tying pieces of blanket around them. One of them must have come loose because Arrow walked with a strange gait—three muffled thumps and then a clop as the unprotected hoof made contact with the hard ground.

He turned his head to follow the dark shape moving away from him.

"Come back, Arrow," he said. At least, he thought he said it. The only sound that came from his mouth was a dry, choking rasp. The horse ignored it. He continued to move away, searching for forage that might contain even a little moisture. Again, Will tried to call Arrow back, but no sound would come. Finally, he gave up. The foreign stars watched him and he watched them.

They seemed to be fading, their cold brilliance dimming. That was unusual, he thought. Usually the stars kept burning till the sun came up. He didn't realize that the stars were burning as brightly as ever. It was he who was fading. After a while, he lay still, barely breathing.

The lion passed within meters of him. Arrow, weakened and dehydrated, was intent on freeing himself from the blanket strips tangled around one forefoot. He never sensed the giant predator until the last second. There was time for one shrill scream of fear, cut off almost instantly by the massive jaws.

Later on, Will would think that he might have heard it but he could never be sure. In fact, it had registered with his subconscious but he was too far gone to stir.

Arrow died quickly and, in doing so, he saved Will's life.

◆ ◆ ◆

Will felt the snorting breath of a horse close by his face, felt the soft-ness of its muzzle as it nuzzled against him and the roughness of the big tongue licking him, the lips nibbling softly at his hand.

For one wonderful moment, Will thought it was Tug. Then his spirits sank as he remembered that Tug was gone, lost somewhere in this wasteland. Arrow must have come back, he thought. His eyes wouldn't open. But he didn't want them to. He could see the glare of the sun even through his closed eyelids, burning down on him once more, and he didn't want to face that. Far easier to lie here with his eyes glued shut. Arrow moved again so that his shadow fell across Will's face, shading him, and he murmured his gratitude.

He tried to force his eyelids open but they were gummed shut in his swollen, sunburned face. He was vaguely surprised to realize that he wasn't dead, but he knew it was only a matter of time. Maybe, he thought, he *was* dead. If so, this certainly didn't feel like any idea of heaven he'd ever been told about and the alternative wasn't pleasant to contemplate. Once again, the horse's muzzle nudged him, as if try-ing to wake him. Tug used to do that, Will recalled. Maybe all horses did it. He didn't want to wake up, didn't want to open his eyes. The effort would be too great.

Funny, he thought, a few hours ago, he didn't have the energy to roll over. Now a simple act like raising his eyelids was beyond him. It would be easier to just lie here sleeping and fade away from it all.

He heard the crunch of footsteps on the sand and rock, close by him. That was strange; he didn't remember anyone else being here. Then a hand slipped under his head and raised it, resting it on what felt like a knee, so that he was sitting half upright. He sighed. He simply wanted to be left alone.

Then he felt something wonderful. Something unbelievable. A cool trickle of water spilled over his dry, cracked lips. He opened his mouth eagerly, seeking more of the wonderful water. Another trickle found its way inside and he tried to rise, tried to reach for the water skin and hold it to his mouth. A hand restrained him.

"Steady," said a voice. "Just a little at a time."

And as he said it, more water trickled into Will's parched mouth and then down his throat. It caught in the back of his throat and he coughed, spitting it out, trying frantically to retain it, knowing that he mustn't lose it.

"Take it easy," the voice said. "There's plenty here. Just take it slowly at first."

Obediently, Will lay back and allowed the stranger to trickle water into his mouth. He was grateful to whoever it was, but obviously the man didn't realize that Will was nearly dead from thirst. Otherwise he would have let the water flood into his eager mouth, he thought, overflowing and spilling down his chin while he gulped it in by the gallon. But he said nothing. He didn't want to offend his benefactor in case he stopped.

He heard an anxious whinny close by and, once again, it sounded to him like Tug. But Tug was gone.

"He's all right," the voice said. Will assumed he was talking to the horse. Nice of Arrow to be worried about him, he thought. They hadn't known each other all that long. He felt a wet cloth wiping gently around his eyes, working on the gummed-up eyelids. Some of the water trickled down his cheeks and he caught it with his tongue, flicking it into his mouth. Be a shame to waste it.

"Try to open them," said the voice, and he obeyed, using all his strength to get his eyes open.

He could see a slit of light and a dark shape leaning over him. He blinked. The action took an enormous effort but when he reopened his eyes it was a little easier and his vision was a little clearer. It was a dark face. Bearded, he saw. Framed by a yellow and white keffiyeh.

The nose was big and hooked and at some time in its owner's life it had been so badly broken that it now sat at a crooked angle on his face. For a moment, the nose held his focus. Then he blinked again and the eyes above the nose caught his attention.

They were dark, almost black. Hooded by heavy eyebrows, deep-set in the face. A strong face, he realized. But not handsome. The big crooked nose saw to that.

"Tha's a big nose," he croaked and instantly realized he shouldn't have said something so impolite. I must be light-headed, he thought. But the face smiled. The teeth seemed inordinately white against the dark beard and skin.

"The only one I have," he said. "More water?"

"Please," said Will, and that wonderful water was back in his mouth again.

And then, wonder of wonders, another face pushed its way into his field of vision, nudging the bearded man aside, nearly causing him to spill the water. For a moment, Will's face was unshaded and the glaring sun caused him to wince away and blink. Then shadow fell across him again and he opened his eyes.

"Tug?" he said, not daring to believe it. And this time, as the horse whinnied in recognition, there was no doubt about it. It was Tug, standing over him, nuzzling him, nibbling him with his big soft lips and trying to be as close to him as was possible.

He butted against Will's shoulder in the old familiar way. The big eyes looked deep into Will's half-closed ones.

See what trouble you get into when I'm not around? they said.

The bearded man looked from the horse to the blistered, burned face of the foreigner.

"I take it you two know each other," he said.

He was half conscious but he was aware of someone spreading a soothing, cooling balm onto the burned skin of his face and arms.

And there was more water, all he could drink—so long as he drank it slowly. He had learned by now. If he tried to drink too quickly, the water was taken away. Drink slowly and it kept flowing. As several people tended to him, he was aware of Tug, always there, always close by. Will drifted in and out of consciousness and each time he awoke, he had a momentary fear that he had been dreaming and that Tug was still missing. Then he would see that familiar, worried face and breathe more easily.

Vaguely, he registered the fact that he had been placed on a litter that was tilted at about thirty degrees from the horizontal. Perhaps it was strapped behind a horse, he thought. Then, as he began to move and he felt the strange slow rhythm of the animal dragging him behind it, he revised his estimate. It must be a camel, he thought. The unusual, long-legged swaying gait transmitted itself through the wood poles and webbing base of the litter to his body.

Someone thoughtfully placed a shade cloth to protect his face and eyes from the glare and he dozed as they proceeded across the desert. He had no idea which direction they were taking. He didn't care. He was alive and Tug was a few meters away, walking slowly beside him, alert to any sign that he might be in danger again.

They could have traveled for half an hour or half a day as far as he knew. Later, he found out that he had ridden on the litter for just over an hour and a half before they reached his rescuers' camp. He was lifted from the litter and placed on a bedroll in the shade under a stand of palm trees. The light filtered gently down through the fronds and he thought he had never been so comfortable in his life. The skin was sore on his face and arms, but more of the soothing balm eased the pain.

Tug stood nearby, watching him attentively.

"I'm fine, Tug," he told the horse. He was relieved that his voice seemed to be getting back to normal. He was still weak but at least now he could form words properly.

He wondered now where Arrow had got to. He hadn't seen the Arridi horse since he had woken again. He hoped he wasn't lost.

"Got to stop losing horses," he said drowsily. "Bad habit."

Then he slept.

Will woke from a deep, refreshing sleep. He was lying on his back, looking up at palm fronds.

He was in a large oasis. He could hear the sound of trickling water close by and the movement and voices of many people. As he swept his gaze around, he saw a camp of low tents had been set up. The oasis, and the camp, sprawled for several hundred meters in either direction. There was a large central pool of water, and other outlying pools and wells surrounding it. People moved about, carrying urns of water from the wells, preparing cooking fires or tending to the herds of goats, camels and horses that he could see. From the size of the camp, he estimated that there must be several hundred people, all dressed in long, flowing robes. The men wore keffiyehs and the women had long scarves draped over their heads, leaving the face uncovered but protecting the head and neck.

"You're awake."

The voice came from behind him and he twisted around to see the speaker. A small, slender woman, aged perhaps forty, was smiling down at him. She carried a flat basket of fruit and bread and meat, and a flask of water as well. She dropped gracefully to her knees beside him and set the basket down, gesturing for him to help himself.

"You should eat," she said. "I'm sure you haven't eaten in some time."

He studied her for a moment or two. Her oval face was evenly featured and friendly. Her eyes were dark and there was an unmistakable light of humor in them. When she smiled, which she did now, the face seemed to be transformed into one of great beauty. Her skin was a light coffee color. Her headscarf and robe were a bright yellow. There was something motherly and welcoming about her, he thought.

"Thank you," he said. He took a piece of fruit and bit into it, feeling the juice spurt inside his mouth, bringing his own saliva alive. He reveled in the feeling, remembering how, just a short while ago, his tongue and throat had been swollen and dry. He had a vague memory of someone repeatedly placing the neck of a water skin to his mouth and admonishing him to drink, but slowly. There was a dreamlike quality to it but he realized it had been real. His rescuers must have thoroughly rehydrated him without actually waking him.

He took another sip of water. He wanted to ask where he was but the question seemed so banal. Instead, he indicated the people moving through the camp.

"What people are these?" he asked. She smiled at him.

"We are the Khoresh Bedullin," she told him. "We are desert people. My name is Cielema." She made the lips-brow-lips hand gesture he had seen Selethen use. He didn't feel up to carrying it off in response. Instead, he made an awkward half bow from his sitting position.

"How do you do, Cielema. My name is Will."

"Be welcome to our camp, Will," she said. As they were speaking, he had suddenly realized how hungry he was and he helped himself to some of the delicious flat bread in the basket. There were also slices of cold roast meat and he took one, wrapping it in the bread and taking a large bite. The meat was delicious, perfectly grilled so that it was still flowing with juices, with a slightly smoky taste from the fire and lightly flavored with delicious spices. He chewed and swallowed, then tore off another huge piece of bread and a second slice of meat, filling his mouth and chewing rapturously. Cielema smiled gently.

"There can't be too much wrong with any young man with such an appetite," she said, and he hesitated, thinking that perhaps he had shown bad manners in wolfing his food this way. She laughed and made a gesture for him to continue.

"You're hungry," she said. "And such enthusiasm is a compliment to my cooking."

Gratefully, he ate more of the food. When the pangs of hunger were stilled, he brushed crumbs off his lap and looked around again.

"The man who found me," he asked. "Where is he?"

She gestured to the middle of the campsite. He realized that he had been placed on the fringe of the camp, probably to assure his uninterrupted rest.

"That was Umar ib'n Talud," she told him. "He's surely involved in very weighty affairs right now. He is our Aseikh."

She saw the incomprehension in his eyes and explained further. "Aseikh is our word for leader. He is the headman of the Khoresh Bedullin people. He's also my husband," she added. "And he knows that our tent needs mending and that I have a carpet that needs beating. This is why he is surely involved in weighty affairs right now."

The hint of a smile touched her mouth. Will had the feeling that an Aseikh might be the leader of his people but, like husbands the world over, he answered to the ultimate authority of his wife.

"I would like to thank him," he said, and she nodded agreement.

"I'm sure he would enjoy that too."

28

"These Tualaghi are good at this," Gilan said as he and Halt swung back into their respective saddles. Selethen was seated on his own mount, waiting to hear what the Rangers had found.

It was the fifth time that afternoon that they had lost the trail left by the Tualaghi war party ahead of them and had to cast around on foot for some faint sign showing the direction they had taken.

Halt grunted in reply as they headed out again. On the first day, the Tualaghi had pushed on without making any attempt to hide their progress. But after that, they had begun to cover their tracks, leaving a small party to follow behind and obliterate the signs left by the main group as they gradually changed direction. Of course, they couldn't manage to remove every trace of their passing, but only trackers with the skill of Halt and Gilan would see the faint signs remaining.

"This is how it's been any time we've tried to follow them," Selethen said. "We'd see their trail clearly for a while, then it would simply disappear."

"Makes sense," Halt told them. "You need daylight to cover tracks like this, just as we need daylight to follow them. The first day, they'd be keen to put as many kilometers behind them as possible. My guess is they ride out before dawn and keep pushing till the middle of the day. Then they rest and continue on in the late afternoon and evening. Then, when they've established a lead over their pursuers, they start all this zigzagging and track-covering." He looked at Selethen. "That's when your trackers lose the trail and you have to give up," he said. Selethen nodded.

"At least this is slowing them down," Gilan put in.

Halt nodded. "They have to travel in daylight, the same as we do. And they're not taking a direct route. My guess is we've closed the gap by half a day."

The two Rangers had been able to cut a few corners in their pursuit. It had quickly become apparent that the Tualaghi, perhaps overconfident in their past ability to confuse Arridi pursuers, had fallen into a pattern of false trails and zigzags. After several hours, the pattern had become predictable and Gilan and Halt had been able to ignore several of the false trails and keep on a more direct route, picking up the real trail some kilometers farther on. It had also quickly become apparent that when the Tualaghi laid a false trail, they would take less effort to cover it. They were good, as Gilan had noted. But they lacked the important element of subtlety.

Of course, it helped that Halt and Gilan could work as a team. When they reached a diversion, Gilan would follow it for a short time, as insurance, while Halt led the Arridi party along the path the enemy had taken previously. The fact that the pursuing party was traveling in the early morning or late afternoon was another piece of luck. The oblique, low angle light made it easier to sight the disturbances and faint hoofprints left in the thin sand covering the desert.

So far, whenever they had adopted this tactic, they had rediscovered the real trail within a few kilometers, at which point Gilan would rejoin them. Fortunately, the terrain was flat and they were able to maintain line of sight communication for considerable distances.

As Halt had said, this had put them half a day closer to the Tualaghi. But he wanted to get closer still. He looked up at the sun, shading his eyes with his hand. It was getting close to the middle of the day, when they'd have to rest from the heat.

"I'm thinking," he said to Selethen, "that this afternoon, the three of us might push on ahead. We'll move more quickly that way and we can leave clear signs for the rest of the party to follow. I want to get close enough by tomorrow night for Gilan to take a look at these Tualaghi."

Selethen nodded agreement. The suggestion made sense. With a party of fifty men, they were limited by the slowest horse in the group. And the continual stop-start nature of their progress, when Halt and Gilan had to search for tracks on the hard ground, added to the time they were taking. Each time they stopped, it took that much longer to reassemble a large party and get it under way again. There was always a girth to be tightened, a stone in a horse's hoof, a piece of equipment needing adjustment, another drink to be taken from a water skin. It might only be a few minutes here and there, but it all added up over a day.

"We'll keep going for a few more kilometers," he said, "then we'll rest. This afternoon, the three of us will go on ahead."

It was a significant indication of the change in their relationship, Halt thought. After his initial suspicions at the scene of the massacre, the Wakir had placed his trust in the two Rangers to guide his party. Now he was willing to isolate himself from his own men and ride ahead with Halt and Gilan.

For his part, the Wakir felt a growing satisfaction at the prospect of dealing a telling blow to the Tualaghi tribesmen. The nomads knew that he had no Bedullin trackers working with him and they were overconfident, as the bearded Ranger had explained. If he and his warriors were able to stage a surprise attack sometime in the next few days, the old enemy might not be so ready to raid in the future, with their apparent ability to disappear into the desert wasteland undermined.

He was in some awe of the ability of the two northerners to read signs on the ground. They had shown him several times what they were looking for, and what they sighted: a faint indentation in a softer piece of sand; a slight scrape of a hoof on a piece of stony ground; a thread from a saddle blanket or robe caught on one of the ever-present scrubby bushes. Tiny signs that he would never notice. Yet their keen eyes read them as if the facts were written on the ground in large letters.

Gilan swung down from his saddle and ran a few paces ahead, staring down at the ground. His bay horse followed obediently behind him, saving him the time needed to run back and remount. The young Ranger reminded Selethen of a searching hound, with his energy and eagerness to follow the trail of the Tualaghi.

"This way," he called, pointing slightly to the left, and the Arridi party swung their horses to follow the direction he had indicated.

After resting through the middle of the day, Selethen and the two Rangers moved ahead of the main party, having arranged to leave signs behind for the others to follow. At every change in direction, they would scrape a large arrow in the ground. Or, if the ground was too hard, they would form an arrow with stones and rocks.

It soon became apparent that the idea was working, and they were moving well ahead of the main party. Yet even when the riders behind them were no longer visible, they could still see the small cloud of dust that marked their presence. Halt frowned thoughtfully as he studied it.

"Best keep that in mind when we get within striking distance," he said. "We don't want them to know we're behind them."

They pushed on through the late afternoon, until the sun was virtually on the western horizon and the light was too uncertain for tracking. Selethen had noticed that the Rangers had increased their pace, sometimes trotting and even cantering when the trail was easier to follow. The sturdy horses they rode showed no discomfort at traveling faster than the slow walk they had been reduced to formerly. His own mount was unbothered by the change in pace, but he was a thoroughbred, from a long line of some of the finest horses in Arridi. Selethen knew that some of the lesser horses ridden by his troopers would have balked at the increased tempo and he looked more carefully at the Ranger's shaggy mounts. Alongside his beautifully formed and groomed Arridi horse they appeared nondescript and shabby. But they had enormous endurance and amazing speed, he thought. In the short term, he believed that his stallion, Lord of the Sun, would probably outpace them. But then their ability to maintain speed kilometer after kilometer would probably begin to tell.

Perhaps I should find out more about these horses, he thought, as he considered the advantages of having cavalry equipped with such uniformly fine mounts.

The main party had been left far behind by the time the three stopped for the night.

They unsaddled, tended to the horses and made camp. Selethen set about gathering firewood for a small signal fire. Halt and Gilan moved to help him but he waved them aside.

"You've been working all day," he said. "I've been a passenger."

He saw the slightly surprised look that passed between them and felt secretly pleased that he had earned their gratitude and, perhaps, a little respect. They were not men to stand on ceremony, he thought, and they knew that true authority came from sharing the hard work, not attempting to place oneself above it. He soon had a fire going and it threw a bright circle of light around them. It would be visible in the darkness for quite a distance, he knew. The following party would have no trouble finding them in the dark.

"That's another thing we'll have to watch as we get closer," Halt said. From five or six kilometers away, the fire would be a bright pinpoint. And before the moon rose, its glow might well be visible in the sky from much farther away.

They ate when the main party finally joined them, three hours after nightfall. As the troops relaxed after their meal, drinking coffee and talking quietly, Selethen moved among them, as a good commander should. He would stop by each small group, dropping to one knee and talking quietly, appraising them of the progress made during the day, checking to see if they or their mounts were having any problems.

Halt and Gilan had been joined by Svengal and the other Araluens. They watched Selethen approvingly as they enjoyed the rich Arridi coffee. They knew the Wakir must be tired and longing to sprawl comfortably on the still-warm ground with a cup of coffee. But he continued to move among his men, with a joke here for an old companion or a word of advice or concern there for a young recruit.

Finally, the tall, white-robed figure completed his rounds. Somewhat to their surprise, he walked toward the spot where they were sitting.

"May I join you?" he said.

Halt made a welcoming gesture. "Please do."

Horace began to scramble to his feet. "I'll get you a cup of coffee," he said, but Selethen waved him back down.

"Sidar will see to that," he replied, and they realized that one of the troopers, anticipating his leader's needs, was bringing a cup from the single small fire. As Selethen sat down, he sighed contentedly, then accepted the cup from his soldier.

He sipped deeply, then sighed again—with the satisfaction that comes from sore, tired muscles that are finally allowed to rest.

"What would we do without kafay?" he asked them, using the Arridi name, and the original name, for the drink.

"If you're a Ranger, very little," Horace replied, and they all grinned. Selethen had already observed that the Rangers were as keen on the drink as any Arridi. The tall warrior seemed to share the same near-addiction, whereas the Skandian usually grumbled over his coffee in the evening, wishing instead for the dark ale of his homeland.

"Don't know how you all keep going without a good drink of ale," he said. "Settles the mind in the evening, ale does."

Evanlyn smiled at him. "Feeling homesick, Svengal?" she asked. The big pirate studied her for a moment, considering his reply.

"To tell the truth, your majesty," he said, "I'm not built for this climate."

Svengal insisted on calling Evanlyn "your majesty" in spite of her protests. She suspected that this was a none-too-subtle leg-pull, in light of the Skandians' known reputation for egalitarianism.

"You're not built for riding, either," Horace added. "I'd say more saddle sore than homesick."

Svengal sighed ruefully, shifting his buttocks for the twentieth time to find a more comfortable spot.

"It's true," he said. "I've been discovering parts of my backside I never knew existed."

Selethen smiled, enjoying the quiet good humor and friendship of these foreigners.

But he hadn't come to chat. He coughed gently and saw that Halt's attention was drawn immediately.

"Something on your mind, Selethen?" Halt asked. They had passed the time when he might have addressed the Wakir by his title or by the honorific "Excellence." Selethen leaned forward, smoothing the sand in front of him.

"As a matter of fact, yes. One of my corporals raised an interesting point while I was talking to the men."

He drew his curved dagger and scratched an *x* in the sand. "Let's say this is our position at the moment," he said. Then he drew a zigzag line back from that position for a meter or so. "And to get here, we've followed the Tualaghi while they zigzagged and diverted and backtracked." He looked up at Halt. "As you pointed out, this gave us the chance to catch up to them."

Halt nodded.

"Yet with all this chopping and changing and to-ing and fro-ing, the Tualaghi have kept coming back to one base course." He slashed a straight line through the middle of the zigzagging line. "And if they continue, it will take them here." He gouged a point in the sand farther along the projected line that indicated the Tualaghi base course.

"And what might be there?" Evanlyn asked. Selethen glanced up at her to answer.

"The Khor-Abash Wells," he said. "The best water source within two hundred kilometers."

Horace frowned at the scrape marks in the sand. "D'you think they need water?" he asked. Selethen turned his gaze upon the young man. His face was deadly serious when he replied.

"In the desert, you always need water," he told him. "A wise traveler never goes past the chance to refill his water skins."

"Is there nowhere else they could do this?" Halt asked. Selethen tapped another mark into the sand with his dagger.

"There are the Orr-San Wells," he said. "They're smaller and not as reliable. And they're forty kilometers farther to the west. If the

Tualaghi's end destination is where I think it is, the Orr-Sans will be too far from their course."

"Where do you think they're eventually headed?" Halt asked him.

"Here." The knife stabbed again, at a point to the right of the mark indicating the Khor-Abash Wells. "They'll top up their water then swing right, toward the northern massif." He scraped a line from east to west. "There are mountains, hills, cliffs, blind canyons. And several towns they could use as a base."

Halt frowned. "I thought you said the Tualaghi were nomads?"

Selethen nodded. "They are. The towns are Arridi towns but the Tualaghi take them over and occupy them for a month, six weeks at a time. Then they head back into the desert again, or farther into the hills."

Halt rubbed his chin reflectively, studying the marks Selethen had made.

"So if you're right and they're zigzagging toward these wells before swinging north to the hills, we could simply stop zigzagging in their tracks and cut straight across country to the wells. With any luck, we could be waiting for them when they arrive."

Selethen met his gaze, held it and nodded. "It's a gamble, of course," he said. "But I can't think of anywhere else they could be heading."

Halt hesitated. He looked around his companions' faces. After all, Erak was a friend to all of them and if he followed Selethen's plan they risked losing track of him altogether. Silently, one after the other, they all nodded. He looked back at Selethen.

"Let's do it," he said.

29

CIELEMA HELPED WILL TO STAND AS HE CAST OFF THE BLANKET and rose from the bed that had been placed under the trees.

She steadied him with a hand under his arm. He swayed groggily for a few seconds, then his head steadied and he stood more firmly. She nodded at him, satisfied that he was well on the way to recovery.

"A strong healthy body restores itself quickly with a little rest," she said. "Come and meet the mighty Umar."

There was an amused undertone to her words. Will realized his feet were bare and he didn't see his boots. His cloak was gone as well. She saw him glance around.

"Your belongings are safe," she told him. She saw him looking for something else and guessed what it might be. The little horse had stayed by his side through the day and night as he had slept.

"The horse is with the rest of the herd. They are being watered and fed," she told him. "It took a while to convince him to leave your side."

Will smiled at the thought. He'd had a moment of panic when he had thought perhaps he had dreamed that Tug was here. Reassured, he looked at his bare feet.

"My boots," he said. "I need my boots."

But Cielema merely smiled and began to lead him toward the center of the camp. "The sand is soft."

She was right. He walked beside her as she held his arm lightly in case he stumbled. The sand, not yet heated by the burning rays of the sun, was cool underfoot. He became aware of a slight burning sensation on his arms and face. He looked down and saw that the red, burned skin of his arms was glistening with some kind of oil compound.

"It's a salve our people have used for years. In a day or two your burns will heal," she told him. He nodded to her.

"Thank you," he said, and once more she smiled at him. He felt a sense of warmth toward this kind, humorous woman. Aseikh Umar was a lucky man, he thought.

As they passed through the camp, he noticed that people stopped to watch him—particularly the children. Such curiosity was only natural, he thought. But there were also smiles and gestures of welcome—the by-now familiar mouth-brow-mouth gesture—and he returned the smiles and nodded his head in greeting.

"Your people are very friendly," he said. Cielema frowned thoughtfully.

"Not always," she told him. "As a rule, we like to keep to ourselves. But everyone is happy when someone is saved from the savage Skylord." She gestured upward and he realized that she meant the sun. He guessed it was a constant enemy and threat to these people.

They were close to the center of the camp now and he could see a group of half a dozen men sitting around in a circle. All of them wore yellow and white checked keffiyehs—like the one he had noticed on his rescuer. Cielema stopped him with a gentle pressure on his arm.

"We must wait," she said. "They are involved in important business."

Her tone was serious, almost reverential. The two of them stopped, some five meters from the group of men. They were all leaning forward, staring intently at an upright rock placed in the middle of the circle. Will thought they must be praying, although no words were being said.

Then, as one, they all slumped back with a roar of disappointment.

"It flew away!" said one figure, and Will recognized the voice. It was the man who had rescued him. "Almost to the top and it flew away!"

He looked questioningly to Cielema and she rolled her eyes at him. "Grown men gambling on two flies crawling up a stone."

"Gambling?" he said. "I thought they were praying."

She raised an eyebrow. "To them, it's much the same thing. The Bedullin will bet on just about anything. It's almost a religion." She urged him closer as the circle began to break up and most of the men moved away. "Aseikh Umar!" she called. "Your visitor has woken."

Her husband stood and turned to them with a wide smile. Will recognized the powerful face and the big, crooked nose. Umar stepped toward him, both hands out. He went to seize Will's forearms in greeting but his wife hissed warningly.

"Careful, buffoon! His arms are burned!"

Realizing his mistake, the Aseikh held both hands in the air in a kind of blessing gesture instead. "Of course! Of course! Please, come and sit. Tell me your name. I am . . ."

"He knows who you are. You are the great fly-gambling Umar. His name is Will."

Umar grinned easily at his wife. Will had the impression that this sort of byplay went on between the two of them all the time. Then he looked back at Will.

"It's good to see you awake. You were nearly finished when we found you! Come and sit and tell me what you were doing." He looked at Cielema. "Beloved wife, will you bring us coffee?"

Cielema raised an eyebrow and looked inquiringly at Will. "Would you like coffee, Will?"

His mouth watered at the thought of it, a sure sign he was recovering quickly. "I'd love coffee," he said.

She made a graceful bow. "In that case, I will bring some."

She swept away, her head held high. Umar grinned after her. Then he turned his attention back to Will and ushered him to the circle of cushions.

"So, your name is Will," he said as they sat cross-legged.

"It is." Will paused, then added, "I want to thank you for saving my life, Aseikh Umar."

The Bedullin waved his thanks away. "It was the horse you were riding that saved your life. And he did so twice."

"Arrow!" said Will, remembering. He hadn't seen Arrow since he'd been rescued. "Where is he? What did he do?"

Umar's smile disappeared. "He's dead, Will. A lion took him during the night. That was the first time he saved you. The lion took him, and not you. We saw its tracks and it passed within two or three meters of where you lay. The horse was obviously moving and making noise so that the lion never noticed you."

"Dead," Will said, saddened. Arrow had been a good horse. Umar nodded sympathetically. He admired a man who cared for his horse.

"He saved your life a second time the following morning," he said. "The vultures gathered to feast on him and we saw them. I came to investigate and . . . there you were." He smiled, back on a more cheerful topic.

Will shook his head gratefully. "Once again, you have my gratitude," he said.

As before, Umar dismissed his thanks. "It's what we do in the desert. In fact, it's considered good luck to save a fellow traveler in trouble." Then his face quickened with interest. "We have your weapons!" he said. He turned and called to a low, wide-spreading tent a few meters away. "Ahmood! Bring the foreigner's weapons!"

A teenage boy emerged from the tent a few seconds later. Grinning, he deposited Will's knives, in their double scabbard, and his bow and quiver. He also set down the folded chart and the northseeker in its leather case. Will stood and buckled on the double scabbard. He felt a sense of completeness. No Ranger was ever totally comfortable without his weapons. Umar watched him carefully, then picked up the unstrung bow.

"I've never seen one like this before," he said. "It must be powerful."

"It is," Will said. Quickly, he settled the bow in front of his left ankle and behind his right calf. Using his back muscles, he bent the bow and slid the string up into the notch at the end. He handed it to Umar, who tested the draw weight, grimaced slightly, then returned the weapon to Will.

"Show me," he said, handing Will an arrow from the quiver.

Will nocked the arrow and looked around for a suitable mark. He noticed a group of boys fifty meters away, playing a game with a small leather ball. They used their feet, heads and bodies to keep it in the air, passing it between them without letting it touch the ground. He started to look for a safer area to demonstrate, then glanced back as something caught his eye. The smallest boy, no more than eight years old, had lost control of the ball, sending it bouncing and rolling until it ended under a flat rock. Laughing, he ran after it and dropped to his hands and knees, reaching for it.

Will drew, aimed and fired in the space of a heartbeat. His arrow flashed across the oasis, missing the boy's reaching hand by centimeters, and ended, quivering, embedded under the rock. The boy recoiled, screaming in terror. His companions echoed his cries, turning to see where the arrow had come from.

A massive fist struck Will backhanded across the jaw. He staggered and fell, the bow dropping from his hands. Umar's face was contorted in rage.

"You reckless fool! Do you think you'll impress me by risking the life of my grandchild? You could have killed him!"

His hand dropped to the massive hilt of a heavy dagger in his belt. Will, stunned by the blow, tried to regain his feet but a savage kick from Umar winded him and sent him sprawling again. In the distance, Will could hear the child, still crying in fright, and a jumble of voices calling out—shouting in surprise and anger and fear.

He heard the faint metallic *shring!* of the dagger being drawn from its scabbard. Then Cielema's voice, shrill and urgent, was carrying above the others.

"Umar, stop! Look at this!"

Umar turned away from the prone figure before him. His wife had been returning with the coffee when she had passed by their grandson and witnessed the incident. Now she was on her knees, reaching for something under the rock. With an effort, she tugged Will's arrow free. With it, held firmly by the barbed broadhead, was the meter-long body of the sand cobra he had shot. The arrow had passed cleanly through the snake's head, killing it instantly.

A second before it could strike at the boy.

The dagger dropped from Umar's hand as he realized what had happened, what he had done. Aghast, he stooped to help Will to his feet.

"Forgive me! I'm sorry! I thought . . ."

Will was still gasping for breath when Cielema reached them, brandishing the dead snake impaled on the arrow.

"What are you doing, you fool?" she demanded. "The boy saved Faisal!"

Umar had hauled Will to his feet and begun to feverishly brush him down, a stricken look in his eyes. He had been about to kill the young man who had undoubtedly saved his grandson's life.

"Forgive me!" he said frantically. But Cielema brushed past him, shoving him away from the young foreigner.

"Get away!" she said roughly. She dropped the dead snake, took Will's jaw in her hands and gently worked it from side to side, her head cocked to listen. "Are you all right?" she asked him. He tried a weak grin, then wished he hadn't when it hurt his jaw.

"Bit swollen," he said thickly. "Bu' I'm all ri'."

She moved quickly to where a jar of water stood outside the large tent nearby. Dipping the end of her scarf in it, she came back and pressed the cool wet cloth against his jaw. Umar tried once more to placate her.

"I'm sorry!" he said. "I thought that . . ." He got no further. She rounded on him savagely.

"You thought? When did you ever think? You were ready to kill the boy! I saw you with that knife of yours!"

Will took her hands and removed the wet cloth from his face. He worked his jaw a little, making sure nothing was broken.

"It's all right," he told her. "No harm done. I'm a little bruised. It was just a misunderstanding."

"Exactly!" Umar told her. "A misunderstanding." Cielema looked at him savagely.

"He saved Faisal's life," she said. "And what did you do?"

Umar went to reply, realized there was nothing he could say that would placate his furious wife, and he dropped his hands helplessly.

It certainly had looked as if the stranger had shot close to his grandson in an arrogant and reckless display of his marksmanship, which was undoubtedly of the highest possible order. He had never seen anyone shoot like that. He looked again at his wife, saw the anger in her eyes and the set of her body and knew that there was nothing he could say.

Will stepped into the awkward silence. "He saved my life, remember?" He grinned a little lopsidedly at the Aseikh. "I'd say that makes us even." He held out his hand to the Bedullin, who took it gratefully, and gripped it.

"You see?" he said to his wife. "There are no hard feelings. It was a mistake!"

Seeing Will's reaction, and his disinclination to hold any sort of grudge, Cielema relaxed a little. She even allowed herself a small, tight smile at the two men as they continued shaking hands.

"Very well," she said. Then, to Will, "But you must tell us anything we can do for you."

He shrugged. "You've already done more than enough. Just give me a day or two to rest and regain my strength; give me food, water and my horse. Then give me directions for Mararoc and I won't bother you anymore."

But the Aseikh was frowning at his words. "Your horse?" he said. "Your horse died. I told you. A lion took it."

Will shook his head, smiling. "Not that horse. Tug. The little shaggy gray that was with you when you found me. He's my horse."

Now it was the Aseikh's turn to shake his head. He was reluctant to cause any disappointment to the stranger. But he had to face facts.

"He's not your horse," he said. "He's ours."

30

Now that they had decided on taking the more direct route to the Khor-Abash Wells, there seemed to be no point in having Gilan, Halt and Selethen ride ahead.

Before dawn the following morning, the entire party broke camp and set out together. Initially, Selethen led them on a long swing due west, before angling back to a northwest course—the base course that the Tualaghi had been following. This gave them enough clearance so that they would avoid running into the Tualaghi war party on one of their westerly zigzags.

With no need to follow the Tualaghi's tracks anymore, they were able to revert to their original travel pattern, riding in the cooler hours of darkness before dawn. In addition, they continued to move northwest after the sun had set, giving themselves an extra hour or two of travel each day. In this way, they were able to gain considerable ground on the enemy. As they camped in the darkness on the second day of direct travel, one of Selethen's scouts rode into camp and reported to his Wakir. Selethen listened, then approached the spot where the Araluen party were sitting, a satisfied smile on his face.

"We were right," he said. "My scout tells me that the Tualaghi force is following a course parallel to ours. They are camped for the night, approximately ten kilometers to the northeast." He glanced meaningfully at the small, semiconcealed cookfire that was all he had allowed for their party. Its light, he knew, would be barely visible from a distance of more than two kilometers. "Apparently, they're convinced that we have lost their trail. They're not worrying about concealing their fires."

Halt scratched his chin thoughtfully. "Of course, under normal circumstances, you would have given up and turned back long ago, wouldn't you?"

The Arridi leader nodded. "Exactly. It seems that our friends are becoming overconfident."

"And overconfidence," Halt added, "can be a dangerous thing." He turned to the younger Ranger, who was relaxing, the small of his back supported by his saddle, the ever-present coffee in his hands. "Gil," he said, "d'you think you're up to taking a look at their camp tonight?"

Gilan smiled and finished his coffee. "Thought you'd never ask," he said. He glanced up at the quarter moon, now low in the western sky. "Moon'll set in half an hour or so. Might as well get going now."

"According to Selethen's man, you should be able to see the loom of their fires from about four kilometers away. Leave Blaze there and go ahead on foot. Make sure you cover your tracks and . . ." Halt paused, aware that Gilan was watching him with a patient smile on his face. "Sorry," he said. If anyone knew how to go about a surveillance job like this, it was Gilan. "You know all this, right?" he added, a rueful smile on his face.

"Right," said Gilan. "But it never hurts to be reminded. Anything in particular you want me to look for?"

Halt thought, then shrugged. "The obvious. See if you can spot Erak. See how they have him guarded. If there's a chance we could break him out of their camp by stealth, I'd rather do that than fight a pitched battle. Numbers, of course. Let's find out how many of them there really are. And anything else you think might be of interest."

"Consider it done." Gilan had hoisted his saddle over one shoulder and was heading toward the spot where their horses were quartered for the night. Horace rose hastily, brushing sand from his knees.

"Hold up, Gilan. Want some company?" he asked.

Gilan hesitated. He didn't want to offend the young warrior.

"Might be better if he went alone, Horace," Halt cautioned. "He's trained to move silently and you're not."

Horace nodded. "I know that. But I can wait back where he leaves Blaze—keep an eye on things. Even I can't be heard from four kilometers away."

"That's debatable," Halt said, perfectly straight-faced. Then he looked at Gilan.

"But he does have a point. Might be a good idea to have some backup close by."

"Fine by me," Gilan said, relieved now that he knew there was no need to offend Horace. "I'll be glad of the company. Let's get saddled."

Horace reached down and seized his own saddle and, together, the two walked toward their horses.

"This is as far as you'd better go," Gilan told Horace. The younger man nodded and they both swung down to the ground. Horace tethered Kicker's reins to a thornbush. Gilan, in the way of Rangers, simply dropped his reins on the ground.

"Stay," he said to Blaze.

Gilan and Horace surveyed the skyline to the northeast.

"They're getting cocky, aren't they?" Horace said. Even at this distance, the glow of the Tualaghi campfires was clearly visible in the sky above the horizon.

"They are indeed," Gilan said. "Let that be a lesson to you. Never assume you've given someone the slip until you're absolutely sure of it."

He unslung his bow and quiver and laid them on the ground. He wouldn't be needing them on this mission and they'd just get in his way. Similarly, he unclipped his scabbarded sword from his belt. That left him with his saxe knife and throwing knife, which were weapons enough.

"Do you want me to loosen Blaze's saddle girth?" Horace asked, and Gilan answered without hesitation.

"No. Leave it as it is. Kicker's too. We may want to get out of here in a hurry if anything goes wrong."

Horace regarded him with some interest. He knew the young Ranger's reputation as one of the finest unseen movers in the Ranger Corps—perhaps the finest. It was said that Gilan could approach to within a few meters of a wide-awake sentry, steal his belt and shoes and leave the man wondering why his pants were falling down and his feet were cold. Horace knew it was an exaggeration—but not by much.

"Are you expecting something to go wrong?" he asked. Gilan looked at him seriously and laid one hand on his shoulder.

"Always expect something to go wrong," he told him. "Believe me, if you're wrong, you're not disappointed. If you're right, you're ready for it. See you in a couple of hours," he said, and melted away into the darkness.

Gilan moved quickly and silently over the rough ground. As he reached the crest of the first ridge between him and the Tualaghi camp, he glanced back once to where the tall figure and the two horses stood waiting. Then he dropped to the ground and rolled silently over the ridge and into the dark area below it, avoiding skylining himself to any possible observer. The only thing that such a person might have seen would have been a low, indeterminate shape that briefly broke the line of the horizon before disappearing.

Once he was safely below the ridge itself, Gilan resumed his feet and headed toward the fires.

The fact that he had such a clear-cut guide was a potential hazard, he knew. It would be too easy to simply continue toward the light of the fires, now becoming more and more visible over the horizon, without taking care that he himself wasn't seen. Overconfidence, as they had all observed, was a dangerous thing. So he proceeded as if there were a score of sentries just out of sight, all alert and all forewarned that someone might be trying to slip past them.

It took more time to do it that way. But he knew it might save his life in the end.

It was an hour later when he reached the Tualaghi camp. As before, he dropped to the ground before the crest of the final ridge, and inched forward, the cowl of his cloak pulled up to shade the white oval of his face.

As his eyes rose above the ridgeline, he whistled silently to himself. The camp was much bigger than he had expected. They had been following a party of around eighty men. There must have been more than two hundred in this camp, and twice as many fires as he had expected—another reason why the firelight had been so obvious.

Either they've rejoined a main party, he thought, or met up with another one.

It didn't really matter which, he realized. The fact was, there were nearly four times as many men as Selethen had. That meant a direct attack was virtually out of the question.

While he digested this fact, his eyes searched the camp for some sign of Erak. It didn't take long to find him. The Oberjarl's burly figure stood out among the slightly built desert nomads. As might be expected, he was in the center of the camp, where he would be hardest for a potential rescuer to reach. The Tualaghi had left their prisoner in the open air, while they spent the night in small, low tents, similar to the ones Selethen's Arridi troops used. Erak was left to make himself as comfortable as possible in the cold night air, with only a blanket for warmth. As Gilan watched, the big Skandian re-arranged himself on the stony ground and the chains securing him became more obvious. Gilan frowned, trying to see what Erak was attached to, then realized that he was chained to not one, but two camels that were lying nearby. He shook his head in frustration. Even after a brief time in Arrida, he had learned how stubborn the hump-backed beasts could be. Chaining Erak between two of them would make it virtually impossible for him to escape. And the bad-tempered animals would provide a noisy warning if anyone tried to tamper with his chains.

So, no direct assault and no way to creep in and release him, Gilan thought. This was getting trickier by the minute.

He had no idea what alerted him to the slight movement. He sensed it more than saw it—right out at the periphery of his vision. Something, or someone, had moved on the long ridge he was occu-pying. But whoever or whatever it might be was four or five hundred meters to the left of his position, where the ridge curved back to the right. He looked directly at the spot now and saw nothing in the uncertain night light. Then he looked to one side of the position, to allow his peripheral vision a chance to see if anything was there. This was an old trick for seeing movement in the dark. The peripheral vision was more reliable.

Now he was sure of it. Something moved. The movement was an abrupt one and that was what alerted him to it. A small shape had slipped back below the level of the ridge. He looked directly at the spot again but there was nothing to be seen. A sentry? He didn't think so. There was no reason for a sentry to behave in such a clandestine manner. And there was no sign of any other sentries this far out from the perimeter. That had been the first thing Gilan had checked when he made his approach. It made no sense for one sentry to be placed where he had seen the movement. Perhaps it had been a small nocturnal animal? It was possible, but he doubted it. Rangers were trained to listen to their instincts.

Gilan's told him that someone else had been observing the Tualaghi camp.

31

WILL FELT THE BLOOD RUSHING TO HIS FACE. "YOUR HORSE?" HE said, his voice a little shriller than he intended. "What are you talking about? You know he's mine."

Cielema was frowning at her husband. But the Aseikh made a helpless gesture with both hands.

"He was yours," he admitted. "But now he's ours. That's the way we do things."

"You steal horses?" Will accused him, and he saw the embarrassment on the other man's face change to anger at the words.

"I will ignore that insult because you're ignorant of the way we do things in the desert," he said. "Do not make the mistake of repeating it."

Cielema stepped toward her husband. "Surely, Umar, you could make an exception . . ." she began, but Umar stopped her with an upraised hand. He turned back to Will, seeing the anger seething in every inch of the slightly built youth's body.

"It's not up to me to make that exception." He turned to Will and continued. "You must understand our ways. You did own that horse originally. No one contests that."

"How could you?" Will said. "There was a spare arrow case on the saddle, carrying arrows identical to that one." He gestured to the arrow that had transfixed the sand cobra, which was still lying on the ground at their feet. It was a calculated move. Will wanted Umar to be reminded that he had just saved his grandson's life.

"Yes. We agree. And it was obvious when we found you that the horse knew you. But that's beside the point. You must have allowed him to escape."

Will was taken aback by the statement. He still blamed himself for letting go of Tug's bridle during the storm. "Well, yes . . . in a way, I suppose. But there was a sandstorm, and I couldn't . . ."

He got no further, as Umar seized the advantage. "And in our law, if you release a horse and it runs off, it is no longer your horse. Whoever finds it owns it. And Hassan ib'n Talouk found it. It was wandering, nearly dead of thirst. He rescued it and cared for it and now it is his horse."

Will shook his head. His voice was bitter. "I don't believe this. I nearly killed myself looking for Tug and you tell me this . . . Hassan ib'n Talouk . . . owns him now, because he found him?"

"That's exactly what I'm telling you," Umar said.

"Umar, we owe this young man," Cielema said, a pleading note in her voice. "Surely there is something you can do?"

Umar shook his head. "Yes, we owe him. And he owes us his life, if you recall. We are even on that score. He has said as much himself." Unhappy as he might be with the situation, Umar felt obliged to respect the laws of his tribe.

"No one else will ever be able to ride him!" Will shouted. Ranger horses were trained so that they could never be stolen by another rider. Before mounting for the first time, a rider had to speak a secret code phrase to the horse.

"Yes. We've noticed that. There is obviously some secret to riding that horse. Unfortunately that has intrigued Hassan even more. I doubt he will give him up."

"Then I'll buy him," Will said.

Umar raised an eyebrow. "With what? You had no money on you when we found you. Have you somehow obtained some in the last few hours?"

"I'll owe it to you. You have my word. I'll pay it. Name the price." He knew he could get Evanlyn to back his promise. But again, Umar was shaking his head.

"How will you pay us? How will you ever find us again? We're nomads. We don't deal in future promises. We deal in gold and silver and we deal in right now when we trade. Do you have gold or silver? No, you don't." He answered his own question with an air of finality. Then, his tone softened a little.

"Our laws say that when we find a man dying of thirst in the desert, we must do everything in our power to save him. We could have just ridden by and left you to die. But our law says otherwise. By the same token, another law says that a horse found wandering becomes the finder's property. You can't take advantage of one law and deny the other.

"It is Hassan's right to keep this horse. That is final."

"This is ridiculous, Umar!" Cielema said angrily. "You will tell Hassan that he must return the horse to Will. You are the Aseikh, after all!"

Umar's lips set in a tight line. "Don't you understand, wife, it is because I am Aseikh that I *can't* do this! If I order him to ignore our laws, how can I discipline anyone in the future who wants to do something similar?"

Cielema looked away angrily, and her tense stance and folded arms spoke volumes about the fury inside her. Will felt a mounting sense of hopelessness.

"May I speak to Hassan?" he asked, controlling the anger in his own voice, forcing himself to speak calmly. Umar considered the suggestion for a few seconds, then shrugged.

"There's no reason why not," he said. "But I warn you, it will do no good."

Hassan was a young man. He couldn't have been much more than twenty years old. He had a pleasant face and a rather wispy beard that he was obviously trying to grow. His eyes were dark and humorous and in other circumstances, Will would probably have liked him.

Right now, he hated him with every fiber of his body.

The young Bedullin was grooming Tug when they found him in the horse lines. Umar and Cielema had escorted Will and as they passed through the camp, word was spreading as to what was happening. Now a small crowd of onlookers followed behind them. It was noticeable that Will was now fully armed, with his saxe and throwing knife, and the massive longbow slung over his shoulder once more.

He heard one whispered comment from the people following behind him as he strode through the camp. "I've heard the foreigner wants to fight Hassan for the horse!" someone said. And the more he thought about it, the more Will found he wasn't opposed to the idea.

Tug nickered happily when he saw Will approaching. He had recognized the sound of his master's stride. Hassan looked up from his work and smiled a welcome. He made the Arridi greeting gesture to Umar.

"Good morning, Aseikh Umar." He looked at Will, saw the anger in the young man's face and wondered what was troubling him. "I see the stranger has recovered. That's good."

Tug tried to move toward his master but Hassan restrained him with a firm hand on his bridle. The little horse balked and looked puzzled. He whinnied shrilly. The sound tore at Will's heart.

"Hassan," Umar began, "this is Will. Will, meet Hassan ib'n Talouk."

Hassan made the polite greeting gesture again. Will responded with a stiff little bow. Once again, Hassan saw the anger and frowned.

"You seem to have recovered, Will," he said. "I'm glad to see it." He wondered what the foreigner was doing here. Hassan, after all, had not been responsible for finding him in the desert. He had only tagged along because the shaggy little horse that he had found some days previously had bolted after the Aseikh when he had ridden out to investigate the vultures. The horse must have caught some scent of his former owner, Hassan thought.

It was obvious that the horse had formerly belonged to the young man they found close to death in the desert. Yet Hassan saw no reason to consider returning the animal, who he had already renamed Last Light of Day, in memory of the time of day when he had found him. "Finders, Owners" was the law of the desert and Hassan and all the Bedullin had seen it exercised many times in the past. He had no reason to think that Will would dispute the fact.

He waited patiently now while the stranger worked to get control of his anger. Finally, Will said in a calm voice: "Hassan, I would like my horse back, please."

Hassan frowned. He looked to Umar for guidance but the Aseikh avoided his gaze. He smiled pleasantly at the stranger.

"But he's no longer your horse. He's mine." He looked to Umar again. "Have you not explained the law, Aseikh?"

Umar shifted uncomfortably. "I have. But the stranger is a foreigner. In his land, the law is different."

Hassan considered this information, then shrugged. "Then I'm glad we're not in his land, because I like this little horse." He hesitated, seeing the unhappy expression on Umar's face. Cielema was beside him, he noticed. She was very stiff-necked and angry-looking too.

"Aseikh Umar," he said, "do you wish me to return my horse to the stranger?"

Umar hesitated for a long moment. He knew that the young man held him in the highest regard. He idolized him, in fact. If Umar were to say that he did wish him to return the horse, Hassan would do so, out of respect for his Aseikh. And that was what stopped Umar from asking him to do so. He knew it would be using his influence unfairly. The horse was Hassan's, and Hassan was not from a wealthy family. It could be years before he could afford another horse.

"I won't ask you to do that," he said finally, folding his arms across his chest.

Hassan looked back to Will. "I'm sorry," he said. He turned away to continue with his grooming.

"I'll pay you for him," Will said abruptly.

Hassan stopped grooming and looked back at him. "You have gold?" he asked.

Will shook his head. "I'll get it. I give you my word."

Hassan smiled again. He was a polite young man and had no wish to be discourteous, but the stranger simply didn't understand how things were done.

"I can't buy anything with words," he said. He wished the stranger would stop being so pushy. But now that he was here, Hassan thought he might well find out something that had been bothering him about Last Light of Day.

"Can this horse be ridden?" he asked curiously. Every time he had tried to gain the saddle, the little gray had bucked him off. He was a mass of bruises.

Will nodded. "I can ride him."

Hassan led Tug forward and handed the bridle to Will. He wanted to see if it were possible.

"Show me," he said. He watched as Will put a foot in the stirrup and swung easily into the saddle. Hassan waited a few seconds. Usually, about now, the little horse would explode into a leaping, twisting, bucking devil. But he stood calmly, ears pricked.

Sitting astride Tug, Will had a momentary urge to set him to a gallop and simply ride off. As if sensing it, the Bedullin tribesmen tightened the circle around him and the moment was lost. Besides, he thought, he had no idea where he was, no chart and his north-seeker was back by Umar's tent. Umar made an unmistakable gesture with his thumb and Will reluctantly dismounted. He put the bridle back into Hassan's waiting hand.

"So there is a secret to riding him," Hassan said. "You will have to tell me."

He smiled, wishing the stranger would simply accept the inevitable. But he saw the refusal in the younger man's angry expression.

"You'll never ride him," Will said.

Hassan shrugged. He looked inquiringly to Umar, wishing he would step in and end this unpleasantness.

"I'll find a way," he said confidently.

"If you won't let me pay you for him, I'll fight you for him," Will said tersely. Hassan actually stepped back a pace, appalled at the lack of courtesy and basic good manners. This time Umar did step in, as a buzz ran around the watching crowd.

"There'll be no fighting!" he snapped. He glared at Will. "What did you have in mind—to stand off fifty paces and kill him with that bow of yours before he comes in reach? That's not fighting. That's murder!"

Will dropped his eyes. Umar was right. But he was torn with anxiety over the loss of his horse. To find him again and then lose him like this was unbearable. Something Cielema had said was moving around in his mind, just out of reach of conscious thought. There was a way, he thought, if he could only . . .

"Besides, if I can't ride him, I'll use him as a pack pony. He's sturdy enough," Hassan was saying.

That was the final straw. The idea that Tug, his intelligent, affectionate, wonderful Tug, would see out his days as a beast of burden was too much for Will to bear. Then Cielema's earlier statement came into clear focus and he knew there was one desperate way out of this.

"I'll race you for him," he challenged. "I'll race Tug against the best horse and rider you have in the camp."

Now there was a definite buzz of interest among the crowd. Umar's head snapped up at the challenge. As his wife had said, no Bedullin man could resist a wager.

"What terms?" Umar asked. Will thought quickly, then took a deep breath and committed himself.

"If I win, I get Tug back. If your man wins, I'll tell Hassan the secret to riding him. And I'll give up all claim to him."

Umar looked around the watching circle of faces. He could see a light of interest and expectation in every eye. This was the sort of challenge that set Bedullin blood racing. Already, side wagers were being negotiated among the onlookers. He looked back at Will, saw the defiant look on the young man's face as he staked everything on one throw of the dice.

"Hassan?" Umar asked, and the young Bedullin nodded eagerly.

"As long as I'm the rider," he said. "And you let me ride your horse Sandstorm."

Umar nodded. Hassan was a brilliant rider and Umar's palomino stallion Sandstorm was far and away the best horse in the tribe.

"Done," he said.

32

"You never saw who it was?" Halt asked as Gilan made his report. The young Ranger shook his head.

"It may not have been a person at all. It could have been a small animal."

"But you don't think so?" Halt asked. This time Gilan hesitated before he answered.

"No, I don't," he said finally. "I would have gone closer to examine the ground but I didn't know if he'd gone or was still in the area—or if he had friends with him. If some kind of ruckus had started, it would have given away everything to the Tualaghi. I thought it was better to come back here and report."

"Yes. Yes, you were right," Halt said, frowning over the news. He looked at Selethen. "Any idea who might be keeping an eye on the Tualaghi?" he asked.

The Wakir shrugged. He'd been considering the question since Gilan had first reported.

"There could be a Bedullin party somewhere in the area. They come and go as they please. If so, it would make sense for them to keep an eye on the enemy."

"Would they be likely to attack them?" Halt asked. This time the Wakir was more definite in his answer.

"I wouldn't think so. They don't usually go looking for trouble and a party of two hundred Tualaghi is a lot to take on."

"I was thinking the same thing myself," Halt said.

Selethen nodded gravely. "Quite so. But if it was Bedullin watching, odds are they would simply move away and give the Tualaghi as wide a berth as possible."

"Do you think he saw you?" Halt asked Gilan.

Gilan shook his head. "No. I only saw him because he moved suddenly."

There was no need for Halt to ask Gilan if he'd moved. He knew his former student would never make such a fundamental mistake.

"You covered your tracks coming back, of course?"

"Of course," Gilan replied. "Don't worry, Halt, I left no sign that I'd been there."

Halt came to a decision. "All right. We can catch a few hours' sleep. We'll push on as usual when it gets a little closer to dawn. See if you can get some rest, people."

Selethen and the Araluens turned and headed for their respective tents. They all knew the value of getting as much rest as the situation allowed.

Unfortunately, while Gilan had left no tracks, the unknown observer had not been so careful, or so skilled. And by the worst possible chance, the path he took when he left the Tualaghi campsite led within a quarter kilometer of the camp where the Rangers and Arridi troops had spent the night.

An hour after Selethen had led the party on their way, Tualaghi scouts, following the tracks discovered near their camp, chanced across those left by the mixed Araluen–Arridi group. They followed them carefully until the Arridi troops came into sight. Then, taking a wide curve to keep from being seen themselves, they hurried back to their own leaders to report that an armed party was traveling on a parallel course to their own.

After a quick consultation, half of the Tualaghi split off and dropped back behind the others, then traveled southwest until they too cut across the trail of Selethen's troops.

They picked up the pace at that point and began moving closer to the unsuspecting travelers. Halt and Gilan, expecting that if any trouble came it would be from the northeast, had no idea that one hundred mounted warriors were closing in on them from the south. Nor were they aware that the lead party of Tualaghi had begun to move faster, and to angle slowly across their path.

The hunters had become the hunted.

They stopped in the middle of the day, as was their custom. It was this pause that gave the Tualaghi leaders their final opportunity to spring the trap they had spent the day preparing.

After the main heat of the day had passed, and before they continued on their way, the Araluens were discussing ideas for a possible rescue operation. Under cover of darkness, either of the two Rangers would be able to make his way into the camp unseen by the Tualaghi. The problem arose when it came to getting Erak out unseen.

"That's why they keep him in the center out in the open, of course," Evanlyn said. "If he tries to escape, he's bound to be seen by someone."

"Plus, you'll need a way to cut him loose from those camels," Horace put in.

"Maybe only one," Svengal suggested. "If you could cut the chains to one, he could ride the other one out of the camp."

"That might be just a little obvious," Gilan said. "The combination of a Skandian and a camel isn't exactly hard to notice—and the last thing we want is a running fight with two hundred Tualaghi."

Halt sat to one side, quietly listening as his friends put up suggestions then rejected them. Most of these thoughts he'd already examined. But there was always the chance that a stray remark might trigger the eventual solution to their problem. Not so far, however. For the moment, the best they could hope to do was continue as they were. If they could reach the wells before the Tualaghi, they might be able to arrange something—exactly what, he had no idea. But experience had taught him that if you waited long enough, sooner or later an unexpected opportunity might arise.

"You're quiet, Halt," Horace said, turning to where the gray-bearded Ranger sat. "Do you have any . . . ?" His voice trailed away to silence as his eyes lifted from Halt to the ridge behind him, some hundred and fifty meters away.

"Good God," he said, in a more urgent tone of voice, "where did they come from?"

The others followed his gaze. They had camped in a large, saucer-shaped depression, concealed from the sight of any Tualaghi stragglers. But the problem with concealing yourself from sight is that others can be concealed as well. Selethen had pickets out, of course, beyond the ridgeline. But later, they would see the bodies of those men lying where the Tualaghi skirmishers had killed them.

For the moment, their attention was fixed upon the line of armed horsemen that had just materialized over the ridge, spreading out in a semicircle across their intended line of march.

Halt swore softly and turned quickly to look behind them. As he had feared, another line of horsemen stood at the top of that ridge. They were trapped between the two parties—each of which was at least one hundred strong. By now, others had seen the enemy as well and the Arridi troops were running and shouting, pointing to the two lines of horsemen who had them trapped. Selethen's voice rose above the others and the moment of panic passed as he began to form his men into a defensive circle, with their horses inside it. The four Araluens and Svengal quickly gathered their weapons and moved to join the Arridi leader.

Selethen cursed bitterly. Only the night before, he had boasted about the Tualaghi's overconfidence—now he had fallen into the same trap. The desert raiders were wily and unpredictable. He should have assumed that they might get wind of the fact that someone was trailing them. A good leader should always plan for the worst.

As Halt and the others joined him, he nodded briefly. There was no point in recriminations, he knew. Now all they could do was create the best defense possible.

"You'll fight them on foot?" Halt asked.

The Arridi nodded. "No point in mounting and trying to charge them. We're too badly outnumbered."

"And you'd be charging uphill," Horace remarked. "All the advantage would lie with them. Let them come to us."

Selethen looked at him, a little surprised. For one so young, Horace had sized up the tactical situation quickly. Most of Selethen's young troopers would have chosen to charge the enemy, he knew. Horace unsheathed his sword now, the blade hissing out of the scabbard.

Svengal was looking around the ring of Arridi warriors. They had their shields locked together and each man was armed with one of the slender lances they usually used from horseback. In addition, each one wore a curved saber for close quarters work.

"Shield wall," he said approvingly. "Good work."

It was a standard Skandian battle tactic and he felt instantly at home. He swung his massive battleax experimentally, the huge, heavy blade making a thick swooshing sound as it passed through the air. For now, he'd stand back. But the minute a gap appeared in the wall, he'd fill it. Any Tualaghi warrior planning on breaking through would have an ugly surprise waiting for him.

Horace looked at him and read his thoughts. "I'll join you," he said quietly, moving to stand shoulder to shoulder with the bearlike northerner. Svengal grinned at him.

"With us two, we could probably send the rest of these boys home," he said.

Gilan and Halt also stood side by side, but in the center of the ring formed by the shield wall. Evanlyn looked at them, her heart thudding nervously in her chest. They all seemed so calm. She was sure her hands were trembling. For a moment, she thought of getting her sling from where it was concealed, but she realized that the two Rangers' longbows would provide more than adequate long-distance firepower. Instead, she accepted a spare shield from Selethen and eased her saber in and out of its scabbard. No need to draw it yet, she thought. She swallowed nervously.

Halt saw her and called softly.

"Evanlyn, come here with us." As she moved to stand beside the Rangers, he gestured to the ridge at their back. "Gilan and I are going to concentrate on the front at first. Keep an eye on the Tualaghi behind us. When they're within fifty meters, let us know and we'll switch."

"Yes, Halt," she said. Her mouth was dry and she didn't trust herself to say more.

Gilan grinned at her. "Make sure we hear you," he said. "There'll be plenty of yelling going on."

He was so relaxed and unworried, she thought. His casual manner helped to ease the butterflies that were swarming in her stomach.

Selethen approached them now. "They'll try the easy way first," he said. "An all-out charge to see if they can break our position."

"Might not turn out to be as easy as they think," Gilan replied, testing the draw on his bow. Selethen regarded him for a moment. Soon, he thought, he would see just how well these two cloaked foreigners could shoot. He had the feeling that he wasn't going to be disappointed.

"Can I suggest you put four of your men with Svengal and Horace?" Halt said. "Use them as a mobile reserve for any place the line is broken."

"Good idea," Selethen replied. He called four names, issued a rapid order, and the men selected dropped out of the shield wall to stand behind Horace and Svengal.

"Good to see you," said the Skandian. "Now give me some elbow room."

They heard the jingle of harnesses as the two lines of riders began to move forward.

"Here they come," Horace said quietly.

33

"THIS IS WHERE WE TURN TO HEAD BACK," WILL TOLD TUG. A tall pole had been hammered into the ground to mark the spot. The little horse studied the marker with interest.

Will turned and looked back toward the oasis. It was now out of sight, hidden by the undulating ground, but he knew it was four kilometers distant. Four kilometers out, four back. Eight in all. He had tried for twelve, then ten. Finally, he had to settle for an eight-kilometer racecourse. He hoped it would be far enough for Tug's stamina and staying power to assert itself over Sandstorm. It would be a close thing, he knew.

The Arridi horse was definitely faster over a short distance. For the first kilometer or two, he would leave Tug behind. But then the Ranger horse would start to reel him in as the Arridi stallion began to slow and Tug maintained his speed.

"We'll win it on the back leg," Will told Tug. He had decided to walk the horse over the course to familiarize him with it, and to give them both a chance to spot any hidden holes or unevenness that might bring them down.

Tug shook his head and whinnied softly. At times like this, Will was never totally sure that the horse was just responding to the sound of his master's voice. He knew better, of course, yet it often seemed that Tug understood every word Will said to him and was agreeing or disagreeing.

Or we'll lose it on the back leg, Will thought. He hoped that the second four kilometers would be enough to let Tug make up the distance he'd lose in the first half of the race. If he could, and they drew level with the Arridi horse and rider, another contest would begin.

Horses like Tug and Sandstorm hated to lose, hated to have another horse ahead of them. As Tug drew alongside Sandstorm, the Arridi horse would dig deep for a greater effort. Tug, meanwhile, would be straining for extra speed to pass the Arridi horse. It would then be a matter of judgment for the two riders, to pick the point where they should let the horses have their heads.

Too soon and the energy and speed would peter out before the finish line. Too late and there wouldn't be time to overtake. Each rider would do his best to force his opponent into going too early. The moment had to be just right or the result would be failure.

Will watched as Hassan put Sandstorm through his paces. He was sure the Arridi rider was holding something back.

They walked slowly back into the oasis. Unlike Hassan, Will had no need to familiarize himself with his mount's little peculiarities. He and Tug knew each other's ways back to front and inside out. A curious crowd of Bedullin watched them as they entered the camp. It was early morning and the race was set for late that same afternoon, when the full heat of day had passed.

He knew that there had been a lot of betting on the race. It was impossible not to hear conversations in the camp, even though he tried to appear aloof to such matters. He also knew that most of the betting wasn't about the actual outcome of the race. It was about the margin by which Sandstorm would win. The Bedullin were familiar with the beautifully formed Arridi stallion that Hassan would be riding. It seemed that none of them gave the shaggy little barrel-shaped horse from the north any chance of winning.

Even though Will had the utmost faith in Tug, faced with such universal disbelief, he found it hard to keep his spirits up. Yet he had to believe they could win—that they *would* win. The prospect of losing was just too awful to contemplate. He had been too impulsive, he thought, when he agreed to risk losing Tug in such a way. Yet time and again throughout the day, when he racked his brains to think of what else he could have done, he came up with no answer. If he were to get Tug back, he would have to risk losing him.

The thought tortured him through the long, heavy hours of the middle of the day. Then, as the sun began to slant down, and the shadows of the palms stretched out farther and farther, it was time.

Will led Tug through the oasis to the start line. Hassan was waiting, mounted on the beautiful palomino, by the line that had been gouged in the sand. Like Will, who had discarded his cloak for the race, he wore shirt, trousers and boots, and a keffiyeh. The headgear would protect the riders' faces from flying sand and dust during the race. He nodded a greeting as Will and Tug moved toward the starting line. Will nodded back. He didn't speak. He couldn't bring himself to wish Hassan good luck. He didn't want Hassan to have anything but bad luck. If Hassan managed to fall off Sandstorm in the first fifty meters and break a leg, Will wouldn't mind in the slightest. Yet looking at the Bedullin youth's easy seat on the horse, as Sandstorm moved nervously, prancing slightly, ears pricked with eagerness for the coming contest, it didn't seem likely. Hassan seemed glued to the saddle, an integral part of the horse.

Will put his foot in the stirrup and swung up astride Tug.

"This is it, boy," he whispered. The horse tossed his head. Will drew one end of the keffiyeh across his face, and twisted the other end over it to hold it in place. Now only his eyes showed, through a narrow slit. The rest of his face was covered. Beside him, Hassan did the same.

Sandstorm pawed the ground eagerly, kicking up small clouds of dust. Beside him, Tug stood stolidly, all four feet planted firmly. The difference between the two horses was all too obvious: one prancing, eager and light-footed, his coat groomed till he gleamed; the other solid, barrel-chested and shaggy. More money changed hands as last-minute bets were made.

"Riders, are you ready?" Umar stepped forward as he called them.

Hassan waved one arm. "Ready, Aseikh!" he called. The Bedullin cheered and he waved to the watching crowd.

"Ready," Will said. His voice was muffled behind the keffiyeh and he had to force the word out through a throat constricted by anxiety. There was no cheer this time. As far as he knew, nobody had bet on him to win—only the distance by which he'd lose.

And that was hardly something they were going to cheer about.

"Move to the line. But remember, if you cross it before the start signal, you will have to turn and go back to cross it again."

Hassan edged Sandstorm forward, crabbing him sideways. This was a tricky moment for him. With the horse prancing and excited, he had to hold back a meter or two from the line to make sure he didn't cross prematurely. Will nudged Tug and the little horse moved quietly to the line.

"Hold there, boy," Will said quietly. Tug's ears twitched in response and he stopped, his forehooves only centimeters from the line. One of the Bedullin, who had been assigned the task of monitoring the start line, crouched and peered closely at the horse's hooves, then straightened as he realized Tug wasn't infringing. But he kept his eyes riveted on the line and Tug's feet. Seeing it, Will touched Tug with one toe.

"Back up, boy," he said. He wasn't willing to take the risk that the judge might be overeager to penalize him. Tug obediently retreated one pace.

"There will be no interference between the riders. If either of you interferes with the other, he will automatically lose."

The two riders, now intent on the course that stretched out before them through the desert, nodded their acknowledgment. There were marshals stationed along the course to make sure neither of them cheated.

"Ride straight to the marker, around it, and ride back again. The start line is also the finish line," Umar said. Neither rider nodded this time. They knew the course. Both had been over it during the day.

"The starting signal will be a blast on Tariq's horn. The minute you hear it, you may start."

Tariq, an elder of the tribe, stepped forward with a large brass horn. He brandished it so they could both see it. Earlier in the day, Will had been made familiar with the note of the horn.

"In your hands, Tariq, and in God's will," Umar intoned. It was the official notice that the next sound to be heard would be the starter's horn. An expectant silence fell over the crowd. Somewhere, a child started to ask a question. Umar looked around angrily and the mother quickly silenced her offspring. Umar gestured to Tariq and the older man raised the large, bell-mouthed horn to his lips.

Will watched him intensely. He saw the Bedullin's chest swell as he took a deep breath. Beside him and slightly behind him, he knew, Hassan would be watching like a hawk.

He tightened his grip on the reins, forced himself to relax his legs around Tug's body. He didn't want to send any inadvertent signal to the horse before it was time.

Now!

The horn brayed its metallic baritone note and Will squeezed Tug with his knees. Hassan yelled as he urged Sandstorm forward. The crowd roared with one huge voice. Then the sound cut off in shock.

Tug shot away from his stiff-legged stance like an arrow, going from stock-still to full gallop in the space of a few meters. Sandstorm, excited and prancing, was left behind, curvetting and tossing his head for the first few paces. Then Hassan clapped his heels into the palomino's sides and he stretched out in a gallop after Tug.

The crowd, silenced momentarily by Tug's incredible accelera- tion from a standing start, began yelling again, screaming for Hassan and Sandstorm to run him down.

Even Will, who was aware of Tug's phenomenal ability to accel- erate, was a little surprised at the lead they had established. Yet he knew that Sandstorm would overhaul them once he hit his stride. But Will hoped the shock of being left behind at the start would force Hassan to overstretch his mount, using up some of the pre- cious energy reserves that would become so important in the last few kilometers.

Behind him, the sound of the yelling tribesmen began to dim. Closer to, he heard the rolling thunder of Sandstorm's hooves on the rocky ground. Tug's ears were up and his legs were churning, throw- ing a plume of sand and dust into the air behind them.

Will touched his neck.

"Take it easy, boy. Pace yourself."

Tug's head tossed fractionally in response. Will felt him ease a little and nodded. Sandstorm's hooves were closer behind him now. The Arridi horse was as fast as lightning, he thought.

Hassan, now a few meters behind them, was worried. He had no idea how fast the foreign horse would be. The horse's lines and configuration gave no hint of his startling off-the-mark speed. And even now that Sandstorm was gaining, he was doing so much more slowly than Hassan would have liked. He urged the horse to give a little more and heaved a sigh of relief as he began to draw alongside the foreigner and the shaggy little gray. The other rider didn't turn his head to look at them, but Hassan saw the horse's eye rolling to view them as they came alongside.

Fast horses hate being led in a race. And this was definitely a fast horse—not as fast as Sandstorm but faster than he had expected. In Hassan's experience, once a horse found itself overtaken and led by another, it would often give in—or overextend itself, trying desperately to regain the lead. Hassan knew it was time to establish his horse's superiority. He flicked the reins against Sandstorm's neck and the palomino found another few meters of speed. He surged forward, away from Tug.

Will felt Tug begin to respond and for the first time he could remember, he checked him firmly with the rein. Tug snorted angrily. He wanted to show this flashy Arridi horse what racing was all about. But he obeyed Will's touch, and denied his own instinctive urge to go all out.

"Not yet, boy," he heard Will say. "Long way to go."

They flashed past the two-kilometer mark, hearing the cheers of the marshals stationed there as they went. The cheers were all for Sandstorm, who was now leading Tug by nearly forty meters. The Arridi horse ran beautifully, Will thought grimly, with a long, powerful stride and perfect rhythm. Forty meters was far enough, he thought. He signaled Tug to increase his pace a little and Tug responded. Will felt a surge of affection for the horse under him. Tug would keep running like this all day, he knew. He wondered if Sandstorm could do the same.

Will had gained five to ten meters when Hassan and Sandstorm rounded the halfway marker. Comfortably in the lead, Hassan had eased his horse's pace a little, knowing that his best turn of speed was behind them now.

He waved as they passed the other rider and horse. There was no response from Will, and Hassan grinned behind his keffiyeh. He wouldn't wave if he were losing, either, he thought.

Around the halfway marker, Tug's hooves clattered on the stony ground, skidding slightly as they turned and set out after Sandstorm. Maybe less than thirty meters separated them now.

"Go now, Tug!" Will yelled, and the horse dug deep into his reserves of strength and endurance and courage and accelerated under him. Will could see Sandstorm through the cloud of dust and sand he was kicking up—appropriate name, he thought grimly. The palomino's flanks were streaked with sweat and his sides heaving with exertion. Slowly, Tug narrowed the gap to the Arridi horse. With two kilometers to go, he moved alongside, the two horses plunging side by side, each head alternately taking the lead, losing it, taking it again as they raced stride for stride, neither able to pull away from the other.

There would be a moment, Will knew, when it was time for the final sprint. Both horses and both riders were aware of it. It was a matter of perfect timing. Too soon and the horse would be exhausted before the finish line. Too late and the race would be lost.

The horses, side by side, glared at each other, their eyes rolling in their heads, whites showing so each could view the enemy. Then Tug surged ahead and Will couldn't check him—to do so now would be to lose speed and Tug had cast the dice for them, sensing the moment. He moved a neck length, then a body length, ahead of Sandstorm, moving faster than Will could ever remember him doing. The drumming of the horses' hooves filled his consciousness. Then he heard Hassan yelling encouragement to Sandstorm and, turning his head slightly, he saw the Arridi horse begin to regain ground on them. Unbelievably, he was on the verge of overhauling Tug yet again.

Then Tug faltered.

It was the slightest break in rhythm and pace but Will felt it and knew it was all over. Sandstorm saw it too and lunged ahead of them, a meter . . . two . . . five . . . the clods of dirt and sand flew up in Will's face, stinging the small area of skin exposed around his eyes, forcing him to grit his eyes almost shut.

There were three hundred meters to go and Sandstorm was fifteen meters ahead of them. Tears blurred Will's vision as he realized he had lost the race—and his horse.

Sandstorm's pace had been too much. The early lead it had given him had been too great. He was twenty meters ahead of them.

And then he faltered.

Will saw the slight stagger in his step, the loss of rhythm, the slackening in the blinding speed. If only they'd waited. Tug had been too eager. But now the twenty-meter lead would be enough to carry the exhausted Sandstorm across the finish line ahead of his equally exhausted opponent.

He had barely completed the thought when he felt Tug accelerate beneath him.

All the power, all the certainty, all the balance was back in his stride as he went to another level of performance, a level Will had never seen before. Tug stretched out and reeled in Sandstorm as if the taller horse were standing still. An amazed Will crouched low over Tug's neck, little more than a passenger. He realized that he had never had any idea how fast Tug could run. It seemed there was no upper limit. Tug would simply run as fast as the situation demanded.

Tug had controlled the race, pretending to falter when he did to goad Sandstorm into a final spurt. The loss of stride and balance had been a feint and Sandstorm had swallowed the bait, accelerating away and exhausting his last reserves just thirty meters too soon. That was the gap between them when Tug rocketed over the finish line.

Will had dismounted and was hugging the little horse's neck when Sandstorm, now slowed to a canter, sweat-streaked and blowing, staggered wearily over the finish line. And now the Bedullin did cheer for the foreign horse. Because they loved good horses and they knew they had just seen one of the best. And besides, since none of the bets were predicated on Tug's winning, nobody had actually lost any money.

Umar took Sandstorm's rein when Hassan slid down from the saddle. Before the young man could speak, the Aseikh slapped him on the shoulder.

"You did your best," he said. "Good race."

Others were echoing the sentiment when Hassan pushed his way through the crowd to offer his hand to Will. He shook his head admiringly.

"I was never going to win, was I?" he asked. "You knew that."

Will, grinning widely, shook his hand. "Actually, I didn't know it," he said. He jerked his head at Tug. "He did."

34

HALT ESTIMATED THAT THERE WERE APPROXIMATELY THIRTY men riding down the slope toward them.

"They're coming this side too," Evanlyn said behind him. A quick glance over his shoulder showed a similar number of riders sweeping down behind them, fanning out to encircle the waiting Arridi troops. Halt faced front again. He and Gilan took a moment to read the approaching speed of the riders. Then they moved as one.

"Now," said Halt quietly, and they both drew and shot once, then twice, then three and four times, lowering the elevation each time to compensate for the rapidly reducing range. After four devastating two-arrow volleys, Evanlyn called out behind them:

"Fifty meters at the back!"

The two archers pivoted one hundred and eighty degrees and sent more arrows ripping into the charging Tualaghi behind them. Already, half a dozen riderless horses were running wildly with the group charging from the front, their riders lying in crumpled heaps in the sand behind them. Now another five joined them from the rear group before they drew so close to the shield wall that Halt and Gilan had to cease fire. Evanlyn marveled at the high-speed accuracy of the two Rangers. Eleven enemy troopers out of the fight in a mat-

ter of seconds! That was an attrition rate no commander could hope
to sustain for long.

Now it was the turn of the men waiting in the shield wall as the
riders crashed into it.

But few of the horses made direct, head-on contact. The bris-
tling fence of lances, their sharpened heads gleaming in the sun,
forced most of them to swerve aside at the last moment, in spite of
their riders' urging and whipping them to continue their headlong
charge. The riders rapidly lost momentum and found themselves at
a disadvantage as the Arridis' long lances thrust up at them. Most of
the riders dismounted, leaving their horses with comrades detailed
for the task, and joined the fight on foot. The battle became a heaving, shoving, hand-to-hand melee, with curved swords rising and
falling, hacking and stabbing along the line. Men cried out in pain on
both sides as they went down, then cried out again as comrades and
foes trod them down in their efforts to reach the enemy.

Horace scanned the shield wall, eyes slitted in concentration,
looking for the first weak spot where the Tualaghi might break
through. To the left front, an Arridi trooper slipped and was cut down
by one of the Tualaghi, who instantly moved into the gap in the line,
hacking wildly to left and right, widening the breach so that two of
his comrades forced their way in and the line began to bulge inward.

Horace drew in a breath and turned to the four troopers with
him. Before he could act, however, there was a bull-like roar from
beside him and Svengal went forward at the run, the huge ax whir-
ring in a circle above his head. Realizing he'd only get in the Skandian's
way if he joined him, Horace relaxed and gestured for the four men
to stand fast as well.

Svengal hit the Tualaghi who had broken through like a battering
ram. He smashed into them with his shield, and in spite of the pressure of the men behind them urging them forward, he hurled them

back, off balance and staggering. Then he began dropping them left and right with sweeping blows of his ax before they could recover.

Almost as soon as it had appeared, the breach in the wall was restored and the line closed up. Svengal returned to the point where Horace was waiting.

"Let me know anytime you need a hand," the young warrior said mildly. Svengal glared at him. There was a dangerous light in his eyes.

Then he was off again as the Tualaghi threatened to break through in another spot, slamming into them with shield and ax, forcing them back, trampling over one who had fallen under his charge. But this time, Horace had no time to watch. He was needed at another trouble spot and he led his four men in a wedge formation, running to the point where another group of Tualaghi had forced their way inside the wall. As Horace approached, one of them went down with an arrow in his chest. Then Horace and his men were on them, forcing them back.

There was no time for fancy swordsmanship. It was shove and cut and cut again and parry with the shield and hit and hit and hit! Horace rained blows down on the Tualaghi with bewildering speed and force, forcing them back in growing panic.

It was a panic that spread through the attackers, and they began to stream away from the shield wall—first in ones and twos, then in larger groups. They retrieved their horses, mounted and fled up the slope, pursued by triumphant jeers and catcalls from the defenders.

Gilan raised his bow and looked a question at Halt, who shook his head.

"Save your arrows," he said. "We'll need them later."

"Can't say I like the idea of shooting men in the back," Gilan agreed. He replaced the arrow in his quiver.

Selethen was approaching them. His white outer tunic was ripped and stained with blood and dirt. He was cleaning his sword blade as he came.

"That hurt them," he said. "You shot well," he added, nodding in acknowledgment to the two Rangers.

"I doubt they'll try another frontal attack," Halt said, and the Wakir nodded agreement. He gestured to the rim of the hill, where a group of three horsemen were watching, raining abuse on the retreating troops as they rode past them. At one stage, the tallest of the three leaned over in his saddle and struck at a retreating soldier with his riding whip.

"Unless I miss my guess, that's Yusal Makali up there. He's one of their more capable war leaders. He's cunning and cruel and he's no idiot. He's just seen what a frontal assault will cost him. Now we'll have to see what he tries next."

"It's cost us as well," Gilan said quietly, nodding to where the Arridi troops were tending to their wounded. There were too many of them for comfort. The Tualaghi may have lost men in the attack, but at least ten Arridi soldiers lay dead or wounded.

Svengal and Horace had moved to join them. Both were cleaning their weapons, as Selethen had done. Svengal's face was still red with battle rage.

"What are they waiting for?" he said, his voice louder than the occasion demanded. "Why don't they get on with it?"

Halt eyed him with concern. "Calm down, Svengal," he warned. He could see that the Skandian, frustrated by weeks of inaction, was close to the berserk rage that could strike a Skandian in the heat of battle. "Odds are they won't attack again. You cost them too many casualties. Good work, too, Horace," he added as an aside. He had seen the young man's devastating counterattack. Horace nodded. His sword was clean now and he resheathed it.

"What do you think they'll do next, Halt?" he asked.

Before he answered, the Ranger squinted up at the sun, now almost directly overhead and hammering down on them.

"I think they'll wait for heat and thirst to do their work for them," he said. "That's what I'd do in their place."

He was right. The rest of the day passed with no further attack from the Tualaghi. Instead, the Araluens and their Arridi comrades sweltered under the blasting heat of the sun.

Their water supplies were low. Expecting to reach the Khor-Abash Wells sometime that day, Selethen had relaxed his normally strict water discipline. Now he estimated that with strict rationing, they had water for two more days.

The Tualaghi, of course, could send riders for all the water they needed. All they had to do was keep watch over the little camp in the middle of the depression. Wary of the accuracy shown by the two bowmen, they kept below the ridge. But from time to time they could be seen briefly as the watch changed and sentries were relieved. Halt had no doubt that their low black tents were pitched just beyond the ridge.

As darkness fell, Selethen drew his men in, shortening the perimeter so that half his force could sleep. At least, that was the idea. An hour after nightfall, the quick, darting attacks began.

There were never more than a dozen Tualaghi involved. But they would rise shrieking from the desert, having crept within a stone's throw of the camp. They would dash in on the shield wall, killing a man here, losing one of their own there, then withdraw, carrying their wounded with them. They were nuisance attacks, pure and simple. But they kept the entire Arridi camp alert and watchful throughout the night, preventing them from resting.

Even though the attacks were feints, each one had to be countered, as Halt and the others never knew when a genuine attack in force might come.

The result was a nervous, sleepless night for the Arridi troops, punctuated by brief moments of violence and sudden terror.

In the light of dawn, Halt turned bleary, red-rimmed eyes to the ridgeline. He could see occasional movement there but nothing that presented him with a worthwhile target. The Arridi had lost four men in the first mass attack, and another two succumbed to their wounds overnight. There were several more wounded and most of these needed water—which was now in short supply. Selethen reluctantly told his medical orderlies to reduce the amount of water the wounded were receiving. It was a hard decision. Water was just about the only comfort they had out in the desert.

He was visiting the wounded when Halt called to him. A white flag was waving over the crest of the ridge.

"They want to parley," Halt said.

The tall rider Selethen had identified as Yusal Makali rode down the slope, accompanied by a rider carrying the white flag. Selethen, with Halt carrying a similar flag, stepped through the line of Arridi warriors and walked to meet them.

"Yusal knows I'll respect the flag of truce. Yet he'd ignore it in a moment if it suited him," Selethen said bitterly. "I wish I could ask you to simply shoot him as he rides in."

Halt shrugged. "We could do it, of course, but that wouldn't solve the problem that we're trapped and outnumbered. And we might not get another chance to negotiate."

They stopped half a dozen meters from the two mounted men. Yusal swung down from the saddle and advanced to meet them.

He was taller than the average Arridi or Tualaghi, Halt saw, standing a good head above Halt himself and some centimeters taller than Selethen. He wore white, flowing robes and a keffiyeh. White was a sensible color in the searing desert heat. But whereas Selethen's robes were all white, Yusal's were trimmed in dark blue. And while the Arridi would wind the ends of the headdress around his face for protection, the Tualaghi left his flowing free. But the lower half of his face was hidden behind a dark blue, masklike veil. Halt had heard the Arridi refer to their enemies as the "Blue-Veiled Riders, the Forgotten of God." Now he understood the reference.

Yusal's skin, what could be seen of it above the mask, was dark brown—burned by years of desert sun and wind. Although the mask covered his lower face, it was obvious that the nose was prominent. His eyes were deep-set and hooded under heavy brows and thick eyebrows. They were deep brown, almost black. They were the only feature Halt could make out, yet he knew he would recognize Yusal again if he saw him without the veil. The eyes were cold, black and pitiless. There was no trace of mercy or warmth in them. They were a killer's eyes.

"So, Wakir Seley el'then," Yusal said, "why are you following me?"

The voice was muffled slightly by the veil. But it was harsh and unfriendly, like the eyes. So much for pleasantries, Halt thought.

Selethen was equally to the point. "You killed twenty of my men when you wiped out the caravan. And you took a prisoner from us. We want him back."

Yusal shrugged. The movement was a contemptuous one. "Come and take him then," he challenged. There was a moment of silence. Then he added, "You're in a bad position, Seley el'then. You're surrounded. You're outnumbered and your water's running short."

The last statement was a guess, of course. Yusal had no idea how little water they had and Selethen wasn't about to inform him.

"We have plenty of water," he said evenly and, again, Yusal shrugged. Selethen's statements meant little to him.

"If you say so. The fact is, you will run out eventually, while I can send for all the water I need. I can afford to wait while thirst and heat start to kill your men. You can't."

He glanced back up the slope that surrounded them on all sides.

"You can attack us if you like. But it's uphill and we outnumber you four to one. There's only one way such an attack will end."

"We might surprise you," Halt said, and the dark, hooded eyes swung to him, studying him, boring into him. Halt realized the unwavering stare and the silence that accompanied it were intended to unnerve him. He raised one eyebrow in a bored fashion.

"You're one of the archers, aren't you?" Yusal said. "But in spite of your marksmanship, once the battle gets to close quarters, numbers will tell."

"You requested this parley, Yusal," Selethen said. "Was it merely to tell us how hopeless our position is? Or did you have something worthwhile to say?" He allowed the same tone of contempt that the Tualaghi had used to creep into his own words.

Yusal looked back at him.

"Surrender," he said simply, and Selethen responded with a short bark of laughter.

"And have you kill us out of hand?" he asked.

The Tualaghi leader shook his head. "You're worth money to me, Selethen. I can ask a large ransom for you. I'd be mad to kill you. And I'm sure there are people who will pay for the foreigners with you as well. I've kept the other Skandian alive for that very reason. Why would I do differently with you?"

Selethen hesitated. The Tualaghi were motivated by greed above all else and he was inclined to believe Yusal. As he thought about it, the Tualaghi leader voiced the alternative.

"Or stay here and die of thirst. It's only a matter of time. When you're weaker, we'll have no problem walking in and taking the weapons from your hands. And if you make me wait, I might not be so charitable."

He turned away, as if disinterested in which course Selethen might choose. The Wakir took Halt's sleeve and led him a few paces away.

"This concerns your people as well. What do you say?" he asked in a low voice. Halt looked at the tall figure standing a few meters away, his back to them.

"Do you believe him?" he asked, and Selethen nodded, a fractional movement of his head.

"A Tualaghi will do anything for money," he said. "At least this way we'll have a chance. As he says, if we wait, we'll grow progressively weaker until we have to give in anyway."

Halt considered the situation. He and Gilan might break through the Tualaghi lines under cover of darkness. But even that wasn't certain. Expert though they might be at unseen movement, the ground was virtually devoid of cover. And scores of eyes would be on watch. And if they did succeed in getting past the Tualaghi, then what? They'd be on foot, with the nearest help many kilometers away. By the time they reached Mararoc to bring help, Selethen and his men would be dead. Evanlyn, Horace and Svengal too. If they surrendered now, they'd all be in reasonable condition and an opportunity might arise to escape or turn the tables on their captors. Better now than later when they were weakened and half mad from thirst.

"Very well," he said. "Let's discuss terms."

35

WILL WAS CHECKING THE STRAPS AND TIES THAT ATTACHED HIS equipment to Tug's saddle when he heard footsteps crunching the sand behind him. He turned to see Umar approaching, a worried look on his face.

"There's something you ought to know before you leave," he said.

It was four days after the race—a race that was already set to become part of the Bedullin verbal history. In that time, Will and Tug had been feted by the tribe, and fussed over nonstop by Cielema. The cheerful, grinning foreigner and his amazing barrel-bodied horse had become popular figures in the camp. Hassan and Will had become good friends too—the young man bore no grudge for being defeated in the race and losing his claim to Tug. The Bedullin were inveterate gamblers, as Will had noticed, but they accepted their losses without complaint.

The friendship was helped along by the fact that Umar, delighted with the outcome of the race, had presented Hassan with a horse from his own herd—a blood relative of Sandstorm. Hassan was overjoyed and had volunteered to guide Will on his way to Mararoc.

The mystery of the faltering northseeker had finally been solved. Asked how he had planned to navigate the trackless desert, Will had shown them the northseeker and explained the secret of its magnetic properties. To demonstrate, he had brought the blade of his saxe knife close to the needle and showed how it wavered away from the earth's magnetic field. It took only seconds for Umar to see the connection.

"You rode by the Red Hills?" he said, and Will confirmed the fact. "But they're almost pure iron—huge deposits of iron. Surely that would serve to make your instrument unreliable."

As Will realized the truth of the statement, he felt a small sense of relief. In the back of his mind, he had still harbored a vague suspicion that Selethen had given him a false map. On top of that, he felt an unreasonable guilt that he had somehow failed Halt's belief in him. Now that he could see a reason for the mistake—and knew that he couldn't have foreseen it—he could lay those fears to rest.

While he had been preparing Tug for their departure, a rider had come in from the desert—dusty and disheveled, riding a tired horse. He had reported straightaway to Umar's tent. Will had watched with no particular interest. Doubtless it was some business of concern only to the Bedullin. Now, however, he wasn't so sure.

He followed Umar to the wide, low tent that he occupied with Cielema. Stooping, he entered and made the required lips-brow-lips greeting gesture. In the past few days, he had become familiar with it.

The tent was floored with a thick carpet, soft cushions scattered across it. He selected one and sat cross-legged on it in the tribe's fashion. A Bedullin he hadn't seen before was sitting on another, eating and drinking eagerly as Cielema plied him with fruit and water. He looked up at Will, then glanced curiously at Umar.

"This is Jamil, one of our scouts," Umar explained, and the

Bedullin nodded in greeting. He was in his thirties, Will estimated, although it was hard to tell with the Bedullin men, whose skin was usually brown and heavily lined by the sun.

"This is the foreigner I told you about. His name is Will."

Again Will made the greeting gesture. It seemed appropriate, he thought. Jamil seemed a little surprised that a foreigner should have a grasp of Bedullin etiquette, and he responded hastily. Will glanced at Umar, a question on his face. The Aseikh gestured to Jamil to proceed.

"Tell Will what you have told us."

Jamil finished eating an orange, licked the last of the juice off his fingers and wiped his mouth with a cloth.

"You were traveling with a group of Arridi soldiers?" he said. It was as much a statement as a question. Will nodded confirmation, his brow furrowing. He sensed, from the man's serious manner, that something had gone wrong.

"That's right," he said.

"And there were other foreigners as well . . . two of them dressed as you are." He indicated the mottled brown cloak Will was wearing. Again, Will nodded. The Bedullin scout shook his head in displeasure at the fact and Will's premonition of impending bad news deepened.

"What's happened to them?" he asked. The Bedullin looked at him a moment, then, thankfully, came straight to the point without any useless attempts to soften the news.

"They've been captured by the Tualaghi," he said.

Will looked quickly at Umar. "The Tualaghi?" he queried.

The Aseikh's expression was one of intense distaste.

"Brigands. Bandits. The Forgotten of God. They're nomads like us but they prey on other travelers and undefended villages. They encircled your friends and captured them. Now they're taking them toward the northern massif, along with Wakir Seley el'then and his surviving men. There was a skirmish," he added in explanation, and Will felt a stab of fear.

"A skirmish? Were any of the foreigners hurt?"

Jamil shook his head. "No. They were taken and chained with the other foreigner. They are captives like him. It seems that—"

Will held up a hand to stop the Bedullin's account. This was all moving too fast for him.

"Just a moment! The other foreigner? What other foreigner are you talking about?"

Jamil nodded apologetically, realizing that more explanation was required.

"The Tualaghi had captured another foreigner. One of the wild men from the north. There was one of them with your group too," he added.

Will's head was spinning. There could only be one person he was talking about. But Erak had been in Arridi hands last he had heard.

"This is crazy," he said. "You must mean Erak. But he was being taken to Mararoc with an Arridi caravan. How has he suddenly turned up with these Tualaghi?"

Jamil shrugged. Umar rubbed his nose thoughtfully.

"Perhaps the Tualaghi attacked the caravan and captured the Northman?" he suggested.

Will nodded to himself, thinking furiously. If that had been the case, Gilan and Halt would have been able to read the signs of the attack. Then they would have set out after the ambushers, with Selethen and his men in company. He shook his head to clear his thoughts. It didn't matter how it had happened, he realized. The plain fact was that it had happened.

He was surprised, however, that Halt and Gilan had been so careless as to allow the Tualaghi bandits to get wind of them.

"Do you have any idea how the Tualaghi learned that my friends were tracking them?" he asked.

This time, the Bedullin's eyes slid away in shame. He hesitated a moment before he could bring himself to answer.

"I'm afraid I led them to your friends' camp," he said. And as Will began to rise angrily from his sitting position, he hastily held out a hand.

"No! Please! It was unintentional! I had no idea your friends were there. I saw the Tualaghi party in the distance and I went closer to find out more about them. They were a much larger party than usual—at least two hundred, maybe more. After dark, I crept close to their camp to see more clearly. That was when I saw the Northman—they had him chained up in the open.

"I left before dawn and headed toward here. I must have passed close to your friends' camp without ever seeing them. But a Tualaghi rearguard scout found my tracks and followed them later that morning—and they led him to your friends. They were traveling parallel to the Veiled Ones, several kilometers away. If I hadn't inadvertently crossed their track, the Tualaghi would never have known they were there."

"How do you know all this?" Will asked.

The scout replied unhappily, "I went back the next day to check further. I had no idea then that my tracks had been discovered. But I saw where the Tualaghi had followed me, saw where they crossed your friends' path and turned to follow them. They must have thought I was part of that group. I'm sorry, Will. I had no idea I was bringing danger to your friends."

Will waved the apology aside. It hadn't been Jamil's fault, he realized. It had just been bad luck—Jamil had been the chance unexpected element that had led to Halt and the others being captured. As Halt had told him so many times, if anything can go wrong, it will.

"You couldn't have known," he said. "Do you have any idea where they might be taking them?" He addressed the question to both Jamil and Umar.

"I'd say they were heading for the massif," Jamil said.

Will looked to Umar, who explained.

"It's a huge range of cliffs and hills and mountains to the northwest. There are Arridi villages scattered throughout the hills and the Tualaghi often ride in and impose themselves on the villagers— stealing their crops and killing their livestock. A party of two hundred would have no trouble taking over a village—or even a small town. Chances are they have one in mind and they'll use it as their headquarters for a month or two. Then, when the herds and food supplies are exhausted, they'll move on."

Will reached into his shirt and produced the map Selethen had given him.

"I've got to go after them. Show me on this," he demanded. But Umar put his hand over the younger man's to calm him.

"Slow down, friend Will," he said. "Nothing will be gained by rushing off into the desert without a plan. The Tualaghi are dangerous enemies. I need to talk with my council and then we'll see what can be done."

Will went to argue but the pressure of Umar's grip increased.

"Trust me on this, Will. Give me an hour," he said.

Reluctantly, Will relaxed, folding the chart and returning it to its hiding place inside his shirt.

"Very well," he said. "An hour. But then I'm leaving."

* * *

Will returned to where Tug waited patiently and loosened the saddle girths so the horse would be more comfortable. Then he sat, his back resting against the bole of a palm tree, his eyes closed, while he tried to make sense of the situation.

Somehow, he would have to rescue his friends. He knew that much. But how? He was alone and he was unfamiliar with the territory. Against that, his friends were being held by two hundred armed bandits—cruel and merciless men who would cut their throats without hesitation. He was a foreigner. He would stand out among the Arridi villagers, if he could even manage to find the correct village in the first place. He realized that he didn't even know where to pick up the trail left by the Tualaghi. And if his recent attempts at navigation were anything to judge by, he'd probably never find them.

He must have dozed, affected by the heat of the day. He was woken by the sound of Umar lowering himself to the sand beside him with a faint grunt of exertion.

"We've talked," he said simply. Will looked at him. There was no hint in his bland expression of what he and his advisers had decided.

"Will you let Hassan guide me to where the Tualaghi captured my friends?" he said.

Umar held up a hand, palm outward, to stop him. "Let me explain. Here are the facts I put to my council. The Tualaghi are no friends of ours. A large war party like this means they're up to no good and they could well attack other Bedullin bands—ones smaller than this. Then there's the matter of Seley el'then. I don't like the fact that he's their captive."

"You know Selethen?" Will asked.

The Aseikh nodded. "We've fought together against the Tualaghi.

He's a good man. A brave fighter. More important, he's an honest man—a man I trust. Those are good qualities to have in a Wakir. There's always the possibility that another man might not be so fair-minded. And a lot of Arridi resent us. They see us as interlopers in their country. Wakir Seley el'then has always treated us well. It might not suit us to have him replaced by someone who is not so honest or fair-minded."

A small flame of hope was starting to burn in Will's chest as the Aseikh continued to analyze the situation.

"Are you saying you'll . . . ?" he began, but once more, Umar made that palm outward gesture to silence him.

"And there are two more points to consider. One: you have become a friend of the Bedullin. You saved my grandson's life and you behaved well in the matter of the race. My people like you, Will. And we take friendship seriously."

"You said two points?" Will interjected.

Umar shook his head, his expression very serious. "As Jamil told you, it was his fault that your friends were captured. If he had not been so clumsy, the Tualaghi would never have known they were there. His fault, his failing, becomes the failing of the tribe as a whole. This weighs very heavily on Jamil's mind . . . and my own."

Will hardly dared to hope that what he was beginning to think might be true. Tentatively, as if by being too positive he might cause the idea to dissolve and blow away on the wind, he said: "So you're saying you . . ."

He couldn't bring himself to finish the statement. Umar did it for him.

"I'm saying we're all agreed. We're going to rescue Seley el'then and your friends from the Veiled Ones." He smiled at the elated young man beside him. "Of course, you're welcome to come along with us if you wish."

36

THE ARRIDI SOLDIERS WERE DISARMED AND MADE TO SIT ON THE
ground, surrounded by over a hundred Tualaghi warriors. Selethen,
the four Araluens and Svengal were led to one side. Their hands
were bound in front of them and they watched as Yusal and two of
his officers walked among the seated Arridi troopers.

"I could kill you all now," he told them. "You know that. But instead I'm going to be merciful."

Halt watched skeptically. "And he knows that if he started killing
them, they'd fight back," he said in an aside to Evanlyn. "Even though
they're unarmed, he'd lose some of his own men." Men who were
certain they were going to die would fight desperately to the end, he
knew. But if there was a ray of hope, no matter how faint, they would
take it.

"I'll keep your horses," Yusal continued, "and we'll take your
boots. Then you can go." Selethen started forward angrily but a
Tualaghi sentry restrained him.

"Go? Go where?" he shouted. The tall war leader turned toward
him, the eyes above the blue mask devoid of any sign of mercy. He
shrugged.

"That's not my concern," he said harshly. "I didn't ask these men to follow me. You did. If I leave them now in the desert, that's on your head, not mine. At least I'm giving them a chance."

"What chance will they have in the desert without water?" Selethen challenged, and Yusal spread his hands in a sarcastic gesture.

"Did I say they would be left without water?" he asked. "I said I'd keep their boots and their horses. I don't want them following us. But the Word of Law says we must never turn a traveler out in the desert without water. Of course they will have water." He gestured to one of his men. "Give them two water skins," he said.

"For over thirty men? And some of them wounded? This isn't what the Law means and you know it, you murderer!"

Yusal shrugged. "Unlike you, I don't pretend to know God's will, Seley el'then. The Word of Law says a stranger must be given water. I don't recall an amount being mentioned."

Selethen shook his head bitterly. "No wonder you're the Forgotten of God, Yusal," he said.

The Tualaghi flinched at the insult as if he had been whipped. He turned and gave a curt order to his men and there was a ringing sound of steel as one hundred swords were drawn and raised over the defenseless Arridi troops.

"Your choice then, Seley el'then. Give the word and my men will kill the prisoners now. Or would you rather they had my mercy?"

His hand was raised to give the command. The muscles in Selethen's jaw knotted as he tried to control his rage and frustration. One of his troops, a lieutenant, looked up and called to the Wakir.

"Excellence, don't worry about us! We'll be all right! We'll find help and come after you!"

Yusal laughed then. "How brave! Perhaps I should kill this one. I wouldn't like to think that such a fierce warrior was dogging my footsteps." He stepped close to the young officer and drew his own sword. The Arridi looked up at him defiantly.

"Your choice, Seley el'then," Yusal repeated. Selethen made a small gesture of defeat.

"Let them live," he said quietly, and Yusal laughed again.

"I thought you might change your mind." He gave another hand gesture to his own men and their weapons were sheathed. Then he leaned down to the young Arridi who had spoken. His eyes, dark and cruel as those of a bird of prey, bored into the soldier's.

"You're brave enough now, boy," he said in a quiet, bitter voice. "But wait till your tongue is dry and swollen so large that it fills your throat so that you can hardly breathe. Wait till your feet are torn and blistered by the heat and the rocks. Your eyes will be blinded by the glare of the sun and you'll wish your leader had allowed me to kill you here and now. Believe me, he's done you no favor today."

The young man's defiant gaze dropped from Yusal's. The Tualaghi war leader snorted in contempt.

"Turn them out into the desert!" Then, to the guards who were gathered around Halt, Selethen and the others, he ordered, "Bring these ones to the camp!"

He turned away, strode to his horse, mounted and rode off toward the crest without a backward glance.

The guards moved in on the small party of hostages. Four of them surrounded Svengal and two more stationed themselves behind him. Obviously, their dealings with Erak had taught them what to expect from the wild sea wolves. Before Svengal could resist, one of the men behind him struck him across the back of the knees with the haft of his spear. The Skandian's legs collapsed under the unexpected blow and he fell to the ground. Instantly, the four were upon him, hobbling his legs with leather thongs so that he could only shuffle along, taking half steps. Then they dragged the big man to his feet again. He glared at them, the rage boiling up inside him. But the sight of the drawn daggers that surrounded him was enough to calm him down. There was no point in suicide, he realized.

Another guard stepped forward and dragged Evanlyn out of the group. Horace went to intercept him but a spear butt rammed into his stomach stopped him in his tracks. He sagged to his knees, gasping for breath.

"The girl is a valuable hostage," Halt warned the guard. "Yusal won't thank you if she's harmed."

The man hesitated. In fact, he had only been interested in the necklace that Evanlyn wore. He seized it now and dragged her off balance as he examined it. But the rounded stones threaded onto the string were worthless marble.

"Keep them!" he snarled. "They're worth nothing!"

He shoved her back with the others, then gave a brisk order. The guards mounted and herded their captives on foot toward the camp, their hands tied tightly before them with leather thongs. Urged on by spear butts and curses, they stumbled on the uneven ground.

One of the guards rode close to Gilan. He had lost three friends to the Rangers' arrows during the attack that morning and he took every opportunity now to crack his spear shaft painfully across the Ranger's shoulders and back. The fourth time he did so, Gilan turned and looked up at him with a peculiar smile.

"What are you looking at, foreigner?" the guard demanded roughly. The smile was a little unsettling. A prisoner shouldn't smile at his captors like that.

"I'm just making sure I can remember you," Gilan told him. "Never know when that might be useful."

The spear cracked down across his shoulders. He flinched, then nodded meaningfully at the Tualaghi rider before he began plodding up the hill once more.

Erak looked up as the hostages were thrust unceremoniously onto the ground beside him.

As Gilan had observed some nights earlier, he was seated on the ground, chained between two noisy, complaining camels. His face was bruised and his hair matted with dried blood. One eye was almost closed and there were whip scores on his arms and back.

"Well, look at what the cat dragged in," he said cheerfully. "What brings you here, Halt?"

"We've come to rescue you," Halt told him, and the Oberjarl looked quizzically at the leather bindings that secured his friends.

"You've chosen a strange way to do it," he said. Then, as he recognized Selethen, his brows contracted into an unfriendly frown. "Nice work, Wakir," he said. There was an overtone of bitterness in his voice as he held up his own manacled hands.

Selethen shook his head. His own bitterness matched Erak's.

"This was not what I intended. I lost a lot of good men," he told the Skandian. Erak considered the statement for a moment, then his expression softened and he nodded. He glanced at Svengal.

"Svengal, my friend," he said, "when I told you to go and get the Araluens, this isn't exactly what I had in mind."

Svengal shrugged. "Don't worry, chief. We've got these Tualaghi surrounded—from the inside."

"Exactly," Erak replied dryly. Then he gestured to the stony ground. "Take a seat, why don't you?"

As the others sat, Evanlyn knelt beside the Oberjarl. Gently, she examined the wounds to his scalp and the massive bruise around his eye.

"Are you all right, Erak?" she asked.

He shrugged. "Oh, I'm fine. They never hurt you so badly that you can't walk. And they're treating me like an honored guest—a handful of moldy dates, some stale bread and a mouthful of water, then a nice walk in the sunshine. Who could ask for more?"

"Any word of Toshak so far?" Halt asked.

Erak's expression darkened. "Not by name. But that swine Yusal hinted that I'd be meeting a countryman soon—and I don't think he meant you, Svengal. I can't wait. If I get a chance to get my hands on Toshak's throat, he'll wish he'd never been born." He looked up at Halt then. "Unlike you to be taken by surprise, Halt. Are you losing your edge?"

Halt raised an eyebrow at him. "From what I've heard, you didn't do so well yourself at Al Shabah," he pointed out, and Erak shrugged.

"I guess we're all getting careless," he said.

"Any idea where this bunch is headed, chief?" Svengal asked.

"They don't exactly consult me. I just drag along behind Matilda there." He jerked a thumb at the nearer of the two camels. "We've become quite fond of each other," he added, glaring balefully at the grumbling beast.

"Odds are we're headed for the northern massif," Selethen said, and Erak looked at him with interest.

"I believe I did hear those words mentioned," he said. "Well, you'd better get some rest while you can. It's a long day when you're walking."

Horace scratched his ear, the movement made clumsy by the fact that his hands were tied together. "What time do they feed us?" he asked. Erak looked at him for a second, then grinned.

"Don't ever change, Horace," he said.

37

Will, Umar and one hundred and twenty Bedullin warriors were on a forced march across the desert.

They rose four hours before dawn, rode until four hours after first light, then rested through the heat of the day. In the late afternoon, a few hours before sunset, they would set out again, riding until well after dark before stopping to rest again. Will estimated that it was around nine in the evening when they would camp for the night. But the two rest periods, one in the middle of the day and the other late at night, gave them plenty of time to water and feed their horses and recover their strength for the next march.

It was a hard schedule but a sensible one. They rode at a steady pace, trotting their horses rather than cantering or galloping. But Will soon realized that they were covering great distances by keeping to the steady pace, even though he was tempted to go faster. As the kilometers reeled by under Tug's hooves, he knew that this would be the better course in the long run.

Umar had decided to act on Jamil's assertion that the Tualaghi were headed for one of the towns in the northern massif. As a result, they were able to plan a straight-line course to intercept the raiders, rather than return to the site of the battle and follow their tracks. This, combined with the prodigious distances they were able to cover each day, meant they were well on the way to overhauling the enemy.

Will had asked Umar and Jamil to show him the location of the massif on his chart. It was farther to the north than the area covered by Selethen's chart. They studied that document with some interest, rapidly seeing its relevance, even though the Bedullin never used charts themselves. Their navigation was based on tribal lore and knowledge, handed down over hundreds of years. As they pointed to landmarks drawn by Selethen, they would refer to places by names such as "river of bright stones" or "Ali's Hill" or "the snake wadi." While some of the names were self-explanatory, the origin of others was hidden in antiquity. Nobody, for example, had the slightest memory of who Ali might have been, and the bright stones that marked the river had long since disappeared—along with the river itself.

This was a war party, so the Khoresh Bedullin women and children had remained at the oasis camp, with seventy of Umar's warriors to keep them safe. The Aseikh was reluctant to reduce his attack force by so many but the desert was an uncertain place and seventy was the minimum number of men he was willing to leave for the protection of his people.

"We'll be outnumbered," he remarked to Will.

"They won't be expecting us," the young Ranger replied, and the Aseikh nodded, with a certain grim satisfaction.

"I'm looking forward to that."

On the third day of travel, the problem of numbers was re-dressed. A forward scout rode back at a gallop to report that he had encountered a party of thirty men on foot in the desert.

Umar, Will and Hassan rode back with him, cantering ahead of the main party. After three kilometers, they came upon the group of men, sitting in the meager shade afforded by a wadi bank and sharing the last of a water skin the scout had left with them.

"Arridi troopers," Umar said, recognizing the remnants of the uniforms they wore. Will noticed that none of the men wore boots, although they had torn cloth from their cloaks and shirts to wrap around their feet for protection. There was barely more than a mouthful each in the water skin and the distribution was being carefully overseen by a young man who still wore a lieutenant's insignia. The group might be ragged and close to exhaustion, but it was obvious they had maintained their discipline. Will wasn't certain but the officer looked vaguely familiar. He thought he might have been one of Selethen's men.

The three riders had carried extra water skins back with them and these were quickly distributed. The lieutenant moved toward Umar and made the traditional greeting gesture.

"Thank you, Aseikh," he began. He recognized Umar's badge of rank, the triple strand of horsehair rope that bound his keffiyeh. "I'm Lieutenant Aloom of the—"

Umar stopped him with a gesture and passed him his own water skin. The young man's voice was dry and croaking. "Drink first, Lieutenant," he told him. "The talking will be easier after that."

Gratefully, the officer raised the water skin to his mouth and drank. Will noticed that even though he must have been parched, he sipped only small amounts of the water, drinking slowly so as not to overwhelm his body with a sudden flood of moisture. The people of Arrida maintained excellent water discipline, he realized, remembering how desperately he had tried to gulp the water he was given when Umar found him.

It was close to the tenth hour of the morning, which was the time Umar would usually call a halt for the first rest period. He signaled to the others to dismount and swung down from his saddle.

"We'll camp here," he said. "The Arridi can use the rest period to recover."

Lieutenant Aloom had quenched his thirst now and told them of the Tualaghi ambush and the ensuing battle; how Halt and the others had been taken prisoner while he and his men had been turned out into the desert by Yusal, without boots and with a bare minimum of water. That had been two days ago.

"You've kept thirty men alive and marching with just two water skins?" Umar queried. There was a note of respect in his voice.

The lieutenant shrugged. "They're good troops," he said. "They understood the need for discipline."

"They have a good officer," Will said. He'd been tempted to interrupt the lieutenant immediately and ask for news of his friends. But he saw that the man was close to exhaustion and thought it better to let him tell his tale in his own time. The lieutenant stared at him for a moment before recognizing him. When the war party had set out from the oasis, Will had adopted Bedullin clothes—baggy trousers, a long flowing shirt and cloak and, of course, a keffiyeh to cover his head and face. But the longbow and quiver slung over his back were unmistakable.

"You're the one they call Will," Aloom said. "We thought you would be dead by now."

Will smiled. "Glad you had such faith in me," he said. Then the smile faded. "Are Halt and the others all right? Is Evanlyn safe?"

Aloom nodded. "They were safe when we left. Yusal talked about ransom, so the girl will be looked after. Chances are he'll want to sell her as a slave and nobody wants to buy a disfigured girl slave. The men won't be so lucky. They'll be beaten, I would expect."

"I agree," Umar said. He turned to Will. "They'll be uncomfortable but it won't be too bad. There's a harsh practicality to it all. Yusal won't allow them to be badly hurt. It would slow them down. The lieutenant is right about the girl too. If there's one thing the Tualaghi are good at, it's looking after their investments."

"Aseikh, may I ask, what are your plans?" the lieutenant asked. He glanced into the distance, where he could see the main party of Bedullin approaching. His keen eyes took in the fact that the group consisted of fighting men only, no women or children.

"We're going after the Tualaghi," Will told him. "Aseikh Umar and his people have agreed to help me rescue my friends."

"And Wakir Seley el'then?" the lieutenant asked.

Umar nodded confirmation. "The Wakir is an old comrade. I don't plan to leave him in Yusal's grubby hands."

They had been sitting in the narrow patch of shade thrown by the wadi's bank. Aloom scrambled to his feet now, with a new light of energy in his eyes.

"Then let us come with you!" he said. "My men and I have a score to settle with those cursed Tualaghi. And I promised my lord that we would return."

Umar frowned. "Your men are exhausted—and half dead from thirst," he said doubtfully. But Aloom was shaking his head before he finished.

"They're fit and in good condition. Let them rest overnight with food and plenty of water. They'll be ready to travel by tomorrow morning, I swear it."

"You're unarmed," Will pointed out.

Aloom shrugged. "Surely your men can spare a few daggers? Most Bedullin carry more than one. And once the battle starts, every Tualaghi you kill will provide weapons for one of my soldiers."

Will and Umar exchanged a glance. "It would be handy to have an extra thirty trained fighting men," Will pointed out. Then he frowned. "But how will they keep up with us? They're barefoot and walking."

Umar dismissed the problem with a brief shake of his head. "They can ride double with my men," he said. "There's only thirty of them. We can rotate them among the force so no horse has to carry double for too long."

Aloom had followed the discussion between them eagerly, his eyes swinging from one to another as they spoke. Now he raised a hand and spoke tentatively.

"One thing," he said. "Four of my men are wounded. We've been carrying them. They're not fit for travel or a battle."

Umar weighed the problem briefly. He liked the idea of having more fighting men under his command and he knew the Arridi troopers would prove capable warriors.

"We'll leave two of my men to look after them," he said, thinking aloud. "We can leave some water with them but we'll need most of what we have. There's a small soak half a day's ride to the east. It will provide enough water for six men. One of my men can fetch water while the other stays here with them. If we're successful, we'll pick them up on the return trip."

He considered his own statement for a second or two, then nodded. They'd lose the evening travel period—five hours. And he'd weaken his force by two men. But in return, he'd gain twenty-six trained soldiers. Better yet, they were soldiers who had a score to settle with the Tualaghi. It was a good trade-off, he thought.

"We'll camp here through the rest of today and tonight," he said. "Your men will have food and all the water they need. Tell them to be ready to travel four hours before dawn."

Aloom smiled. "They'll be ready," he said.

38

THE NORTHERN MASSIF LOOMED OVER THEM, ROW AFTER ROW OF cliffs and hills climbing eventually to a plain high above. The open desert had given way to a narrow road, running between rocky outcrops and cliffs and angling upward through the first foothills. At an elevation a hundred and fifty meters above the desert floor, there was a level section cut by nature into the sheer walls of the cliffs, cutting back to run in a rough north–south alignment. The town of Maashava stood there.

The town was a market center for the Arridi farmers who lived and worked in the foothills and the plains below the massif. Its normal population was around five hundred, but it grew to eight or nine hundred in market weeks, when herdsmen and farmers came in from outlying areas and neighboring hill villages to trade their goods.

It was a perfect temporary base for the Tualaghi warriors—large enough to provide accommodation for them and forage for their animals, and well stocked with foodstuffs brought into the market and stored in the town's warehouses.

The buildings were the usual white-painted mud-brick houses, mostly single-story structures with flat roofs where the occupants could enjoy the cool air at the end of the day and, on occasion, sleep during the hottest nights. But there were also many dwellings cut into the face of the cliffs themselves—their entrances weathered and worn by the years, indicating that they were ancient. For the most part, these were used as storehouses for the food and other goods traded in the town. But some were dwellings and, as the prisoners filed into the town behind their guards, Halt saw several where the signs of human occupation were obvious: women, burdened with jars containing the family's water supply, climbed access ladders to the higher entrances, and the smoke of cooking fires issued from carefully cut smoke holes in the face of the rock. On some, washed garments had been hung on long, slender poles and pushed out into the hot air to dry, the clothes fluttering like pennants in the slight breeze that moved through the canyons.

The three-day march to Maashava hadn't been a pleasant one for the prisoners. They had been led on long ropes tied to the saddles of their guards, forced to jog awkwardly in order to keep up. If anyone fell—and inevitably they did, since they were kept off balance by having their hands tied together in front of them—he was immediately surrounded by riders jabbing with lance points or striking down at them with the butts of their spears.

After a few kilometers, Halt noticed that the riders of the horses they were tied to were expert at sudden, unexpected changes of pace or direction, calculated to throw the prisoners off balance so that they would fall.

Evanlyn was the exception. As Selethen had predicted, the Tualaghi saw her as an investment to be protected and she suffered none of this brutality. She was even given a small horse to ride, although her hands remained bound and the horse was led by a Tualaghi warrior, constantly on the alert for any sign that she might try to escape.

The two Rangers fared the worst. They were foreigners and so regarded with contempt by the Tualaghi. Worse, their uncanny accuracy during the brief attack had made them hated men. Most of the Tualaghi had at least one friend who had suffered at the wrong end of a Ranger arrow and the two longbows carried by Halt and Gilan marked them out as the culprits.

Both men were bruised and battered by the time they reached Maashava. Halt's left cheek was a massive bruise and the eye was nearly closed, courtesy of a Tualaghi fist. Gilan had bled profusely from a head wound inflicted by a small club. The crusted blood matted his hair and face.

It seemed that the presence of the two Rangers diverted the Tualaghi's attention from their original victim—Erak. He and Svengal were generally left alone, aside from the almost casual beating with spear butts when they slipped and fell. Selethen also fared better than the others. Yusal knew his value as a hostage, whereas the Araluens were an unknown quantity in that area.

Horace, fit, athletic and light on his feet, gave their guards the fewest opportunities to beat him, although on one occasion an angry Tualaghi, furious that Horace misunderstood an order to kneel, slashed his dagger across the young man's face, opening a thin, shallow cut on his right cheek. The wound was superficial but as Evanlyn treated it that evening, Horace shamelessly pretended that it was more painful than it really was. He enjoyed the touch of her ministering hands. Halt and Gilan, bruised and weary, watched as she cleaned the wound and gently patted it dry. Horace did a wonderful job of pretending to bear great pain with stoic bravery. Halt shook his head in disgust.

"What a faker," he said to Gilan. The younger Ranger nodded.

"Yes. He's really making a meal of it, isn't he?" He paused, then added a little ruefully, "Wish I'd thought of it first."

Halt's one good eye glared around at him. Muttering under his breath, the gray-haired Ranger shuffled away.

"Young men!" he snorted to Erak. "They think a pretty face can cure every ill."

"Some of us can remember back that far, Halt," Erak told him with a grin. "I suppose that's all far behind an old hack like you. Svengal told me you were settling down. Some plump, motherly widow seizing her last chance with a broken-down old graybeard, is she?"

Erak, of course, had been told by Svengal that Halt had recently married a great beauty. But he enjoyed getting a reaction from the smaller man. Halt's one-eyed stare locked onto the Oberjarl.

"When we get back, I'd advise you not to refer to Pauline as a 'plump, motherly widow' in her hearing. She's very good with the dagger she carries and you need your ears to keep that ridiculous helmet of yours in place."

Now the joking was stilled as they stumbled into Maashava at the end of an exhausting day's march. The Arridi townspeople looked at the new arrivals with dull, uninterested eyes. They had no sympathy for the prisoners. The Tualaghi's invasion of their town would leave them penniless and hungry. It would take several seasons to replace the food and other provisions that the invaders were helping themselves to.

The town was in shadow, as the sun was now hidden behind the high cliffs. They were led through the main square, where the market was held, to one of the warehouse caves at the rear of the town. The long lead ropes were removed and their hands were untied.

"Looks like we've arrived at wherever we're going," Horace said.

A Tualaghi cursed him and told him to hold his foreign tongue.

The prisoners were shoved unceremoniously into the empty warehouse and a guard was mounted outside the entrance. A few minutes later, food, water and blankets were brought to the captives. Then the outer door was slammed shut and locked and they were left alone.

Less than an hour later, they heard the rattle of a key in the lock and the door swung open. It was now full dark outside and the interior was lit by a single candle. In the doorway, they could just make out a dim, bulky figure. Then he shoved through the narrow door, having to turn sideways to do so, and strode into the center of the large room they were in. A half dozen armed Tualaghi followed him, fingering the hilts of their curved swords, looking around the room, alert for any sign of rebellion from the prisoners. Finally, Yusal entered as well. But none of the prisoners had eyes for him. They were all watching the heavily built, bearded Skandian who had led the way into their cell.

"Toshak!" Svengal said. Angrily, he started to rise from the sand floor of the cave. Immediately, three of the Tualaghi drew their swords and the familiar warning *shrrrinnng* noise rang through the cave. Erak's hand shot out and gripped Svengal's forearm, forcing him back down.

"Sit easy, Svengal," he said. "Can't you see he wants an excuse to kill you?"

"Very astute, Erak," the renegade replied. His voice was surprisingly smooth and well modulated for a Skandian. Most were seamen and used to having to bellow above storm and wind. Toshak gestured to the guards and the swords were returned to their scabbards.

Yusal, his lower face still shrouded by the blue veil, watched the interplay between the two big men, his head moving from one to the other, his dark eyes unblinking.

Like a hawk, Halt thought. Then he amended the concept. Or a vulture.

"So, Toshak, you're finally showing your face. I thought you'd turn out to be the cowardly traitor behind all this." Erak's voice was even and controlled. But he couldn't match the smoothness of his enemy's delivery.

Toshak smiled. "As I say, Oberjarl, very astute. But of course, anyone can be clever in hindsight. It's a pity you didn't show such keen perception a little earlier. You might have avoided my trap. You hardly gain any credit for saying 'I knew it was you all along' when I walk into the room, do you?"

"Whether I knew or not, the fact remains, you're a traitor. And you deserve to die."

"Well, yes. But, of course, one man's traitor is another man's patriot, as they say. And I'm afraid any dying is going to be done by you."

"Which means you'll lose the ransom money," Halt interrupted. He looked at the Tualaghi leader. "How does your comrade in arms feel about that? Do you want to give up sixty thousand reels of silver, Yusal?"

The Tualaghi stepped forward, his eyes blazing with anger. He measured himself against the Ranger, and glared down at the shorter man. His finger jabbed Halt in the chest, emphasizing his words.

"You do not call me Yusal!" he snapped. "You address me as Aseikh Yusal or as Excellence. Do you understand me, you insolent foreigner?"

Halt cocked his head to one side, considering the question, even though it had been rhetorical. "What I understand," he said, "is that there is very little about you that is excellent and that Aseikh is a term of honor. There's nothing honorable in a man who hides his face behind a blue woman's hanky."

The fury flared more brightly in Yusal's eyes. Halt was watching them carefully. He always watched an enemy's eyes and, in Yusal's case, they were the only feature visible.

As Yusal swung his fist backhanded at him, Halt was ready. He swayed slightly to his right and the blow passed by harmlessly. Yusal, expecting to meet resistance, staggered with the follow-through. Burning with fury, he stepped closer to Halt to strike at him again. Toshak raised his hand to stop him.

"Wait!" he said. He peered more closely at Halt, studying the swollen, bruised face.

"You're the Ranger. Halt, aren't you? I remember hearing about you now. You made trouble in Skandia three years ago and now you're here. You just get in the way on every continent, don't you? And I suppose that's the other one who was in Skandia with you?"

He gestured to Gilan. Truth be told, Toshak had never seen either Ranger. He simply knew that Halt's assistant had been a younger man.

"Actually . . ." Gilan began. But Halt cut him off.

"That's right," he said quickly. Gilan looked at him, a little surprised. But he said nothing further. Toshak turned to Yusal now.

"These are the archers? The ones who killed so many?" he said.

The Tualaghi nodded. "My men wanted to kill them. But they might be worth a ransom."

Toshak shook his head. "Nobody will pay to have them back," he said. "Rangers are troublemakers. And they're dangerous. Best they're killed as soon as possible."

"I can ransom them!" Evanlyn said in the deathly silence that fell over the room. "I'm a . . . diplomat. I'm close to the King of Araluen. I can arrange to have a large ransom paid for these men."

Toshak eyed her curiously. He hadn't actually been present in Hallasholm during the war with the Temujai.

But he had heard tales of what had taken place: wild stories about a girl who had been with the Rangers—a high-ranking Araluen girl. It could be this one, he thought. Then he shrugged; her identity was immaterial. What was important was what had been found in her belongings.

"You'll do that anyway," he said. "Whether we kill them or not."

Evanlyn opened her mouth to argue, then stopped as she saw what he was holding: the draft for the Silasian Council.

"It's worthless without a seal," she told him.

"But you know where to find one, don't you?" he asked.

Evanlyn met his gaze unflinchingly. Just before they had surrendered, she had hidden the seal under a rock outcrop in the saucer-shaped depression. She was glad now that she had done so. She said nothing, not trusting her voice.

Toshak nodded. Her silence confirmed his suspicion. He turned to Yusal.

"Aseikh Yusal, how would you convince this girl to find the seal she appears to have misplaced?"

Yusal's eyes crinkled and the veil moved slightly over his face. Evanlyn realized he was smiling. The Tualaghi had watched the captives closely all the way to Maashava. He hadn't missed the byplay between the girl and the young warrior. He pointed to Horace now.

"If we began to peel the skin from this one, I think she might remember," he said. He chuckled. His harsh, unpleasant voice made it an ugly sound.

Evanlyn froze, looking helplessly at Horace. She could never stand by and see him tortured.

But if she made out the warrant, they would all die anyway.

"Toshak?" It was Svengal, his voice soft and questioning. The rebel Skandian looked at him, his eyebrows raised. Svengal continued.

"How about you and me, we have a little wrestle together? Just for fun."

"Fun?" repeated Toshak.

Svengal smiled winningly. "Yes. I think it would be such fun to tear that ugly head off your shoulders. And your beaky, blue-faced friend's too." He spat the last words out, switching his glare to Yusal.

Toshak raised an eyebrow.

"You should have kept your mouth shut, Svengal. I might have let you live. But now I see how determined you are, well . . ." He paused, looking around the tense group who faced him. "Let's just recap where we stand, shall we?" he said. He indicated Selethen. "The Wakir is going to be ransomed. He gets off lightly but I have no argument with him. On the other hand, I do have one with Erak and Svengal, so they're going to die. You two Rangers as well." He pointed at Horace next. "You're going to have your skin peeled and the young lady here is going to pay us a large amount of money for the privilege of listening to your screams." He smiled around at them all. "Have I missed anyone? No? Well, have a nice night thinking on it."

The smile disappeared. He jerked his head at Yusal and the two of them turned. Then the Tualaghi leader, struck by a thought, stopped and turned back. He held up his left hand as if asking for their attention and moved back toward them.

"There was one more thing," he said. Then he spat an order to his guards and two of them gripped Halt by the arms, forcing him forward and down until he was on his knees in front of Yusal. The Tualaghi Aseikh then rained closed-fist blows on Halt's face, left and right, striking again and again until the Ranger's face was cut and bleeding and his head lolled to one side. Toshak watched, amused. Erak started to move forward to intervene but the point of a saber in his belly stopped him. Finally, Yusal stepped back, breathing heavily.

"Let him go," he told the men holding Halt. They released him and he crumpled to the sand, facedown and semiconscious.

"Not so light on your feet now, are you?" Toshak said to the slumped figure. Yusal uttered a short bark of laughter and together they turned and left the room. The guards, hands on their weapons, backed out after them, slamming the door. In the ensuing silence, the prisoners heard the key rattle in the lock.

Gilan let go a deep, pent-up breath and moved quickly to kneel beside his semiconscious friend. Gently, he rolled Halt over and began cleaning the mixture of sand and blood from his face. Evanlyn joined him, her hands light and delicate.

Horace brought over the water skin that had been left with them and handed it to Evanlyn. He watched as she gently washed Halt's face. Horace was worried. He had never seen Halt defeated before. He was always in control of the situation. Halt always knew what to do next.

"I think we're in big trouble," he said. Then they all started as Halt moved, raising his hand and trying to sit up. Evanlyn held him down and he stopped his efforts. But he spoke, his voice thick and somewhat slurred by his swollen mouth and face.

"They're forgetting one thing," he said. There was a light of defiance in his one good eye. The other was now completely closed.

The others all exchanged a glance. They could see no positive side to their predicament.

"And what might that be, Halt?" Evanlyn asked, willing to humor him.

Halt caught the tone in her voice and glared at her. Then he said, with some force:

"Will's still out there somewhere."

39

〜〜〜〜〜〜〜〜〜〜〜〜〜〜〜〜

THE FIRST LIGHT OF THE SUN WAS STRIKING THE WHITE-PAINTED houses of Maashava when Will and Umar finally reached a vantage point above the town.

They had climbed for several hours in the predawn dimness, following narrow animal tracks to one side of the township, then angling back until they emerged fifty meters above it, with a perfect view of the comings and goings of the townspeople.

Now they surveyed the town. A low wall ran around three sides. The fourth was protected by the cliffs themselves. There were watchtowers raised at intervals along the wall but there was no sign of any sentries. Will remarked on the fact and Umar shook his head contemptuously.

"The townspeople are too lazy to mount guards and the Tualaghi believe there's no enemy within hundreds of kilometers."

Smoke from cooking fires was rising from many points around the town. Mixed with the acrid wood smoke was another aroma that set Will's taste buds alight. Fresh coffee was being brewed in kitchens throughout the town. Men and women were beginning to stream out of the town, heading down the winding road to the flatlands below, or to terraced fields on the mountain side itself. Will pointed to them and raised his eyebrows.

"Field-workers," Umar said in response to the unspoken question. "They grow maize and wheat on the flatlands, and fruit and some vegetables in the terraces."

There was no shortage of water in Maashava. A series of wells tapped into an underground stream that ran through the mountains. Some of this was piped to the terraces, some all the way down to the fields. It was a complex irrigation and cultivation system and Will had seen nothing like it in his time in the dry, arid country.

"Who built all this?" he asked.

Umar shrugged. "No one knows. The terraces and aqueducts are hundreds, maybe thousands of years old. The Arridi found them and restored the town."

"Well, in any event, they give us an opportunity," Will said. Umar glanced at him and he continued. "With all those workers moving in and out each day, we can infiltrate some of your men into the town. I figure if they go in in ones and twos, we could get up to fifty men in over the course of a day."

"And then what?" Umar asked.

"They could make contact with the townspeople and hide among them. Surely the people of Maashava will welcome anyone who wants to get rid of the Tualaghi once and for all?"

Umar looked doubtful. "Not my men," he said. "They'd stand out as outsiders. The locals wouldn't trust them. They'd be just as likely to betray them to the Tualaghi."

"But why?" Will's voice rose a little in his frustration at the answer and Umar made urgent gestures for him to keep his voice down. Sound carried a long way in the mountains. "Sorry," Will continued, "but why would they betray you? You're all the same nationality, aren't you?"

The Bedullin shook his head. "We may live in the same country, but we're different tribes. We are Bedullin. They are Arridi. Our accents are different, so are our customs. In general, Bedullin don't trust Arridi and the Arridi reciprocate. My men would be recognized as Bedullin as soon as they spoke."

"That's ridiculous," Will growled. The thought that people could be divided by such minor differences was an affront to intelligent behavior, he thought.

Umar shrugged. "Ridiculous maybe. But a fact."

Will stared at the town below, watching as more people moved out into the street. He gnawed thoughtfully on his thumb.

"But you sent a man in there last night?" he said.

Umar nodded. One of the Bedullin scouts had slipped over the wall after dark. He'd leave again that night and report on what he had heard in the town.

"One man. It's easy for one man to go unnoticed, particularly as he doesn't have to speak, merely listen. But we'd never hope to get fifty men in there without someone noticing the different accent." He decided it was time to change the subject and pointed to one of the openings in the cliff face, at the rear of the township. Unlike others of its kind, where the doors had been thrown wide open to receive the fresh morning air, this one remained closed and barred, and a dozen Tualaghi warriors lounged around it.

"That storeroom must be where they're holding your friends."

Will held his hands up to his eyes, shrouding them to focus his attention as he peered at the strongly defended door.

"I'd say you're right." He thought for a few minutes. "Wonder if there's any way we could break them out."

Umar shook his head. "Even if you got to the storeroom undetected, with enough men to overpower the guards, you'd be seen and heard. Then you'd have to fight your way out through the town again."

Will's eyes went upward to the sheer cliffs towering behind the town.

"What about coming in from above? And going out the same way?"

Umar considered the idea. "Might work. But you'd need ropes. Lots of ropes. And we don't have them," he concluded.

Will nodded. "Best way then is to be waiting for them to bring Halt and the others out of that prison," he said, almost to himself.

"There's only one reason I can think of that they might do that," Umar said. "That's if they were going to execute them."

Will looked at him for several seconds before speaking. "Well, that's a big comfort," he said.

Yusal had appropriated the largest and most comfortable house in the town for his own use. It was the home of the town headman and Yusal also forced him and his family to wait on him and his bodyguards. The man and his wife were terrified of the veiled nomad leader and Yusal enjoyed the fact. He liked striking fear into other people's hearts. And he enjoyed belittling people like the headman and his wife, destroying their dignity and authority by forcing them to perform menial servants' duties for him. Yusal sprawled at ease on a pile of thick cushions in the main room of the house.

The headman had just moved through, lighting oil lamps and candles against the gathering dusk. Yusal insisted on having two or three times as many of each as was necessary. Oil and candles were expensive and hard to come by in a town like this. He liked seeing the dismay on the old man's face as they were used in such a profligate manner. In a few weeks, Yusal would use up three months' supply. But it was of no concern to the Tualaghi leader. When the oil and candles and food ran out, he'd move on.

The woman entered to serve him coffee. As he demanded, she

went down on her knees to offer him the cup. He took it from her, then glared at her until she lowered her eyes. Then he raised the blue veil that covered his mouth and tasted the coffee. Using the sole of his foot, he shoved her away, sending her sprawling on the mud floor.

"Too weak," he said.

Face averted, the woman crawled on her hands and knees from the room. She had quickly learned not to look at the Tualaghi war leader's face when he raised the blue veil to eat or drink. The first time she had been slow to avert her eyes, he had had her savagely whipped.

In fact, there was nothing wrong with the coffee. The headman's wife was an excellent cook and all Arridi women learned to make good coffee as children. But it gave him an excuse to reassert his authority and Yusal enjoyed that.

His good humor evaporated as the main door of the house opened to admit Toshak.

Yusal glared at him now, hastily replacing the veil across his mouth and nose.

"You should wait," he said. "You should be announced and you should await permission to enter."

Toshak shrugged carelessly. "I'll remember that," he said in an offhanded manner that told Yusal he didn't care a fig about it. "Tell me," he added curiously, "do you ever take that veil off?"

He'd seen the quick movement as he entered. He wondered about the blue veils that the Tualaghi wore. Yusal was the only one who never seemed to remove his.

"Yes," Yusal replied flatly, in a tone that told Toshak there would be no further discussion. In fact, there was no concrete reason why Yusal wore the veil all the time. Some believed that his face was horribly disfigured, others that it was not the face of a human. He kept

the veil on to keep the rumors and the uncertainty alive. It added
to the aura of power and mystery that helped keep people in fear
of him.

Toshak took a small object from inside his vest and tossed it to
the Aseikh.

"Look what I've got," he said. "I left a few men behind to search
the foreigners' campsite. They just came in with this."

Yusal turned the object over in his hand. It was a small box containing the missing seal that Evanlyn had carried.

"I figured she must have had it with her and it was nowhere on
her or in her belongings. That left only one possibility: she hid it
before they surrendered. It was a pretty barren site, so it wasn't all
that hard to find."

Beneath the veil, Yusal smiled in deep satisfaction. He decided
he could forgive the northerner for his boorish manners.

"That is excellent. Well thought out," he said.

"Now we can complete the warrant," Toshak pointed out. "That's
sixty-six thousand reels of silver."

"Thirty-three thousand each," the Tualaghi whispered, savoring
the words and the amount. But to his surprise, Toshak shook his
head.

"Sixty-six thousand for you," he said. "I don't want any of it.
Consider it compensation."

"Compensation? For what? What do you want me to do?" Yusal
asked. He wasn't accustomed to having people hand over such
massive amounts of money. But Toshak had decided it was worthwhile. He would be Oberjarl and that was worth an investment of
thirty-three thousand reels.

"Forget the ransoms," Toshak told him. "I want all the prisoners
killed."

Yusal's eyes widened in surprise. "All of them?"

The Skandian nodded confirmation.

Yusal considered the idea. Seley el'then would be worth a lot, he thought. But nowhere near sixty-six thousand reels. And the Wakir had been a thorn in Yusal's side for some years. It would be a far more pleasant world without him. A replacement might not be so energetic about pursuing the Tualaghi when they raided.

Yes, he thought, a world without Seley el'then would be a better place. As for the Skandians and the young Araluen, he had no qualms there. But it would be a pity to kill the girl.

"Why the girl?" he asked. "She'd be worth a lot in the slave markets."

"I want them all dead because I want no loose ends," Toshak replied. "The girl has influential friends in Araluen and the Araluens are friends of Erak's. Slaves can escape or be on-sold and, when I'm Oberjarl, I don't want any rumors starting that I was behind Erak's disappearance. If she's dead, there's no chance of that."

Yusal nodded. It made sense, he realized. The chance that the girl might one day escape and find her way back to Araluen was a slim one. But it was a chance. Better in situations like this to be sure. Besides, he thought, a mass execution would be a good lesson to the people of Maashava. Like the blue veil, it would add to Yusal's own legend and mystique.

"Very well," he said eventually. "But if we're going to kill them all, we might as well make an occasion of it."

Toshak shrugged. "Do as you wish," he said. "Occasion or not, as long as they're all dead, I'm happy."

40

"THEY'RE GOING TO KILL THEM—ALL OF THEM?" WILL ASKED incredulously. He and Umar were back at the Bedullin camp in a blind canyon to the north of Maashava. Sharik, the Bedullin spy who had spent the day inside the crumbling walls of Maashava, nodded in confirmation.

"That's the word among all the Tualaghi I saw. They're announcing it to the townspeople. Making quite a big thing out of it, apparently."

Umar pursed his lips thoughtfully. "It's what you'd expect of Yusal," he said. Will turned his horrified glance on the Aseikh.

"But you said he'd rather make a profit out of them!" he said. Umar shrugged.

"Normally, yes. But perhaps this man Toshak has offered him something in return."

Sharik had also told them about the presence of a Skandian in the Tualaghi camp—a man who seemed to be on equal terms with Yusal. Will knew it must be Toshak. Svengal had told them weeks ago in Araluen that Erak suspected Toshak was behind the betrayal.

Umar continued now: "And Yusal enjoys any opportunity to show how merciless he can be. It helps keep his victims subdued. A multiple execution here will be remembered for years. Word will spread and it will make his task easier next time he takes over a village."

Will was thinking furiously. What could Toshak have offered the Tualaghi to convince him to give up the ransom money? There could only be one logical answer.

"He's found the warrant and Evanlyn's seal," he said, almost to himself. Umar and Sharik regarded him curiously.

"The warrant?" Umar asked, and Will explained quickly about the ransom payment they had arranged for Erak. The Bedullin leader nodded agreement.

"That could be it. An amount like that would be enough to convince Yusal."

Will looked to Sharik again. "Did you get any idea when they might be holding the executions?"

"On Sixday," the spy replied. "The usual time is between the ninth and tenth hour if it's to be a ceremonial execution."

Sixday was the sixth day of the week. It was a nonworking day, preceding Sevenday, the day for religious observances. On Sixday, food and trade markets were set up in the town square and people relaxed and enjoyed themselves. At least, Will thought, they did when their town hadn't been invaded by a nomad raiding party.

"So we have two days," Will said. A thought struck him. "Will they cancel the market?"

Umar shook his head. "Not at all. The more people out and about to see the executions, the better, so far as Yusal is concerned."

Will massaged his chin with his hand, his thoughts racing. "That could work for us," he said abstractedly. "The more people about, the easier it will be to infiltrate some of our men."

"I told you," Umar interrupted him. "My men will be recognized as outsiders as soon as they speak."

"Yours, perhaps," Will replied. "But aren't you forgetting we have twenty-five Arridi troops with us?" He saw understanding in Umar's eyes and hurried on, his thoughts spilling out even as they formed. "We could pair each one with one of your men. They could mingle with the farmers bringing in their produce for the market. Some could even go in the night before. The Arridi does all the talking so the townspeople don't react to a Bedullin accent. That'd give us fifty men inside the town."

"That could work," Umar agreed. "Good work, Sharik," he said, realizing that the spy was tired and there was no need to keep him from his bed. "Go and get some food and rest now." Then he looked to where Hassan was sitting nearby, listening intently to the discussion. "Go and find the Arridi lieutenant," he ordered. "Bring him here."

When the idea was explained to Aloom, he agreed eagerly. The lieutenant had promised Selethen that he and his men would survive the desert, and come after him to rescue him. Now they had that opportunity being handed to them and he accepted instantly.

He was also keen to meet with Yusal again—this time with a weapon in his hand. But there was one detail that Will and Umar had overlooked. He gestured at Umar's keffiyeh.

"You'll need to change those," he said. "Your men all wear keffiyehs with a yellow and white check. The Maashava people wear plain white."

It was a good point. The Bedullin were all so accustomed to their headwear that it was easy to overlook it. Umar nodded his head several times, acknowledging the point.

"We'll make white ones," he said. "We can use the cloaks of the men who aren't entering the town. Plenty of white cloth there."

"I think you should go in the night before," Will told Aloom.

"I'll come with you. I need to look over the town and find a vantage point to shoot from. If anyone questions us, tell them to keep their mouths shut."

"You might also suggest that they can feel free to lend a hand when the fighting starts," Umar said dryly, and Aloom shook his head in reply.

"Doubtful," he said. "The townspeople won't raise a finger to defend themselves. And government officials aren't popular in towns like this. Odds are they're looking forward to the execution."

"Where do you want me?" Umar asked. He had unconsciously deferred to Will's authority in this matter. Umar was a warrior whose skill lay in fast-moving cavalry raids in open country. The business of planning a close-quarters, street-to-street engagement in a town was new to him and he sensed the young foreigner knew what he was talking about.

"You'll lead the rest of the force into the town when we give you the signal." Will quickly sketched a rough map in the dirt with the point of his saxe. "There's a small gully to the northern side of the town—we saw it this morning."

He glanced up at Umar and the Aseikh nodded. He remembered the spot. "We'll get your men into cover there the night before. It's only seventy meters or so from the town. We'll wait till they've brought Halt and the others out . . ." He paused and looked at Aloom for advice. "How do they normally do that? All together or one at a time."

"All together," Aloom told him. "They'll bring them out a little before the ninth hour."

Will was unable to still his morbid sense of curiosity. "How do they plan to execute them?" he asked. "Will they be hanged?"

Umar shook his head. "It's not the custom here. We use the sword. Yusal will have them beheaded."

A sick dread clutched at Will's stomach as the Aseikh said the words. He had a horrible image of Halt and Horace and Evanlyn kneeling before the headsman's sword. His stomach churned at the thought of it. His breath came faster and he closed his eyes, trying to blot out the horror of it. What if I fail? He heard the question echoing in his mind. What if I fail?

He felt a firm grip on his hand and opened his eyes. Umar had leaned closer to him and had placed his hand over Will's.

"We're not going to let it happen," he said. There was a conviction in his voice that eased the sudden, horrified panic that had gripped Will. His breathing slowed and he steadied himself, nodding in gratitude to the desert warrior. Umar saw confidence returning to the young man's eyes once more and he released his hand.

"Do you have any thoughts about where you'll position yourself?" Umar asked.

Will nodded. "I'm thinking on one of the watchtowers along the north wall."

He'd need a position with a good overview of the market square where the executions would take place. And he'd need an elevated position so that he'd have a clear shot. Yusal would probably concentrate his men in the immediate area of the execution site to stop any trouble. He wouldn't be expecting it to come from a hundred meters away.

"Good idea," Umar agreed. He and Aloom both regarded the young man with interest. Umar had seen the accuracy of Will's shooting. Aloom had seen Halt and Gilan's skill. If the young Ranger was half as good as his companions, it would make for an interesting morning, he thought.

"You plan to shoot Yusal then?" Aloom asked. He was in fact hoping that he might get the chance to deal with the Tualaghi leader, but he realized he wouldn't be too disappointed if Yusal ended up on the wrong end of an arrow. Will chewed his bottom lip thoughtfully, staring down at the plan of the town he had sketched in the sand.

"Probably," he said. "My first priority will be the executioner. He's not getting anywhere near my friends. I'll want our fifty men to mingle with the crowd, as close to the execution site as possible. As soon as the executioner's down, they can keep the Tualaghi busy until Umar and his men arrive. I'll keep Halt and the others covered in case anyone else decides to try his luck as an executioner. If Yusal's still around, I might arrange to spoil his day."

"I'll need a sign so I know when to attack," Umar pointed out.

"One of my men is the company bugler," Aloom replied. "As soon as he sees Will shoot the executioner, he can sound the signal."

"That should do it," Will said. "But let's cut a few corners. Keep watch on the tower. Once you see me climbing up to it, start moving your men out of the canyon. Nobody'll be watching in that direction. They'll be watching proceedings in the market square."

"Right." All three men were staring at the rough map in the sand while their minds went over the details. It was a relatively simple plan, Will thought, and that was a good thing. Simple plans were less likely to go wrong.

Umar looked up and studied the young man's face.

"If you're going in the night before, we might need to darken your face a little," he said. He took Will's face between finger and thumb and turned it from side to side, studying it in the moonlight. Will was tanned after his time in Arrida but his skin was nowhere near as dark as the average Bedullin. His brown hair and dark eyes would pass muster, but not his complexion.

"Maybe we can use a little kafay to darken your skin," he said thoughtfully, then added, with a grin, "It's a pity your nose isn't bigger."

Will grinned, remembering his unintentional insult when he

had regained consciousness in the desert and found Umar bent over him. Then the Aseikh turned to Aloom.

"You'd better brief your men, Captain. I'll pick out twenty-five of my best warriors to go with them. They can start pairing off and getting to know each other tomorrow."

Aloom started to rise, then hesitated. "Captain?" he said. "I'm a lieutenant."

Umar shook his head. "I just promoted you. You might have to throw your weight around with the townspeople. And nobody ever listens to a lieutenant."

Aloom allowed himself a smile at that. "Too true," he said. "Too true."

41

For the past day, the prisoners had been hearing the sound of hammering. Something was being built in the market square, but with the large door remaining closed and locked the entire time, there was no way of knowing what was going on.

The chance to find out came when the guards arrived with their evening meal. Evanlyn watched as they set down the cold coffee, flat bread and a meager handful of dates. One of them caught her watching and grinned at her, but the grin was not a friendly one. Then he raised a thumb and drew it across his throat in an unmistakable cutting gesture. Unnoticed, Horace had sidled close to the open door so that he could look out onto the town below. Now, as they turned to leave, the two guards shoved him roughly back to join the others.

"I didn't like the look of that," Evanlyn said.

"You'll like it less when you see what they're building," Horace told her. "It's a big raised platform at the end of the square, with steps running up to it."

"Like a stage?" Evanlyn suggested. "Maybe they're planning to put on a play?"

"Or an execution," Horace said.

◆ ◆ ◆

Will and Aloom joined the throng of field-workers making their way back into the town. There were Tualaghi guards at the gateway, of course, but they took little notice of the Arridi workers streaming past them. In all the years that the Tualaghi had been forcing themselves on towns and villages in outlying areas, they had never encountered any real opposition. They were always careful to leave the occupants just enough to live on and regroup with after they left. And they usually didn't return to a town for several years after they had ransacked it. As a result, the Arridi people had come to accept the sporadic invasions as part of life. Not pleasant, but not worth dying over.

In the crowd around them, Will recognized at least three Arridi–Bedullin pairs. He glanced at Aloom and saw that the lieutenant had noticed as well.

"Let's find a coffeehouse," he said quietly. "My back's getting tired."

Both of them were burdened by large bundles of firewood. They'd spent the afternoon gathering it from the gullies and canyons in the surrounding area. In contrast to the treeless desert, the foothills of the northern massif had a sparse cover of spindly trees and bushes. The underground streams that honeycombed the hills provided sufficient water for the vegetation to grow.

The firewood bundles were useful props. They would be able to sell them to one of the inns or coffeehouses in the town, which would make them instantly welcome. The Arridi always needed firewood. Plus they helped disguise Will's slightly foreign appearance as he moved through the gate past the Tualaghi guards. He walked with his head bowed and his back bent under the load, keeping his eyes and face down.

Yet there was an even more important reason for carrying them.

In the center of Will's bundle was his unstrung longbow and quiver of arrows.

They crossed the town square, Will glancing sideways at the large platform built at the western end. Its purpose was unmistakable.

"Looks like they're ready," he whispered, and Aloom nodded agreement.

"Let's move away from here. We're too exposed out in the square."

They dived into one of the narrow streets that led away from the market square and its ominous wooden platform. Neither of them had any idea where they were going. But they both knew better than to look uncertain. They walked steadily, following the twisting path upward as the street matched the natural incline of the land.

He felt Aloom's hand tugging his sleeve and he looked to where the Arridi lieutenant was pointing down a side alley.

There was a two-story building, larger than its neighbors, about thirty meters away. A signboard hung out over the alleyway, with Arridi symbols painted on it in fading characters.

"There's an inn," said Aloom, and led the way toward the building.

They had opted to spend the night in an inn. The other pairs would spread themselves out among inns or coffeehouses in the town. Obviously, there wouldn't be enough of them to accommodate fifty extra men. But it was normal practice in a market town like this for the buildings that lined the sides of the market square to set up canvas awnings, projecting out into the square itself. The itinerant field- and market workers who came into town for market day would bed down for the night under their shelter. So would many of the Arridi–Bedullin pairs.

That meant they'd be on hand in the market square the following morning, which was where Will wanted them when the fighting started. Aloom and Will, however, wanted to be close to the wall and one of the watchtowers that Will had selected as a vantage point.

There was a lean-to stable beside the main building. They entered it, lowering their bundles of firewood to the ground. Will reached inside his and quickly withdrew his longbow and quiver, secreting the weapons in a manger half filled with old hay. There were a few animals in the stable—two horses and a ragged-looking donkey. They looked up incuriously at the newcomers, then went back to chomping on their hay.

"Obviously they don't have too many guests. We should be able to get a room here," Aloom said. They slung the bundles over their shoulders once more and marched to the inn's front door.

They entered the main room of the inn. In Araluen or Gallica, this would have been the taproom, where the patrons drank ale or wine. But the majority of Arridi avoided alcohol, choosing to drink strong bitter coffee instead. Will laid the bundle of firewood down and glanced around the room. There were eight or nine men seated at low tables, mostly in pairs or threes. They looked up at the newcomers, then, seeing they didn't know them, went back to their conversations. One man sat apart. He was overweight and he continued to stare at Will as Aloom went to the bar and negotiated a meal and a room for the night in return for the firewood and a small amount of money.

"Haven't seen you around before," the innkeeper said, once the bargaining was done. There was a note of inquiry in his voice. Aloom met his gaze unblinkingly.

"That's probably because I keep myself to myself," he said. His tone was less than friendly and invited no further discussion. Country people in Arrida, he had told Will, went to great lengths to keep their own business private—although, conversely, they loved sticking their noses into other people's affairs.

The innkeeper accepted the rebuff philosophically. He poured two cups of coffee and placed them on a wooden tray, along with a plate of fresh flat bread, several spiced dips and four skewers of grilled lamb.

Aloom brought the food and drinks to the table Will had selected and they began to eat.

As they did, Will could feel the fat man's gaze still on him.

"We're being watched," he said quietly to Aloom. The Arridi officer glanced up and made eye contact with the fat man.

"Something on your mind, friend?" he said sharply.

The man was unabashed. "You're strangers around here," he said.

Aloom nodded. "That's because we heard you spend a lot of time here," he said rudely.

"So where have you come from?" the man asked. Aloom fixed him with an unfriendly stare. He shifted on the cushion and removed the dagger, still in its scabbard, from his belt. He placed the weapon on the table before him.

"I don't believe that's any of your business," he said. Then, in an aside to Will, loud enough to be heard, he added, "Typical small-town busybody. Always minding other people's business for them."

Will grunted and filled his mouth with bread and hot lamb, avoiding the need to reply.

"Does your friend ever say anything?" the fat man asked. Aloom set down the piece of bread he had just rolled around several chunks of meat and gave an exasperated sigh.

"I heard him say 'oops!' once, when he cut the ears off someone who was asking too many questions." Some of the other guests looked up and nodded in appreciation.

Obviously, the fat man wasn't popular in the coffeehouse.

"Leave it, Saoud!" one of them called across the room. "Let the people eat their meal."

There was a general chorus of agreement and the fat man looked around, his distaste for his fellow guests all too obvious. He sneered at them all, then finally settled back on his cushion and drank his coffee. But his eyes stayed on the two strangers.

When they finished their meal and headed for the upper floor, where their room was situated, Will could still feel the man's eyes boring into his back. He wondered if they should do something about him.

Aloom sensed his uncertainty. "Don't worry," he said as they mounted the stairs, "by tomorrow, he'll have forgotten all about us. He'll have something else to gossip about."

Will wasn't so sure.

42

THE KEY RATTLED IN THE STOREROOM LOCK. THE PRISONERS glanced up. It was morning, a few hours after first light, and they were accustomed to having the first meal of the day delivered about now. They had fallen into a routine. The day was divided by the three meals they were given. The food was unvaried and uninteresting— usually yesterday's flat bread, stale and tasteless, and a handful of dates—not enough to provide any of them with a real meal.

But at least there was coffee and, even though it was served luke-warm at best, Horace, Halt and Gilan appreciated it. Svengal and Erak, of course, bemoaned the absence of strong ale. Svengal sometimes thought longingly of the half-full cask he had left behind on *Wolfwind*, several weeks ago. He wondered how his men were faring in Al Shabah. Probably a lot better than he was here, he thought morosely.

The others were nursing thoughts of their own. Gilan was still wondering about the platform Horace had reported seeing. Executions, the young warrior had said. Gilan knew that he and Halt were decidedly unpopular with their captors. If anyone were going to be executed, he thought, it would be the two of them. But he faced the thought philosophically. Rangers were accustomed to being in tight spots. They were also used to being the principal targets for their enemies. He had lived with the possibility of an event like this for years. All he could do now was wait for an opportunity to escape.

Horace remained calm. He had faith in Halt and Gilan and he knew that if there was a way out of this predicament, they would find it.

It was the fact that their captors came for them at the time when they normally served breakfast that caught them all by surprise. Expecting two men to enter the storeroom laden with a tray of food and a jug of coffee, they were caught unawares when a dozen men, swords drawn, dashed through the open doors and took up stations around them.

Halt, sitting with his back against the wall, went to rise.

But the point of a curved saber stopped him, pressing none too gently into his throat.

"Stay where you are," the Tualaghi captain ordered him. He gestured to the seated Ranger, his eyes never leaving Halt's face. "Hands out front," he said. Then, to one of his men, as Halt complied: "Tie him."

Halt's hands were quickly tied in front of him. Initially, as the Tualaghi went to tie them, he tried to tense the muscles in his arms and wrists, hoping to relax them later and cause the ropes to loosen slightly. But the Tualaghi captain was wise to the old trick. He rapped Halt sharply across his knuckles with the unsharpened back of his blade.

"That's enough of that," he ordered harshly. Halt shrugged and relaxed his hands. It had been worth a try. Around the room, he watched as the others had their hands similarly bound. Why all of them? he wondered. He and Gilan, he could understand. Maybe even Horace. But the others were valuable hostages. He felt a sinking sensation in his stomach as the others were dragged to their feet.

Then the captain gripped the rope that secured his hands together and hauled him upright as well.

"Where are we going?" he demanded, but the man simply laughed and shoved Halt toward the door.

Will and Aloom slept relatively late. Most of the other guests had risen, breakfasted and left shortly after first light.

However, reasoning that they had to wait until the ninth hour, they had decided that there was no point rising early and then attracting suspicion by loitering in the vicinity of the watchtower on the crumbling wall. Consequently, they entered the main room of the inn an hour after most of the other guests had departed.

Most of them. The fat man from the night before was still in his room. He had watched, his door held open just a crack, as the two young men made their way down the hall to the stairs. Saoud was a vain man. He was a wealthy cloth merchant and he owned several stalls in the marketplace, all manned by his paid staff. The actual business of dealing with customers was beneath Saoud these days. He was too wealthy and too important for such crass dealings. Instead, he spent his time in coffeehouses, where he expected to be treated with the respect due to a rich, self-made man.

All of which added up to the fact that he hadn't liked Aloom's brusque, disrespectful manner the previous night. And he hadn't liked the fact that others in the coffee room had joined in on the strangers' side.

There was something suspicious about those two, he thought. And he knew people who might be pleased to hear about it.

As Aloom and Will descended the stairs to the coffee room below, he quietly emerged from his room, closing the door gently behind him, wincing at the noise the lock made as it slipped home. Would they have heard him?

No. He could hear their voices floating up the stairway as they talked, without interruption or pause. Walking carefully, staying close to the wall to avoid having floorboards squeak under his bulk, he moved to the stairs himself.

He paused as he heard the main door of the inn open and close. For a moment he thought the two men had left. Then he heard the older one speaking to the innkeeper. So the younger one had gone outside for something, he thought. But what?

He edged his way down a few more stairs, his ears alert for any sound of his quarry returning. Then he heard the front door again and saw the younger stranger moving past the hall at the bottom of the stairs, into the coffee room again.

This time, he was carrying what looked like a long staff, wrapped and tied in canvas, in his right hand. Saoud frowned. He had never seen a staff like that before. Moving carefully, he went down the rest of the stairs and let himself out into the street through a side door.

There was another alleyway a few meters to the right, even smaller than this one. He hurried to it, moving gratefully into the shadows, then settled down to wait for the two men to leave.

A few minutes later they emerged from the inn and turned left, heading north. Saoud watched them curiously, then followed them. It was already thirty minutes past the eighth hour and the majority of people in Maashava would be heading for the market square. Even though they might have no argument with the prisoners who were scheduled to die, an execution was a spectacle and most people wanted to watch it.

Why then were these two heading away from the square? There was nothing of interest on the northern side of the town—just a confusing jumble of falling-down, rat-infested hovels. And the crumbling old wall itself, of course, with its ramshackle watchtowers.

Turning abruptly, the fat cloth merchant retraced his steps.

Talish might be interested to hear this, he thought. Talish was a Tualaghi warrior—a minor authority in the nomad band, who usually traveled with two henchmen to do his bidding. They had quickly established a reputation among the Arridi townspeople as thieves and extortionists. Somehow, they always seemed to divine where wealthy Arridi merchants had hidden their money or their best products. In fact, it was Saoud who told them. He had established an alliance with the three Tualaghi. In return for their leaving his stalls and storehouses untouched, he informed on his neighbors and competitors.

There was a coffeehouse that they frequented, by the edge of the market square. Saoud increased his pace, his fat body wobbling as he hurried through the narrow streets to find the Tualaghi thief. If Talish didn't seem interested in the two men, he'd tell him they were carrying a purse full of gold. That would definitely get the Tualaghi's interest.

Later, if Talish were frustrated or angry at the absence of the gold, it would only work against the two strangers. And as far as Saoud was concerned, that was all to the good.

Will and Aloom picked their way through piles of rubbish and fallen masonry. The northern section of the town was in the worst state of disrepair. The houses had been left to rot and collapse and had been taken over by squatters—the poor, the unemployed, the criminally inclined. From time to time, they saw faces peering furtively through crumbling doorways at them. As soon as they were spotted, the observers would pull back into the shadows of the houses.

The streets here were narrow and wound in a haphazard fashion as they detoured around houses that had collapsed and had simply been left where they fell—gradually deteriorating into shapeless mounds of masonry. Will had lost his sense of direction some time back. He hoped Aloom knew where they were heading. The Arridi lieutenant certainly led the way confidently enough.

Will heaved a sigh of relief as they eventually emerged from a twisting, confusing alley and he saw the remnants of the north wall ahead of them.

Originally, there had been a wide, clear footpath along the inner base of the wall, with buildings not permitted to encroach within three meters. But over recent years, people had built hovels and lean-tos against the wall itself—often using the collapsed mud bricks that had formed part of the wall to build their dark little hutches.

They had come farther east than they had planned, forced into one winding, random detour after another as they had picked their way through the ruined houses. Now Will saw that the watchtower he had picked out as a vantage point was some two hundred meters away. He recognized it by a roof beam that had collapsed and caught on the railing of the observation deck. The beam stuck out at an acute angle.

He looked up at the sun. It was climbing higher into the eastern sky and the tower was a long way away. There was another one closer to them, barely fifty meters away. By the time he picked his way past the lean-tos and the fallen piles of rubble, he might reach the original tower too late. It had taken them longer than they had estimated to traverse the ruined part of the town.

He gestured to the nearer tower.

"That'll have to do," he said, and Aloom nodded. He was looking worried.

"It's getting late," he said. "They'll be starting any minute."

Half running, they picked their way through the chaos of fallen masonry and hovels toward the nearer of the two watchtowers.

43

UMAR CROUCHED BEHIND A LARGE GRANITE BOULDER AT THE head of the gully, his eyes screwed up, intent on the watchtower that he and Will had selected the day before. The half-fallen beam made it easy to distinguish from its neighbors.

There was a movement behind him and he turned to see Hassan. The young man had made his way forward from the position farther back in the gully where the main Bedullin force waited quietly.

"Any sign of him, Aseikh?" Hassan asked.

Umar shook his head. "He should be in position by now. It's nearly nine."

"Maybe the executions have been delayed," Hassan suggested.

Umar scratched his beard reflectively. "Maybe. But I can't see that devil Yusal giving up such a chance to impress the locals." He held up a hand for silence, his head turned slightly to listen. From inside Maashava, the deep, rhythmic booming of a bass drum carried to them on the gentle morning breeze. "No," he said. "The execution's going ahead. What the devil has happened to Will and Aloom?"

"Shall I bring the men up, Aseikh?" Hassan asked. Umar hesitated. Chances were there would be no one looking in this direction and they could get a head start down the dusty track that led to the town. But he rejected the idea. All that was needed was one curious pair of eyes to see them and the alarm would be raised.

"We'll wait for the Ranger," he said.

Surrounded by guards, the seven prisoners were led down a long earthenware ramp from the storehouse cave to the streets of the town itself.

Shoved and buffeted, they stumbled over the uneven ground, strung together in a long line, forbidden to speak to each other. For the most part, the Arridi townspeople watched them with a mixture of apathy and morbid pity. Yet, as always in such a crowd, there were those who chose to jeer at the prisoners and throw stones, clumps of earth or garbage at them. Halt glared at one group of young men in their twenties. They had obviously been drinking. They stumbled and staggered together, their eyes red and their jaws slack as they hurled insults at the line of prisoners. Halt turned and looked back over his shoulder at Selethen, the next in line behind him.

"I thought your religion banned alcohol," he said.

Selethen glanced with distaste at the noisy, catcalling group and shrugged.

"There's a low element in every society," he said. "People like that are simply too glad that they're not the ones being led to the block today."

A guard stepped forward and stung the two men with a knotted rope end.

"Hold your tongues!" he yelled at them. "No talking, we said!"

They emerged onto the square itself now. It was thronged with people and their escort had to shove to make a path for them. Half those watching were Tualaghi, Halt saw. They were enjoying them-

selves, hoping the prisoners' nerves would break at the last moment
and cause them to cry for mercy.

Not that they'd be listened to. The concepts of pity and mercy
were unknown to the Tualaghi.

On the far side of the square, close beside the raised timber platform which they could now see clearly for the first time, the deep
booming of a drum had begun. It continued in a slow rhythm, like
the beating of a great heart. It was a signal for the crowd around
them to redouble their noise.

The single file of prisoners was forced through the crowd until
they were standing by the steps leading to the platform.

Halt looked up. Yusal stood above them, dressed today in flowing robes of dark blue, his booted feet spread apart, hands on hips.
As ever, his face was concealed behind the dark blue veil. Only his
eyes were visible, as cold as ever. He turned to the crowd now, scanning the faces before him, waiting for silence to fall.

Gradually, the shouting died away to an occasional exclamation.
Then those too were stilled as Tualaghi soldiers in the crowd struck
out at anyone who interrupted their leader. An unnatural silence fell
over the square.

"Bring the prisoners up," Yusal said, his harsh voice now heard
clearly in all corners of the square.

The guards urged their captives forward and Halt led the way up
the rough steps to the platform. He felt the stairs shudder under his
feet as Selethen mounted them behind him and Svengal followed
behind the Arridi.

Yusal grabbed Halt's shoulder as he went to move along the platform, making way for those who were following.

"You stay here," the Tualaghi told him. "You will be first."

There was an angry growl of approval from the Tualaghi warriors in the crowd. The other prisoners might provide sport and diversion with their executions. The two Rangers were hated.

The drum, which had temporarily ceased its ominous booming, began once more.

As Gilan climbed to the platform, following Erak and Evanlyn, Yusal gestured for him to stand beside Halt. Another murmur of pleasure came from the watching Tualaghi.

There was a bustle of movement in the ranks of the crowd below them and Toshak shoved his way through to the front. He grinned up at Halt.

"This is where you get it in the neck, Ranger!" he called.

Halt ignored him, looking away, scanning the crowd, hoping beyond hope that he might see Will somewhere. He still had an unreasoning faith that his apprentice had survived and that he would not let them go to their deaths without attempting a rescue of some kind.

Vaguely, he was aware of Erak replying to Toshak, inviting him up onto the platform.

"Even with my hands tied, I'm sure I could break your treacherous neck for you, Toshak!" he said. Toshak grinned infuriatingly.

"I'll take your head back to Skandia, Erak," he said. "I'll use your skull as an ale tankard."

Yusal glared at the two northerners. He had a sense of theater and occasion and a flair for the dramatic. But their uncultured, noisy bickering had no place here.

"Be silent!" he commanded. Toshak glanced at him, shrugged indifferently and leaned against one of the support poles to the platform. Yusal, satisfied that there would be no further interruption, held up one hand.

"Let Mussaun stand forward!" he shouted. The cry was taken up by the Tualaghi around the square.

"Mussaun! Mussaun! Mussaun!"

The shouting echoed off the building fronts, keeping pace with the incessant booming of the drum. Some of the Arridi were caught up in the moment and joined their voices to the chorus. They had seen executions before. They had a good idea what was about to happen. The shouting grew in intensity, volume and urgency.

Then a massive figure appeared on one side of the square, standing high above the heads of the spectators. For a moment he seemed to be floating in the air, then Halt realized that he was on a large wooden shield, being borne at shoulder height by four Tualaghi as they forced their way through the crowd toward the execution site.

The drumbeat intensified in pace and the shouting went with it. Mussaun was a giant of a man, clad entirely in black. His long, flowing robe billowed on the early morning breeze and the tails of his black keffiyeh trailed behind him as the four warriors carried him forward. The lower half of his face was covered by the ever-present dark blue Tualaghi veil.

His hands, crossed in front of his chest, rested on the hilt of a massive, black-bladed, double-handed sword.

Will and Aloom had reached the nearer tower as the drumbeat began, deep and sonorous.

"They're starting!" Aloom cried. "Get moving! We haven't much time!"

Will said nothing. He stripped the canvas wrapping from his longbow, bent it behind his right calf, anchoring it in place with his left ankle, and slid the bowstring up into its notch, grunting slightly with the effort of overcoming the bow's fifty-kilogram draw weight.

He tossed his cloak to one side, revealing the quiver of two dozen arrows over his shoulder, slung the bow alongside it and started to climb up the rotten timber framework of the tower.

It was slow going. In spite of Aloom's exhortations to hurry, and his own growing sense of urgency, he knew he had to pick his hand- and footholds carefully. The tower was in worse condition than he had expected and there was an excellent chance that it might collapse under a hurried movement.

He'd gone up four meters, past the top of the wall itself, and was stepping carefully to one last crosspiece before he gained the observation platform.

The drumbeats were now coming faster and faster. Then a chant from hundreds of voices carried to him:

"Mussaun! Mussaun! Mussaun!"

"Who the blazes is Mussaun?" he muttered to himself, inching carefully along a decidedly untrustworthy timber brace.

He was poised in midair, his foot reaching out tentatively for the more solid-looking platform, his weight supported by his arms so that he was utterly helpless, when he heard a voice from behind him.

"Who are you? And what are you up to?"

He looked down. Aloom was below him, facing back the way they had come. Ten meters away, three Tualaghi warriors watched them suspiciously. Behind them, smiling vindictively, was the fat merchant they had seen in the inn the previous night.

44

The giant executioner balanced easily on the shield, borne on the shoulders of four Tualaghi warriors as they made their way through the crowded market square toward the execution site. As he passed through the crowd, hands were raised and weapons brandished by the Tualaghi in admiration of the massive figure.

The four bearers stopped beside the execution platform and Mussaun stepped lightly onto it. As he did so, another bout of cheering rose up.

Now that he could see him more closely, Halt realized that the executioner really was a giant. He stood well over two meters in height and his shoulders and body were built in the same massive proportion. He whipped the huge two-handed sword up until it was raised vertically above his head and paraded along the front of the platform, ignoring the line of prisoners and brandishing the sword to the assembled crowd.

Again the cries of his name echoed out.

"Mussaun! Mussaun! Mussaun!"

He marched along the front of the platform to the far end, then back to the center again, drinking in the adulation of the crowd. Then, when he stood at the center, he raised the sword to the fullest stretch of his arms, reversed it with a flick of his powerful wrists and drove it, thudding, point-first into the platform.

He stepped back a pace, leaving the sword stuck into the wood, slowly quivering.

Then he reached up to the lacing that secured his outer robe, quickly released it and swung the robe out and away from his body, letting it fall in a heap behind him.

He was clad now only in a pair of wide, billowing trousers, gathered at the waist and each ankle, and the black keffiyeh and dark blue face veil of the Tualaghi. His bare torso gleamed slightly with oil and now the hugely muscled arms, chest and abdomen could be seen clearly.

He stepped forward and, without any apparent effort, flicked the sword free of the wood, then spun it around his body and head in a bewildering series of high-speed arcs and circles. He handled the huge sword as if it were a toy, but to anyone who knew weapons and could estimate the weight of the long, heavy, tapering blade, it was an impressive display that spoke volumes about the strength and coordination of arm, body and wrist muscles. The highly polished black blade caught the rays of the morning sun and flashed and dazzled the eye, moving so quickly that at times it seemed more like a solid black disc than a narrow blade.

"Mussaun! Mussaun! Mussaun!"

The cries went up again and this time, more of the Arridi joined in, mesmerized by the strength and power and charisma of the Tualaghi giant.

Mussaun was pleased to play to the crowd. He began dancing from side to side, delivering overhead cuts, side cuts and deep thrusts with the massive sword, letting it flicker and sweep with all the speed of a snake's tongue. Back and forth he went, from left to right, then back to the left again.

Then he leaped high in the air and delivered a huge, arcing downward cut with the sword, miming the decapitation of a kneeling victim. The point thudded into the wood planks and again he released it and leaped back, leaving the sword quivering from the force of the blow.

As quickly, he seized the two-handed grip and jerked it free again, then began knee-walking from side to side, dropping to a knee with each stride, and all the time keeping the sword spinning, flashing and cutting. The chanting of his name intensified, with the cadence of the chant matching the rhythm of his movements.

From his kneeling position, he leaped high in the air, spinning as he came down to face the line of victims, carving an invisible X in the air with two diagonal sweeps of the sword. Then he spun once more to face the crowd. For all his size and strength he was amazingly light on his feet. He signaled to one of the men who had carried him to the platform and the warrior reached to a nearby market stall and retrieved a melon. He tossed it high into the air above the giant.

The sword flashed in two opposing diagonal cuts. The first cleaved the melon in two pieces. The second sliced through the larger of the two before the sections of fruit dropped to the platform with a wet thud.

Unbidden, the soldier now lobbed another melon and this time Mussaun halved it with a horizontal sweep, followed instantly by a vertical cut through one of the pieces.

The crowd howled its delight.

Mussaun responded by passing the sword, spinning, from one hand to the other, maintaining the rhythm as he passed it from right to left hand then back again, holding it by the long hilt, close to the crosspiece, controlling it with the strength of his hands and wrists.

He tossed it, spinning, high into the air, caught it as the hilt came around. Then, leaping high, he spun one hundred and eighty degrees in the air and brought the sword down in a savage splitting stroke at the captive who happened to be facing him.

By chance, it was Horace.

The crowd fell suddenly silent as the huge figure leaped, spun and struck. They expected to see the foreigner split from head to shoulders, at least. But at the last moment, with an amazing display of strength and control, Mussaun halted the downward stroke so that the massive blade merely touched Horace's hair.

The crowd yelled, then fell silent as they realized that the young foreigner hadn't moved, hadn't flinched. He hadn't tried to raise his bound hands in a futile attempt to ward off the terrible blow. He had merely stood, rock steady, watching the executioner with a disdainful look on his face.

Horace's pulse was racing and adrenaline was surging into his system. But he showed no sign of it. He had somehow realized what was coming as the huge man had leaped and spun before him. The coordination of the back stroke with the turn had alerted Horace, and he had determined that he would not move a muscle when the stroke arrived. It took enormous strength of will but he had managed it. Now he smiled.

Prance and leap all you like, my friend, he thought, I'll show you what a knight of Araluen is made of.

Mussaun paused. He frowned as he stared at the smiling young man before him. In times past, that movement had invariably resulted in the victim's dropping to the ground, hands above head, screaming for mercy. This youth was *smiling* at him.

"That was really very good," Horace said. "I wonder, could I have a go?" He held out his bound hands.

It was as if he really expected Mussaun to pass him the sword. The executioner took a pace back, bewildered. He felt the situation was moving out of his control. Then matters became worse as the two bearded Skandian ruffians joined in.

"Nice work, Horace," Erak said, chuckling delightedly.

Svengal echoed the sentiment. "Well done, boy! That's set Horrible Mussaun back on his haunches!"

With a scream of rage, Mussaun turned on the two guffawing Skandians. The sword spun over his head, then he swung it in a flat, horizontal arc, this time straight at Erak's neck. As with Horace, he halted the blow only millimeters from the Skandian. But, like Horace, Erak showed no sign of flinching.

Instead, he turned to his cohort and said in an approving tone, "Nice control, Svengal. The man's got good wrists. I'd like to see him with a battleax in his hands."

Svengal frowned, not totally agreeing.

"I'd like to see him with a battleax in his head, chief," he said, and they both guffawed again.

Mussaun sensed a growing impatience and puzzlement in the crowd. The chanting of his name had died down as they showed their respect for the courage of these foreigners. Arrida was a hard land and violent death was a daily occurrence. The Arridi and Tualaghi both admired those who could face it with such aplomb. It was vital, Mussaun knew, that he regain the mob's respect. He paced along the line of captives, looking for the weak link.

And saw the girl.

45

Suspicion turned to certainty in the eyes of Talish, the Tualaghi thief, as he glanced up and saw Will hanging from the watchtower framework, his longbow and quiver slung over one shoulder.

The Tualaghi didn't recognize the young man but he recognized the weapons. He had seen bows like that before, when he and his friends had charged the Arridi campsite.

"He's one of the foreigners!" he yelled, drawing his sword. "Get him!"

His two henchmen moved forward with him, their own swords ringing clear of their scabbards. Aloom stepped clear of the wall, discarding his cloak and drawing his own weapon to bar their way.

"Keep going, Will!" he called. "I'll take care of them!"

But there were three of them, all seasoned fighters, and they crowded upon him, swords flashing, rising and falling as they attacked. Aloom gave ground stubbornly before them but he was fighting a losing battle. He set his back to the stones of the wall and desperately parried the storm of blows that rained upon him. Inevitably, one of the swords broke through his defense and he was cut badly on the upper part of his sword arm. Then another stroke slashed across his thigh and he stumbled, recovering just in time to avoid a horizontal slash at his throat.

Hanging awkwardly above him, there was no way Will could unsling his bow in time to help. Even if he could have done so, he couldn't have shot, hanging by his arms. Yet he could see his friend would be dead within seconds. Aloom's parries were growing clumsy and awkward now and he was cut again, this time across the forehead so that blood ran into his eyes, half blinding him.

From the square, Will heard the crowd's chanting grow weaker, and then all was silent. He didn't like the sound of that silence.

Will hesitated for a second. Aloom would die if he didn't help him. But the change in tone of the crowd told him that events in the square had built to a climax. He might even now be too late . . .

But Aloom was here and now, and fighting desperately to save him. There was no question about what he should do. Measuring the distance, he released his grip and let himself drop to the uneven battle below him.

He landed feetfirst on the shoulders of the Tualaghi leader. The man gave a cry of shock and pain and crumpled beneath the force of Will's body. Will heard the snap of bones breaking somewhere, then a sickening thud as the bandit's head slammed into the hard, rocky ground. Will rolled forward to cushion the shock of landing, although the greater part of the force of his fall had been broken by the Tualaghi's body.

He leaped to his feet as the other two bandits turned on him. Shocked by his unexpected action, they hesitated a second— and that was a second too long. Will stepped into them, closing the distance so that he was inside the reach of the nearest man's sword.

Always move forward if you have the option. Halt had drummed the lesson into his brain hundreds of times. A man going forward has the momentum to control a battle. Now Will acted spontaneously, his saxe knife hissing out of its scabbard as he drew and lunged in one smooth, continuous movement, taking the closest man in the center of the body.

The Tualaghi gave a short cry, half surprise, half pain, and sank back against the wall, his sword dropping from his hand and clanging against the stones.

There was still one Tualaghi to take care of.

As Will had dropped from the tower onto the shoulder of the first bandit, Aloom had sunk gratefully back against the wall, trying to stanch the flow of blood from the multiple sword cuts to his arm, leg and body. He saw the third Tualaghi was within reach now and tried to lend a hand.

Coming to his knees, he slashed at the bandit, but his stroke was weak and poorly coordinated. The Tualaghi saw it coming and parried it easily, sending Aloom's sword spinning away out of his grip. Then he raised his own sword to finish off the Arridi. He was an experienced fighter and he judged he had time for one quick killing stroke before he must turn and face the foreigner.

Will threw the saxe underhand, following through to the target automatically, in a movement that had been drilled into him, over and over again, in the past five years.

The Tualaghi, arm raised for the killing stroke, was totally defenseless as the saxe knife flashed across the distance separating him from Will. He felt a heavy impact in his side, an impact that staggered him.

Then a huge pain flamed up around the point of impact and he wondered what it . . .

Then nothing.

Will started toward Aloom. Then he stopped. From the square, voices were calling again.

* * *

Rage had built up in Mussaun like water behind a dam. He released it now with a lingering scream of hate as he leaped for the girl, sword raised. Then the blade was sweeping and cutting across her, beside her, above her head, thudding down into the planking by her feet so that the floor of the platform shook with the force of his blows. He cut the air about her, the sword never more than a few millimeters from her. It was a terrifying, terrible display of rage and strength.

The girl didn't move.

Evanlyn stood stock-still, knowing she must not move, must not cringe or flinch or blink while the terrifying weapon hissed past, barely a hairbreadth from her face and body. Any one of those blows would cut her in half, she realized. Yet she forced herself to show no fear. She knew how the others' courage in the face of this man's show had upset him, and she determined not to give him an inch of satisfaction.

She stood, eyes open but deliberately unfocused as the razor-sharp blade, nearly a meter and a half long, hissed and whooshed around her face and neck and body.

And finally, it was Mussaun who was defeated. He stepped back, lowering the sword. His body gleamed with perspiration. His eyes above the mask showed his utter bewilderment. And the crowd was silent.

Then one voice, from somewhere in the middle, called out. "Release her!"

And another joined in, and another. Until a growing section of the crowd were echoing the sentiment. Mostly they were Arridi. But Yusal's eyes narrowed in rage as he saw several of his own men raising their hands and calling for Evanlyn's release.

Furious, he stepped forward, drawing his own sword to emphasize his words.

"That's enough!" he shouted. "Enough!"

Behind him, Halt realized that this was a moment of maximum danger for Evanlyn.

Yusal might well choose to make a swift end of her here and now to still the chance of any further protest on her behalf. He would have to take the focus away from her and concentrate Yusal's anger on himself. Forcing a tone of utter boredom and disdain into his voice, he stepped forward, calling loudly to the Tualaghi leader:

"Yusal, this is getting very boring. Can we get on with it, please?"

Yusal rounded on him, Evanlyn forgotten. This was the man his soldiers hated, he knew. This was the way to recover control of the situation. Nobody would call for Halt's release. He pointed his sword now at the gray-bearded, shaggy-haired figure.

"Kill him!" he ordered Mussaun. "Kill him now!"

"Release her! Release her!"

Will heard the distant shouts and realized they must be about Evanlyn and for a moment felt a surge of hope. They were going to release his friends. Then Yusal's hard, uncompromising tones cut across the voices of the crowd.

"That's enough! Enough!"

Aloom, face screwed up in pain, gestured weakly for Will to climb back up to the watchtower.

"Go! Go! Hurry! There's no time!"

He coughed and scarlet blood stained the front of his robe. But he continued to point to the watchtower and Will knew he was right. He could tend to Aloom later, but now he had to rescue his friends and signal Umar to bring the rest of his men to the attack.

Heedless of the rotting wood that groaned and splintered beneath his movements, he scrambled up the tower. Whereas before he had moved slowly and carefully, this time he moved at lightning speed, reasoning that the less time he put his weight on a hand- or a foothold, the less chance there would be that it might collapse beneath him. Several beams, in fact, splintered and shattered after he had stepped clear of them and on to the next. The pieces clattered to the ground below.

"Kill him now!" Will heard Yusal's shouted order and he knew, somehow, that he was talking about Halt.

Then he was on the relatively solid footing of the tower platform. He shrugged the bow off his shoulder into his left hand. His right hand automatically sought an arrow from the quiver and had it nocked on the bowstring before he was even aware of performing the action.

From his vantage point he could see across the low, flat-roofed houses of this section of the town to the square. Beyond the milling heads of several hundred spectators, Halt was being dragged forward and forced to kneel beside the executioner's block. His companions stood in a line behind him. Yusal stood to one side, a grim figure with his dark robes and veiled face. On the other side was a monster. A giant Tualaghi, bare to the waist, head and face covered. Hugely muscled, gleaming with oil, holding an immense sword in two hands.

There was Halt kneeling.

The executioner stepped forward. He raised the sword over his head.

Will drew the arrow back until the tip of his right forefinger touched the corner of his mouth. His mind and senses analyzed the shooting situation in fractions of a second. Range? A little over a hundred and twenty meters. The arrow tip raised slightly in his sighting picture. Wind? Nothing to worry about.

The executioner was almost at full stretch now, measuring his stroke before the sword started down. Will knew this shot had to be right. There would be no time for a second attempt. He shrugged away a moment of confidence-sapping uncertainty.

Worry that you might miss a shot and you almost certainly will, Halt had taught him.

He heard the long sigh of expectation from the crowd, emptied his mind of doubt and allowed the bow string to slide free of his fingers, almost of its own volition, sending the arrow on its way.

46

GILAN WATCHED HELPLESSLY AS THE MASSIVE SWORD ROSE higher and higher in Mussaun's two-handed grip. The young Ranger's face was twisted in a grimace of impotent horror. He was watching his friend and teacher about to die, torn by a combination of grief and frustration that he was unable to do anything to prevent it. He tried to cry out Halt's name but the word choked in his throat and he felt tears running freely down his cheeks.

The sword rose higher still. Any moment, it would begin its downward, cleaving path.

But then, inexplicably, it continued to rise, going past the vertical, past the point where the executioner should have begun his killing stroke.

There was a sudden chorus of surprise from several points in the crowd.

The sword continued up and over as the executioner, arms fully extended above his head, slowly toppled backward, falling with a plank-shuddering crash on his back. Only then did those on the platform see what had been visible to the crowd in the square: the gray-shafted arrow buried deep in the executioner's chest. The huge sword fell free as Mussaun hit the planks, stone dead.

"It's Will!" Gilan yelled, scanning the crowd feverishly to see where his friend was concealed.

Kneeling by the block, Halt lowered his head, closed his eyes and whispered a prayer of thanks.

Around them, pandemonium erupted. Yusal watched, amazed, as his executioner fell dead before him. Then he saw the arrow and knew instinctively where the next shot would be aimed. Sword still in hand, he hesitated a second, tempted to finish off the kneeling figure. But he knew he had no time. He turned to his right to escape.

The second arrow was already on its way before the first struck Mussaun down. The moment he released the first shot, Will knew, with the instincts of a master marksman, that it was good. In less time than it takes to say it, he nocked, drew, sighted on the black-robed figure of Yusal and released.

It was the turn to the right that saved Yusal's life. The arrow had been aimed at his heart. Instead, it took him in the muscle of his upper left arm as he turned away. He screamed in pain and fury, dropping his sword as he clutched at the wound with his right hand. Stumbling, he lurched toward the rear of the platform to escape, doubled over in pain, holding his bleeding left arm.

Will, high on his vantage point, saw the movement and realized he had missed. But he had other priorities for the moment. Yusal was out of the picture, but there were still armed Tualaghi all over the platform, threatening his friends. His hands moved in a blur of action as he nocked, drew, shot, nocked, drew, shot, until half a dozen arrows were arcing over the square, and the guards began dropping with shrieks of agony and terror.

Four of them went down, dead or wounded, before the others regained their wits. Faced with the prospect of staying on the platform, exposed to the deadly arrows of the unseen archer, they chose to escape, leaping from the platform into the square below.

Already, a series of individual battles had begun as the infiltrating pairs of Bedullin and Arridi troopers threw off their cloaks, drew their weapons and struck out at the nearest Tualaghi warriors. The square was soon a seething, struggling mass of clashing warriors. The townspeople of Maashava attempted to escape from the killing ground, but many of them were wounded as the Tualaghi, fighting for their lives, not knowing where the sudden attack had come from, simply struck out blindly around them.

On the platform, a few guards remained. But not for long. Erak and Svengal combined to pick one bodily off the ground and heave him into three of his comrades. The four bodies crashed over and rolled off the edge of the platform into the struggling mob below. Gilan, meanwhile, had seized Yusal's fallen saber and was cutting through Evanlyn's bonds with its razor-sharp edge.

Horace, taking in what had happened, reacted with all the speed of the trained warrior he was. He dashed forward to where Halt was struggling his way clear of the block, raising himself to his feet and slipping his bound arms up over the block. Horace helped him untangle himself, then turned him toward Gilan, a few meters away, now releasing Erak and Svengal from their bonds.

"Gilan'll cut the ropes," he said, giving the Ranger a shove to send him on his way. Then the young knight scanned the square and the space beyond it for a sight of his friend. He saw a figure high on a watchtower on the wall. The clothes were unfamiliar but the longbow in his hand was unmistakable. Taking a deep breath, Horace yelled one word.

"Will!"

His voice was trained to carry over the din of a battlefield. Will heard it clearly. Horace saw him wave briefly. Horace held both his bound hands in the air above his head for a few seconds, looking up at them. Then he bent forward and placed them on the far side of the execution block, pulling them as far apart as he could to expose the ropes that held his wrists together. He turned his face away, closed his eyes and prayed that his friend had got the message.

Hissssss-Slam!

He felt the bonds part a little, opened his eyes and saw the arrow quivering in the wood of the execution block. Will had cut one of the three strands holding Horace captive. The other two were still intact.

"You're slipping," Horace muttered to himself. But the answer to the problem lay in the form of the razor-sharp broadhead on the arrow. It took only a few seconds for Horace to cut the remaining ropes with the keen edge, leaving his hands free.

In the square below them, a small group of half a dozen Tualaghi had reorganized and were heading in a fighting wedge toward the stairs leading up to the platform. Horace reached down and retrieved the massive two-handed executioner's sword, testing its weight and balance with a few experimental swings.

"Not bad," he said.

As the first two Tualaghi mounted the stairs to the platform, they were met by a sight from their worst nightmare. The tall young foreigner charged them, the huge sword whirling, humming a deep-throated death song. The leading warrior managed to catch the blow on his shield. The massive blade smashed into the small circle of metal and wood, folding it double on his arm. The stunning impact of the blow sent him tumbling back down the stairs, crashing into the two men who were following him.

Another, slightly to Horace's right, drew back his own sword to strike—but the return blow was already on its way and it caught the Tualaghi's blade a few centimeters from the hilt of the sword, shearing it off. This nomad was made of sterner stuff than his comrades. Barely pausing to react to the massive damage done to his weapon, he dropped it and charged forward, ducking under the sweeping flight of the two-handed sword as Horace brought it back. As he came, he drew his belt dagger and slashed upward in a backhanded stroke, catching Horace high on the shoulder.

A thin red line formed immediately, then blurred as blood began to well out of the cut. Horace barely felt the touch of the blade but he felt the hot blood coursing down his arm and knew he'd been wounded. But there was no time to worry about it now, with the Tualaghi inside the arc of his giant sword.

Yet there was more to the sword than its long blade and Horace simply brought the massive brass-pommeled hilt back in a short, savage stroke, thudding it into the man's head. The keffiyeh absorbed some of the blow, but not enough. The man's eyes rolled back into his head and as Horace put his shoulder into him, he sailed back off the platform, landing on the struggling heap that had fallen at the bottom of the steps.

Horace stood at the top of the steps, feet wide apart, the sword sweeping back and forth in short, menacing arcs. Having seen the fate of the last group of men who tried to mount the steps, none of the other Tualaghi were anxious to try their luck.

Halt and Selethen stood toward the rear of the platform. Gradually, the square was emptying as the Maashavites found their way into the alleyways and streets that led from it. The struggling, fighting groups of Arridi, Bedullin and Tualaghi were rapidly becoming the only ones left in the square. And the Tualaghi's numerical superiority was becoming obvious.

"Nice of the townspeople to lend a hand," Halt muttered. He and the Wakir had both armed themselves with swords dropped by the fallen guards. Gilan had a sword as well and the two Skandians were brandishing spears—also the former property of their guards. Evanlyn removed the broad leather belt she had been wearing, unlacing a length of leather thong that had formed a decorative crisscross pattern on the belt. Halt glanced at her curiously, wondering what she was up to.

Then Selethen spoke and his attention was distracted from the girl.

"They're used to submitting, not fighting. They think only of themselves," the Wakir said. He had expected no more of the people of Maashava. He had heard how some of them had even cheered his upcoming execution.

Gradually, in response to a prearranged plan, the Arridi and Bedullin warriors were falling back to form a perimeter around the execution platform. Selethen glanced around the square, a worried frown on his face.

"There can't be more than fifty of them," he said. "Where did they come from?"

"Will brought them," Halt answered. He gestured to the semi-collapsed watchtower, where he had finally caught sight of a small figure perched among the crossbeams, a longbow ready in his hands. Halt waved now and his heart lifted as the figure returned his salute. With no immediate targets to seek out, Will was conserving his arrows, hoping for another sight of Yusal.

"Will?" Selethen said, his face puzzled. "Your apprentice? Where would he find men to rescue us?"

Halt smiled. "He has his ways."

Selethen frowned. "A pity he didn't find a way to bring more then."

"Do you think we should go down and lend a hand?" Halt gestured to the stubborn line of fighters forming a perimeter around the base of the platform. Selethen looked at him, cut his sword back and forth experimentally to test its balance, and nodded.

"I think it's time we did," he said.

Hassan grabbed Umar's shoulder and pointed to the left of the tower they had been watching.

"There!" he said. "He's on that tower!"

They had heard the sudden silence from the town that greeted the death of Mussaun—although they had no way of knowing the reason for it. Then they had heard the clash of weapons and the screaming of the crowd. Obviously, the battle had started, but there was still no sign of the foreigner on the watchtower. And there had been no signal from Aloom's bugler. As luck would have it, he had been struck down, almost by accident, in the opening seconds of the battle. As most soldiers learn sooner or later, if something can go wrong, it will.

Then Hassan had noticed movement on the adjoining tower as Will opened up with his high-speed barrage of arrows, and had drawn Umar's attention to it.

"He's on the wrong one!" the Aseikh complained. Hassan shook his head.

"So what? He's on a tower. What are we waiting for?"

Umar grunted and drew his sword. He turned to the men crouched behind him in the gully.

"Come on!" he shouted, and led them, yelling their war cries, out onto the dusty track to Maashava.

Gilan moved into the thin rank of defenders ringed around the platform and began wielding the unfamiliar curved sword as if he had been using one all his life. The speed and power of his slashing attacks cut through the Tualaghis' defenses like a knife through butter. Men fell before him, or reeled away, clutching wounds in pain, sinking slowly to the ground. But, in spite of the confusion around him, Gilan was searching the veiled faces for one in particular—the man who had taken such pleasure in beating him on the road to Maashava.

Now he saw him. And he saw recognition in the man's eyes as he shoved his way through the press of fighting men to confront the young Ranger. Gilan smiled at him but it was a smile totally devoid of any warmth or humor.

"I was hoping we'd run into each other," Gilan said. The Tualaghi said nothing. He glared at Gilan above the blue veil. Already imbued with a deep hatred of these foreign bowmen, he had seen another half dozen of his comrades fall before their arrows this morning. Now he wanted revenge. But before he could move, Gilan spoke again.

"I think it's time we saw all of your ugly face, don't you?" he said. The curved sword in his hand flicked almost negligently up and across, with the speed of a striking snake.

It slashed the blue veil at the side, where it was attached to the keffiyeh, cutting through it and letting the blue cloth fall so that it hung by one side.

There was nothing extraordinary about the face that was revealed—except for the fact that the lower half, usually covered by the veil, was a few shades lighter in tone than the browned, wind- and sunburned upper half. But the eyes, already filled with hate for Gilan and his kind, now blazed with rage as the Tualaghi leaped forward, sword going up for a killing stroke.

It clanged against Gilan's parry, and the Tualaghi drew back for another attack, attempting a hand strike this time. But Gilan caught the blade on the crosspiece of his own weapon, then, with a powerful twisting flick of the wrist, turned the other man's sword aside and went into a blindingly fast attack. He struck repeatedly, the strikes seeming to come from all angles at virtually the same time. The sword in his hand blurred with the speed of his backhands, forehands, overheads and side cuts.

The Tualaghi was an experienced fighter. But he was up against a swordmaster. Gilan drove him back, the defenders on either side of him advancing with him to protect his flanks. The Tualaghi's breath was coming in ragged gasps. Gilan could see the perspiration on his face as he tried to avoid that sweeping, glittering blade. Weakened, he dropped his guard for a moment and Gilan, stretching and stamping with his right foot, drove forward in a classic lunge, the curved sword upturned by his reversed wrist, and sank the point deep into the Tualaghi's shoulder.

Gilan withdrew his blade as the other man's sword dropped from his hand. Blood was beginning to well out of the wound, soaking the black robes. Gilan lowered the point of his sword. As if by some unspoken agreement, the fighting around them stopped for a moment as the other combatants watched.

"You can yield if you choose," he said calmly. The Tualaghi nodded once, his eyes still burning with hate.

"I yield," he said, his voice barely above a whisper. Gilan nodded. He stepped back and his foot twisted as he stepped on the arm of a Bedullin warrior who had fallen earlier in the battle. He glanced down. His eyes were distracted for no more than a fraction of a second, but it was enough for the defeated Tualaghi. With his left hand, he drew a curved knife from his belt and leaped forward at the young Ranger.

There was a massive whistling sound, then a great *whump!*

The Tualaghi stopped in midleap, seeming to fold in half over the huge blade Horace had swung in a horizontal sweep. Horace withdrew the sword and the warrior crumpled to the stony ground of the square, with no more rigidity or resistance than his bloodsoaked robes themselves.

"Never take your eyes off them," Horace said to Gilan, in an admonishing tone. "Didn't MacNeil ever tell you that?"

Gilan nodded his thanks. The lull in the fighting that had come when he thrust at the Tualaghi now continued as the two groups of enemies stood facing each other. It was a moment when the Arridi–Bedullin force might have claimed victory but for a voice ringing out across the square.

Yusal was rallying his troops for one last effort.

47

"RIDERS OF THE BLUE VEIL! TUALAGHI WARRIORS! LISTEN TO me!"

Yusal's harsh, grating tones rang out over the market square in the sudden silence that had greeted the pause in combat. As one, Tualaghi, Arridi and Bedullin all turned to look at him.

He was on the eastern side of the square, standing on a market stall so he could address them. Halt noted the rough bandage wound around his upper arm. The bandit war leader had made his way clear of the execution platform in the confused moments when Will had begun shooting. Now he had managed to regroup. A force of twenty men stood around him, weapons ready, faces covered by the ubiquitous blue veils.

The square was empty now of townspeople—except for those who had been caught up in the battle between the two forces and now lay in crumpled heaps on the stony ground.

Perched high on the watchtower, Will heard the Aseikh's words too. But Yusal was hidden from Will's sight by the buildings along the northern side of the square.

"Look around you! Look at the enemy! There are barely forty

of them!" Yusal continued. And he was right. The raiding force had been hard-pressed in the battle and many of them had fallen, never to rise again. The remainder were grouped defiantly in front of the platform where Halt and the others were to have been executed.

"We outnumber them! If we work together, we will crush them!"

There was a sullen growl of assent from the throats of the Tualaghi warriors. They, too, had lost men in the hard fighting. But they had started with a four-to-one superiority and they had maintained the ratio. As Yusal made his point, they began to realize that it was well within their power to crush the small band who opposed them.

"Seley el'then! I will give you one chance. One chance only. Throw down your weapons and surrender!"

Selethen laughed harshly. "Surrender? Do you think we believe you'd show us mercy, Yusal?"

Yusal spread his hands in front of him. "I'll offer you the mercy of a quick death," he replied. "Otherwise, you'll linger for days in agony. You know my men are masters of slow torture."

Selethen looked sideways at Halt. "That's true enough," he said quietly. "I think we'd do better to die with our weapons in our hands."

Halt went to reply, then stopped. Somewhere close by, he could hear a faint humming noise—a hum that gradually rose in pitch and intensity. He had no idea what it was. He shook his head, dismissing the strange sound.

"I'm with you," he said. "We'll fight on. You never know when something's going to turn up."

Yusal waited for Selethen's reply. When he realized none was forthcoming, he raised his arm above his head, preparing to give the signal to his men for one final, overwhelming attack on the smaller group.

"Very well. You've rejected my offer. Now you'll pay. Tualaghi riders, let—"

His words were cut off in a strangled grunt of pain and his hands flew up to his forehead. A solid smacking sound could be heard clearly around the square. Then Yusal's hands dropped and revealed a mask of blood covering his eyes and upper face, flowing down to soak into his blue veil. He took one faltering step, missing the edge of the stall he was balanced on, and fell full length to the hard ground below. He lay there, unmoving.

The Tualaghi stirred uneasily. Their leader had been cut down in midsentence. Yet there had been no evident weapon that had struck him—only that ugly smacking sound followed by a river of blood flowing down his face.

The desert riders were superstitious. They believed that djinns and devils and spirits all lived in these ancient mountains. Now one of them, virtually out of thin air, seemed to have struck down their leader with terrifying force. They began to back away from the defensive line of Arridi and Bedullin warriors, muttering to one another.

One of Yusal's lieutenants, braver than the rest, sprang up onto the stall in place of his leader and tried to rally them.

"Tualaghi warriors!" he yelled, his voice breaking. "Now is the time for—"

Again there was a meaty smack and, like Yusal, the man's hands flew to grasp at a sudden, vicious wound that appeared on his forehead. He lurched, grabbed for the stall's awning, missed and fell to the ground. He knelt there, doubled over, clutching his face and moaning in pain.

This time, Halt saw Evanlyn, at the rear of the platform, slowly lowering the sling. She caught his eye and gave him a smile. He noticed that the necklace of heavy marble stones was no longer around her throat.

"Well, what do you know about that?" he asked of no one in particular.

Demoralized, confused and filled with superstitious fear, the Tualaghi began to back away.

Then there was a chorus of battle cries and the clash of weapons as Umar and the rest of his force burst into the square. The Bedullin warriors fanned out quickly into a half circle and the Tualaghi found themselves suddenly surrounded, with Umar and his men at their back and the forty determined defenders before them.

The Tualaghi were essentially bandits and thieves. They would fight without mercy, but only when the odds were solidly in their favor. A four-to-one advantage was the sort of ratio they looked for in a battle. When the numbers were virtually even, and with no leader to spur them on, their eagerness for battle tended to fade away.

Slowly at first, then with increasing frequency, their weapons began to fall to the ground at their feet.

"There's one last little thing to take care of . . ." Erak said.

Umar's troops had disarmed the remaining Tualaghi and were busy subduing them, tying their hands behind their backs and leaving them seated cross-legged in the square. Yusal had been bound and taken under guard to the storeroom he had used as a prison. The Aseikh was still dazed and only semiconscious. The heavy marble stone from Evanlyn's sling had left him with a severe concussion.

"Toshak?" Svengal answered him.

Erak nodded. "Toshak. The treacherous swine has stolen off somewhere in all the confusion."

"He was in front of the platform when the whole thing began," Halt pointed out.

Evanlyn nodded. "But he started to move toward those colonnades when Will began shooting," she said. She looked around. "Where is Will, anyway? What's keeping him?"

Will knelt in the rubble beneath the watchtower, his bow and quiver discarded, Aloom's head resting on his knee. The Arridi lieutenant was dying. The loss of blood from his multiple wounds had been too great. As Will had dropped lightly from the wall to tend to him, he glanced up and saw the fat trader who had betrayed them, still standing, frozen to the spot, watching them.

"Find a surgeon," he ordered, and as the man hesitated, he repeated the command. "Go! Get a surgeon! Do it quickly!"

The fat man's eyes betrayed him. They slid away from Will's and he turned to go. Will's cold voice stopped him.

"Wait!"

The man turned back. Still he would not make eye contact with the Ranger.

"Look at me," Will commanded and, slowly, the man raised his eyes. "If you run away, if you don't come back, be certain that I will hunt you down," Will told him. "I promise you won't enjoy that."

He saw the fear of certain retribution slowly overcoming the treachery in the man's eyes and the trader nodded quickly. Then he turned and slunk off into the alley behind him.

Aloom was muttering feverishly. Will unstrapped the small canteen from the Arridi's belt and trickled a few drops of water into the man's mouth. Aloom's eyes cleared for a few moments and he looked up at Will.

"Did we win?" he asked.

Will nodded. "We did," he assured him. He saw the relief in Aloom's eyes. Then the lieutenant tried to struggle to a sitting position, and Will had to restrain him gently.

"Rest," he said. "There's a surgeon coming."

Aloom took several ragged breaths. Then a new thought occurred to him and he rasped out more words. "The Wakir . . . is he safe?"

Again Will nodded.

"He's fine. I saw him with Halt when it was all over. Something happened to Yusal," he added inconsequentially, still trying to understand what had gone on in the square. He had heard Yusal's voice suddenly cut off in a cry of agony. Yet he knew none of his friends had a bow with them.

Aloom drifted into a state of delirium again, as if the news that his lord was safe was enough for him. His arms and legs began to twitch and his breath came in ragged bursts.

Will heard a soft patter of footsteps approaching in the alley and reached for the hilt of his saxe knife. He had recovered it from the body of the dead Tualaghi when he first climbed down from the wall.

Two figures emerged from the shadows of the alley and he recognized the fat trader. Beside him was an older man, carrying a leather satchel over one arm.

"This man is a healer," the trader said, and his companion came forward, dropping to his knees beside the muttering lieutenant. He looked around, saw Will's discarded cloak lying close by and rolled it into a makeshift pillow. Then he placed it under Aloom's head, allowing Will to move free. He examined the wounded man briefly, looked up at Will.

"Your friend?" he asked.

Will nodded. He'd only known Aloom for a few days but the

man had held off three swordsmen to give Will the chance to save the others. You couldn't ask more of a friend than that.

The surgeon shook his head.

"I can give him something to ease the pain—nothing more," he said. "He has lost too much blood."

Will nodded sadly.

"Do it," he said, and watched as the healer took a small vial from his satchel and allowed several drops of a clear liquid to fall into Aloom's mouth, onto his tongue. In a few seconds, Aloom began breathing more freely. His chest rose and fell more evenly. Then the breaths came more slowly until, finally, they stopped.

The surgeon looked up at Will.

"He's gone," he said, and Will nodded sadly again. He glanced up and saw the trader watching him fearfully. The man obviously was remembering how he had betrayed the two strangers to the Tualaghi. Now one of them was dead and the other had shown that, young as he was, he was not a man to cross. The trader wrung his hands together and moved forward, pleading for mercy. He dropped to his knees.

"Lord, please . . . I didn't know you were . . ." he began.

Will cut him off with a contemptuous hand gesture. The man had betrayed them, he knew. But he had also returned with a surgeon. Suddenly, Will felt there had been enough killing on this day.

"Oh, go away," he said quietly. "Just . . . go away."

The man's eyes widened. He couldn't believe his luck. He rose slowly, turned away. Then he hesitated, making sure Will hadn't changed his mind. Finally, reassured, he scuttled into the alley. Will heard his soft shoes pattering on the broken stones for a few minutes, then there was silence.

The surgeon regarded him with sympathy. He had laid Aloom out with his hands folded over his chest. Will retrieved his cloak—

Aloom had no further use for it. He spread the lieutenant's own cloak over his still form, covering his face. Then he felt in his purse and handed the surgeon a silver coin.

"Stay with him?" he asked. "Watch over him until I come back."

He reached down, retrieved his bow and quiver and headed off down the alleyway to the market square.

48

TOSHAK PEERED AROUND THE CORNER OF A NARROW STREET leading onto the square. The beginning of the wide thoroughfare that led to the main gate was forty meters away. He looked now and saw Erak and his friends moving toward the colonnades that lined the far side of the square. Somebody must have seen him running in that direction.

He smiled grimly. He *had* gone that way initially. But then he'd doubled around, cutting through a maze of streets and alleys to emerge back here. He had a horse saddled and ready, in a stable a few doors back from the square. Now his enemies were moving away, leaving the way clear for his escape. And the Rangers, he noted with satisfaction, were without their cursed longbows. All he needed to do was fetch the horse, lead it to this corner, mount and ride for his life.

Once he was out of Maashava, who knew? He'd have a head start, a fresh horse and plenty of water. He'd make for the coast sixty kilometers away. His ship, *Wolfclaw*, was moored in a little bay and he was an experienced stellar navigator. He'd travel by night so those accursed Rangers couldn't track him. In two days, he could be on board.

But first, he had to get out of Maashava. And this was looking like his best chance. He backed slowly away from the corner for a few paces, then turned and ran lightly to the stable.

"The trouble is, he could have gone anywhere once he made it this far," Horace said. Halt nodded, chewing his lip reflectively. Beyond the colonnades that lined the market square, they found a maze of narrow, winding streets and crowded buildings.

"We'll just have to keep looking till we find him," he said. "At least he'll be easy to spot."

"What's all that shouting?" Evanlyn interrupted. From the square, they could hear voices raised, calling the alarm. In a group, they ran back through the rear door of the coffeehouse they had just left, then out onto the square once more.

"It's Toshak!" Svengal yelled.

Diagonally opposite them, the Skandian traitor was seated astride a rearing horse, striking left and right with a battleax at a group of Bedullin warriors who were trying to stop him.

He beat his way clear, leaving two of the warriors lying ominously still, and set his horse toward the wide entrance to the road leading to the main gate. Svengal ran forward a few paces and launched his spear after the retreating horseman, but it was a futile gesture and the missile landed with a clatter, twenty meters short.

Then Halt heard that strange humming sound again, rising gradually in pitch. He glanced around to see Evanlyn, feet braced apart, whirling the long leather sling around her head, letting the speed build up.

"He's wearing a helmet," he cautioned. Toshak had been prepared to fight his way clear. He was fully armed and Halt knew that the sling would be useless against his heavy iron helmet.

"I know," said Evanlyn briefly, her brow furrowed in concentration.

Then there was a whistling slap as she cast the heavy marble ball after the fleeing Toshak. It flew across the square, too fast for the eye to follow, and slammed painfully into the target she had set herself—the horse's rump.

Stung by the sudden burning impact, the horse reared and lost its footing on the cobbles of the square. It staggered sideways on its rear legs, trying to regain its balance. The unexpected, violent movement and change of direction was too much for an inexperienced rider like Toshak and he slid backward over the horse's rump, falling with a crash on the cobblestones.

"Good shot," Halt told Evanlyn. She grinned.

"I figured he'd sit a horse as well as most Skandians," she said.

Momentarily winded, Toshak regained his feet to find himself surrounded by a ring of vengeful Bedullin. The desert warriors circled him cautiously, kept at bay by the threat of the massive battleax. A true Skandian, Toshak hadn't released his grip on the weapon when he fell.

He eyed the circle of enemies now, determined to sell his life dearly. Toshak might be a traitor but he was no coward.

"All right," he said, to nobody in particular. "Who's going to be first?"

"I think that would be me."

Erak shouldered his way through the Bedullin warriors and stood facing his enemy. Toshak nodded several times, and smiled. He knew he was going to die but at least he'd have the satisfaction of taking the hated Oberjarl with him. He glanced down scornfully at the Tualaghi saber Erak was carrying. It looked no bigger than a dagger in the Oberjarl's massive fist.

"You're fighting an ax with that toothpick, Erak?" he sneered. Erak studied the weapon and pursed his lips. He looked around the watching circle and saw a better alternative. He removed his keffiyeh and wrapped it around the palm and fingers of his left hand. Then he set the saber down and reached his right hand out to Horace.

"D'you think I could borrow that bodkin of yours, Horace?" he said.

Horace stepped forward, reversed the huge executioner's sword and placed the hilt in Erak's outstretched hand.

"Be my guest," he said.

Erak swiped the long sword back and forth several times, then nodded in satisfaction.

"That'll do," he said. "Now step back, everyone. I've got work to do."

The circle of spectators quickly backed off several paces as he launched himself at Toshak, the sword swinging down in a blow that would have split the traitor down to the waist.

There was a massive ringing clang as Toshak caught the blow on the top of his double-bladed ax head. He twisted his wrists, jerking the sword to one side, then it was his turn and he swung in a flailing round arm blow with the ax.

Erak leaped back just in time, the heavy double-bladed head whooshing through the air only millimeters from his ribs. He was already counterattacking with the sword and this time Toshak swayed to one side, letting the huge blade slice down just clear of him, striking sparks from the stones on the ground.

He tried an overhead cut and now Evanlyn understood why Erak had bound his hand with the keffiyeh. He gripped the blade with his left hand and the hilt in his right to block the force of the ax blow. A grip on the hilt alone wouldn't have provided sufficient leverage to stop the massive ax.

The two men strained against each other for several seconds, their weapons locked together. They were both massively built, each one as powerful as an ox. But Erak had been a prisoner for some weeks now and his strength was reduced by the meager diet and the punishment he had taken from his captors. In a straight-out contest of brute strength like this, Toshak had the advantage and he began to force the Oberjarl back, a pace at a time.

Realizing he was overmatched, Erak struck out quickly with a flat-footed kick to Toshak's thigh. The blow staggered the traitor and Erak was able to spin away, leaping suddenly to avoid a lightning-fast ax stroke as Toshak recovered his balance.

Then they rushed at each other again and stood toe to toe, hammering blows at each other. Parrying and blocking, sliding to one side to evade each other's weapons, they beat at each other in a final trial of strength and speed. There was no science or subtlety to it. Each used the advantage his weapon gave him—Erak the extra reach of the sword, Toshak the massive weight of the battleax.

And it was that weight that began to tell as he rained blow after blow down at Erak, forcing the weakened Oberjarl onto the defensive.

Svengal watched in an agony of concern as his leader began to give ground, a few centimeters at a time at first, then in gradually greater amounts. A light of triumph came into Toshak's eyes as he saw the Oberjarl faltering, felt him giving way. He redoubled the effort he was putting into his strokes, feeling Erak's weakening resistance, seeing his knees buckle slightly with each blow. Now Toshak was swinging two blows to Erak's one and the momentum of the battle was with him and it would only be a matter of time.

Erak's eyes were haunted and his breath came in ragged gasps.

He caught one final, overpowering ax blow on the blade of the sword and the massive force behind it buckled his knees and drove him back and down onto the cobbles.

There was a groan from the spectators as they saw the Oberjarl fall. Toshak leaped forward with a snarl of triumph, the mighty ax rising in a two-handed grip for the killing blow. Then he saw something strange.

Erak was smiling.

Too late, Toshak realized he had been tricked. Erak was nowhere near as tired and clumsy as he had seemed. And he was holding a weapon with a much longer reach than any battleax. With a mighty roar, Erak used his left arm to thrust himself up from the cobbles while he drove the sword deep into Toshak's unprotected body. Then, releasing the sword, he sidestepped the ax stroke that came half a second too late and watched his enemy, impaled by the terrible sword, stagger, drop his ax and fall to the ground.

Toshak's eyes were wide open in pain and fear. His fingers scrabbled awkwardly on the cobbles and he was mouthing something to Erak. The Oberjarl understood and nodded. With the toe of his boot, he nudged the ax alongside his enemy's scrabbling hand. Toshak's fingers closed over the haft and he nodded once.

Skandians believed that if they were to die in battle without a weapon in their hand, their soul would wander for all eternity. Even Toshak didn't deserve that.

"Thank . . . you . . ." Toshak sighed, the words almost inaudible. Then his eyes closed and he died.

"You should have left him to wander," Svengal said coldly. Erak looked at him, eyebrows raised.

"Would you?" he asked, and Svengal hesitated. At the end, Toshak had fought well and that counted for a lot with Skandians.

"No," he admitted.

49

THE LONG COLUMN WOUND SLOWLY ACROSS THE DESERT, HEADING
for the oasis where the Khoresh Bedullin tribe were camped.

The mounted Bedullin warriors herded a file of manacled
Tualaghi prisoners before them, the bandits forced to walk while
their captors rode. The Tualaghi, no longer the scourge of the desert,
were a pitiful, footsore group—more like beggars than the feared
raiders they had been. In a final symbol of their downfall, Selethen
and three of his officers had walked among the bandits, tearing
the blue veils from their faces and throwing them to the ground.
Mindful of the way they had treated his bodyguard, the Wakir also
removed their boots, letting them hobble on cut and bruised feet for
the journey.

Unlike Yusal, however, he provided them with sufficient water.
Before the party left Maashava, Selethen had called the people together in the market square. Standing above them, on the platform
that had been intended for his execution, he harangued the crowd,
reminding them of how they had cried for his blood only a few days
earlier. The townspeople hung their heads and shuffled their feet
guiltily. He assured them that he would be in contact with the Wakir
of their province and that a heavy tax would be levied. The first part

of this would be a requirement for Maashava to refurbish its walls and watchtowers and organize an effective defense force, he told them. The Maashavites nodded gloomily. The walls were in a parlous state and repairing them would mean months of hot, heavy work. But, philosophically, they accepted his words. He was right, after all. They should be better prepared to defend themselves against future marauders.

There was at least a little good news to brighten the townspeople's spirits: Selethen decided to leave thirty of the Tualaghi captives behind to do the heavy work.

"They'll have a hard time of it," Erak said to the Wakir when he heard about that arrangement. Selethen turned pitiless eyes on him.

"They slaughtered the men escorting you, remember?" he said coldly, and Erak nodded. He had no real sympathy to waste on the Tualaghi.

The remaining prisoners would be taken from the Jass Par Oasis to Mararoc, where they would spend their lives at hard labor. Selethen had negotiated with Umar for an escort of Bedullin warriors to conduct them there. Umar agreed readily. He would be glad to see so many potential enemies taken away and kept in chains. Like Erak, he had no sympathy for them.

The returning war party, and its additional members, received a noisy and enthusiastic greeting when they arrived at the oasis. The Bedullin women stood in two welcoming lines, shrilling a welcome in an eerie, ululating chant, as their menfolk rode slowly back into the massive grove of trees.

The Tualaghi prisoners, following behind, were greeted with an ominous silence. They shuffled past the double line of silent women, their heads bent and their eyes down. They were still unaccustomed to showing the world their faces and they were only too aware that their lives rested on a knife edge.

Their former leader, Yusal, traveled on a litter behind a camel. He was still concussed from the massive blow he had taken to the forehead when Evanlyn's heavy marble missile had struck him. On the infrequent occasions when he regained consciousness, he raved and gibbered. Sometimes he was even seen with tears running down his cheeks. Evanlyn regarded the result of her handiwork with some misgivings.

"Do you think he'll recover his senses?" she asked the healer who had accompanied the Bedullin war party. The older man touched the massive blue and yellow bruise that disfigured the Tualaghi's forehead and shrugged.

"Head wounds are uncertain," he told her. "Maybe tomorrow he'll improve. Maybe in a year. Maybe never." He smiled at her. "Don't be too concerned, young lady. He doesn't merit any pity."

She nodded. But she wasn't completely comforted. She didn't like the fact that she had reduced a man—no matter how evil he might be—to a drooling idiot.

Her spirits recovered on the second night back at the oasis, when the Khoresh Bedullin organized a feast of welcome and celebration.

They ate spiced roast lamb, and peppers blackened in the fire until their tough outer skins could be peeled away, then stuffed with flavored rice and a cereal the Bedullin called couscous—light and fluffy, spiced with saffron and cumin and cardamom and garnished with plump sultanas and thin flakes of toasted almonds.

There were other delicious dishes of mutton or chicken, cooked in strange conical clay cooking pots called tagines and mixed with more spices, dates, apricots and root vegetables. The cone-shaped lids of the tagines retained the flavored steam from the cooking liquids, rendering the meat so succulent and tender that it fell from the bone.

The meal was eaten with the hands, and pieces of fresh flat bread were torn up to make implements. It was a delicious, greasy-fingered evening of eating to excess—a piece of indulgence the group felt they owed themselves after the hardships of their desert campaign.

Halt, Gilan, Evanlyn, Horace and the two Skandians were given a prominent position in the circle sitting around the massive fire. Selethen and Will, however, were in the principal places of honor, seated to the right of Umar and his wife, Cielema, respectively. Evanlyn smiled at Horace and jerked her thumb toward the young Ranger, currently engaged in animated conversation with the Bedullin leader and his wife. The two older people roared with laughter at something he had said and he ducked his head, grinning, pleased that he had amused them.

"He lands on his feet wherever he goes, doesn't he?" she said, a trifle wistfully. Horace looked across the fire at his old friend and nodded.

"People like him," he replied. Then he added, "There's a lot to like, after all."

"Yes," Evanlyn said, her eyes fixed on Will. For a moment, studying her, Horace saw a brief shadow of sadness pass across her face. He jogged her with an elbow, a little more enthusiastically than good manners dictated.

"Sling us a peach, will you?" he said. She raised an eyebrow at him and grinned.

"You don't mean that literally, do you?" she said. He smiled, glad to see she had shaken off her melancholy. He held up his hands before his face in mock horror.

"Please! Spare me that!" he said and they both laughed.

The Bedullin, as a general rule, didn't use alcohol, but out of deference to the two Skandians, several flasks of arariki, a brandy made from fermented dates and peaches, were provided. Now Erak and Svengal, at their own insistence, decided they would perform a sea chanty for the enjoyment and education of the assembled group. They stood on rather unsteady legs and began to bellow out the ribald tale of a penguin who fell hopelessly in love with a humpback whale.

Since the desert-dwelling audience had never seen either animal and so had no idea of the discrepancy in their sizes, much of the humor fell flat. So did much of the melody. But they applauded the enthusiasm of the singers, and the sheer volume at which they performed, and the two sea wolves resumed their seats, confident they had upheld the honor of Skandia.

Halt was quiet, Gilan thought. But then, Halt usually was quiet at events like this. Halt's eyes were intent on the animated young face of his apprentice as he talked and laughed with the Bedullin Aseikh and his wife.

"He did well," Gilan said, and Halt turned to him, a rare smile touching the bearded face.

"He did," he agreed.

"Told you he would," Gilan said, grinning.

Halt nodded acknowledgment. "You did. You were right."

Gilan shifted to face Halt more directly, remembering something Halt had said some days previously.

"But you knew, didn't you? You said to us when we were in Maashava that Yusal had forgotten that Will was out there. So you knew he'd survived. How was that?"

Halt's face grew serious as he considered the question. "I think 'knew' is too definite a term. I sensed it. I've always had a sense about Will. There's a feeling of destiny to that boy. I've felt it since the first day he joined me."

"And now it's nearly time to turn him loose," Gilan said gently. He saw a mixture of sadness and pride competing in Halt's eyes. Then the grizzled Ranger sighed.

"Yes, it is," he said.

After the feast broke up, Evanlyn's party sat with Umar and Selethen around a smaller fire. Cielema passed around coffee.

"Perhaps it's time we talked a little business," Selethen began, his eyes on Evanlyn. "There is the small matter of Erak's ransom."

He paused hopefully, waiting for Evanlyn to produce the money draft and her seal ring. Both items had been recovered from Yusal. Evanlyn, however, showed no sign of doing so.

"His ransom?" she asked, and he nodded, anxious to move things along.

"Yes. You agreed to ransom him. I'm sure you can recall that," he added, smiling expectantly.

Evanlyn nodded several times, went to speak, then stopped, her hand raised in midair. Then, as if uncertain, she said to the Wakir, "Just explain the concept of ransom to me if you would?"

Selethen's smile faded. He had hoped to hurry through this matter and have it settled before anyone thought too deeply about it. It seemed he wasn't going to get away with it.

"I think we all know what a ransom is," he said evasively.

Evanlyn smiled at him. "Humor me. I'm an addle-headed girl."

Across the fire, Cielema hid a smile behind her hand. Umar, who had been told the background to this discussion by Will, leaned forward helpfully.

"If I might assist here. A ransom is paid by one party when a second party is holding a third party hostage."

"That's a lot of parties," Horace whispered to Will, and the young Ranger grinned.

"S-o-o-o," Evanlyn said, "if I were the first party, I would pay an agreed amount to the second party who is holding the third party? Is that correct?"

"Correct," Selethen said. He had the uncomfortable feeling that he was about to be outsmarted—and by a young girl. Evanlyn frowned at him, a puzzled expression on her face.

"You can't really expect me to pay sixty-six thousand reels of silver to Yusal, can you?"

"To Yusal!" the Wakir exclaimed, coming close to choking on his coffee. "Why in the name of all that's holy would you pay it to Yusal?"

Evanlyn spread her hands in an ingenuous gesture. "Well, he was the second party, wasn't he? He was the one holding Erak hostage when we found him. Not you," she added, after a significant pause.

"That's a technicality," Selethen said, trying to sound confident. But he still had a sinking feeling that he was being outsmarted. He thought it might be a good tactic to change the subject, then work back to the ransom question at a more favorable time. "Besides, Yusal's future is yet to be decided," he said.

"That's a good point," Halt put in. "What's going to become of Yusal?"

Selethen gestured toward Umar. "That's for the Bedullin to decide, I would say. What do you want to do with him, Aseikh Umar?"

Umar shrugged. "I don't want him. You can have him if you want him."

Selethen smiled for the first time since this discussion had begun.

"Oh yes, I want him. The man is a killer and a rebel and we have a cell ready and waiting for him in Mararoc. He's been a thorn in our side for longer than I can remember. With him out of the way, the

Tualaghi will be a lot easier to handle. As a matter of fact, the Emrikir has been offering a substantial re—"

He stopped himself a fraction of a second too late, realizing he had said too much. He feigned a fit of coughing to cover his lapse.

Evanlyn waited till he finished, then tugged at his sleeve, forcing him to make eye contact.

"A substantial 're—,'" she said, mimicking his hesitation. "Would that be 'reward' that you were going to say?"

"Yes." The word was forced out from between Selethen's reluctant lips.

"Now let me get this straight," Evanlyn said thoughtfully. "Who actually captured Yusal? I mean, who actually defeated him?" She looked up at the stars, her brow knitted in thought. Then it cleared and she said happily, "Oh, I remember! I did! With my little sling!"

"She's right," Umar said, grinning fiercely. "If anyone has the right to determine his fate, it's her."

"So I'd be entitled to that 'substantial reward' you mentioned?"

Selethen was in an awkward position. If they had been conducting this discussion at Al Shabah or in Mararoc, he would have had the negotiating advantage that came with a large number of armed men to uphold his argument. But the only large force here was Bedullin—and their leader seemed to be in agreement with Evanlyn. On top of that, the Wakir admitted, there was a lot of validity to her claims. He hadn't been holding Erak when the Skandian was rescued—and the Araluen princess was the one who had brought Yusal down. Technically, the Tualaghi war leader was her prisoner. Technically, she owed Selethen nothing and he owed her the reward. This wasn't how he'd planned things, he thought. Not at all.

"All right, let's get down to it," said Evanlyn, dropping the little-girl act and suddenly becoming all business. "Selethen, I believe we do owe you something. But not sixty-six thousand reels. And we definitely owe Umar and the Bedullin something because, without them, Erak would still be Yusal's captive."

"We didn't do it for money. We did it for friendship," Umar said, indicating Will when he mentioned friendship. Evanlyn nodded acknowledgment.

"You can always give it back if you like," she said, and, as Umar hastened to make a negative gesture, she smiled. "So here's the offer: I'm willing to pay Umar and his people twenty thousand reels for their help."

She paused, taking in the looks of agreement and approval around the fire. It was a fair sum. She went on:

"I'll pay the same amount to you, Selethen. Twenty thousand. I think you're owed something." Before the Wakir could say anything, she added, "And I'll forego the 'substantial reward' for Yusal. You can have him. Keep him. Cut off his ears. Drop him down a well if you like. I don't want him. Is that fair?"

Selethen hesitated, then his own sense of justice cut in. The offer was effectively more than forty thousand. She could have offered nothing and got away with it.

"It's fair. I accept gratefully," he said. Then he smiled. "Obviously, I am in the presence of a master negotiator," he added and inclined his head toward Evanlyn.

Erak nodded his approval too. He thought Evanlyn had handled the entire matter with great statesmanship. Stateswomanship, he corrected himself.

"You're very generous, Princess," he said, smiling indulgently at her. Evanlyn looked at him, one eyebrow raised.

"No, I'm not," she said. "You are. You're repaying the forty thousand to my father, remember?"

"Oh, yes . . . of course," Erak said. He felt a stabbing sensation in his heart. Skandians often had that sensation when they lost money. Suddenly he didn't feel like smiling anymore.

The meeting broke up shortly after that and Evanlyn strolled back to her tent, her hand resting lightly on Halt's arm. When they were out of earshot of both Bedullin and Arridi ears, she turned to him, a little anxiously.

"So, Halt, how did I do?"

Like all of them, she thought, she wanted Halt's approval above all else. He turned that grim, bearded face on her and shook his head slowly.

"Lord forgive me, I've created a monster," he said.

Then he smiled and patted her hand gently. "And I'm very proud of you."

EPILOGUE

WILL AND HALT SAT FACING EACH OTHER, ON EITHER SIDE OF the plain wooden table in Halt's cabin on the edge of the woods.

For the fifth time in the past few minutes, Will glanced down to make sure his uniform was clean and neat, the leather of his belt and double scabbard waxed and shining. As unobtrusively as he could, he reached up and smoothed his hair. Then he checked his fingernails, making sure that in the forty seconds since he'd last checked them, they hadn't somehow become encrusted with dirt and grease.

"It's not a fashion parade," Halt said. He seemed totally at ease. But then, Halt always seemed at ease. Will, on the other hand, was nervous as a cat. There was one thing he was grateful for and that was that he didn't have to wear the new formal uniform that Crowley had devised for Halt's wedding. Tradition said that apprentices wore their normal everyday uniform for Graduation Day. Will doubted that he could have kept the white silk shirt and the fine leather tunic clean on such a day. By now, he would surely have spilled something on himself.

"Wonder what's keeping Crowley?" Halt said idly. And, as if on cue, they heard footsteps on the small verandah at the front of the cabin. The door opened suddenly and Crowley bustled in, head down, a leather folder tucked under his arm.

"Right! Right! Sorry to keep you waiting! Got held up on the way but here I am at last, eh?"

At the sudden appearance of the Corps Commandant, Will had jerked up out of his seat to stand to attention. Now he wondered why, since he had never before felt it necessary to do so in Crowley's presence. Crowley looked at him, a little puzzled, and motioned him back into his seat.

"Sit down, Will. There's a good fellow," he said.

"Yes, sir," replied Will, and Halt's eyebrow shot up in surprise.

"He's never called me sir," he said.

"Probably trying to get on my good side," Crowley replied.

Halt nodded sagely. "Probably."

Will glanced from one to the other, nervously wetting his lips. He wasn't sure what he'd expected of Graduation Day. He had assumed there would be more of a ceremony. More a sense of occasion. But then, they were *Rangers*—and Rangers weren't big on ceremony. Maybe Graduation Day was like any other day. Except you graduated.

Crowley pulled another chair to the table and sat, spilling papers out of the leather folder, taking out a quill pen and a sealed inkwell. He uncorked the ink and began flicking through the pages, muttering to himself as he read the official forms.

"Right! Let's get on with it! All right . . . you . . . Will . . . have trained as apprentice to Ranger Halt of Redmont Fief these last five twelvemonths and blah blah blah and so on and so on. You've shown the necessary level of proficiency in the use of the weapons a Ranger uses—the longbow, the saxe knife, the throwing knife."

He paused and glanced up at Halt. "He has shown that proficiency, hasn't he? Of course he has," he went on, before Halt could answer. "Furthermore, you are a trusted officer in the service of the King and so on and so on and hi diddle diddle dee dee . . ." He glanced up again. "These forms really carry on a bit, don't they? But I have to make a pretense of reading them. And so forth and so on and such like." He paused, nodded several times, then continued.

"So basically . . ." He flicked a few more pages, found the one he was after and then continued, "You are in all ways ready to assume the position and authority of a fully operational Ranger in the Kingdom of Araluen. Correct?"

He glanced up again, his eyebrows raised. Will realized he was waiting for an answer.

"Correct," he said hastily, then in case that wasn't enough, he added, "Yes. I mean . . . I do . . . I am. Yes."

"Well, good for you. So . . . one other detail. You know we need to give you more of a title than Ranger Will because there are three other Wills in the Corps. It's not a problem that applies to Halt, of course, because there's only one Halt.

"Normally we'd use your family name but you were an orphan. So in your case, we looked for a name that reflected your achievements over the past five years. We looked at Will Boar Killer." He made a gesture of distaste. "Didn't like that. Someone suggested Will o' the Bridge to commemorate the destruction of Morgarath's bridge. But it sounded too much like will-o'-the-wisp, so we let that one go as well.

"Finally, your mentor"—he nodded to Halt—"suggested a name that had to do with one of your most meaningful contributions to the Kingdom. He pointed out that you were one of those instrumental in the creation of the treaty between Araluen and Skandia—a very important milestone in our country's history. So the suggestion is that you be known from now on as Will Treaty. How does that suit?"

Will looked to Halt, who nodded almost imperceptibly. "I like that very much," Will said. "Thank you, Crowley ... sir," he amended, feeling the occasion required formality.

"Excellent! So Will Treaty you shall be!" Crowley wrote the name at the bottom of a form and swung it around to face Will, handing him the quill pen. "Just sign there at the bottom and we're done."

He watched as Will scratched his signature at the bottom of the parchment form, then slapped his hands on the tabletop in satisfaction.

"There, all done! Congratulations, Will, you're a Ranger now. Well done! Is there anything to drink?" He addressed the last part to Halt.

Will sat stunned. That was it? He'd expected ... he didn't know what he'd expected but he certainly hadn't expected this breezy, off-the-cuff "Sign here and you're a Ranger" approach.

"Is that all?" he blurted out.

Crowley and Halt exchanged slightly puzzled glances. Then Crowley pursed his lips thoughtfully.

"Um ... it seems to be ... Listed your training, mentioned a few achievements, made sure you know which end of an arrow is the sharp part ... decided on your new name ... I think that's ..." Then it seemed that understanding dawned on him and his eyes opened wide.

"Of course! You have to have your Silver ... whatsis, don't you?" He took hold of the chain that held his own Silver Oakleaf around his throat and shook it lightly. It was the badge of a Graduate Ranger. Then he began to search through his pockets, frowning.

"Had it here! Had it here! Where the devil is it ... wait. I heard something fall on the boards as I came in! Must have dropped it. Just check outside the front door, will you, Will?"

Too stunned to talk, Will rose and went to the door. As he

set his hand on the latch, he looked back at the two Rangers, still seated at the table. Crowley made a small shooing motion with the back of his hand, urging him to go outside. Will was still looking back at them when he opened the door and stepped through onto the verandah.

"Congratulations!"

The massive cry went up from at least forty throats. He swung around in shock to find all his friends gathered in the clearing outside, around a table laid for a feast, their faces beaming with smiles. Baron Arald, Sir Rodney, Lady Pauline and Master Chubb were all there. So were Jenny and George, his former wardmates. There were a dozen others in the Ranger uniform—men he had met and worked with over the past five years. And wonder of wonders, there were Erak and Svengal, bellowing his name and waving their huge axes overhead in his praise. Close by them stood Horace and Gilan, both brandishing their swords overhead as well. It looked like a dangerous section of the crowd to be in, Will thought.

After the first concerted shout, people began cheering and calling his name, laughing and waving to him.

Halt and Crowley joined him on the verandah. The Commandant was doubled over with laughter.

"Oh, if you could have seen yourself!" he wheezed. "Your face! Your face! It was priceless! 'Is that all?'" He mimicked Will's plaintive tones and doubled over again.

Will turned to Halt accusingly. His teacher grinned at him.

"Your face was a study," he said.

"Do you do that to all apprentices?" Will asked.

Halt nodded vigorously. "Every one. Stops them getting a swelled head at the last minute. You have to swear never to let an apprentice in on the secret."

He touched Will's sleeve and pointed.

"But only the luckiest, or the best, get this."

Will looked in the direction he indicated and felt a lump rise to his throat. Side by side, Alyss and Evanlyn were walking slowly across the clearing toward him, carrying a small red satin cushion between them.

Alyss, tall, poised, ash blond and beautiful in her elegant Courier's robe.

Evanlyn, tomboyish, grinning, honey blond and beautiful in her own way.

And on the cushion between them, gleaming in the errant rays of the late afternoon sun that found its way through the trees, lay a simple Silver Oakleaf amulet on a chain—symbol of everything Will had been striving for in the past five years. Now his.

The two girls lifted it from the cushion and together draped it over his bowed head while the assembled crowd cheered themselves hoarse. Then, driven by the same impulse, they kissed him—Alyss on the left cheek, Evanlyn on the right.

And then glared daggers at each other.

"Let's get this party started!" said Crowley hurriedly. And catching Will by the arm, he drew him down to the group of friends waiting to congratulate him.

It was a party that would go down in the annals of Castle Redmont. The last guests were still celebrating as the sun began to rise. Will and Horace, his oldest friend, sat on the little verandah watching the last dancers stagger out of the clearing and head for home.

"Do you feel like a Ranger at last?" Horace asked him.

Will shook his head. "I feel absolutely overwhelmed by the whole thing," he said. Then, after a few seconds, he confided, "You know, a few weeks back, I didn't think I was ready for this."

"And now?" Horace prompted.

"Now I know that if you wait till you think you are ready, you'll wait all your life."

The young knight nodded. "I couldn't have put it better," he said. "That's exactly how I felt when we came back from Skandia and Duncan knighted me. 'I'm not ready,' I kept wanting to say."

"But you were," Will said.

Horace nodded. "Yes. Maybe our teachers do know what they're doing, after all. Halt thinks the world of you, you know. When we were in prison in Maashava, he knew you'd turn up to get us out. He must have been proud to see you graduate today. Following in his footsteps."

"They're big footsteps to follow in," Will said. "Crowley said it best today: there's only one Halt."

Horace looked at him very seriously, appraising him, thinking of all he had learned about this remarkable young man in the past five years.

"You may not ever be exactly like him," he said. "But you will be Will Treaty—and that's more than enough for the rest of us."

Then the two friends leaned back and watched the sun rise clear of the trees.

"Best time of the day," said Will.

"Yes," Horace agreed. "What's for breakfast?"

The story continues in . . .

RANGER'S APPRENTICE

BOOK EIGHT: THE KINGS OF CLONMEL

1

SOUTHERN CLONMEL, THE ISLAND OF HIBERNIA.

The farmers had risen at first light, bringing in their cattle for milking, and releasing the sheep and chickens that had been kept overnight in the barn to protect them from nocturnal marauders.

The leader of the bandits crouched among the trees and smiled grimly to himself. Today, the inhabitants of this little group of farms would have more to worry about than animal predators. Today, real danger lurked inside the tree line, concealed from the eyes of the farmers as they went about their routine tasks.

His men had been in position since long before first light. A less experienced leader might have chosen to attack at dawn. Most people thought that was the best time for a surprise attack. But the bandit knew his business. Farmers rose early. They were wide-awake at dawn. They were prepared for unexpected danger, even if it were only a fox or a marauding wolf. And they often had tools ready at hand—axes and spades and scythes—that would serve as makeshift weapons in the event of an attack.

It was better, he knew, to wait until they had finished their early morning tasks and were heading in to breakfast. The sun would be up by then and warm on their backs. They'd be relaxed and a little weary from their labor, and looking forward to the hot meal their wives had waiting for them. Their defenses would be down and that was the best time to attack them.

He saw the nearest pair, who had been repairing a fallen fence rail, stop now and lay their tools down. One called to a group of three a little farther away. He stretched, his hands rubbing his back where the muscles were stiff. The bandit couldn't make out the reply, but the tone was clear. It was good-humored, amused. Just a typical morning out in the fields.

The bandit leader gave a satisfied nod as he saw the men begin walking to the largest building. The little hamlet was probably a family settlement—mother and father in the big house; their offspring with their families in the smaller houses that had been built nearby. The one big barn served all of the families. He'd heard the high-pitched voices of several children chattering earlier on. A welcoming curl of wood smoke rose from the chimney and he knew that the wives would all be gathered in there, preparing a communal breakfast. He picked up the mouthwatering aroma of bacon frying.

At that moment, the door to the farmhouse opened and the oldest woman emerged. She moved to an iron barrel hoop hanging from a post and beat a rapid tattoo on it with a hardwood stick. The message was clear: Breakfast is ready. Not that the farmers needed telling. They were all on their way by this point.

The bandit reached into his pocket and found a bone whistle. He raised it to his lips, sensing the men closest to him stirring as they saw the movement. Then he blew a loud, piercing blast and rose from concealment, drawing his sword and yelling as he ran forward.

His men followed, charging into the open from three sides around the settlement. They were fierce, terrifying figures, wearing half armor and carrying weapons. Bloodcurdling war cries rose into the morning air as they ran forward.

The farmers were frozen in surprise for a moment. Then one of the younger ones was first to react. He reached for the ax he had just leaned against a water trough. Before he could raise it, an arrow flashed across the clearing and buried itself in his throat. He gave a choking cry and staggered, falling half into the trough. The water rapidly began to turn red with his blood.

"Inside the house! Quickly! Maeve, get the—" the father called. But it was already too late. The first of the raiders was upon him and a sword thrust cut off his words. His face showed surprise, then pain, as he sank to the ground and lay, unmoving.

His killer leaped over the body and shouldered the door of the farmhouse open. It was a mistake. The woman who had rung the breakfast gong was waiting with a pot of freshly boiled water, which she flung in his face.

He screamed in agony and lurched to one side, dropping the bloody sword and throwing his hands up to his face. But the woman didn't have long to savor her momentary triumph. The raider following him struck swiftly with his sword and cut her down, her body falling across the threshold and preventing those inside from closing the door.

The remaining men outside tried in vain to stave off the attack. But they were fighting with their bare hands and didn't stand a chance. In rapid order, they were surrounded and cut down by the raiders, without pity or compassion. They were badly outnumbered and their attempts to protect their women and children were to no avail.

The bandit leader stood back a little from the group who surrounded the fallen bodies. He'd seen one of the farmers dart aside and into the barn.

Now he reappeared, his gaze intent on the men surrounding the dead and dying members of his family. He had a long pitchfork in his hands and he raised it as he ran forward.

He never saw the bandit leader. He only felt the searing agony of the sword thrust into his side, underneath his raised arm. He tried to cry out but was unable. He fell facedown.

"You should have run when you had the chance," the leader said.

Inside the house, three women cowered in the large kitchen as half a dozen men forced their way in.

The women saw the bloodied swords and knew their menfolk were gone. One of them raised her hands in entreaty.

"Mercy," she pleaded. But there was no mercy that day.

The raiders, oblivious to the splashed blood and sprawled bodies around them, helped themselves hungrily to the platters of hot, sizzling bacon and fresh baked bread that had been laid out for the men's breakfast.

"They won't be needing it," one said. He added, "And it's a sin to waste good food."

The others laughed as they crammed the food into their mouths. But one stood aside, his head cocked, listening. From the adjoining room, he could hear a furtive hacking, scraping sound. He crossed the kitchen and pushed the inner door open with the blade of his sword.

It was dimmer in the bedroom, with no window in the far wall, and his eyes took a second or two to adjust. Then he made out three forms, kneeling by the back wall. A woman, a boy, and a girl, the children about ten years old. The woman was frantically hacking at the wall with a heavy kitchen knife. Now she stopped, looking up in horror at the silhouette that filled the doorway. Strangely, the raider paused and waited as she attacked the wall with new vigor, creating a hole large enough for the children to squeeze through. He watched impassively as she shoved the two wriggling young ones through the exit she'd created.

"Run, Seamus! Run, Molly!" she said.

Then she heard the sound of a footstep and looked up to see the tall figure approaching her. She wondered vaguely why he'd given her time to let the young ones escape. Then she stood and looked the stranger in the eye, facing him calmly.

"The Holy Man warned us you would come," she said bitterly. "We should have listened."

He drew his sword back and smiled—an ugly grimace of a smile that was without any vestige of pity.

"Yes. You should have," he said, and brought the sword down.

In the trees, a figure stood watching the attack. He was tall, with shoulder-length white-gray hair. His eyes were a piercing blue and he wore a dull gray woolen cloak over a white, full-length robe. He watched as two children appeared at the end of the largest house— a boy and a girl. They paused uncertainly, but the men grouped around their dead kinsmen were facing away from them and they remained unseen. The tall man smiled as the boy took the little girl's hand and led her stooping and running to the tree line at the far side of the clearing.

"Good," he said, nodding his approval. "Leave a few survivors to spread the word."

Turn the page for a preview of

BROTHERBAND
CHRONICLES

BOOK ONE: THE OUTCASTS

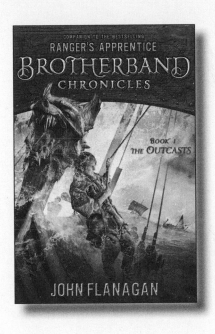

Twelve years prior . . .

Wolfwind emerged from the predawn sea mist like a wraith, slowly taking physical form.

With her sail furled and the yardarm lowered to the deck, and propelled by only four of her oars, the wolfship glided slowly toward the beach. The four rowers wielded their oars carefully, raising them only a few centimeters from the water at the end of each stroke so that the noise of drops splashing back into the sea was kept to a minimum. They were Erak's most experienced oarsmen and they were used to the task of approaching an enemy coast stealthily.

And during raiding season, all coasts were enemy coasts.

Such was their skill that the loudest sound was the *lap-lap-lap* of small ripples along the wooden hull. In the bow, Svengal and two other crew members crouched fully armed, peering ahead to catch sight of the dim line where the water met the beach.

The lack of surf might make their approach easier but a little extra noise would have been welcome, Svengal thought. Plus white water would have made the line of the beach easier to spot in the dimness. Then he saw the beach and held up his hand, fist clenched.

Far astern, at the steering oar, Erak watched his second in command as he revealed five fingers, then four, then three as he measured off the distance to the sand.

"In oars."

Erak spoke the words in a conversational tone, unlike the bellow he usually employed to pass orders. In the center section of the wolfship, his bosun, Mikkel, relayed the orders. The four oars lifted out of the water as one, rising quickly to the vertical so that any excess water would fall into the ship and not into the sea, where it would make more noise. A few seconds later, the prow of the ship grated softly against the sand. Erak felt the vibrations of the gentle contact with the shore through the deck beneath his feet.

Svengal and his two companions vaulted over the bow, landing catlike on the wet sand. Two of them moved up the beach, fanning out to scan the country on either side, ready to give warning of any possible ambush. Svengal took the small beach anchor that another sailor lowered to him. He stepped twenty paces up the beach, strained against the anchor rope to bring it tight and drove the shovel-shaped fluke into the firm sand.

Wolfwind, secured by the bow, slewed a little to one side under the pressure of the gentle breeze.

"Clear left!"

"Clear right!"

The two men who had gone onshore called their reports now. There was no need for further stealth. Svengal checked his own area of responsibility, then added his report to theirs.

"Clear ahead."

On board, Erak nodded with satisfaction. He hadn't expected any sort of armed reception on the beach but it always paid to make sure. That was why he had been such a successful raider over the years—and why he had lost so few of his crewmen.

"All right," he said, lifting his shield from the bulwark and hefting it onto his left arm. "Let's go."

He quickly strode the length of the wolfship to the bow, where a boarding ladder had been placed over the side. Shoving his heavy battleax through the leather sling on his belt, he climbed easily over the bulwark and down to the beach. His crewmen followed, forming up behind him. There was no need for orders. They had all done this before, many times.

Svengal joined him.

"No sign of anyone here, chief," he reported.

Erak grunted. "Neither should there be. They should all be busy at Alty Bosky."

He pronounced the name in his usual way—careless of the finer points of Iberian pronunciation. The town in question was actually Alto Bosque, a relatively unimportant market town some ten kilometers to the south, built on the high, wooded hill from which it derived its name.

The previous day, seven of his crew had taken the skiff and landed there, carrying out a lightning raid on the market before they retreated to the coast. Alto Bosque had no garrison and a rider from the town had been sent to Santa Sebilla, where a small force of militia was maintained. Erak's plan was to draw the garrison away to Alto Bosque while he and his men plundered Santa Sebilla unhindered.

Santa Sebilla was a small town, too. Probably smaller than Alto Bosque. But, over the years, it had gained an enviable reputation for the quality of the jewelry that was designed and crafted there. As time went on, more and more artisans and designers were drawn to Santa Sebilla and it became a center for fine design and craftsmanship in gold and precious stones.

Erak, like most Skandians, cared little for fine design and craftsmanship. But he cared a lot about gold and he knew there was a disproportionate amount of it in Santa Sebilla—far more than would normally be found in a small town such as this. The community of artists and designers needed generous supplies of the raw materials in which they worked—gold and silver and gemstones. Erak was a fervent believer in the principle of redistribution of wealth, as long as a great amount of it was redistributed in his direction, so he had planned this raid in detail for some weeks.

He checked behind him. The anchor watch of four men were standing by the bow of *Wolfwind*, guarding it while the main party went inland. He nodded, satisfied that everything was ready.

"Send your scouts ahead," he told Svengal. The second in command gestured to the two men to go ahead of the main raiding party.

The beach rose gradually to a low line of scrubby bushes and trees. The scouts ran to this line, surveyed the country beyond, then beckoned the main party forward. The ground was flat here, but some kilometers inland, a range of low hills rose from the plain. The first rose-colored rays of the sun were beginning to show about the peaks. They were behind schedule, Erak thought. He had wanted to reach the town before sunup, while people were still drowsy and longing for their beds, as yet reluctant to accept the challenges of a new day.

"Let's pace it up," he said tersely and the group settled into a steady jog behind him, moving in two columns. The scouts continued to range some fifty meters in advance of the raiding party. Erak could already see that there was nowhere a substantial party of armed men could remain hidden. Still, it did no harm to be sure.

Waved forward by the scouts, they crested a low rise and there, before them, stood Santa Sebilla.

The buildings were made of clay bricks, finished in whitewash. Later in the day, under the hot Iberian sun, they would glisten and gleam an almost blinding white. In the predawn light they looked dull and gray and mundane. The town had been built with no particular plan in mind, instead growing over the years so that houses and warehouses were placed wherever their owners chose to build them. The result was a chaotic mass of winding alleys, outlying buildings and twisting, formless streets. But Erak ignored the jumble of houses and shops. He was looking for the repository—a large building set to one side of the town, where the gold and jewels were stored.

And there it was. Larger than the others, with a substantial brass-bound wooden door. Normally, Erak knew, there would be a guard in place. But it seemed his diversion had achieved the result he wanted and the local militia were absent. The only possible resistance could come from a small castle set on a cliff a kilometer away from the town itself. There would possibly be armed men there. But the castle was the home of a minor Iberian nobleman and its location here was a mere coincidence. Knowing the snobbish and superior nature of the Iberian nobility, Erak guessed that the castle lord and his people had as little to do with the common tradesmen of Santa Sebilla as possible. They might buy from them, but they wouldn't mix with them or be eager to protect them in an emergency.

They headed for the repository. As they passed a side street, a sleepy townsman emerged, leading a donkey loaded with what seemed to be an impossibly heavy stack of firewood. For a few seconds, head down and still half asleep, the man failed to notice the force of grim-faced, armed sea wolves. Then his eyes snapped open, his jaw followed suit and he froze in place, staring at them. From the corner of his eye, Erak saw two of his men start to detach from the main body. But the firewood seller could do them little harm.

"Leave him," he ordered and the men dropped back into line.

Galvanized by the sound of Erak's voice, the man dropped the donkey's halter and took off back into the narrow alleyway from which he had emerged. They heard the soft sound of his bare feet flapping on the hard earth as he put as much distance between himself and the raiders as he could.

"Get that door open," Erak ordered.

Mikkel and Thorn stepped forward. Mikkel, whose preferred weapon was a sword, borrowed an ax from one of the other sea wolves and together, he and Thorn attacked the heavy door. They were Erak's two most reliable warriors, and he nodded appreciatively at the economy of effort with which they reduced the door to matchwood, placing alternate ax strokes precisely where they would do the most good, each building on the damage the other had caused. The two men were best friends. They always fought together in the shield wall, each trusting the other to protect his back and sides. Yet they were a contrast in body shapes. Mikkel was taller and leaner than the average Skandian. But he was powerful and hard muscled. And he had the reflexes of a cat.

Thorn was slightly shorter than his friend, but much wider in the shoulders and chest. He was one of the most skilled and dangerous warriors Erak had ever seen. Erak often thought that he would hate to come up against Thorn in battle. He'd never seen an opponent who had survived such an encounter. Belying his heavy build, Thorn could also move with blinding speed when he chose.

Erak roused himself from his musing as the door fell in two shattered halves.

"Get the gold," he ordered and his men surged forward.

It took them half an hour to load the gold and silver into sacks. They took only as much as they could carry and they left easily the same amount behind.

Maybe another time, Erak thought, although he knew no subsequent raid would be as easy or as bloodless as this one. In retrospect, he wished he'd caught hold of the firewood seller's donkey. The little animal could have carried more of the gold back to the ship for them.

The town was awake now and nervous faces peered at them from behind windows and around street corners. But these were not warriors and none were willing to face the fierce-looking men from the north. Erak nodded, satisfied, as the last of his men, each laden with two small but heavy sacks, emerged from the repository. He breathed a small sigh of satisfaction. It had been easy, he thought. Easier than he had expected.

Laden as they were, they couldn't maintain their previous jog as they followed the path through the scrubby undergrowth back to the beach. At least a dozen of the townspeople followed them, as if unwilling to let their gold and jewels simply disappear from sight. But they kept their distance, watching in impotent fury as the sea wolves carried away their booty.

"Thorn, Mikkel, bring up the rear. Let me know if there's any change," Erak said. It would be all too easy to become complacent about the men shadowing their footsteps, and so miss any new threat that might arise.

The two men nodded and handed their sacks of loot to other crew members, then faded to the back of the column.

They marched some twenty meters behind the main party, turning continually to keep the following townspeople in sight. Once, Thorn faked a charge at a couple who he felt had come too close, and they scampered hurriedly back to a safe distance.

"Rabbits," said Mikkel dismissively.

Thorn grinned and was about to reply when he caught sight of movement behind the straggle of townspeople. His grin faded.

"Looks like we've got some rabbits on horseback," he said. The two raiders stopped to face the rear.

Trotting toward them, following the rough track through the undergrowth, were five horsemen. The newly risen sun gleamed off their armor and the points of the spears they all carried. They were still some distance behind the raiders but they were coming up fast. The two companions could hear the faint jingle of their horses' harness and their equipment.

Thorn glanced back to the main party of raiders. They were about to enter a narrow defile that led down to the last stretch of open ground to the beach. He let out a piercing whistle and saw Erak stop and look back. The rest of the party continued to move as quickly as they could.

Thorn pointed to the riders. Uncertain whether Erak could see the new enemy, he held up his right hand, with five fingers extended, then brought it down in a clenched fist close by his shoulder—the signal for "enemy." He pointed again to the riders.

He saw Erak wave acknowledgment, then point at the entrance to the defile, where the last of his men were just passing through. Thorn and Mikkel both grunted in understanding.

"Good idea," Mikkel said. "We'll hold them off at the entrance."

The high rock walls and narrow space would encumber the horsemen. It would also prevent them from flanking and encircling the two sea wolves. They'd be forced into a frontal attack. Normally, that might be a daunting prospect, but these were two experienced and deadly fighters, each secure in his own skills and those of his companion.

They both knew that Erak would not abandon them to this new danger. Once the gold was safely at the ship, he'd send men back to help them. Their job was only to buy time, not to sacrifice themselves so the others could escape. And both men felt confident that they could hold off a few country-bumpkin horsemen.

They doubled their pace, covering the ground to the defile. Behind them, they heard a ragged cheer from the townspeople as they saw the raiders seemingly running for their lives ahead of the avenging horsemen, who urged their horses to a gallop, determined to catch these interlopers before they could escape into the narrow gully.

The two warriors had no intention of escaping. Rather, as they reached the defile, Mikkel and Thorn turned and drew their weapons, swinging them experimentally as they faced the approaching riders.

Like most Skandians, Thorn favored a heavy, single-bladed battleax as his principal weapon. Mikkel was armed with a long sword. Both of them wore horned helmets and carried large wooden shields, borne on the left arm, with a heavy center boss of metal and reinforcing metal strips around the edges. They presented these to the oncoming riders, so that only their heads and legs were visible—as well as the gleaming sword and ax, still moving in small preliminary arcs, catching and reflecting the sunlight as the two warriors stretched their muscles.

It seemed to the horsemen that the shields and swords blocked the defile entrance completely. Expecting the Skandians to run in panic, they were somewhat taken aback now at this show of defiance—and at the confident manner of the two men facing them. They drew rein about thirty meters short of the two men and looked at each other uncertainly, each waiting for one of the others to take the lead.

The two Skandians sensed their uncertainty, and noted the clumsy way they handled their spears and small round shields.

There was none of the easy familiarity that could be seen in an experienced fighter.

"I think these boys are still wet behind the ears," Mikkel said, smiling grimly.

Thorn nodded. "I doubt they've seen any real fighting."

They were right. The horsemen, who had come from the castle in response to a messenger who had run all the way from Santa Sebilla, were young and only half trained. They were all from well-to-do families. Their indolent parents had always supplied their every whim: new chain mail, a sword with a gold-chased hilt, a new battle horse. They viewed their training in the knightly arts as more of a social activity than a serious one. They had never before faced armed and determined warriors like these two, and it suddenly occurred to them that what had begun as a lighthearted expedition to send a few ill-bred raiders running in panic had quickly turned into a potentially deadly confrontation. Someone could die here today. So they hesitated, uncertain what they should do next.

Then one, either braver or more foolhardy than his fellows, shouted a challenge and spurred his horse forward, awkwardly trying to level his spear at the two Skandians.

"Mine, I think," said Thorn, stepping forward a few paces to accept the charge. Mikkel was content to let him do so. Thorn's long-handled ax was the more effective weapon against a horseman.

Thorn summed up his opponent through slitted eyes. The youth was bouncing around in his saddle like a sack of potatoes, trying to steady his spear under his right arm and keep it pointed at his enemy. It would be ridiculously easy to kill him, Thorn thought. But that might simply rouse the anger of his companions. Better to humiliate him.

Bracing himself, he caught the spearhead on his shield and flicked it easily to one side. Then he slammed the flat of his ax into the shoulder of the charging horse, throwing it off balance. As it stumbled, he drove forward with his shield, hitting the animal again and sending it reeling to one side. The horse struck the rough rock wall beside the defile and lost its footing, crashing onto its side with a terrified neighing. The rider barely had time to clear his feet from the stirrups and avoid being pinned under the fallen horse. He fell awkwardly to one side, his small shield underneath him. He scrabbled desperately at the hilt of his sword, trying to clear the long blade from its scabbard. When it was half drawn, Thorn kicked his arm and hand, finishing the action and sending the bared sword spinning away out of his grasp.

The young rider looked up at Thorn with terrified eyes. He flinched uncontrollably as he saw the terrible war ax arcing up and over. Then it slammed into the hard ground, a few inches from his face. The Skandian's eyes, cold and merciless, held his. Then Thorn said one word.

"Run."

The young Iberian scrambled clumsily to his feet and turned to escape. As he did, he felt a violent impact in his behind as Thorn helped him on his way with his boot. Stumbling and crying in panic, he blundered back to where his companions were waiting, their horses moving uneasily from one foot to the other, the riders' fear communicating itself to the animals.

Behind him, the boy heard the two Skandians laughing.

Thorn's instincts had been correct. The apparent ease with which he had dealt with the rider was far more disconcerting than if he had simply killed him. By letting him live, he had shown the utter contempt with which he and his companion regarded these neophyte warriors. Such disregard made the Iberians even more uncertain.

"I think you've made them nervous." Mikkel grinned at his friend.

Thorn shrugged. "So they should be. They shouldn't be allowed out with pointy sticks like that. They're more danger to themselves than anyone else."

"Let's see them off," said Mikkel. "They're starting to annoy me."

Without any warning, the two Skandians brandished their weapons and charged at the small group of horsemen, screaming battle cries as they went.

The shock of it all was too much for the demoralized group of riders. They saw the terrifying warriors charging across open ground at them and each one was convinced that he was the target they were aiming for. One of them wheeled his horse and clapped spurs to its flanks, dropping his spear as his horse lurched suddenly beneath him. His action was infectious. Within seconds, all four horsemen were steaming across the plain in a ragged line, the riderless horse with them, and their dismounted companion stumbling awkwardly behind them, encumbered by his thigh-high riding boots, spurs and flapping, empty scabbard.

Mikkel and Thorn stopped and rested on their weapons, roaring with laughter at the sight.

"I do hope they get home all right," Mikkel said and Thorn laughed all the louder.

"Are you ladies ready to join us?" It was Svengal, sent back with five men to reinforce the rearguard. "It seems you don't need any help."

Still laughing, Thorn and Mikkel sheathed their weapons and walked back to join Svengal and the others at the mouth of the defile.

"You should have seen it, Svengal," Mikkel began. "Thorn here simply frightened them away. The sight of his ugly face was too much for them. It even made a horse fall over."

Svengal let go a short bark of laughter. Hurrying up the defile at the head of the reinforcements, he had seen how Thorn dealt with the charging rider. He was impressed. He knew he could never have pulled that move off. In fact, he couldn't think of anyone other than Thorn who might have managed it.

"Well, you played your part too," Thorn was saying in reply. "Although I must admit I *was* magnificent."

"I'm not sure that's the word I'd—" Mikkel raised his arm to clap his friend on the shoulder when the spear hit him.

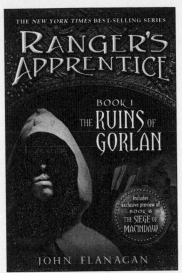

RANGER'S APPRENTICE

BOOK ONE: THE RUINS OF GORLAN

The Rangers, with their shadowy ways, are the protectors of the kingdom who will fight the battles before the battles reach the people. Fifteen-year-old Will has been chosen as a Ranger's apprentice. And there is a large battle brewing. The exiled Morgarath, Lord of the Mountains of Rain and Night, is gathering his forces for an attack on the kingdom. This time he will not be denied.

RANGER'S APPRENTICE

BOOK TWO: THE BURNING BRIDGE

On a special mission for the Rangers, Will discovers all the people in the neighboring villages have been either slain or captured. But why? Could it be that Morgarath has finally devised a plan to bring his legions over the supposedly insurmountable pass? If so, the king's army is in imminent danger of being crushed in a fierce ambush. And Will is the only one who can save them.

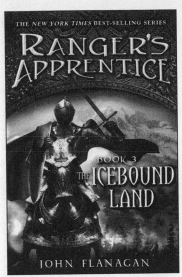

RANGER'S APPRENTICE

BOOK THREE: THE ICEBOUND LAND

Kidnapped and taken to a frozen land after the fierce battle with Lord Morgarath, Will and Evanlyn are bound for Skandia as captives. Halt has sworn to rescue his young apprentice, and he will do anything to keep his promise—even defy his king. Expelled from the Rangers he has served so loyally, Halt is joined by Will's friend Horace as he travels toward Skandia. But will he and Halt be in time to rescue Will from a horrific life of slavery?

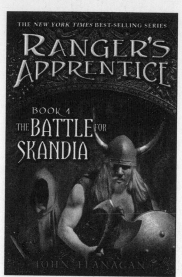

RANGER'S APPRENTICE

BOOK FOUR: THE BATTLE FOR SKANDIA

Still far from home after escaping slavery in the icebound land of
Skandia, young Will and Evanlyn's plans to return to Araluen are
spoiled when Evanlyn is taken captive, and Will discovers that
Skandia and Araluen are in grave danger. Only an unlikely union can
save the two kingdoms, but can it hold long enough to vanquish a
ruthless new enemy?

BOOK FIVE: THE SORCERER OF THE NORTH

Will is finally a full-fledged Ranger with his own fief to look after. But when Lord Syron, master of a castle far in the north, is struck down by a mysterious illness, Will is suddenly thrown headfirst into an extraordinary adventure, investigating fears of sorcery and trying to determine who is loyal to Lord Syron.

BOOK SIX: THE SIEGE OF MACINDAW

The kingdom is in danger. Renegade knight Sir Keren has succeeded in overtaking Castle Macindaw. The fate of Araluen rests in the hands of two young adventurers: the Ranger Will and his warrior friend, Horace.

BOOK SEVEN: ERAK'S RANSOM

In the wake of Araluen's uneasy truce with the raiding Skandians comes word that the Skandian leader has been captured by a dangerous desert tribe. The Rangers—and Will—are sent to free him. Strangers in a strange land, they are brutalized by sandstorms, beaten by the unrelenting heat; nothing is as it seems. Yet one thing is constant: the bravery of the Rangers.

BOOK EIGHT: THE KINGS OF CLONMEL

When a cult springs up in neighboring Clonmel, people flock from all over to offer gold in exchange for protection. But Halt is all too familiar with this group, and he knows they have a less than charitable agenda. Secrets will be unveiled and battles fought to the death as Will and Horace help Halt in ridding the land of a dangerous enemy.

BOOK NINE: HALT'S PERIL

The renegade outlaw group known as the Outsiders may have been chased from Clonmel, but now Rangers Halt and Will, along with the young warrior Horace, are in pursuit. The Outsiders have done an effective job of dividing the kingdom into factions and are looking to overtake Araluen. It will take every bit of skill and cunning for the Rangers to survive. Some may not be so lucky.

BOOK TEN: THE EMPEROR OF NIHON-JA

Months have passed since Horace departed for the eastern nation of Nihon-Ja on a vital mission. Having received no communication from him, his friends fear the worst. Unwilling to wait a second longer, Alyss, Evanlyn, and Will leave and venture into an exotic land in search of their missing friend.

RANGER'S APPRENTICE

THE LOST STORIES

Some claim they were merely the stuff of legend: the Rangers as defenders of the Kingdom. Reports of their brave battles vary; but we know of at least ten accounts, most of which feature Will and his mentor, Halt. There are reports of others who fought alongside the Rangers: the warrior Horace, a courageous princess named Evanlyn, and a cunning diplomat named Alyss. Yet this crew left very little behind, and their existence has never been proven. Until now, that is . . . behold the Lost Stories.